# FIGHT
# FOR
# DEMOCRACY

# FIGHT FOR DEMOCRACY

Barrie Edward

*Riverhaven Books*

*www.RiverhavenBooks.com*

*Fight for Democracy* is a work of fiction. While some of the settings and names mentioned are historically accurate, any similarity regarding characters or incidents is purely coincidental. In particular there is no secret hotel suite on the twenty-second floor of the Custom House.

Copyright© by Barrie Edward 2019

All rights reserved.

Published in the United States by Riverhaven Books
www.RiverhavenBooks.com

ISBN: 978-1-951854-00-3

Printed in the United States of America
By Country Press, Lakeville, Massachusetts

Cover art by Katelyn
Designed and edited by Stephanie Lynn Blackman
Whitman, MA

*This novel is dedicated to those fans who insisted on a sequel to Death of Democracy. Most vociferous, my wife Anita, my editor Stephanie Blackman, author Gin Young, and my sometimes transcriber Pauline Bedford.*

*In the years of writing this book, sometimes real life events have overtaken my inventive mind - sometimes after, sometimes before finding their way to the page.*

Also written by
Barrie Edward

*Casablanca Connection*

*Death of Democracy*

## Prolog

President Anders had entered the White House by eliminating his competition. Congressional seats had been won by means of extortion, dirty tricks, and ballot box fraud.

The agenda of the new Congress was support of Muslim regimes and abandonment of former allies. Britain, France, and Germany had been similarly compromised. The result was the withdrawal of all allied and United Nations troops from Middle Eastern nations, which had now reverted to Muslim dictatorship. An Arab Nations congress had convened in Baghdad and expressed the goal of world domination.

In the United States, Mathew (Mac) McDougal had tried to alert the country to the danger. Forced to flee, he joined an underground organization dedicated to the return of democracy. The Sons of Freedom had been branded terrorists by the new government.

In Texas, a previous presidential hopeful was resisting a subpoena for her arrest on charges of treason; conspiracy, and complicity to murder while an alleged member of the Ku Klux Clan.

## Chapter One

"Twenty-five!"

Ellie May Joseph had spat the words, and her husband Jim, the only other occupant of the room, glanced up briefly from the corporate agreement he was reading.

Spectacles perched on his nose and a red pencil poised over a clause in the agreement, he marked the paragraph to reread later and looked up, saying nothing. Just waiting for her to continue.

The dominant map of Texas behind her was truly representative of where her heart would always call home. Her taste for Southwest décor, complete with burnt orange walls and predominately yellow rugs in a Navaho Indian design, spoke volumes.

"Twenty-five!" she repeated as she rifled through the papers and charts that surrounded her.

"Twenty-five months that this..." She paused to filter her thoughts into words.

Jim had heard them all before, along with many that were not flattering of the incumbent President of the United States.

"...that this person has been in office," she continued. "Twenty-five percent unemployment, according to government estimates." She harrumphed her disbelief of the veracity of anything that came from the government. "...Twenty-five percent approval rating, according to social media sites..." She nodded her approval of this statistic. "…and twenty-five days since he had Mathew McDougal assassinated."

"The newspaper said that it was a firefight," Jim interjected.

"The newspapers also said that Mac was a terrorist and that government agents were trying to arrest him in connection with a litany of crimes; including incitement to riot, killing David White, and supporting the FBI's most wanted criminal…Ellie May Joseph."

"Your point?"

"My point…first, when is dissent a criminal act? Second, where did freedom of speech go? And third, Mac McDougal was on live television in Boston when David White was murdered, murdered by the same agent sent to arrest Mac. And fourth, Ellie May Joseph has committed no crime – I'm the Attorney General for Texas and a former presidential candidate. And Mac's support of the effort to run this terrorist out of the White House is an act our Founding Fathers would have approved!"

"Ah, yes, the original Sons of Liberty."

"The Sons of Liberty," agreed Ellie May.

"You missed twenty-five dollars a gallon for gasoline and twenty-five states that you need to convince that you might make a better president than Anders."

"Better president?" Ellie May exclaimed. "Lassie would make a better president!"

"Twenty-five states is the bigger hurdle since Anders has those with a large black population believing that you were the first female member of the Ku Klux Clan. I'd think that campaigning in urban areas with the active militia ready to shoot you on sight would also present a challenge," Jim pointed out.

"Did every state approve militia?" she asked.

"Not to mention his arming them. The crime rate in some areas has escalated instead of decreased. Stores are now barricaded, and if they do open it's just for a few daylight hours. Looting is rampant, armed robbery is no longer investigated, and gang warfare is a fact of life."

"And don't forget that the President blames all of this on the previous administration," Ellie May added.

"You didn't mention foreign policy. There were twenty-five countries represented at the Islamic conference last month."

"I think that you have just depressed me even more," she said, adding another line to the list of twenty-fives she was compiling.

"I can't do this Jim."

"Then who can?"

"I don't know. People expect someone to the extreme right to run. You know that would result in civil war."

"What do you call what is happening in the streets?" Jim asked.

"If I get elected president, or anyone for that matter, how does this…this…state of affairs get reversed?"

"One thing at a time El; let's get you elected first."

"First I need to get on the ballot."

There was silence in the room. They were both thinking of how they were to achieve the seemingly impossible. If there were federal warrants for their arrests and they could not leave Texas, how were they to campaign, raise money, gather support, and have access to national TV and other media?

A knock on the door raised them to high alert. It was a familiar knock: three, then two raps, representing the Lone Star State emblem. The familiarity of the knock allowed Bobby Joe, head of their security, to be admitted with a push of a button.

"How y'all doin' today?"

"Well, Bobby. And you?" asked Jim.

"Fine...everything quiet, as I like it. There's a man, says his name is Mark Hughes, checked into town. Says you will see him."

Mark Hughes...Ellie May stopped to think through the implications and how much they already knew. It was a name from the past campaign when Mark Hughes headed a political action committee with ties to defense contractors. If this were the same person, there would be valuable information of the outside world, outside of Texas.

"Check him out, then invite him for breakfast. Bring him out at seven tomorrow."

\*\*\*

Mark had been recruited by Mathew McDougal to raise money for a presidential campaign. Mac had also spoken to Ellie May about funding for a rerun.

Ellie May Joseph had run on the Republican ticket and had been beaten by a strong Democrat Party candidate, Marjorie White. But Marjorie had resigned after her husband David had been murdered, leaving the current occupant – her former vice-presidential candidate – in the White House.

Now that Mac had been gunned down, was the deal still on the table? Mac had been sparse on the details. Maybe there would be more information...if this was indeed Mark Hughes. Ellie May switched from her "twenty-five list" to a fresh sheet of paper and began writing a list of questions for Mark Hughes.

\*\*\*

Mark Hughes, in a comfortable Austin hotel room,

was also compiling a list. His was a list of questions for Ellie May Joseph and her advisors; it was a long list of subject matter to be covered.

To get this far into Texas and this deep into the Joseph stronghold had taken several days. Trying to take the conventional route was virtually impossible; certainly impossible for him, as his name was on the government's watch list.

Mark had been a political action committee fundraiser. His clientele of mostly defense industry or industrial machine manufacturers had kept him busy and enjoying a lavish lifestyle. One of the major beneficiaries of his fundraising had been the Republican presidential candidate: Ellie May Joseph. The fact that he had also provided support for her opponent Marjorie White was a case of hedging his clients' bets.

The election two and a half years ago had been hijacked by Arthur Anders, who had immediately embraced Islam and changed his name to Mohammed Al Adana. Since the new president had accepted no PAC money or any donations, he was not beholden to Mark. The fact that he had withdrawn troops and all but eliminated the defense budget had resulted in many of Mark's clients filing for protection in the bankruptcy courts. These clients had reneged on pledges made with Mark and had led to his personal bankruptcy.

Reflecting on those dark days, with no money and suspecting that he was on a hit list, he recalled being rescued by a phone call from Helen Harvey. Mrs. Helen Harvey McDougal, he corrected himself. Mark and Helen had been lovers until they parted to their separate careers. When she became a media director for Marjorie White, a previous presidential hopeful,

Helen had reunited with her former lover, Mathew McDougal, an investigative political writer and journalist. Mac and Helen had subsequently married and gone into hiding after the election of President Mohammed Al Adana. The phone call from Helen, which had rescued him, had resulted in a meeting in Las Vegas, resurrected his career, and led him by a circuitous route to Texas.

Mark went back to his notes and stopped. The phrase "What happens in Vegas…stays in Vegas" passed through his head. At no time did it ever seem more appropriate. There were no notes from that meeting. The fact that they had ever been in Nevada had been expunged from all records. He would not write it down now, nor mention the names of the infamous people also at the meeting.

The next morning, Mark was met by Betty Jo Williams, the wife of Bobby Joe. She had become a full-time driver for the Josephs. It was a means of staying close to her husband, and her personality and female intuition was another quiet line of defense against infiltration.

President Mohammed Al Adana had made Ellie May Joseph public enemy number one, and Mark Hughes was in the top ten. The fact that they were meeting would be of great interest in Washington and would certainly create a wave of speculation.

Betty Jo was driving a Cadillac SUV with tinted, bulletproof windows. She would drive directly into the Joseph's underground garage. These precautions were against the intrusive eyes of the drones which appeared regularly over Texas.

Stepping out of the car, Mark walked through a body scan and retrieved his briefcase on the other side.

Over six feet tall, Mark was good looking and lean.

The lean was due to his step down from high living and his reallocation of extra time used for running and staying in shape. He was only slightly taller than Ellie May Joseph, who was wearing cowboy boots with heels, a brightly colored blouse, and tight jeans, tucked into the boots. Jim Joseph introduced himself and Bobby Joe who was leaning against the wall to his right.

"Welcome to our home. Or is it our prison?" Ellie May said, moving forward and smiling. "Mathew McDougal said that you were one of the white hats and that we could trust you. That's a good enough introduction for me."

"That was kind of him," said Mark relaxing. He wasn't used to being in a meeting where everyone was visibly armed.

"Before we get to why you are here, please tell us how you know Mac." Ellie May had turned her now all business blue eyes on Mark. "Please, sit down. Coffee?"

"Yes, please...black."

Mark sat opposite Ellie May and Jim Joseph. Sheila Hutchins, the campaign media manager, and Allyn Cherwin, introduced as the treasurer, joined the meeting during the initial formalities and conversation. Ellie May still had pretty much the same team as she'd had for her initial election bid, though her chief of staff had gone back to his old position as the CEO of an offshore drilling company.

Mark explained that he'd known Mac in Washington where they were in similar social circles. He made light of their dating the same woman, Helen Harvey, and their subsequent rivalry; he summarized conversations that they had shared during the primaries, then explained how Anders accepted no money and how information provided by his PAC to Congress often found its way into foreign hands. Specifically, he told them in detail how a bill containing "pork" benefits from most of the states and twenty-five million dollars of kickbacks had been stripped of these attributes.

After protests that this was probably good, he shrugged unapologetically and explained that it was the inside knowledge use that was his concern.

Everyone in the room was involved in politics, so there was no surprise. The open admission added to Mark's credibility.

The others in the room shared reminiscences of Mac and Helen and the shock of their being killed.

"Rumor is that he survived," said Mark.

"Sons of Liberty posted that," said Sheila. "Probably propaganda! They've been posting articles out of Boston under his pseudonym Peter Doath."

"How do you know that it's not him?" asked Allyn.

"I recognize his style and Helen Harvey's. Mac wrote as Deep Throat; Peter Doath is his anagram byline. He didn't write those articles."

"There's no way anyone survived that conflagration," Bobby Joe added, shaking his head.

"There's also no way that scene was created by two agents sent to 'talk' to him," interjected Ellie May.

There was general scoffing at the official report that said that two federal agents sent to interview the outlaws had been fired upon and, in the exchange of gunfire, a large cache of ammunition had exploded. They generally agreed that Mac was a writer and not a fighter and that there were no arms except perhaps a hunting rifle in the house. The reports of large numbers of armed soldiers in the area had been deemed credible by those who controlled the media.

Ellie May brought the meeting back to the present. "What brings you to Texas, Mark?"

"A number of things," he said, taking out his notes. "We needed to meet so we need to work out how we are going to communicate and fund your campaign."

"As you can imagine, we have a number of questions ourselves. Let's put our questions out there and then spend the rest of the day answering them," suggested Ellie May. "First, I'm not sure I should or can run. Second, who is funding this campaign? And third, what will I owe them?"

"My backers have the same first question," said Mark. "Before I leave Texas at the end of the week, I need sufficient evidence of that resolve."

"Who are these backers?" asked Allyn.

Mark hesitated too long and had to buy time. "What did Mac tell you?"

"That Mark Hughes would be responsible for funds and to trust him."

"That's a lot of responsibility and very little information," said Mark. "I won't go into who, but it will be enough."

"I'm the treasurer of this event and need to know," said Allyn.

"You're the treasurer and need to work out an expense budget and cash flow reports to cover the next eighteen months," Mark corrected.

"How am I supposed to budget for a person not yet committed, not able to leave Texas, with no agenda, platform, election team…nothing?"

"Improvise," Sheila Hutchins replied to Allyn, then, looking to Mark, she asked, "How do we get our message out?"

"I really don't know, but since Mac was a member and supporter of the Sons of Liberty, they would be your natural window to the rest of America. I'll admit within these walls that I'm also a member of the Sons of Liberty in Montana.

"We're working on a communication system, but so far the government has infiltrated every network. I think we can persuade one of my clients, who launched a satellite, to give us an access that cannot be breached. A code would be known only to one person in each chapter and one here."

"New campaign financing means naming all contributors," Jim Joseph stated, thinking of the legal obstacles. "What do we report to stay within the law?"

"That the money comes from the same source as the president," said Mark.

"Is that true?"

"As a matter of fact, it is," stated Mark. "You don't want to know," he added in response to their questioning looks.

\*\*\*

The president had used money from the Muslim Brotherhood in Turkey, laundered from U.S. aid programs, to gamble on elections which they had 'fixed'. Mathew McDougal had uncovered and reported on this deception to no avail. He had gone to Mark for funding to bet against the president and the Brotherhood, using the same tactics of intimidation to ensure that the Sons of Liberty candidates won. Hal, the bookie, was running a 'book' in Las Vegas and the owners of casinos on the strip had promised that they would use their influence to guarantee the election of Ellie May Joseph.

Mark couldn't tell these people that all they had to do was stay alive. Besides which, that would take a great deal of vigilance and even more luck.

The first test was to be the election of a New

Mayor in New York. The previous mayor had died in a suspicious accident after criticism of the administration and a known supporter of the president was running for the office. The Sons of Liberty had persuaded, and were protecting, a popular female candidate in opposition. The Las Vegas connection was defusing propaganda against her and building a case against the Democrat. The book had taken in nearly two million at four-to-one odds, which the Brotherhood had matched with eight million dollars, laundered through several offshore jurisdictions.

The game was on!

## Chapter Two

Communication was the subject at the Sons of Liberty meeting in Boston. The latest newsletter had been intercepted and they were debating the bad luck, the backlash, and more importantly how to bypass the intercept.

The publishing of newsletters and the transfer of information was still being handled out of Massachusetts Institute of Technology. So far the source had not been discovered, due to the large number of similar facilities in the Boston area – universities, colleges, teaching hospitals, all had hundreds of potential sites.

The committee meeting had begun with a reprise of what was happening locally. The woman who had taken the working name of Paula Revere, an attractive graduate student at Harvard, was talking. Her father, a professor and the leader of the Boston group, sat opposite in an armchair.

The room was large and comfortable, located on Beacon Hill, not far from the State House. There was a coal fire in the grate which occasionally spit quietly and cast a warm glow against the wood paneling. Portraits looked benignly down on the eight occupants.

"We have to be able to get our message out. We have to get information in, and we have to be sure that the information travelling between the groups has not been modified," she said.

"Many of us do not have the expertise to know how to do that," her father's concerned voice replied.

"But you can help by using the expertise that you do have: the ability to analyze and interpret. The ability to work on codes, protocols, and language skills; these are all important."

"There appears to be some of the same concerns from other groups, and if we are to coordinate, we can combine our resources and information," said Sean Lynch, known to the members as Patrick Henry. Sean was a lawyer and a lifelong Democrat with contacts throughout the state government.

"Are you suggesting a summit or a series of clandestine meetings?" asked Paula.

"It has to be a summit. We should plan it here in Boston, hidden in plain sight," Sean explained.

"Invite the whole world to a summit meeting to discuss how to prevent the government from seeing our communications?" asked a large woman using Betsy Ross as her code name. In social circles she was known as Marian Willett, philanthropist, trusteeship at the Museum of Fine Arts, and sponsor of the local cancer campaign.

"Something like that." Sean smiled. "No, I was thinking about a discussion on the second amendment."

"Seriously?" added the man known as Benjamin Franklin, a Harvard professor. "We need to piggyback onto a conference and then send the invitation to the other known groups from the list that Mac sent to us before the fire."

"There's the annual computer conference in April, which gives us a month to put it together," said Paula.

"MIT is always represented, so I can join their conferees."

"We should set up a breakout meeting for those members who we can identify."

"There will be spies," warned Marian.

"We will be very careful," Paula assured her.

The rest of the evening was engaged with the logistics of inviting groups from around America to register at the conference. It was finally decided that there would be two mailings: the first a brochure for the conference, and the second a newsletter without naming the conference. This should ensure that only the recipients would understand the importance of the previously received brochure.

The meeting became energized. They needed a sympathetic, well-known attendee to organize the breakout sessions that were being proposed. In order to keep it limited, it was voted that only Paula Revere, who would be using her real name, would register and that any recruits that she encountered would be given a pass to the Harvard Peabody Museum and its famous glass exhibit. The pass would be marked, and her father would then meet the recruit to assess their loyalties and patriotism. This fight would be fought in cyberspace, and the youngest, brightest computer minds were coming to Boston.

## Chapter Three

In New York City, the mayoral race was dividing into two distinctive positions. The administration's candidate, Daniel Boots, was forty-one, handsome, and articulate. His career at a Manhattan law firm had seen him working extensively in the banking industry. The fact that he had never been sought for a partnership was due to his lack of imagination and his inflexible exercise of vacation and holiday time. It was known that annually he traveled in January to Africa or the Middle East. His political platform was a slavish agreement with the politics of President Al Adana and the terrorist-controlled Congress. His rallies were carefully scripted and controlled. The local militia was always prominently on display.

The opposition was provided by Joyce Milner, a fifty-seven-year-old widow. Her husband, a firefighter, had been at Ground Zero on September 11th, 2001. Although he had survived that day, the result had been affected lungs and a sense of guilt that he had survived where so many had died. The resulting depression had led to his death from a massive stroke four years later.

Joyce was matronly, she'd been brought up in the Jewish faith and married Jim Milner against her family's wishes. She'd enjoyed a happy marriage with no children, despite their desire to have them. After Jim's death, she had dedicated more time to charitable work, which her brothers and parents approved of, and to the Republican Party, which they did not. Permanently cheerful, she was a decent speaker.

The Sons of Liberty had persuaded her to stand as a candidate for mayor of New York. She was not told until later that she had, in fact, been their fourth choice. The other persons who had been approached had been afraid to accept the challenge in spite of the strong promise of protection.

The stubborn streak in Joyce had been some of the reason for her acceptance. She had assumed, correctly, that it would send her family into orbit.

Protection had begun immediately upon her declaration. The announcement, made at an NYFD fundraiser, had been popular. Immediate endorsements from the firefighters and police unions had ensured coverage in local, national, and international media.

The next day her protection intercepted an explosive device in her mail. It was small: a warning. But it had the opposite effect on Joyce. She defiantly threw herself into training. A speech coach was provided; a speech writer helped with press releases and interviews with reporters. Other coaches arrived for updates in politics, constitutional subjects; dieticians helped her determine meals which would trim her figure to be more camera-friendly in a too-superficial world; secretaries kept her correspondence up to date. Computer experts checked her equipment daily. It was a trial run, with all of the attention to detail that was going to be necessary if they were to be successful in removing the incumbent president.

Joyce Milner was overwhelmed with the attention. It was just as well that she could not see the global implications. Every minute was programmed for her, including conversations with family and friends.

"Hello. This is Joyce Milner; how can I help?"

"Joyce dear, this is your mother."

"Hi, Mom. How are you? How's Dad?"

"We're okay. It's a little nerve wracking having all the attention from the reporters and TV personalities. They're telling us that you have no chance and that you should drop out of the race."

"Thanks, Mom. I knew I could count on your support," said Joyce ironically.

"Then you'll drop out?"

"No, Mom. Sorry!"

"That nice man, Daniel Boots, came by yesterday and asked for our vote as loyal Democrats and as Americans. We told him that of course we always vote Democrat. Dad and I both signed his papers."

"Well, Mom, thanks for stabbing me in the back. Give my love to Dad."

"Will we see you for Seder?"

"No, I'll be busy." Joyce was crying – for the use and abuse of her parents by the Democrat Party, for the preparation and hard work which seemed to be steps forward and steps back, for the lack of understanding and support of her parents, for the loss.

"Joyce." A heavyset man entered the room.

"Yes, Ray?"

"You know we listen to your calls?"

"I guess, but sometimes I forget."

"Well the latest call, your mother; word is that Boots is preparing an ad that says that your chances being nil was recorded in an interview with your parents where they endorsed Boots' campaign."

"Those dirty…" Joyce was angry and confused.

"We have to get in front of this," said Ray.

"I don't want to make my parents a ball in a ping-pong match."

"You have no choice. Boots is going to put them in play. We have to immediately spin this; if we can preempt, then even better. But we have to do it now, Joyce!"

"Okay."

"Good, because I have a sympathetic reporter on the way and my team is working on a statement."

"Ray…" she began. "Never mind. I know you said it would be rough."

"Less than ten days."

"But, Ray, do I really have any chance?"

"You're a shoo-in."

Although Ray Bryant was not privy to everything, he knew that the Sons of Liberty were the conduit and that through their contacts, unions in New York were going to forego centuries of backing Democrats in order to support Joyce Milner, an unknown Republican candidate. Ray knew with an instinct of thirty years in the business that his recruitment and the recruitment of his talented, expensive team had not been compiled in order to lose. Losing was not an option for Ray, who depended upon results to get his next job.

In Las Vegas there was a flurry of interest in the candidacy of Daniel Boots. This time it was not matched, since the contacts the bookies had sensed a 'testing.' Someone was looking for the matching funds. The result of the additional betting on the Democrat resulted in his rise in the polls. There was now a week to go. The same gremlins warned of a new attack on Joyce Milner, and this caused tension in the morning meeting.

"Joyce, you have a television interview today, and I think there must be a trap there. The interviewer is refusing to divulge the direction of her questions."

"Should we anticipate and cover the expectations?" asked Jenny, another member of the team.

"I think that would take too much attention from what we need to talk about." Ray Bryant had taken control. "The main thing is to learn from Marjorie White, a more seasoned politician than you are, who lost her cool. Joyce, don't lose your cool."

"What about the drop in the polls?" asked Jenny.

"We need to allay the fears of our supporters and be strong, positive."

\*\*\*

Carole Cooper was a young, attractive, ambitious television reporter, a lean and mean interviewer. The lean came from her daily 5:30am workout at the gym. The workout included kick boxing. The mean came from her ambition. Graduating from Columbia, Carole stayed in New York City. It suited her style – vibrant, never sleeping; a city with wealth and influence. Her language skills and good looks had secured a position at the United Nations' building. At first she'd been a guide and then a liaison for some of the delegates. A mistake going out with a foreign, married diplomat had led to leaving the international arena. The diplomat helped secure a position in the media covering the United Nations and now to her national television personality status.

Looking down at her hands, she remembered the pounding that she had given the bag that morning. It was a wonder that she hadn't split her knuckles. Her hands were swollen and red; she continued rubbing moisturizing cream into them. It was more like a wringing of her hands.

The past had reappeared. It always did. How many times had she pinned some helpless man or woman, executive or politician, with the past? At first it had appeared innocuous, just a passing remark; as she had been changing into workout clothing, the only other occupant of the changing room had spoken to her. It was a typical, for her, beginning of a conversation.

"Don't I know you?" the woman asked.

Carole looked across at an attractive woman in her thirties.

"You probably recognize me from television."

"No; you were at the United Nations."

Carole looked more closely at the woman. Foreign, she thought and tried to place her face.

"I am Mrs. Sindar. Mrs. Serdar Sindar."

Carole blanched. A name that she had forgotten, now back in her life. Coincidence? Not likely! Still she waited; there was no need to plead guilty before a charge had been laid.'

"We know you're interviewing Joyce Milner tonight. You are to destroy her on air. You will attack and humiliate her or your career is over. A list of subjects will be in your office this morning." The woman slammed a locker and then left without another word or opportunity for Carole to respond.

Looking down at her hands, she realized that she was a pawn. All this time she had seen herself as a queen, in control. Now she realized that the "we" Mrs. Sindar had mentioned held all of the cards. Carole was playing the wrong game – this wasn't chess; it was a loaded hand of poker, and she couldn't win against the house.

The voice over announced to the live audience and the television viewer that they should welcome "our host Carole Cooper."

Carole looked attractive; she had chosen for this interview to dress in black. It was her mood; everything that she had picked out had been black –

from her underwear and shoes to her stockings and a dress, longer than usual, to the knees, and higher than usual at the neck.

"Good evening, ladies and gentlemen, and welcome to our show. I want to introduce the Republican candidate for mayor of New York City. Welcome with me Joyce Milner."

There was desultory applause. A veteran would have noticed that the audience was less than normal; there had been no encouragement to applaud, and that the audience, unlike any other in recent history, was predominantly male.

"Thank you for joining us this evening."

"Thank you for having me."

The banal formalities continued.

"You were married to one of the heroic firefighters who died on 9/11?"

"Yes, we were married for ten years."

"No children?"

"No, unfortunately we were unable to have any."

"It was a mixed marriage?"

"No, it was traditional. A man and a woman." Joyce responded testily. She had been warned about traps and was sensing a test right up front.

"I was referring to the fact that he was Catholic and you're Jewish."

Joyce smiled and sensed a moment of indecision in the interviewer.

"Well?" asked Carole.

"Well what? Did you ask a question or make a statement?"

Carole Cooper was experienced enough to change course. "Passover is in a few days. Will you celebrate with your family?"

"Passover is a very special time in the Jewish

religion and is usually spent with family, as you will remember from your own traditions Carole."

Carole Cooper did not like being reminded of her Jewish upbringing and had not celebrated with her family since she had left for college. She was losing control of the interview, quickly.

"Your mother does not expect you this year. Is that true?" she put as much emphasis in the question to suggest that this might be similar to giving up one's first-born child.

"Not sure, Carole. This campaign is certainly taking on a life of its own."

"The polls do not expect you to win. Even your own parents are voting for Daniel Boot."

"The voting booth, to my knowledge, is still a personal, private privilege that Americans enjoy. New Yorkers will exercise that privilege in a few days, and I certainly did not come this far along in order to roll over. In golf terms, I have no intention of laying up; we are hitting for the green. My campaign is going until the last vote is counted." Joyce was feeling confident. The training, the speech therapy, the practice had been well worth the while.

Carole Cooper was tapping the envelope in front of her. This interview had been a disaster so far.

"We'll take a break now and when we come back examine the experience of the candidate and some of the issues facing New York."

Off the air. Carole smiled at her guest and stated, "Two minutes, Joyce," then turned away, leaving one hand securely on the envelope.

A psychologist had been assigned to Joyce's team and he walked up to her now and whispered. "Be careful; she has something in the envelope that she is waiting to spring on you. Remember, stay cool; do not walk away, no matter what it may be."

"I remember, thank you."

"Just doing my job. You have done very well so far. Don't let your guard down."

A light was flashing and Carole Cooper, make up refreshed, turned again to talk to the camera.

"Welcome back to our show where our guest tonight is the Republican candidate for mayor of New York, Joyce Milner." She paused briefly. "Joyce, before the break, I promised viewers that we would talk about issues facing New York. We know that you have strong views on family, although you're seemingly estranged from your own."

"Well, Carole, I just spoke to my mother this morning, so I think your description 'estranged' is a bit off course. To the issue, however, I believe that children have the right to be safe and that family is at the heart of our society."

"But you chose to give your son up for adoption instead of providing a home for him."

Joyce Milner was stunned. No one knew about the son that she had given up while in college. The strong urge to get up and flee was only held in check with great difficulty. How was she to answer? The truth? Some of the truth? Then she remembered the training. Sit still, with a serious look on the face, and turn the subject.

"My son was so loved that I gave him up to provide for him a life that at that time, as a teenager, I could not possibly provide. I loved him enough to give him life. I loved him enough to give him up."

"So you have had no contact with him since you gave him up for adoption? You therefore have no idea if what you just said is true?"

"I trusted that the adoption agency did their job."

"If you have had no contact, how do you know that? I have documentary proof that he is thirty-seven years old and in prison for murder."

Joyce gasped, momentarily stunned. "Carole, I think that this unfounded, unnecessary, outrageous claim belongs on a different television show. Let's talk about the facts. There are seven hundred thousand people out of work in New York; there are over three hundred thousand who are either homeless or living in pitiful conditions with no heat. I want to bring jobs to New York, bring back business. I will do that with help from firefighters like my husband and police officers. There has to be an end to this lawlessness. We must take back the streets."

Carole may have hated herself at that moment more than at any other time in her life, but she remembered the threat to ruin her own career and pressed forward.

"These issues are all family related, and you have no actual experience of a real family, have you?"

"Thank you, Carole, for finally discussing my qualifications. Families are not always whose bloodlines we share; people are what is important. Family values, jobs for those families, futures for their children; futures through education; reopening schools; making those schools safe."

Carole Cooper had one more piece of information. She wanted it to impact, to resonate and be at the end of the program. She called for a station break and left her seat to talk on her cell phone.

Joyce sat, and once again her aide and psychologist came to her side.

"Great job, Joyce. Just a few more minutes after the break." The words were reassuring, the eyes behind the words were questioning. "Don't let your guard down now. The team is already working on a press release for after the program. Remember hang in, stay the course."

"Okay, Josh." Joyce smiled weakly.

The red line winked and then went steady.

"Back here in New York, this is Carole Cooper and my guest is Joyce Milner, Republican candidate for the position of New York mayor. Before the break, Joyce, we were talking about families and family values. You hold these very high do you not?"

"Yes, I do, Carole."

"Will you stand by your son when he is executed?"

"We appear to be back where we were just a little while ago – away from the real issues impacting the voters. I'm not in a position to respond to your unfounded claims regarding my son, but we live in a country moving away from execution." Joyce was tempted to ask where this was going but remembered not to ask a question, particularly one to which she did not know the answer.

"Well it appears that your son is charged in the murder of a security officer, and I'm sure that you know that the president has introduced the death penalty for crimes which include the death of our police and militia, while carrying out their duties. Where do you stand on the death penalty?"

"Life is sacred."

"Yes, life is sacred, Joyce, and I know that this has been your platform. Your husband lost his battle with issues following an alleged terrorist attack on the World Trade Center in 2001. You have been an advocate for women's rights."

"Two things, Carole. Excuse me for interrupting." Joyce could feel a flush but could not stop.

Carole Cooper sat back and the camera caught her

looking like a cat who had just found the cream.

"The terrorist attack on the World Trade Center was not 'alleged'; it was real and involved planning by a foreign terrorist group and was implemented by a terrorist cell. My husband died as a result of that attack, from the inhalation of material from the building as he worked to free those living and recover those who had perished. Secondly, I am not running on women's issues; my campaign is broad based. It is focused on the fact that with thirty percent unemployment, rampant crime, and twenty-five percent inflation, this city is a powder keg."

"Joyce, we understand these things, and the government is working on them."

"The federal government is not able to work on these issues alone. New Yorkers have to work on these issues."

"Before we wrap up the program, I would like to come back to your comment that family and family values are sacred. Did you mean that?"

"Of course."

"You will excuse my skepticism; your son, who you gave up for adoption, is now in prison for murder, and you also had an abortion."

Joyce sat stunned. There was a silence which suggested guilt; there was a glance to the side which looked like flight.

"I had a miscarriage, not an abortion."

"But you went to a clinic in Connecticut, a renowned abortion clinic."

"I went to a clinic in September 2001 when I miscarried. All of the hospitals were full of victims of a terrorist attack."

"According to Dr. Smith…"

"What happened to doctors' privacy?" Joyce was

outraged.

"Well, that is all that we have time for this evening. My guest has been the Republican candidate for New York mayor, Joyce Milner. We have heard her values on families and unfortunately the facts of her own family actions; the estrangement from her own parents; the giving up of a son whose life is in balance on a charge of murder, and the abortion of another child. Not exactly a family model. Good night from Carole Cooper and the entire New York News team."

The camera had turned to Joyce Milner who was trying in vain to communicate. The microphone had been turned off and her gestures looked like pleading.

Carole Cooper walked quickly away and went to the ladies' room where she vomited. She looked in the mirror and did not like what she saw.

# Chapter Four

"A disaster, a disaster, a disaster!"

"Joyce, calm down; it's not helping," Ray Bryant was looking more disheveled than usual. He was sweating profusely and looked like he had not slept.

He hadn't!

It was the day following the interview with Carole Cooper. The entire team was meeting at the headquarters set up in downtown Manhattan. It was luxurious; it had been a brokerage firm before the current administration. The staff had been cut by ninety percent and moved out, leaving all the furniture. The space had been donated to the Milner campaign.

"Then what do you call it, Ray? Even a brilliant media director such as yourself could not spin it as a win."

"We have to face the press this morning and make a statement."

"You mean I need to admit that I'm worthless and that I quit."

"There will be no talk of quitting," a voice from outside the immediate circle spoke with quiet authority.

"Okay, Harry, then…" Joyce was cut off by the man walking forward.

Harry Taylor was tall, blond, and nearing sixty. He

was still handsome and still commanded respect. Harry had held positions in various governments, as undersecretary usually. It was known that undersecretaries did all the work, made all the decisions, and left the spotlight and the comradery to others. Harry Taylor, now a professor at Columbia, was in charge of this operation. He was also the head of the Sons of Liberty in New York. There was a price on the head of Papillion. Harry Taylor was Papillion.

"It was a set-up."

"You said that she was a friend, that the interview would be smooth." Joyce was looking accusingly at Ray.

"It was," said Harry. "Until someone got to our interviewer."

"She has to show some toughness," Ray said defensively.

"Ray, you've been up all night with a group of people; what have you got that are facts?" asked Harry.

Ray saw a chance to show his worth. He was being paid a good deal of money and who knew in these uncertain times where the next job might be.

"First, the son; a fine young man, grew up in Nutley, across the river, went to Rutgers on a soccer scholarship, graduated and worked as an accountant in the city. He married his high school sweetheart, two kids. They had been separated for a few months as things got tough. He moved into the city and was out with friends after work when a militia group stopped them. The story gets a little hazy after that. The militia says that some of the women were inappropriately dressed and tried to arrest them. Other witnesses say that the militia were fondling the women and jeering at the men's' complaints. Anyway, there is no dispute over the fact that Jeff, your son, hit the militia man."

"The story sounds like provocation and reaction," said Harry.

"True, except that the militia man died," said Ray.

"Of a punch?"

"There was a question of whether the militia man was drunk or on drugs, but it never came up at trial."

"What can we do?" asked Joyce.

"First things first: get you elected, and then acquit him with a fair trial," said Harry, trying to bring the focus back to the current problem.

"What else, Ray?"

"It is true that the White Plains Wellness Clinic does perform abortions. It is not illegal. It is also true that it is a first-class gynecological and obstetrics clinic. Tried Smith at home, no good; he has been bought."

"So, Joyce, who else knew why you went to White Plains?"

"My parents; they paid the bill."

"And that's where the lead came from. Anybody else? Your husband?"

"No, it was September 11th. Frank was in a building that was falling down on live television. I got pains, called the hospital, they were not even answering the phones. There was just a message that the caller should try elsewhere. 911 was jammed. It was insane."

"So how'd you get there?"

"My sister-in-law; she lived down the street and came over. She's a waitress and had heard of a clinic out of the city. We got in her car and drove. They wanted money before they'd do anything, so Sara called my parents; they agreed to cover my check."

"Get on it, Ray," ordered Harry. "Have Sara clean,

smart, and well-rehearsed for the press conference."

"She won't thank you," Joyce stated. "She probably worked last night."

"We'll send Sean."

"Can't. Sean is on Carole Cooper," said Jenny.

"Find someone. Send a limo; it always works," said Ray.

"I think that we have something to work with. We'll be back in half an hour."

"Ray, will you be at the conference?" asked Harry.

"Of course."

"Then get a shave and a clean shirt. Don't want them to think that you were up all night, do we?"

Ray left with a grin and was already calling home for fresh clothes to be brought to the office.

"Jenny, Sean! What's happening?" asked Harry.

"Carole Cooper didn't show up at the gym this morning; first time in anyone's memory. Funny thing though. A woman arrived at the gym yesterday in a large Mercedes, went in, then five minutes later came out."

"Description?"

"Attractive, fortyish, Middle Eastern."

"Now we know how, but why and with what?"

"What do you mean?" asked Jenny.

There was no answer, as Harry was into thoughts that took him into his own world of espionage and counter espionage.

\*\*\*

The press conference started contentiously with the same questions as the previous night but, asked in the argumentative manner of a reporter who will have the lead-in, the best five minutes on the evening news. Five minutes to prove that they were knowledgeable and tough.

Joyce took control of the room, raising her hands to quiet the media as she'd been instructed. "Ladies and gentlemen of the press, allow me to speak, and then I will answer your questions once I'm done."

The rumble of the crowd ceased.

"Who I am now, and my position on many issues, has been molded by my experiences. We all grow and change. But I stand by my decision to allow my son to have a good life. And those of you worth your salt will have certainly discovered exactly what my team did. My son grew up in a loving family, went on to have a decent, law-abiding life, and is – in truth – in jail for protecting women from harassment by a member of a militia, not someone sworn to uphold the law. I appreciate Carole Cooper bringing this matter to my attention so that I can work towards ensuring that all of our good citizens are protected by the true laws of this country rather than by the martial law which has made too many fearful to live their lives. As I stated last night, we need to take back these streets and reembrace family values."

She paused as Sara Gallagher made an entrance and embraced her sister-in-law as a friend might. Joyce noticed that the team sent to pick Sara up had stopped at a beauty salon on the way downtown. Normally a blowsy effervescent person, the transformation had done nothing to curb her bubbly nature but, taking some of the height and brightness out of the dyed blonde hair, made her seem more mature. Friends, after seeing her on television, would remark that she could have been a star and that she should be on one of those reality shows.

"I should introduce my sister-in-law, Sara Gallagher, who drove me to the White Plains Clinic on 9/11 as my husband was on duty at Ground Zero, the

World Trade Center attacked by terrorists that awful day. She will confirm my version of events and has agreed to be available for your questions. Sara."

"Good morning. September 11$^{th}$ was the worst morning of my life. My phone kept ringing. First, my mother, hysterical that Frank, my brother, was in the building that was on fire. Then other friends and my sister in Hartford, asking if I knew anything. It was awful." Tears streamed down her face at the memory. She pulled a tissue out of her pocket. "About one o'clock Joyce called and said that she had just heard from Frank, he was not in the building. We were laughing and crying on the phone when she cried out in pain. 'The baby,' she said. 'Sara, the baby, can you come now?' I dashed over right away. The news said that the hospitals were closed to all except emergency vehicles. I remembered overhearing a customer talk about this clinic and where it was so, when I got to the house, I got Joyce in the car and drove straight there. Joyce miscarried in my car; that's the truth."

A flurry of hands went up and Ray, peering out, selected a known reporter.

"Did you know that it was an abortion clinic?"

"No, not 'til last night. The sign said Gynecology and Obstetrics."

Sara was looking straight into the eyes of the reporter with her own hazel eyes, reflecting no guile. These were the eyes of a waitress, one who had seen and heard all the facts of life and had taken them at face value. Never condemning any of life's mistakes, never repeating secrets entrusted to her.

Another reporter asked, "Do you consider Joyce Milner a friend or were you a convenient relative?"

"Joyce has always been a friend. We don't see as much of each other as we should, but that's what happens."

"Did she ask you to come here and tell this story?"

"She asked if I would be willing to come and tell the truth. I was happy to."

"Did she pay you to come here today?"

"No, though someone paid for my hairdo. Do you like it?"

A few reporters chuckled.

"A little extravagant luxury," a well-known male reporter sneered.

"I have my hair done every week and colored once a month. This morning it was a mare's nest. Not extravagant; I wouldn't appear in public how it looked earlier. After waitressing all night, I didn't have the energy to make it presentable myself."

This conversation having nothing to do with politics quieted the crowd until Ray intervened. "One more question perhaps?"

"Will you vote for Joyce Milner, when her family will not?"

"Yes, I will. While her family doesn't appreciate her politics – they're longtime Democrats, I don't vote for the party, but rather for the person. I know Joyce will be a bright beacon for New York."

That appeared to be the final word. With a few more flashing bulbs and a hug from Joyce, she left the podium.

Joyce Milner reached the microphone.

"Thank you, Sara. Thank you for your promise to vote for me." Joyce was much more relaxed now; the anxiety over what might have been asked and answered was over.

"Are there any more questions or can we move on? I have a busy day ahead as do all of you," she smiled.

A hand was raised.

"Yes?"

"Did your campaign pay for your sister-in-law's hair styling?"

"No, it did not. Sara asked if she could do her hair if she was going to appear on television. I believe that the salon was gracious. Since you're interested, I can now give them an endorsement; it was 'Hair Today' on High Street.

"I want to conclude this press conference with the promise that regardless of the attempts to besmirch and belittle my character; that I am in this race all the way. This is not about my family; this is about my commitment to the citizens of the number one city in the world. New York will improve, and its citizens will be better off when I am mayor. Thank you; God Bless America!"

Ray Bryant was beaming as she left the podium. He gave her a perfunctory pat on the back and then waded into the sea of reporters. They had come to gore the sacrificial lamb and were leaving with a more human story for their newspapers and the evening news.

\*\*\*

Joyce's campaign found it interesting that the primary television stations gave airtime to Sara Gallagher and then the early broadcasts had the closing statement of Joyce Milner. The later broadcasts were apparently burying that story. Harry learned that the reason the stations gave was that the statement was blatantly political. It was replaced by a rerun of Daniel Boots welcoming the new head of the New York militia. Harry shook his head and wondered how many voters would be fooled by the fake news propagated by the government's stronghold on the media. Freedom of the press was no longer allowed to exist. The truth was simply pulverized into soundbites that would slide down the throats of those uneducated enough to not know the difference.

\*\*\*

The balance of the week was chaotic for the Milner campaign. The first issue arose when the militia stated that they wanted the execution of Jeff, the son of Joyce Milner, to take place immediately and showed up at Sing Sing. Anticipating this move, the governor had been persuaded to move him to Attica. Thwarted, the Brotherhood had put a price on his head. The union guards at Attica were told of the problems that might ensue if there were any injury to the prisoner. A brief for a retrial was submitted to the state supreme court. This was designed to start a process to free Jeff Drysdale. Joyce met Jeff's estranged wife and her grandchildren.

The meetings where Joyce Milner spoke were all broken up by the militia, making false claims that the meeting participants had started the fracas. As a result the numbers were down at the gatherings. The meetings all included at least one question about her jailed son and her visit to the abortion clinic. The police were providing protection but were frequently outnumbered by the militia.

The Sunday prior to the election date, polls were predicting a landslide victory for Daniel Boots. The Sons of Liberty and Mark Hughes were matching betting in Las Vegas, getting two and sometimes three-to-one odds.

Harry Taylor was busy. He had Sean following Carole Cooper and others had followed Mrs. Sindar. The tape of the television interview between Carole Cooper and Joyce Milner was played and replayed. The size of the envelope, the unease of the questioner, all were scrutinized. He had an idea; it was not yet a plan. All of his chess experience was going to be utilized and hopefully result in 'checkmate'.

The black-hearted media queen was his target. His knight, Sean, was tracking her while other pieces were tracking the bishop, the messenger, the Svengali. But Harry knew that capturing the queen would only be a battle victory; to win at chess, one needed to be victorious over the king. And that was a much longer game to play.

\*\*\*

Sunday night arrived and all was in place. It would now be enacted in front of millions of viewers. There had been some further dirty tricks during the week, but the opposition seemed to be confident of a win. Harry needed them confident; he needed their guard down. In Vegas, the opposition was also confident of a win and never stopped to wonder where the funds bet against them had originated.

Sunday night had been designated as a final push by the Boots campaign. It was an interview on prime-time television. The interviewer, Carole Cooper, had been chosen and it was expected that the same parties would influence a positive outcome for them. Harry Taylor was counting on it.

The first move was where Mrs. Sindar was stopped by a police car on the way to meet Carole Cooper. She never noticed that the brown envelope had been switched, that the questions which the interviewee had rehearsed were now on Harry's desk.

Inside the new envelope, which was held until the second half of the program, were questions together with a sealed white envelope with instructions. On the envelope was written, *Hand it to the candidate and ask him to explain the contents.*

"Mr. Boots, your strong showing in the polls reflects your broad experience as opposed to the limited experience of your opponent."

It was not a lead in that had been rehearsed, but it was a friendly lob.

"Yes, I believe that's true. I have practiced law for fifteen years, representing many of the cities' finest companies."

"But you never made it to the partnership level. Why is that?" asked Carole.

Again, the question raised no flags except in Harry Taylor's living room where he sat on the edge of his seat and in a penthouse condominium where Sindar and two other men looked anxiously at each other.

"It may have to do with the pro-bono work which I have undertaken and my commitment to immigration reform." Daniel Boots was now looking around at the exits.

"Yes, I am told that you take a month every year to help out in Africa and the Middle East."

"That is correct," he breathed and relaxed.

"In fact, it may surprise you that we have photographs of your work." Carole reached for and opened the white envelope handing it to Daniel Boots. "Can you tell the audience exactly what it is that you are doing?"

A photograph fell out of the envelope. Carole Cooper screamed. Daniel Boots, white as a ghost, stood up, almost fell, and although his mouth was moving: no words came out.

The picture showed a naked Daniel Boots receiving oral sex from a boy of about ten while two other boys stood in the background. Sean, standing in the production studio, made sure that the image stayed on the television screen for ten seconds. The network later could not explain how this had been allowed to happen. Sean had paid the crew very well. Very well indeed.

In the penthouse in Manhattan, there was blind fury and expletives in three languages.

In a much smaller room, Harry poured himself a small, single malt whiskey, raised the glass.

"Checkmate!"

\*\*\*

The television switchboard immediately lit to capacity. The social media sites went viral. Images had been prepared in case the network had somehow suppressed the pictures; they were released within seconds of the moment that New York had been shocked.

The next day the world awoke to controversy.

A spokesman for Daniel Boots said that the photographs were faked and that they could prove it. Although there was sympathy for this, a question asked where, if these were faked, was the proof of where the candidate had been every year for a month. No answer was given. The bigger the silence, the bigger the slide.

The candidate did not appear. He did not defend. Daniel Boots hid.

\*\*\*

Carole Cooper was found dead in her apartment Monday afternoon. There was no autopsy, no inquiry; suicide was the official verdict. Mrs. Sindar was gone from New York, back to Turkey her husband claimed; there was no evidence of her leaving New York or having arrived anywhere.

## Chapter Five

It was just before ten o'clock Tuesday night in Texas when the concession statement was read in New York by a spokesperson for Daniel Boots. The candidate had not been seen all day, and the concession could have been read within five minutes of the polls opening. The statement was held until the East Coast television stations had closed. Cameras in Joyce Milner's headquarters had shown a host of volunteers celebrating all evening. The police and five other department spokespersons had been interviewed ad nauseam; the storyline was of their having voted for the Republican candidate after a lifetime of supporting Democrats. The overwhelming message was that law and order was their business, and a safe and secure New York was good for them, their families, for New York, and for the United States.

Ellie May and Jim Joseph had watched through a satellite feed from their ranch all evening.

"That was a good win," said Ellie May.

"It was a loss for Boots rather than a win for Milner," her husband stated reflectively, thinking of the wider implications rather than the Republican win.

"I wonder," he started. "I wonder if labels tie us down?"

"What do you mean?"

"Republicans looking at life differently from

Democrats," he paused. "I was impressed by the woman who spoke for the police force about law and order being the cornerstone; not a red or blue label."

"You think we should be starting a new party?"

"No, that doesn't work. Tea Party, Green Party... for some reason voters want the comfort of a party they know. Plus any new party seems to have a narrow agenda."

Ellie Mae was not fully convinced. "What if we started the American Party?"

"It might be like painting a target on your back. The current administration could run a Republican and a Democrat for the same seat, split the vote three ways. It would also be easier to rig the vote. The counting in Florida could take four years; by then it would be time to vote again."

"Worth chucking at the wall?"

"Yep, why not? Some of the great minds that we have working with us might make it stick."

"Look, look. Joyce Milner is about to speak."

\*\*\*

Joyce Milner looked radiant. She may have been exhausted, but there was no question that this was a moment that she had not expected.

"Friends," she waited for the cheering to quiet a little. "Friends, thank you. Thank you for believing in me through my own doubts.

"Thanks to the police and to the firefighters who keep this great city safe. Without their support, none of this was possible; none of this was thinkable. My commitment to them and to you is to take back the streets of New York. After I am sworn in tomorrow, the militia of New York City is to be disbanded; its members will have forty-eight hours to return their weapons to the armory."

There was wild cheering and cameras were trained on two police officers in the room who were smiling at the statements of support.

\*\*\*

In Texas there was, in contrast, quiet.

"I wonder if she knows what she is up against," Ellie May spoke quietly. "The militia is endorsed by Washington; they can send in the military in support of the militia."

"The militia units were approved by the states."

"Okay, so the National Guard goes in."

"She's talking again."

\*\*\*

In New York the cheers had died down again.

"The police will be given all the support they need to bring back law and order. When people ask, how we will pay for this, I will point to the prosperity that will follow a safe environment. We will pay for it from the police details, no longer to be afforded free to visiting politicians. If they are politicians, then they belong in Washington; if they are shopping, then they must provide for themselves." Joyce Milner turned and smiled to someone in the wings. When the camera swung around, they had gone.

"This has been a long campaign, and this has been a very long day; make no mistake, this is going to be years of very long days. I hope and pray that with your strength we can make a difference.

"I have no more prepared words; but I will be here until I have thanked everyone in this room personally. God bless you all; God bless America."

\*\*\*

"Do you think the National Guard will go in?"

"They may be ordered in, but I suspect that like here in the West there are areas of New York where they won't go."

"So what do you think, Jim?"

"I think that it has begun."

"Begun?"

"The fight. The fight to take back our democracy."

"She is a target; right?"

"Right. She and her family, friends, advisors, supporters…"

"On that cheerful note," said Ellie May ruefully, "I think that I am going to bed. I want to be awake early enough to get the East Coast reaction to the new Mayor of New York."

\*\*\*

Wednesday morning newscasts were confused, contradictory, congratulatory, and conspiratorial all at the same time.

It was clear that the administrative view was that somehow the election had been stolen from them, but how? They had control of the media, control of the process; they had attacked, they had subverted, they had backed their candidate with real material. Financing had not been spared. It was such a slam dunk that it had to be a mistake, and the quicker they corrected it, the better. The governor called for an inquiry.

The problem with an inquiry was that one of the prime witnesses was dead. Evidence from another source, even if extorted before she disappeared, was not necessarily helpful.

Some programs followed Joyce Milner's progress through the morning as she visited every fire station and every precinct in the city. She was heavily supported by police, and her progress was announced by sirens, car horns, and truck air horns. There were few news items about the death of the news anchor. It had quickly been deemed a suicide, no autopsy, and a quick cremation. The swiftness had been questioned by the supporters of the Sons of Liberty. An inquiry found that the arrangements had been authorized by her parents as soon as they had arrived in the city. The documents were on official paper, although no one recognized the signature. The funeral director said that it seemed a little unusual, but all of his paperwork was in order.

The head of the militia stated that he and his army would be back on the streets protecting the citizens of New York. The governor ordered the National Guard to assemble.

It was a powder keg.

\*\*\*

In Texas Ellie May was scribbling notes. Sheila Hutchins, her public relations director, sat quietly watching and occasionally writing a comment of her own.

"Sheila, we have to get some messages to New York. We must be able to communicate; first congratulations, then a link."

"I've been thinking. We can send congratulations out for everyone to see. It will show support and also endorse the promises that Milner has made."

"Okay. I have some thoughts here. Let's put it on paper, edit, and get it on the evening news."

"That shouldn't take long with three pages of notes you've written." Sheila was smiling. "This is the first positive news in a long time. Progress at last."

"How about the other communications that we are working on?"

"I don't know."

"Isn't Ginny working with that team?"

"She may be my daughter, but that doesn't mean

she tells me everything. Mark Hughes is down in Austin too, isn't he?" Sheila was deflecting the perceived criticism of her daughter.

"Yes, they're both going to the computer conference. Let's ask them to stop in New York. In fact it will be better for them to take ground transportation into Boston," said Ellie May, immediately making a note for herself.

"I'll go see what I can find out. I'll draft a statement of congratulations, and I'll ask Mark and Ginny to come by the ranch to give us an update on their progress." Sheila silently left the room.

Ellie May sat back in her chair at the desk. The chance to sit and think alone was a luxury she now only enjoyed in bed. Recently she'd been too tired for that contemplation.

Now she turned off the intercom, shut off her cell phone, and took the phone jack out of the wall.

It was true that it was a beginning, the fight to return democracy to the greatest country on Earth.

She closed her eyes and analyzed her situation. What right did she have in determining that there was a role for her? Had she earned that right? A few words spoken in defiance and hiding behind a wall of Texas Rangers wasn't enough. Joyce Milner stood up to be counted. She was still standing, now with a target on her back.

Sure, she was setting up a network of communications. She had also made a deal with the devil. There is no such thing as a free lunch, and the cost of running for President of the United States had been exorbitant. And that was the cost to lose the race. Was she sure that she had the fortitude to win? The will? The courage? Someone had to; otherwise it was not a democracy.

Democracy: rule of the people. Terrorist: opposing an elected government. Was it true that this government was the will of the electorate? Arguably! Then why was she referring in conversation, in her notes, and even in this quiet reflection to the beginning of a fight for democracy? Surely she was looking to join a terrorist gang and President "What's-his-name" would in actuality be fighting for democracy.

No! No! No! Opposing a political party with a message different from the other side was healthy. Unfortunately many people had unhealthy things happen. So what? Joyce Milner showed the way; stand up, have a message, let the people hear it.

Put a target on your back.

Ellie May felt better now and plugged the telephone back into the wall, reactivated the intercom.

"Has Sheila finished the press release? Let's put another cat into the pigeons!"

It took half an hour until everyone was satisfied with the press release and another half hour before the production team could set up the video part of the program. In the meantime a telephone link was set up to New York.

"Joyce Milner? This is Ellie May Joseph calling to congratulate you and your team on a resounding victory."

"Do you know…?" Joyce Milner started to say.

"That this conversation is being recorded," finished Ellie May. "Probably for quality assurance purposes," she said sarcastically.

"Thank you for your congratulations, although given the present claims against you, I'm not sure that your endorsement is going to sit well."

"True, but then the claims against me have the

same source as the claims made against you during your campaign."

"And Boots?"

"It appears to be the same brown envelope source." Ellie May was aware that she was revealing that she had noted the brown envelope and that she was suggesting that they were from the same person or persons did no harm but might sow additional doubts.

"Thank you for calling. I had no idea that my little campaign was so important."

"It was, and is, of tremendous importance to the future of our country. I look forward to meeting you and talking again soon. God Bless America."

Ellie May and her media advisors listened to the message which Ellie May had recorded, to the telephone conversation with Joyce Milner, and they watched the video analyzing what the Democrats were saying about presentations. They were energized at finally doing something positive. Ellie May was the most energized, which she attributed to her twenty minutes of personal quiet reflection.

Mark Hughes and Ginny Hutchins sat with the whole re-election campaign committee. An agenda had been prepared and the first item was a report from Ginny, who had inherited her mother's energy and forthright manner of communicating. It was interesting that where her mother had tempered her blunt speech in her career as public relations director, Ginny had not. It was as if the hours spent in the Austin Astrophysics lab alone was just the building of a dam ready to burst into words.

"The idea is great. The results have been less than glorious. In fact they stink. Every time we solve a problem, another arises."

Mark interrupted, "The satellite is working fine."

"That's like saying that the computer works, but we can't find any compatible software. Okay, so the satellite works," she admitted, "most of the time; but the passwords are too complicated and have to be reset. It takes time, and we're all getting tired. The group is starting to fall apart."

"Can we get into the networks?" asked Sheila.

"Yes, we can hack into the networks for short bursts, about five minutes at a time. We have to hit them one at a time or someone may figure out, by triangulation, which satellite we are using."

"It seems one five-minute burst to all the networks would have more clout," Allyn contributed.

"If they found our satellite, they would blow it out of the sky!"

"Point taken." Allyn looked suitably chastened.

"And the password issue?" asked Alistair Kirk, the chief of staff in the previous campaign, now on temporary leave from his company.

"We're working on a book code based on the Bible," Ginny explained.

"And roughly how should it work?" Alistair was practical and knew that there would be issues.

"Basically from the television broadcasts. If the broadcast begins with a word beginning with the letter D, then the book is Deuteronomy, P is psalms, etc. Then later there would be a number. One would mean chapter one, part one, and the code is the first nine letters."

There were hands up with questions, but Ginny continued anticipating them.

"The King James Bible will be used, and if there is no message or the site is closed; then the broadcast will begin with a letter that does not relate to a book in the Bible."

There were no more questions as all of the avenues appeared to be covered.

"We have a lot to work on. Thanks, Ginny." Ellie May was moving along. "Next, is sending messages out. Sheila?"

Sheila pulled out a large folder and started preparing her presentation.

"First thing is that we have to present a candidate," she paused, "Ellie May, that is you, and there is no turning back."

Ellie May nodded a lot more confidently than she felt.

"Then we have to take the high road. Meaning, no dirty tricks."

"None?" asked Mark Hughes.

"Well, none from here. If the Sons of Liberty have events that they publicize, there is little that we can do, but from here we should be squeaky clean."

"We ask for a debate."

"Are you nuts? Or were you thinking of neutral ground, like on the moon?" Jim Joseph asked, protective of his wife.

"No, my idea is that we get them to agree to show up, and then we beam Ellie May from our studio here, as if she were in the room. The experts Mark brought in tell me that it *is* possible."

"Won't it identify our satellite?" asked Alistair Kirk.

"No, we'll use the network satellite."

"It can be done?" asked Jim Joseph.

"Yes."

"Good enough for me."

"We'll use the same technique to rally in all of the states."

"Will the militia be a problem?"

"Of course. All the more reason why we need to communicate securely. The Sons will have to thwart the militia."

"Funding?" Ellie May was changing the subject. She had spent three hours the previous day in making a detailed agenda.

"Seems to be working well," said Allyn Cherwin.

"The investors are encouraged by the success in New York and even though the stakes were small, it was a win and now we are playing with the oppositions money," said Mark.

"Even after expenses?" asked Alistair.

"Expenses were surprisingly low. Both candidates were exposed on television most days and so there were few political ads."

"It worked once. It may not work again."

"I think it will. The opposition got rid of what they thought were the culprits without knowing what happened." Mark was confident.

"Let's not assume anything but the worst," said Ellie May.

"They may have questioned and tortured those women before killing them," said Bobby Joe.

Ellie May nodded in agreement to the security chief dressed in full Texas fashion – jeans, ten-gallon hat, boots, and revolver.

"Who are you talking about?" asked a shaken Ginny.

"The announcer and the diplomat's wife," said Bobby Joe.

"But the papers said it was suicide…"

"Hmmph! Don't you believe it." Bobby Joe was very sure after witnessing the happenings during the last presidential campaign.

"Which brings us to the danger that you and Mark

will be in when you're in New York." Ellie May was speaking to Ginny.

Sheila instinctively put her hand on her daughter's arm.

"New York? I thought we were going to Boston."

"You are, but I, we need you to make a detour and deliver some support and some of our thinking to New York. We expect you to meet the mayor and Papillion, the leader of the Sons of Liberty, in New York, along with a certain underworld figure from the old Bonanno gang."

"Does Mark know this?" asked Ginny, looking earnestly from one face to another.

"Some. The reason we want you both at this meeting is to be able to take the latest and strongest first-hand experience out of Texas." This was Ellie May at her political best. Getting people to do things that they did not want to do. "We have plenty of time. The conference in Boston is two weeks away."

"Well… not exactly a lot of time," Sheila stated.

"I have a feeling that I'm not going to like this," Ginny admitted.

Ginny was new to politics. She was unaware of all the previous meetings, discussions, and decisions in spite of her mother being involved…or maybe because Sheila had shielded her daughter from the danger that they had been and were still in.

The room was quiet. Everyone knew a little of the expedition, some knew all of the pieces, but this was the coming together of the sum of the parts.

Ellie May took a drink of water. She realized that this was, in many ways, the most important conversation in which she would ever participate. She had to convince these people in the room to follow her. She needed their 100% loyalty, 100% energy,

100% dedication to this course of action.

"We'll announce on July 4th that we are forming a new political party, the American Party." She waited for the buzz to quiet down. "We'll announce to the world that day that the agenda is to bring back all of the ideals that the original drafters of the Constitution had in mind, but updated to the twenty-first century. Ginny, you and Mark are going to bring this message to the Sons of Liberty. I need their support and commitment. There is a draft manifesto, but it will require input from every state."

"You expect us to go to every state?" Ginny was in shock.

"Of course not. Just as many as we can fit in. Western States will have a different ambassador."

"But, but, but…Do you know how many states are east of Texas?"

"Let's quickly cover the logistics of this trip and groups that we must meet.

"First, you will go out of Port Arthur on a fishing boat and be transferred in the Gulf to another boat which will take you into Louisiana. Tomorrow night you will meet the Sons of Liberty, then leave and go through Mississippi to Mobile."

"Why not Mississippi?" asked Mark.

"We have no reliable contacts there.

"It's also important that you leave immediately after every meeting. No socializing, no stopping. After Mobile; a cruise again to Tampa, Florida, then up the coast road to Savannah, Charlestown, and Raleigh, then to New Jersey and New York."

Mark had been listening and counting the stops or, as he was figuring, the non-stops.

"You mentioned cities and then New Jersey, not Newark. Is there a reason?"

"Very clever, Mark. Yes, I want you to stop and see Marjorie White. I want you to deliver a message, and I want her to be ready to join the American Party."

It was clear that this was news to just about everyone in the room.

"She is under house arrest," said Alistair Kirk.

"I expect that a man with Mark's resources can overcome that small inconvenience."

The understatement brought a chuckle to the room, a smirk to Mark's face, and a scowl to the face of Ginny Hutchins.

"Then to New York with a message for the mayor and, finally, on to Boston."

"I think that you missed a few states," Ginny said a little sarcastically.

"For a leisurely trip home," Ellie May said gently, recognizing that this was a lot to ask of a twenty-five-year-old who had been outside of Texas just twice before this trip in her entire life.

## Chapter Six

They left inauspiciously and unnoticed from Port Arthur. The fifty-foot fishing boat smelled of rotten fish and diesel. No amount of cleaning was going to rid the vessel of decades of catches. Nothing could disguise the smell from long lines baited with shellfish, neatly laid on the rear of the boat. The smell of diesel fuel filled the air as the stack blew irregular puffs of smoke which rose and fell as the breeze from the west knocked down the proof that the whole scene was impatient to be gone. Gone from the tethers of shore and out into the gulf where a new adventure lay. It was always a match, man testing his wits and experience with Mother Nature.

Mark and Ginny were both carrying small suitcases. It was to be a challenge to manage all that was to come with just a few changes of clothing. It had been easier for Ginny, fresh from college, than Mark who was used to fresh shirts every day, together with fresh underwear, socks, and shoes to match his different suits. He had to choose one suit and as much underwear as he could find, together with slacks and the blue jeans he was wearing. They were indistinguishable in their waterproof slickers and heavy sweaters from the other men on the dock and on deck; only the stumble as Ginny managed the gangplank gave away their inexperience.

The captain, leaning from the bridge, watched as they headed below, then with a whistle the stern line was dropped as the gang plank rolled ashore. He reversed without looking, a practice to swing the end away as the front line was dropped. Into the current he accelerated. They were late, but rushing was not going to get them there any faster. Clearing the harbor with the current, the westerly wind was immediately apparent. He pushed the throttle and felt the comfortable throbbing of the engines through his feet and looked into the darkness. Nothing but rolling sea. He looked at his instruments; all normal. A sailor came onto the bridge.

"Take over, Al, while I welcome our guests."

"Who are they, Captain?" On the boat he always called him captain even though they were brothers-in-law.

"Didn't ask, nor should you. Forget you saw them; Billy should too!"

Billy was Al's son and the only other sailor on board. A family business, the familiarity stopped at the dock. Al grunted acknowledgement. He would be told what he needed to know.

The captain entered the cabin below. It was small. This was a working boat, not built for pleasure. There was a table, four cups, three with cracks in them, and a refrigerator. Above was a cupboard that contained coffee, tea, and sugar. Billy was sat at one side of the table on a bench that doubled as a bunk, which was shared and used in shifts. Billy was about twenty, lithe and muscular with an open face. He was facing and looking with obvious interest across at Ginny Hutchins.

"Billy, go topside."

"But…" the reluctance was obvious as he scooped

his coat and put it on in one motion while heading for the door.

Addressing his passengers, the captain told them, "Make yourself comfortable. You'll be with us for about four and a half to five hours. Try to sleep. This is the easier ride. Big rollers coming straight down the Gulf. When you leave, if I guess your destination correctly, you'll be going across the waves. That'll be bumpy."

"Thank you, Captain. I am…"

"Don't tell me. I don't want to know. I was asked, I owed a favor, and I've been paid." The captain rose to leave. "I'll keep Billy out of here while you're aboard. "There is only one head though." He nodded to the far door and left.

"Head?" Ginny asked Mark.

He laughed and replied, "Bathroom."

An hour later Billy came downstairs.

"Making tea for the Captain. Want some?" He looked around for Ginny.

Mark nodded towards the head. The sounds were of retching.

"Yes, please. I hope no one needs the head."

"I'll make a tea for her, too. It'll help."

Billy made tea with some precision but no finesse. A battered can that had a spout received several spoons of loose tea, then it was filled to the rim with boiling water from an equally old kettle. He took a large package from the refrigerator.

"Sandwiches," he said needlessly. "Want one?" he asked anxiously. "Only we didn't expect you."

"No thanks," said Mark. "And I don't think that the girl will have the stomach for it either."

"I'll make soup before we fish, maybe water it down some."

It was both a hospitable comment suggesting a sharing and also perhaps a question, anxious in some way to know how long this intrusion was going to last.

"Thanks," said Mark, answering neither question.

Hearing the noise, Ginny emerged from the head. She looked ghastly.

"Making you a cup of tea," said Billy, as he picked up the only unchipped mug and poured from the battered pot. He put in two spoons of sugar and passed it into her reluctant, trembling hands.

"It's hot. It'll help."

Billy poured three more cups with sugar and headed out with the package of sandwiches.

Mark looked around. There were no more cups or mugs.

"Looks as if we're sharing."

Ginny sat still with both hands around the mug, had a small sip then handed it to Mark. She laid in a fetal position on the bunk.

Mark put a cushion under her head and covered her with the coat that she'd worn onto the boat. He washed the mug, which had smelled slightly of vomit, and poured very dark tea into it. The thought of sugar made him taste the liquid without. He immediately realized that it needed sugar, added some, then after another sip added a heaping teaspoon.

Mark watched the sleeping Ginny as he drank. There was nothing in her life that had prepared her for this adventure. There was nothing in his life that had prepared him either. He looked at his watch and, putting on his coat, went up to the bridge.

The three fishermen stood looking into the darkness; their faces were lit bluish from the lights on the instruments.

"Looks black. What is there to see?" asked Mark.

A nod from the captain caused Al and Billy to leave.

"Take the cups, Billy."

After they'd left, he continued. "Forget his head if it were loose."

Mark looked out at the heaving seas, the swells seemed enormous and, as they crested, the view was of the swells as far as the darkness allowed. The instruments glowed while the radar quietly chipped in recognition of other boats out of sight.

"Headwind has us behind schedule," the captain said. "We're still an hour and a half from where we're to rendezvous."

"Is that a problem?"

"Which?" The captain was contemplating and looking out of the port side. "Gump won't be happy, but he'll wait. The headwind will make a transfer a little more complicated than it should be."

"Gump?"

"Yes," said the captain. "He loved that movie, and he was a wide receiver, so all his teammates called him Gump and it stuck. Good man. Got his own boat and his kids all work it."

"Do you have any kids, Captain?"

"Girls. Billy will get the boat if there are any fish left, or any that we're allowed to catch. Speaking of girls, is your companion any better?"

"Sleeping."

"Good. While the boys are down there, I'll give Gump an idea of how long we're going to be."

They were in fact an hour late, and the transition from one boat to another took twice as long as they'd expected. The two boats were lashed together. A boson's chair was created and, with much swinging and several bruises, Mark, Ginny, and their bags were transferred. The boats separated and then were pushed together with a force that sent everyone to the floor. Fortunately everyone was wearing a safety line and the net result was more bruising and several expletives.

"Don't you go and make a habit of this," shouted Gump to the captain.

It seemed unlikely that the words were heard, but he must have guessed at the meaning as the captain raised his hand in farewell – a friendly gesture.

Gump and his three sons were all hewn from the same mahogany. Black and solid, the three boys were in their late teens and early twenties. They introduced each other, the youngest pointed to his older brother and said, "Lump." The brother reciprocated by turning to the next, "Pump," while making a gesture with his arm, "and Hump" as he swiveled his hips.

The youngest brother launched himself at the older sibling. Having anticipated the move, there was a scramble until Gump intervened.

"Boys, we got guests; take it below."

With a few pushes, they filed out of the bridge. Gump looked at Ginny and Mark with some interest for several minutes.

"Gump…is it okay if I call you Gump?"

"Everyone does," he said, the Alabama accent soft and slow.

"Gump, thanks for the help. I'm not sure what you know."

"I know you come from Texas. I seen the boat. I was told to pick up a package and given the GPS. Glad it weren't drugs; I don't transport drugs."

"We…"

"I was told not to ask. I told the boys don't ask and don't tell nobody."

"You must have been at sea."

"Yep, Margaret, that's my daughter, she called to tell me what I needed to know. She and her momma, they do the business thing. Margaret said she made a deal, get some bills paid. Jest had the engine overhauled, not paid for yet what with the limits and all."

Mark nodded his understanding.

"Three boys. Boat won't support four families," he sighed, then realized that he was digressing. "Margaret, she's going to accounting school. She's smart. Boys are smart too, but they all thought they were going to Alabama on a scholarship. They big, two hundred pounds, and can do 4.5, but they get hit by somebody three hundred and doing the forty yards in 4.4, then fishing don't look so bad."

"Your refit bill is paid," said Mark. "And you have diesel for the season."

"Texan, I take it," said a smiling Gump.

\*\*\*

It was almost noon when they pulled into port. The rest of the boats returning had been unloaded. Putting the boat next to the waiting truck, it took less than half an hour to unload as the boys worked without rancor. When they'd finished, they took off together towards a restaurant as Gump moved the boat to its slip.

"You boys get lost or something?" a taunt from the deck of the bar.

"Hump was in the head for most of the trip," said the oldest brother, which caused the younger brother to launch himself at his sibling. The ensuing scuffle was a sufficient distraction for Ginny and Mark to leave the boat with Gump who carried their bags and threw them into the bed of the pickup.

"Get in; behind the front seat." Margaret had the

pickup started.

"Here's some fish for Momma," Gump told her. "I'll go and sort out the boys."

Gump put a newspaper wrapped fish in the front seat as the truck pulled away.

Margaret was clearly from the same family, as she had her brothers' same build. A pretty girl, Mark gauged her weight was close to two hundred pounds on a six-foot body.

"Thank you, Margaret," said Mark.

"No thanks needed. We got paid. Didn't know how we were going to pay that bill. Now hush till we get out of the yard."

The truck slowed at the gate.

"Hiya, Margaret. Going to the dance Saturday?"

"Sure, Clarence; and you?"

"Gonna save a dance for me then?"

"Only iffen your wife lets you onto the dance floor without her."

"What you doing down here? Your daddy's late today."

"Yeah, heavy swells, I guess. Just picking up the tally and some fish for supper." She gestured to the package.

"Worried that the Seven C's might have been the boat that went down."

"What boat?"

"Some boat out of Port Arthur caught fire, exploded, went down."

Ginny gasped.

Margaret put the truck noisily into gear and pulled away through the now open gate.

"See you Saturday, Clarence."

They left the yard and Margaret pulled over. Her face was no longer pretty as she turned around. "You trying to get me and my family killed? Are you out of your freaking minds?"

"I'm sorry," said Mark.

"Not you. That sniveling, stupid girl."

Ginny was sobbing as she tried to speak.

"It's just that…"

"Listen, I don't give a…!" Margaret turned and, banging the gears, drove with barely controlled fury in a jerky style that threw her passengers around.

"This is not…" Ginny dissolved into a quivering mess.

The truck stopped suddenly. They were in the parking lot of a supermarket. Margaret had calmed a little and was now anxious to pass on the burden that she'd taken. It was so easy to make a deal with the devil when your back was against the wall. The deal had seemed to be too good to be true. But what choice did she have? Her father could lose his boat if they couldn't pay for the refit that had been necessary.

Then she thought, what of her passengers? She knew nothing of them, but apparently someone had been choosing to follow them. They were still in danger. The guy understood that, but the wimpy girl would need to grow up fast. She must be important.

"I got you a Chevy, keys are in the ignition, papers in the console. Take the road east out of town. You might want to stop somewhere, freshen up, and change as you both have a distinctive odor."

They got out of the truck and into the Chevrolet Impala. The bags went into the trunk.

"Good luck!" Margaret stuck out her hand. She was younger than Ginny but appeared at that moment more mature, more in charge.

"Thanks," said Mark taking her hand. "Anything you see or read about us in the future is likely untrue."

"Thank you," said Ginny. "I'm sorry to have acted so childishly. You're right, but those innocent people..."

"They were killed, murdered. They were innocent. It wasn't your fault. It was the fault of the murderers. I hope that your trip or mission can bring retribution to those who committed the atrocity," said Margaret.

"Bless you, Margaret."

"You too. Goodbye!"

## Chapter Seven

A week later Ginny and Mark were in Florida. They would have needed to think very hard to describe the twists and turns that they had taken, the motels or hotels that they'd been in, and the checking in and out with names that corresponded to the credit card used to pay for the room. Sometimes the reservations were made by local supporters; sometimes it was when they could go no further, the next sign that said vacancy or accommodation next exit. When they stopped on the road, a wink and cash ensured that no identification was asked for. Meals were taken at places in which cash was expected, fast food or small family-run restaurants. There was very little trail for anyone to follow. They had spoken to Baton Rouge and New Orleans on consecutive days then drove down to Mobile in Alabama for a meeting and to Pensacola to board a large powerboat bound for Florida. Eighteen hours later they'd arrived.

It had been difficult. They were always on alert. They were almost arrested in New Orleans. Mark was immediately anxious when he saw that about a hundred people had packed into the hall. He asked that his name not be used when he was introduced. The speech asked for support of Ellie May Joseph. He praised the organizers and thanked the crowd. The first question was related to where he was from and he answered, "Not Texas," which drew some guarded laughter. The second question was shouted from the back. "Where do we get in touch with you and with Ellie May Joseph? Why doesn't she come here herself?"

Mark noticed that the companion of the man asking the questions was sending a text message and holding the phone to take a photograph. He ducked out of sight and off the stage. Mark found the leader of the Sons of Liberty group and his contact there in New Orleans.

"That man has infiltrated your group. Tell him that Ellie May will be in touch with him. We have to leave now."

Mark found Ginny who was staying close by. "Let's go."

"But, what about dinner?"

"Now!"

Exiting the building, Mark was glad they'd parked a couple of streets away. As they walked, they heard police cars converging on and surrounding the building they'd just vacated.

"Remember that we were told not to hang about. That's why."

Now in Florida they were meeting with Emilio Gonsalves, who had been elected, in spite of strong opposition and even stronger physical intimidation, into the US Senate. He had taken the oath of office while still in a cast.

Mark had met Emilio at the Democratic Convention in Boston some two and a half years before. Ginny was introduced and was surprised to hear her real name.

"Ginny Hutchins, meet Emilio Gonsalves, US Senator."

"I'm very pleased to meet you. Are you by chance related to Sheila Hutchins?"

Ginny glanced at Mark who subtlety nodded his permission to answer. "Yes, my mother…"

"What a tyrant," Emilio chuckled.

Ginny stood up white with fury. "How dare you call my mother a tyrant, and you serving in a government which has been perverting justice and obliterating the rights of its citizens?" She was shaking as Mark took her shoulders and sat her down.

"Emilio is a good guy, Ginny. Your mother spoke for a Republican challenger when Emilio supported Marjorie White, the Democrat's candidate."

Emilio sat beside her and placed an arm around her shoulders.

"Sorry, Ginny. I thought that my politics were all anyone spoke about. A little arrogant of me. I meant no disrespect. In fact, the opposite. A strong challenge and a strong debate make a strong country. I've tried and will continue to try to engage my fellow senators in a debate of policies which affect us all, Democrat or Republican."

Ginny looked up at this man and realized he was a small man in his seventies. The Florida sun and his daily workout made him look younger.

"Ginny," Mark turned to look at the two emotion filled faces, "Emilio was the first person to agree to run against our common enemy and one of the first to win. His life is in constant danger, and he has escaped assassination more than once."

"Why?"

"Why what? Why run or why not resign?"

Ginny shrugged, "Why?"

"Well, my country needed me, and that sounds patriotic doesn't it? The truth happens to be close to that. Mac asked me to run. He promised me protection. We both knew that there is no way of guaranteeing safety. My wife had died, and I have no children or other family remaining, so I had nothing to lose. I said yes, I would ride the white horse into Washington. I was so well known in Florida that I scraped into office in spite of ballot rigging, intimidation, extortion, and every dirty trick that can be played," he chuckled. "It has its moments. Filibustering to an empty Senate at my age is not fun. Now I don't get called!"

"I'm sorry," said Ginny. "I'm tired. I'm scared."

"We've arranged for you both to stay with Dot Gallaher. She was my campaign manager and was treasurer of the Democratic Committee here in Florida for about twenty years."

"That's kind."

"Well, you probably didn't come all the way from Texas to listen to an old man prattle. What do you want?"

"Straight down to the subject," said Mark, reaching for his briefcase.

"At my age, I no longer buy green bananas."

"We have something to give, something to share, and something to take." Mark took an envelope from a hidden pocket in the side of his case and placed it on the table under his hand. "First, we have to give you some codes in order for you to communicate with Ellie May or others in our national network. We're also going to share with you who some of these contacts are."

"Some, not all?" asked Emilio.

"For your protection and theirs. Some of these contacts are phony, so we can tell if your list has been hacked or compromised."

Emilio harrumphed his displeasure.

Mark ignored him.

"And third, I need to take from you a pledge." Mark paused to allow his next words the gravity he intended. The whole dangerous meeting had been planned for this very moment. "A pledge that if Ellie May Joseph forms a new political party, that you will join her in opposition to the incumbent president."

"Is that all? I thought you were going to ask me to be a Republican!" Emilio tried to lighten the somber silence.

"No, we're asking you to be an American." said Mark seriously.

"Is it treasonous?"

"Starting a new political party?"

"No. Inciting a revolution?"

"Provided for by our founding fathers."

"I need to think," said Emilio. "What's in the envelope? Cyanide pills if I say no?"

"A letter to you," said Mark, handing it over.

Emilio opened the letter, pulled out reading glasses, and read.

"Son of a…" he looked up. "She assumes that I will say yes and wants my input into a manifesto. Who else has a 'Dear Emilio' letter?"

"No one," said Mark. You're the first. We have two more to deliver."

"No point in asking who."

"No, no point."

\*\*\*

Dot Gallaher was a pleasant, smiling woman who had played golf in the morning with her regular partners. It was clear that she and Emilio had been friends for many years. Their chatter covered quickly their aches and pains, status of shared acquaintances, the status of legislation in Washington, and the opinion of the membership of the Windermere Golf Club – of the legislative body as a whole and individually.

"I stopped by the marina and picked up fish. Is that all right?" Expecting no dissent, she was already washing four pieces of fish.

Ginny turned green and quickly left the room.

"Dot, I think that Ginny will just eat salad. We had a bad experience in the Gulf."

"Oh, a little seasick?"

"No, a very, very bad experience; people died. People died helping us, so perhaps we should leave."

"Definitely not. We've had a few attempts at intimidation and are not intimidated."

"Well, we'll need to be careful the next few days," Mark stated.

\*\*\*

Ginny had fallen asleep in a lounge chair by the pool. When she woke feeling much better, she asked whether they could walk the beach, maybe swim. Dot told her that she would be instantly recognized as a visitor since the native Floridians did not swim unless the water temperature exceeded seventy-five degrees.

"I'll go with you," said Mark.

"I need to be alone. I need to think."

"Then I won't talk. I won't walk with you. But I did promise to watch over you." Mark smiled at her as she gestured her disbelief.

"Well, you just heard what a tyrant your mother can be."

This time she laughed. "Okay, but don't even think aloud."

The beach was deserted, and they walked for an hour before heading back to the gated community. As they got nearer, it seemed that there were more people around. Rounding the corner, it was clear that the attraction was a fire at Gallaher's condominium. Mark started to run and then a sense of preservation made him stop. A running man would draw attention to him and to Ginny. They stood, shoulders touching, at the end of the cul-de-sac with a group of gawkers until most of the firefighters and all of the gawkers left.

"What happened, Dot?" Mark asked.

"Burnt the steaks!"

"We were having fish; try again."

"Coupla guys came by and threw an incendiary through the window. Lucky for us, we were watching. Someone pulled an alarm and the first responders seemed disappointed that we were not engulfed. Then they searched the place."

"Were they looking for us?" asked Ginny.

"Looking for someone."

"First responders or same two people as threw the bomb? How'd they get through the gate?"

"They may have been the same. The bomb was thrown from a golf cart. You can by-pass the gate with a cart. Everyone has them."

"We have to leave at once," Ginny said.

"Ginny, dear, they're still watching for anyone leaving, and since they already searched here, this may be the safest place in Florida. Luckily, we had your luggage contents stashed in the washer and dryer, so they found nothing." Dot paused. "Besides, I have all of this fish to cook and eat."

\*\*\*

"They were nice people," Ginny said to Mark.

"Who?" asked Mark, obviously thinking of other things.

"Everyone we met in Florida: Emilio, Dot, Jack,

Warren, the whole group that we met last night."

"Mmmm," Mark asserted without comment.

They were back on the highway headed north. Mark was thinking of the attempt to find them. For a while they might have been assumed to be at the bottom of the Gulf. Now it was clear that somewhere there was a leak, a spy. It had been agreed that Emilio would take their message to Miami and that they would head north to Savannah. A rental car had been provided along with enough gas to make it unnecessary to stop for a couple of days, until they were north of Charleston.

"Do you know what I was thinking?"

"Huh?" Mark was brought out of his thoughts.

"When we were at the beach."

"Which beach?"

"How many beaches have we been on?" she looked across and saw that she had finally engaged him. "I was thinking of all the extraordinarily brave people we have met. Heroes; even you."

Mark glanced across and saw that she was blushing. He looked back at the road.

"Brave people all over the United States. Then there is me." Ginny sighed. "I'd decided that I was going to be a lot braver, not a hero, but brave. Then I saw the fire trucks and fell apart inside."

"I thought that it was brave of you not to show your fear, to suppress your anxiety, and to meet all those men and women last night."

"Patriots," she said.

"Depends which side you are on."

"Patriots don't throw bombs at old ladies in retirement communities."

"Don't let Dot hear you call her an old lady," said Mark with a chuckle.

"Can I call her a patriot?"

Mark nodded. "I think she'd like that."

After riding in silence for several minutes, Ginny looked at him earnestly. "They'll be okay, won't they?"

"Of course. They're patriots!"

"Even patriots get killed," said Ginny returning to silence.

\*\*\*

It took them four days to reach Washington where they had a contact, who was to return the rental car. The stops had been productive and the route a little circuitous; rather than the obvious cities, they had met at smaller communities where representatives travelled to meet with them. It was encouraging to be met with enthusiastic welcomes. Sticking to their plan after meeting, they left as quickly as practical. The reason given, that it was safer for all, was accepted as they all had stories of close calls or beatings for their political stances.

In Washington they stayed with Martin Konrad, a giant of a man with whom Mac had shared his initial concerns regarding manipulation of congressional and the presidential races.

Martin was a computer genius and entertained Ginny for hours with his exploits. Together they were relaxed and plotted methods of communicating secretly. In a challenge they hacked each other's computer through a third computer in a Middle Eastern country and then, opening a file, retrieved a coded message.

Mark found that his only purpose seemed to be in the provision of contacts and acquiring the latest software. This was fine as he needed time to meet with several congressmen, identified by Emilio Gonsalves as being against the current occupant of the White House. These men and women were Democrats, Republicans, old, young, dedicated, and stalwarts of many political campaigns. The harassment stories were similar. Their resolve immoveable. Their admiration for Ellie May Joseph unanimous.

Spring was in full bloom in the parks, but the tourist attractions were empty. Throughout the city there were signs of crime but not lawlessness, signs of neglect but not decay. The stores all had security gates and blinds. There were few people on the street. There were potholes. There was uncollected refuse that had been picked clean of anything edible or useful. And there were fewer cars than Mark had ever seen there before.

The complaints that Mark voiced just a few years ago about the criminals on the street, the pollution, the noise, he now wished that he could raise them again.

Mark had called Ann Gold and arranged to meet at Paula's Café. When they arrived and sat in a back-corner booth, he said, "Ann, this is Ginny. Ginny, Ann Gold, a reporter and a friend, who knows anything and anybody in the city."

"How y'all doing?"

"I'd recognize that voice anywhere. How's your mother?" asked Ann.

"How….?"

"I told you," said Mark chuckling at Ginny's questioning look and Ann's look of triumph. "That expression on your face was all the proof she needed to confirm an intelligent guess."

Ann Gold had lost about one hundred pounds since Mark had last seen her less than three years previously. She looked ghastly.

"You must be a friend of Mac's," said Ginny.

"Shhh." Ann looked fearfully around. "That name can get you arrested, beaten, or worse."

Ginny smiled a smile of disbelief. "You can't get arrested for saying a name."

"I've been to the Armory, the militia headquarters, about fifty times in the last couple of years, and the question is always the same. They leave me without food or water for hours, punch and beat me. If they hadn't been satisfied each time that I don't know where Mac or Helen are, then I would still be in there, dead or barely alive. I manage to convince them that I know people and things and they let me go. It's barbaric." She paused and looked sadly at her hands. "I can't work and am going slowly through my savings and rapidly out of my mind."

"Ann, is he still alive?" asked Mark.

"I'd say no, dear boy, but apparently they suspect otherwise. If they knew something different, why do they keep asking if I know where they are?"

"Martin said the same thing," said Ginny, now chastened.

"What can I do for you, Mark?" Ann studiously ignored Ginny, clearly not having forgiven her earlier remark.

"You know Ellie May Joseph," he stated. "She's going to run again. We need coverage, positive coverage. There are some good people in Congress. They need good positive coverage too."

"There are some bad people too."

"Yes, Ann, bad too, but we know who they are through Emilio Gonsalves."

"I know them too."

"Will you support Ellie May?"

"Yes, if I can. But how?"

"I'll have Martin Konrad meet you and together

you can produce a cyber newspaper."

"Like the one out of Boston."

"Similar. The difference is that it will be here in Washington where policy is made."

"Policy is destroyed here too, Mark. Yes, I have to do something."

"I'm not going to tell you it won't be dangerous."

"So is running out of money," Ann retorted without irony. "Heck, I get hauled in just for being me. I know it can be worse, but it can't be much worse."

Mark and Ginny left the next day by train for New York.

## Chapter Eight

Trouble started before they got to the train station. One of the members of the local chapter of the Sons of Liberty had offered to drive them to their destination. It had appeared genuine, and may have been. Mark was careful, so he'd declined.

In the lobby of the hotel, he called for a taxicab and gave the address as further down the street.

Ginny and Mark left by the rear of the hotel and met the taxi which was late. Mark asked to be taken to the bus station and talked to Ginny about Chicago, how she was going to enjoy the 'windy' city. The driver talked about how business was terrible and that it was barely a living and many drivers and taxi services had just quit.

At the bus station, even though Mark had paid and tipped well, the driver had not met his eyes. Had they been recognized?

Ginny waited at the curb for a cab to drop a fare at the bus station. Mark stood out of sight, scouring the area for unusual activity. It was several minutes, but seemed to be ages, before a cab came. Mark put the bags in the back and gave the driver a fifty-dollar bill and the train station destination. As he suspected, the sight of cash meant that the flag stayed down. This journey would not be reported. They pulled away as police descended on the bus station. Mark was right to be a worried man.

They were late. Less than five minutes to departure. In spite of the lateness, Mark insisted that they go to the toilets and change, then they would board the train separately and sit apart. With just a minute to go, a slender girl with a head scarf around her head sat on the train next to an elderly woman similarly dressed. Mark sat further down, dressed in clothes that he'd last worn on the fishing boat.

In Baltimore, a group of armed militia got on the train. They swaggered through carriages harassing the women and checking tickets and identification. Mark could see Ginny's frightened eyes above the scarf; he tried to look reassuring. Some of the militia appeared to have been taking drugs; they were "confiscating" cell phones, computers, jewelry, and watches. This was good as it was a distraction from their purpose.

The men reached Ginny who handed her ticket and identification, as did the elderly woman.

"How come you have different names?" asked the bearded man who appeared to be in charge.

"What's it to you?" snapped the elderly woman as Ginny lowered her face.

"We have to ask."

"You got the same name as your mama?" The man looked again at the identifications, luckily both had Washington addresses.

"Where are you going?"

"You are holding our tickets...fool!"

The man threw them down and looked up as the other members of the militia were paying a lot of attention to a man and woman in their twenties. The militiamen were relieving them of their jewelry and then asked for cash. Told that they had none, one of the men grabbed the young woman's breast.

"Maybe it's in here!" he leered.

The woman screamed, and the young man punched the leering militiaman in the face.

"Not good!" The militiaman raised his gun and shot the man.

"These are the people we want," he announced. "Traitors, members of the Sons of Liberty, terrorists."

They dropped the dying man and the hysterical woman from the train.

Mark looked at Ginny. She was glaring at him with accusing eyes, just slits with tears glistening. He knew she was now thinking of the horrors that were to follow for the young woman and feeling guilty that it was not her.

*Who is the traitor?* Mark was thinking, as it was clear that the militia knew who they were looking for and where. They were looking for Mark and Ginny and knew that they were headed for New York. Fortunately for Mark they had no good photograph. Bad luck for the young couple in the wrong place. Pressing charges was not an option, not at this time. First and most importantly was their mission which would hopefully put an end to this kind of behavior.

The rest of the journey was a somber, silent traverse of Pennsylvania, New Jersey, and into New York. No one pointed at the sights. No one flinched as trains swooshed in a reverse traverse. No one looked as people alighted, as people departed. The conductor checked tickets in silence.

\*\*\*

New York was a revelation. There was noise, a bustle, an excitement that they had not seen since they left Texas. Was that only a few weeks ago?

Outside there was a group, a gang wearing a distinctive arm band. The gang was checking passengers, especially young men and women. Ginny had wisely walked out with her companion; both had covered faces. The leader had his eyes on Mark and started forward just as a police car with four officers stopped in front of them. The officers asked the leader for his identification and the reason for being at the station. A second unmarked police car stopped and the officer approached Mark.

"Welcome to New York, sir. We understood that there would be a young lady."

Mark didn't like this. "And you are?"

"I'm sorry," said the man sincerely. "The mayor asked that I make sure you kept your appointment with her this afternoon. Inspector Ellis, sir."

The man seemed legit.

"And your young lady?"

"The one in disguise," said Mark nodding.

Inspector Ellis spoke to his companion and fellow police officer. "Jameson, go and ask that young lady for her papers. Make a fuss, then escort her to the hotel."

"Yes, sir."

Turning to Mark, Ellis explained, "We're still having a problem with militia and informal gang hits, but we're getting better. It won't take long to get back to just the petty muggings, robberies, domestics, etc." He spoke without rancor, without emotion. It was obvious that he was a policeman looking forward to being allowed to police.

"This afternoon, the mayor?"

"Yes. I will pick you up around four. Does that work for you?"

It sounded to Mark as though it would be okay whether he agreed or not.

\*\*\*

The mayor, in person, was as ordinary and down to earth as she appeared on television.

"Welcome to New York. I still have a hard time believing I was elected. My advisors..." she looked around conspiratorially, "...say you were 'the money' and that I should be nice to you...to both of you."

"Thank you, Madame Mayor."

"Joyce is fine. My mother still doesn't believe I'm mayor; she calls and asks when my coffee break is." She laughed.

It was clear that she enjoyed her job. Mark knew from his sources that she was listening to her advisors; that the city had turned around for the better in a matter of months – not years as predicted.

"Mayor Joyce, two things before we start. Number one: this young woman, whose current name I forget, is more important than I am as she is going to help your people to communicate directly on a secure line with our people. Secondly, we were compromised in Washington and there are people there who must be warned immediately." Mark paused and looked directly at Inspector Ellis. "Those men at the station were looking for us, and they knew who they were looking for. They may even have been carrying photographs."

"I'll go check into that. We took them in for questioning and found some weapons."

The mayor turned toward her aide. "Gerald, can you take the young lady and introduce her to our communications center?"

He nodded and, as they were leaving the room, Ginny told him, "I need only one person there to interview to ensure they're capable, then I'll educate only that person. The fewer people who know how we communicate, the better."

With just Mark left in her office, her mood changed. Joyce confided, "There have been three assassination attempts on my life. A couple of threats on Sara, on Gerald, even towards my parents, and my parents are in lalaland. I have to keep up the façade for them."

"Then why? How do you manage?"

"I think of my husband running towards the World Trade Center. I think of all the other firemen, police officers, the medics, running toward terrorism not away. If they can do it, then God willing, I can too. So, what can I do for you?"

"It's perhaps what we can do for each other," said Mark.

"Well, as I understand it, you're the instrument of my being mayor, so this must be payback time."

"That's old politics." Mark liked the fact that whatever was on Joyce's mind came out, no apologies. "I need a few things."

"Ah ha," said the mayor reaching for a notepad.

"No record, no writing. First, I need to see Marjorie White."

"The Democrat's former presidential candidate?"

"Yes."

"She's under house arrest, down the Jersey shore."

"Yes. I need to see her, and nobody should find out."

"Not possible."

"We have a couple of weeks, so we can think of something."

"Anything else?"

"Yes, I need you to openly support Ellie May Joseph when she announces her presidential bid."

"Is she nuts?"

"No nuttier than you."

"If I'm here, she has my support."

"And then, after we meet Marjorie White, I need you to spirit my friend and me out of your fair city."

"Done! Tonight I'll send a car and we'll eat New York Style. What do you like?"

"You decide," Mark said. "Anything but steak."

## Chapter Nine

Mark and Ginny had several days in New York City. The shops and museums were all new and exciting even though without the crowds of the past. Mostly the shoppers were foreign entourages. The pacts and trade with Middle Eastern Countries showed at the stores of Fifth Avenue – Made in America was apparently no longer in fashion. The value was in imported goods. Not that there was a cacophony of ringing from the cash registers since all the transactions involved the discreet handing over of pieces of plastic, the efficient exchange of foreign funds from far flung financial institutions, for American goods manufactured in some other foreign nation.

There was security everywhere. The stores had all assigned visible watchers, augmenting the cameras and machines programmed to alert with ear shattering sirens that a shopper had not removed the stores security device. Mark and Ginny had been assigned plain clothes police officers.

Ginny shopped and Mark stood close to the exit, watching. He wasn't looking for anything, just watching. He knew that the police officers were armed, but this did not excite the attention of the store. He wondered which of the people passing were similarly armed, in violation of the law forbidding concealed weapons. He concluded that a small army could be in plain sight.

In contrast, the museums and art galleries were quiet. It occurred to Mark that there was an opportunity to meet quietly with anyone at one of the many venues. On the other hand, they were exposed, and it would be easy to follow people in empty buildings.

Mark's thoughts turned to the coming days. Contact had been made through intermediaries inviting Marjorie White to attend and speak at a political gathering. The "minders" were persuaded by two points. First, she would be going alone, leaving her two sons and her parents down by the shore. The second was that the other speaker would be Vice President Flores, and the presentation was to be to a group of attaches from foreign countries and specially invited guests. The argument made to the organizers was that Marjorie would lend weight to the gathering and bring in some countries that would normally boycott a meeting designed to prop up the current US administration.

Six days until the meeting, and Mark and Ginny needed to be in Boston the day after. They were spending a great deal of time together as it was safer to eat with two police officers. They met regularly with Joyce and her family, though this was kept to a minimum as it was obvious that they were being watched.

The next night they were seated at a neighborhood Italian restaurant with Joyce Milner, her sister-in-law Sara, and Sara's husband. The owner, Mario Bertolino, was personally taking their orders for food. A carafe of red wine and a carafe of white wine were being passed around with a good deal of conviviality. The police escort, two officers in uniform, were seated nearby, and a police cruiser, with two more officers, sat outside the front door. There was no anticipated threat since the neighborhood was predominantly Italian.

Mario was patiently explaining that he would be bringing appetizers for the table and that he had no idea what they might be as his brother, Mike, in the kitchen had not told him what he was putting together. Mario explained it could be expected to be anything from antipasti to mini pizza to bruschetta.

"Please, if you tell me what you like, Mike will cook."

"Could we see a menu?" asked Ginny.

"No! No menu. What do you like?"

"I'd like to see a menu."

There was general laughter and congeniality. "Then go to fast food," said Mario to more laughter.

"I'll go first," Sara jumped in. "Veal Saltimbocca, fried spinach, linguini."

Sara's husband had put up his hand to be next. The door opened and the police escort looked up, alert. Two men dressed as police officers walked in, turned toward the diners, and shot Mario in the back, then Patrolman Dan Murphy in the head, followed by Officer Dee Figurello in the arm. Officer Figurello, though on the floor and bleeding, fired at the gunmen as two officers rushed in from the car and started firing. The gunmen ran, still firing, through the kitchen and into the night.

The next half hour was nonstop sirens.

Mario and Mike's restaurant was filled with police officers. The medics and ambulance attendants were pushing through the policemen in order to tend to the injured.

The chief of police and his deputy arrived and

created some semblance of order with the uniformed officers outside, organizing traffic and preparing to deal with morbid sightseers. Television crews parked and made it difficult to keep the street open for the ambulances and escorts to make their way through.

Officer Figurello refused medication until she had given a statement. In it she declared that they were sitting ducks as soon as the men entered. Her statement, filled with expletives, questioned how they got past the cruiser outside and she called them every name that she could, all at the top of her voice.

The detective inspector was patient.

"Officer Figurello, can you describe the men?"

"Police officers," she said. "Bastards!"

"Real or dressed as officers?"

She closed her eyes in thought – or reflecting the pain from the three injuries that were visible.

"We have to cut off your uniform," a medic was saying.

"Then cut, you stupid…Real! They were real. Real or recently real. White, six feet, six-one. One has a nine mill from my gun in his leg. When you bring him in, tell him I have a whole clip for his balls."

She stopped and grimaced. "Can I have that juice now…please?"

"Very good, officer. Good luck!"

"Thank you, sir." Her voice was now a whisper.

Ginny had been screaming since the first shot was fired. Mark asked one of the medics to give her a sedative. It worked and now she was giving an occasional whimper.

"Mark, I didn't agree to be shot."

"You weren't shot," he said calmly.

"I'm covered in blood!"

"Yes, fortunately for you, not yours. Unfortunately

there are people here dead and hurt, so snap out of it. The police will need a statement."

"I didn't see anything. You threw me to the floor and jumped on me." She stopped. "You're covered in blood, Mark. Are you hurt?"

"Not badly. Mario took the brunt of the attack. The mayor was saved by Mario moving and by Bill standing and pulling a gun I didn't know he had. I think Bill is hurt too, but I don't know how severely."

"So whose blood?"

"Mario's mostly."

The mayor was fuming. "I'm so embarrassed that this happened."

"Not your fault, Joyce."

"They want me gone badly."

"How do you know you were the target?"

"This wasn't the first attack, but it was certainly the most professional."

"Maybe it was us. Or a chance to get all of us." Mark was reluctant to admit that there was a target on his back and Ginny's. He knew he'd be forced to examine the scare, which had all been over in less than half a minute, more than once.

Mark was accompanied in an ambulance by a detective along for his statement of the event.

"We were laughing at something when the door opened. We were about sixty or seventy feet away. I couldn't see who entered, but it happened so fast that Dan didn't even have time to draw his gun. I heard a shot, then his face was all blood. I pushed Ginny, who was sitting on my right, to the floor and dove on top. There was a lot of gunfire, and I saw the other officer, Dee, shoot at the men. She shot, hit him at the back of the knee, which was all I could see. He shouted, then that's when the other officers came running through the door. The two gunmen were both hit, I think."

"Not what you think, sir. What you know."

"One was definitely hit in the back of the knee."

"Thank you. Anything else?"

"Do you know who they are?"

"We're working on it."

\*\*\*

They were three hours at the hospital even though they'd been given priority treatment. It had been clear that Ginny was suffering from little more than post traumatic shock. Mark had also been lucky. The bullet intended for his head had hit his sheltering arm, gone through, and grazed his neck.

There were, however, blood tests, urine tests, questions about tetanus shots, allergies, and his whole family history that the hospital needed. The staff wasn't satisfied until they had prodded, cleaned, inoculated, bandaged, and issued verbal and written instructions. The doctors wanted to make them stay overnight for observation and only relented after assurance that there would be medical and security personnel at the hotel.

Television coverage treated the event as an assassination attempt. The target was assumed to be the mayor, and the assassins those who opposed her inclusion of women in the government. The mayor spoke to the cameras before being brought to the hospital. She did nothing to disillusion the experts even though she knew more.

The reporter spoke to the camera. "The victims were identified as a police officer and the restaurant owner Mario Bertolino; also badly injured were another police officer and Bill Gallagher, the mayor's brother-in-law, who is in critical condition. Sara Gallagher and two other visitors to New York were also hit in the barrage. Their condition is not known at this time. Details are sketchy as no one here is talking to anyone. We expect the police commissioner to read a statement in about half an hour. Back to you, Steve."

"Rosemary, was the mayor hurt and does the latest incident cause her to think of resigning?"

"Steve, the mayor was hit in the leg, I believe, as she was on a stretcher with an inflated leg bandage. They were also applying ice to her head before she came on camera. In answer to the question of resigning, I think that the opposite is true. She is resolved to get to the bottom of this. As the doors of the ambulance closed, she was heard to instruct her officers to 'go bring the bastards in.'"

The station was too slow to delete the "b" word, and it would provide the headlines for every newspaper in the country as well as countless tweets.

It was while they were at the hospital watching the television news coverage that the second event occurred that was to have a profound effect on their lives.

"We'll bring the police commissioner's press conference live. In other news: Boston today saw riot police called to Fenway Park. We have no coverage as all television crews were barred from the area, so the tweets that we have seen are unverified. It appears that a number of factors led to a confrontation between students and the militia."

The screen displayed a reporter outside of Fenway who stated, "It was Patriots Day in Boston, a holiday, an afternoon game against the New York Yankees and eighty-four degrees. Militia attempted to arrest a female student from Boston University as she entered Fenway Park in shorts and a tank top. Male students quickly intervened, and the noise brought more men from surrounding bars. The militia fired into the crowd, then quickly left as an angry mob chased them to their armored vehicles. It is feared that six people are dead or seriously injured.

"This is the latest in a number of confrontations with the militia around the country in which it is suspected that people were killed or arrested.

"The game between Boston and New York was cancelled."

Mark looked across at Ginny, then he scanned the room before he spoke. "This is not likely to end any time soon."

"But perhaps it is the beginning of the end," said Ginny.

"I was talking about unrest in Boston which, by the way, is where we're headed next," said Mark.

"And I was thinking more like Winston Churchill."

In spite of the pain he was feeling, Mark was forced to smile, as it was now Ginny exhibiting a positive reaction.

***

Mark, having taken his pain relief medication, was preparing to collapse onto the bed in his hotel room. He didn't expect to sleep with so many thoughts in his head. They were trying to sort themselves out, but the pain meds were doing their job.

There was a knock on the door between his and Ginny's room. He walked over. The door was designed to lock from both sides.

"Who is it?" he asked.

"Me."

The voice was Ginny's but distraught. He opened the door. Even in the half-light he could see that she wore only a light nightgown.

"I can't sleep. I see blood. I see masked people. I

see people hiding, ready to jump out…We're going to be all right, aren't we? Tell me that we are going to be okay."

"We're going to be just fine. We have the might of right on our side."

Through tears she said, "I'm so afraid. And I hate that I'm such a cry baby."

"Shhh." He held out his arms. She fell into them, now silently sobbing. He felt her slowly relax.

"Can I sleep in here tonight?" she asked.

"Of course. I can sleep in the chair."

"No, I need you close."

He walked her to the bed, and she got in under the covers. Mark sat down on the other side of the bed and looked at her for a long time. His medication kicked in and he barely pulled the covers over himself before he was asleep.

Four hours later Mark awoke to a throbbing in his arm. He reached for his medication and realized that Ginny had wrapped herself closely around him. He was trying to remember how this had happened while extracting himself from the entanglement. The pills had the required effect on his arm, but for fifteen minutes his thoughts were everywhere, mostly on the events at Mario's Restaurant.

Ginny was whimpering in her sleep and he imagined that she was also reliving that minute or two. Mark touched her face gently. She smiled and, without waking, was quiet.

Just before ten, Mark ordered them both breakfast – just toast and coffee. They'd missed dinner the night before, but neither of them had much of an appetite.

While they were waiting for room service, the television brought them up to date as the police had been busy all night.

"This morning the bodies of two men in police uniform were found in the East River. Both had been shot execution style in the back of the head. It is believed that these are the two men who tried to assassinate the mayor last night as she dined in a community restaurant.

"A search of the men's homes found that their families had been murdered, with knife wounds. At one address, the bodies of a woman aged thirty and two children aged seven and nine, while at the other home a woman said to be twenty and pregnant was found. Names are being withheld pending notification of next of kin."

There was an update on the condition of those injured in the restaurant. No mention was made of Mark or Ginny. Bill Gallagher remained in critical condition. Sara Gallagher was stable. The mayor had been treated and released. Officer Figurello, who was being hailed a hero, had her left arm amputated and would be in the operating room again to remove two other bullets lodged in her abdomen, one of which was life threatening. The television showed a line of blood donors asking to contribute to her recovery. Fifty percent were in uniform.

Breakfast came and was eaten in silence.

Ginny was smiling. When she had awoken, she and Mark were in each other's arms. They made love by mutual consent, without speaking.

Then, after breakfast, they did it again.

## Chapter Ten

There was a great deal of media coverage of the attack on the mayor and her family over the next week. Fortunately, forgotten were the two unnamed victims. They were happy to be left to heal and discover they shared a mutual attraction.

Over breakfast the next day, Ginny said, "I've concluded that I'm twenty-five. Enough of these tears and screaming. What's the worst that can happen? I can be killed; I can die. We'll likely both be killed together. I can live with that."

Mark convulsed with laughter.

"What?" asked Ginny.

"You said, 'I can die. I can live with that.'"

She laughed hearing her own words.

His face grew serious. He reached for her hand, and said, "What I couldn't deal with is if you were to die and I were to live."

There was silence as she took his hand. Then they kissed and made their way back over to the bed.

\*\*\*

Three days later, Mark and Ginny watched the funerals, which were shown live on television.

Mario's brother spoke in rapid Italian into the camera.

"I think," said Ginny, "that he asked the mafia to avenge his brother's death."

"Doesn't he know that the mafia doesn't exist? Besides that, there were two bodies found in the East River."

"Maybe he knows that they weren't behind the attack."

"Everybody knows that!"

Dan Murphy's funeral was attended by every policeman and fireman not on duty, including some from twelve other states. When the coffin reached the altar of St. Patrick's followed by his family, Officer Dee Figurello's wheelchair turned and she saluted her fallen comrade. There was a gasp as it was evident that she had lost her left arm and was unable to stand. That she was alive was a tribute to her strength, just as it was obvious that she was barely holding on.

The mayor attended the funeral and, against advice, left her own wheelchair and walked on the arm of her police commissioner behind the family. She gave a eulogy in her own style. Never a polished speaker, these were her people and she had been here before.

The mayor arrived at the hotel later that day.

"Great speech, Mayor," Mark said.

"Easy since it was all true. These brave, dedicated people going out every day, their families not knowing..." she trailed off into her own memories. She finally said, "Hold on to every day!"

"Amen," said Ginny looking at Mark.

"What gives here?" asked the mayor. "Never mind," she quickly added, correctly interpreting the look.

They talked some more about the disturbance in Boston and other parts of the country.

"That reminds me. I have a way of getting you to Boston on Thursday. One of the police crews was from Maine; they drive through Boston. A member of the force knows the captain who came down and persuaded him that they might have a mechanical problem and be home Thursday lunch time. So it's all set; they'll leave you at a police station north of Boston where they have a friendly relationship."

"Thank you. And then?"

"Your host in Boston can pick you up there."

Now all they had to do was successfully complete their reason for staying in New York. It was never going to be easy, but when they saw the four men assigned to go everywhere with Marjorie, it looked impossible.

Ginny came up with the solution.

"Get me into a police uniform. I'll place myself at the entrance to the ladies' room, then suggest that she needs to stop there before the presentation. I'll deliver the information and the message."

It was the only plan they had.

Everything was running late. Flores, the vice president, was held up due to an accident on the airport exit road. A helicopter was called and then grounded when a thunderstorm appeared over the city.

In Lincoln Center the crowd was hot as they had been asked to be at the theater early to go through metal detectors. Mark had been searched with nothing to find. The mayor had taken extra precautions, even in her own city.

Marjorie had been delayed by the same thunderstorm which added to the tension. Contingency plans were discussed and were getting more and more fanciful when she finally arrived. She was ushered into a dressing room where the men went in. One stood at the door, and one remained at each at the end of the corridor.

The moment came and the television personality who would introduce the participants walked into Marjorie's dressing room.

"Mrs. White."

"Marjorie, please."

"Marjorie, I'll introduce you as a former vice president forced to leave office due to family obligations. Is that satisfactory to you?"

"Not the truth, God forbid," said Marjorie ironically. "John, I ask that you change obligations to duty. I think that obligations suggest that I let my family interfere with my duty to this country." She glanced at the guard who was speaking into a small microphone.

"Yes, report that please." She paused, then continued. "Don't worry, I'll say the right things as long as my family is being held hostage."

The television anchor had pretended not to hear as he scribbled the change on his clipboard.

"Time to go, Marjorie. We're running a little late."

They stood and walked out together. The guards arranged around the two: John continued to babble about nothing. As they rounded the corner he slowed.

"Marjorie, before we start, you might want to use the restroom."

"I'm fine."

"Marjorie," he put his hand on her arm. "It may be the last chance for you; and the country," he added in a low voice.

Marjorie White stopped and changed direction, noting that there was a female police officer on guard at the door.

One of the guards moved to follow Marjorie. The female officer stepped in front of him.

"Ladies' Room."

"She's escorted everywhere."

"Not by you in there."

"What if…"

"I'll escort her."

The man shrugged and stepped away.

"Don't be long," said the largest of the guards, all of whom were giants compared with the diminutive police officer.

Once inside, Marjorie looked around.

"I'm Ginny Hutchins. You know my mother, Sheila, who works for Ellie May Joseph."

"Okay, so what's so important that I risked my family's lives?"

"We're here to save your lives."

"How?"

"Listen carefully. Here's a new cell phone. At six pm exactly, Eastern Time, dial 999. It will pick up a dedicated satellite link. If you use it at any other time, no one will answer. Leave a message. In a true emergency, we'll try to help."

"What else is so important that I should come to New York?"

"One, that people see you. Number two, we need you to support Ellie May Joseph when we ask, and number three… a question…"

"What are you doing in there?" called a guard.

"Just washing my hands." Marjorie turned on the faucet.

"What question?"

"Would you consider running with Ellie May Joseph against the incumbent president? Representing a new party, The American Party?"

"You're joking!"

"Take this," Ginny handed her a folded piece of paper, "and call 999 at six pm tomorrow night.

Marjorie stuffed the folded piece of paper into the waistband of her skirt and tucked the phone into her jacket pocket. They exited the restroom.

The guard gave Marjorie a suspicious look and then, seeing nothing out of place, continued to escort her to the stage.

There was a greeting of Marjorie White and Francis Flores, which was aired nationally, and the image of bonhomie was seen around the world. The whispered dialogue was not.

"Marjorie, you're looking well. Retirement suits you."

"Frank," Marjorie knew that he preferred to be called Francis, "Hopefully *you* can get to enjoy retirement soon. Very soon!"

"Ha-ha! Still enjoying the little joke."

"Some joke – imprisoned by your radical goons where the principal exercise is genuflecting to the West."

"You mean the East?"

"No, the West Wing of the White House."

They parted and sat.

"Tonight's topic of discussion is on The Failure of Supply-Side Economics in a Global Economy and to present their views we have the Vice President of the United States, Francis Flores, and former Vice President Marjorie White, who retired from politics in order to concentrate on her duty to her family.

"We begin with Marjorie White who will explain how we were wooed by supply-side, then the administration's view of the success of the new economy, and then both of our speakers will be asked to suggest improvements going forward. Finally, we'll invite questions from our audience."

The audience was predominantly male. It had also

been made clear that there was a delay in the feed should Marjorie try to decry the current administration.

Marjorie White was an experienced speaker and knew the value of eye contact, even if it was the eye of a lens projecting the image into the homes of Americans across the country.

"Good evening, my fellow Americans. I apologize for the rain delay.

"We have had Reaganomics here in the US and Thatcher economics in the UK. These were Republican and conservative plans. There is no correlation in a democratic government. This, then, is the failure of a supply-side economy to properly account for the working people."

There was a polite applause due to a board indicating that the audience should approve. Marjorie continued in a speech which was professional and might have been a basis of a campaign speech. There was applause when, after twenty, minutes she sat down.

Since Marjorie's speech had covered most aspects of the issue, Francis Flores' talk lacked anything new but gained frequent applause. His manner of speaking was stilted as he read from a script which had been written for him. He spoke of the inroads made in making the world a safer place, without saying where or for whom. He praised the president and Congress for their foresight and compassion in conserving the assets of the United States and making the country 'mean and lean.'

The future was addressed by Marjorie White, noting that 'mean and lean' meant no goods on the shelves.

"The citizens of this great country believe that the

Global Economy has benefited to their detriment. The truth is that supply-side economics works best in an inflationary economy. We're experiencing deflation as the rest of the world catches up."

It was almost enough for the censors to cull but the sheer logic, the obvious truth, took them by surprise.

Marjorie continued. "The unemployment rate is unacceptable and will soon match the rest of the world's average. We must lead the world out of this morass with forward thinking, decisive action, and singularity of purpose. And with national pride."

In other times and to a more neutral audience, her words would have been popular, but since the applause board stayed down there was only a smattering of clapping from the rear of the hall.

Francis Flores again took out his notes. "The economics of this government is working. Unemployment is down to an average of eight percent throughout the country."

Mark could just imagine the people in Texas and those members of the Sons of Liberty receiving the regular update and being aghast at this hubris.

"There may be pockets of unemployment, maybe as high as twenty percent, but the average as published just last week remains below eight percent."

There was sustained applause.

"We are supporting, in a free world, those countries in the Middle East, Africa, Europe, and Russia who have replaced dictators with the rule of law found in the Koran."

Again, the audience applauded.

"This, then, is the future. I thank Mrs. White for pointing out that there is still work to be done to create a unified, global economy based on the needs of its people."

He looked out to a standing ovation.

"Thank you, both," the host stated. "Questions?"

There were a couple of planted questions directed at Francis Flores, who glanced at his notes for the answers. They were easy lobs without barbs, without any purpose other than to elevate the Vice President.

"Mr. Vice President, will you continue the policies of the administration when you're president?"

Marjorie seethed at the question, assuming the election results eighteen months in advance. She listened with her political smile fixed to her face as the reply was read from the manifesto according to Mohammed Al Adana, the current resident on Pennsylvania Avenue.

"We have time for one final question before summaries. Perhaps one for Mrs. White or for both of our guests." The moderator was clearly trying to bring some balance to the debate.

A hand rose and Marjorie White recognized the face without placing a name. Mark turned and recognized the academic who he knew was the secret head of the local Sons of Liberty. He was also one of the very few who knew the true purpose of Mark's visit and the invitation to Marjorie White.

"Mrs. White, will you be returning to politics and, if so, what changes would you propose?"

The question was dangerous. A wrong answer could result in peril for Marjorie and her family. Glancing across, she could see Francis Flores lean forward for the answer. There was an expectant hush in the auditorium. Mark held his breath.

Marjorie, with all her years of experience, appeared calm, but there was no doubt that she understood the implications of the question and her answer.

"I have no intention of seeking any office as a Democrat, or for that matter as a Republican." She gave a smile to the audience and then spoke to the camera."

"My efforts, my future focus, will be on America, and on working for an America which is strong and united. Divisions must be healed across the country. Divisions in our cities must be eliminated. There have to be efforts to bring these divisive elements together, and that is something which I shall be pleased to work to bring about together with anyone who asks. Just ask. Show me the way, and I am ready to work."

There was a smattering of applause, and Mark realized that he was attracting attention by his enthusiastic clapping. He stopped. But he couldn't stop smiling. The question had been answered on live television. The answer had been heard in Texas and in Las Vegas.

A short summation of the purpose of the debate followed with Francis Flores repeating the global efforts aimed at aid into the Middle East. Marjorie spoke of having a solid American base with which to expand a global economy – supply and demand, not a demand by supply.

The host thanked his guests and the audience, then the cameras turned off.

The vice president was ushered out, without a word or a smile, as soon as the camera light went out. Marjorie was escorted to a rear entrance without the opportunity of speaking with anyone.

Mark, Ginny – no longer dressed as a police officer, and the mayor were exultant.

"Did you know that she would be asked the question?" asked Ginny.

"Not a hundred percent sure," Joyce said. "But

there were several hundred people in the audience with the question on a card. It happened that the announcer had interviewed the professor many times over the years, recognized a familiar face and was confident in asking. It helps that the producer of the program is also a Son of Liberty."

"Well, that was a successful meeting," said Mark. "Although I think that it's clear that the present administration, and what they perceive as the next administration, is focused on a global Islamic economy."

"Is that bad? We've been dealing with different religions and new religions for hundreds of years. What's different?" one of the police officers asked.

"True, we traded with Europe, South America, and Asia with their various religions. We traded with Communists recently, with Israel, with Pakistan. The difference is that we traded, we negotiated, we grew richer. Hopefully so did they; now we're trading without negotiation, and we're giving our assets and, more importantly, our jobs to a single group with a single aim. The aim, an Islamic Empire."

## Chapter Eleven

The dark oak paneling and the rich carpets made the room seem quiet. The portraits looking down at the scene were bearing silent witness to history. They had watched for years. Theirs was a critical, cynical view of the contemporary world as they, wigged and crinolined, looked down on a solemn group of activists. There was no fire in the grate, but by mutual assent nine people were focused on the speaker standing in front of the fireplace while one of his forebears, with a remarkable resemblance, looked over his shoulder from the wall.

Professor Sanderson, known by members of the Sons of Liberty as Ben Franklin, was tall with short grey hair. He was standing with one arm behind his back and one by his side, reading glasses twirling in a long sinewy hand.

"We welcome you both to Boston." He nodded toward Ginny, who sat in a Queen Anne style chair, and Mark standing at the back of the room. "I wanted you to meet my immediate team as soon as possible. The logistics of your stay and your safety, I might add, are of paramount importance to us and our movement."

He spoke as a professor might speak to his students and with a choice of words as carefully as a politician. He went around the room introducing Betsy Ross,

Paula Revere, and John Hancock…all pseudonyms.

When he had finished, Mark asked, "Who is Peter Doath?"

There was a silence as they all looked at each other.

"I am," said Paula Revere.

"I am," said John Hancock.

"I am," said Betsy Ross amid a chorus of "I am."

Mark smiled. There was solidarity here. They were faithful to each other, a strong team. His eyes had not left Paula Revere and now, meeting his eyes, she blushed.

"Peter Doath was Mathew McDougal. Since he was killed…"

Mark was interrupted by a very large lady with an extremely cultivated voice, who had been introduced as Betsy Ross.

"Assassinated!"

Mark continued "… who was assassinated, then I assume that someone else assumed the mantle and that someone is in this room."

"Perhaps a reasonable assumption," Ben Franklin spoke. "So?"

Mark stood still thinking. If he needed to know, they would tell him. Since they had not said, he didn't need to know.

"So… I have stories from New York City that need to be disseminated by a reliable source."

"Not tonight," said Ben Franklin. "Tomorrow."

The group disbanded.

Ginny was tired. It had been a long day with the trauma of leaving New York in secret and saying goodbye to friends. She and Mark had left the hotel to see Joyce; this had been routine. A police cruiser had taken their belongings from the hotel and met them in the parking garage underneath the mayor's office. The cruiser was from Maine, and the blackened windows ensured that they were not seen by the spies that were known to be everywhere.

Now Ginny looked over at Mark who was looking at Paula Revere; when he turned and found her watching, she stood.

"I have to get some sleep. Thank you all for your hospitality. I expect to see you all tomorrow or soon." She left the room.

There were questioning looks. Mark shrugged.

"A long day, a long story," said Mark. "Ginny is critical to our organization, but she didn't expect that our trip would be this dangerous or this tiring."

"Understandable," said the professor, still standing before the grate.

The next day Ginny's mood was no better. Mark and Ginny were seated in the dining room having breakfast, which consisted of cereal and fresh toast.

"I suppose you talked about me when I left."

"Not really," said Mark.

"Not really? Then you did."

"Only to say your contribution is invaluable."

"Right." Ginny gave a harrumph of disbelief.

The ensuing silence was broken when Paula entered the room with a bowl of fruit. "We don't often get fruit these days," she peeled back a banana and ate with obvious relish.

"Good of you to let us stay here," said Mark in his best diplomatic voice.

"Not many choices really. Word is out that Mark Hughes is a dangerous terrorist loose on the East Coast."

"So, dangerous for you, too – to agree to our staying."

"I suppose." It was said in a matter of fact way. "But how many times can they kill us for our beliefs, our work, our limited contribution?"

"Better for a sheep than a lamb?" Mark smiled.

"Better not at all!"

"Well, we have a lousy track record," said Ginny a little peevishly. "Boats sink with nice people on board and good people get shot to pieces right in front of you…Right in front of you."

She stood and ran from the room.

"Those are pretty tame atrocities considering the militia sanctioned by this administration," said Paula.

"Except that the first was after we'd left the boat, and the second shooting was by two police officers, who were then eliminated by someone – probably the militia."

"I want to record your stories and distribute them. We have all morning. Father is lecturing and will meet here with just two others this afternoon. I'm writing as Peter Doath and Leonard Vallice. Originally it was to prevent the authorities from confirming that with Mac's death they had silenced the source of protest, then it made sense to give continuity to the cause."

"Then why the charade last night? Everyone claiming the penmanship."

"It's a precaution. Anyone caught and tortured cannot say for certain if it is one or many people."

"So why tell me?"

She shrugged and blushed a little. "I need to go to the school."

"Master's program?"

"Doctoral, although I am doing a second Masters too."

"A glutton for punishment. I couldn't wait to see the last of my school and teachers. The feeling, I believe, was mutual."

'Paula' left laughing.

Mark continued drinking his coffee and reading the daily newspaper. The news was obviously edited and censored. Local news reports of robberies were reported when the criminals were apprehended by the militia. Crime statistics showed that crime was down, although anecdotal evidence from the previous evening's conversation suggested differently. The discrepancy may have been accounted for by the crimes committed by the militia.

The international reporting was much the same. The oil-rich Middle East was struggling as global business dried up. Mismanagement of funds added to their problems. Aid continued pouring in and disappearing. There was a restlessness in the world. Business news, Mark noted, was reported in a style similar to the style of New York, that there was low unemployment except for pockets with problems and you, the reader, happened to be in one wherever you were. There was to be a new corporate tax levied. Since the Stock Exchange had been closed, it was difficult to judge the effect that this might have. Dividends were already heavily taxed, and now this new tax would soak whatever remaining cash was in the corporations' bank accounts.

Mark cleared his dishes and went in search of Ginny. After an extensive tour of the house, he concluded that she must have gone out.

"I hope to goodness she's careful," he spoke aloud.

Two hours later he was increasingly concerned and checking the street every few minutes. When she finally walked through the door in a nonchalant manner, he blew up.

"Where the hell have you been?"

"Out for a walk."

"Have you any idea how dangerous it is?"

"I was careful to stay on the busy streets," she said defiantly.

"Not for you. For the rest of us! Nobody gave you the right to jeopardize the lives of these people."

She gave him an icy stare.

"The police have a notice out, photos and a description of us, and you could have led them to this door! You are thoughtless and inconsiderate."

"I'm sorry. I had to get out after seeing you and Miss 'two if by sea' talking as if I wasn't there."

"Hannah Sanderson is our hostess. Hannah Sanderson put together this meeting of patriots from all over the country. Hannah Sanderson took up the mantle of Mathew McDougal and continues a defiant newsletter. Hannah Sanderson is probably number one on the list of people that this administration would like to see disappear. I hate to disillusion you, but we may or may not be in the top ten. The difference is that we, you and I, could lead them to one through twenty, and they know what we look like."

"Finished?" Ginny's face was flushed.

Mark looked at her with some disbelief.

Ginny's façade crumbled; she looked in vain for a trapdoor to open, a way out of the room. The enormous weight was just now occurring to her.

"I'm sorry. So sorry. That was really stupid of me!" She ran out of the room.

Mark didn't bother to follow her.

\*\*\*

After a light lunch, Mark met with Paula Revere, her father Benjamin Franklin, and Betsy Ross.

Ben gave apologies for Patrick Henry, who couldn't get away from the office without a fuss.

Mark guessed that Patrick Henry was in fact Sean Lynch, a lawyer, who had been a college roommate and close personal friend of Matthew McDougal.

They sat for three hours going over the conference details and logistics, the security plans to prevent infiltration. The members of the Sons of Liberty to whom Mark and Ginny would present the details would be separated from the conferees who had signed for the same breakout session; they would be interviewed by Ben Franklin and Betsy Ross before entering the auditorium with their fellow members. The Sons of Liberty conferees would have the same material as those taking the legitimate lecture.

It was foolproof, or as tight a plan as any that could be devised. The conference was just two days away and conferees were arriving. They were being watched by good guys and bad guys. The good guys had the advantage of knowing who they were looking for and were really there, at the hotels, to see if there was any interest from those on the other side.

Ben Franklin had left the room and now returned.

"Let's retire to the kitchen. I have a pot boiling and some clams and lobsters ready to go to their reward. Actually, it's our reward." He smiled.

"Would you go and see if our guest is going to join us?" he said, speaking to his daughter and nodding toward the stairs."

Hannah came back down a few minutes later. "No, she's apparently not hungry and seems quite distraught." She looked over at Mark who was looking carefully at a bottle of wine.

"French, Sancerre," he read, ignoring the questioning look.

\*\*\*

"That was very, very good," Betsy Ross declared.

"Can't get lobster like that in Texas I bet."

"I'm not from Texas," said Mark.

"Can't get lobsters like that anywhere except New England." She was adamant. "How are things in Texas? They going to secede?"

"More than likely, they'll be thrown out," said Ben Franklin.

"Wait until I get my note pad," Paula said. "Then you can tell us all your story, and I can get it out to the rest of the country. Maybe a special addition to the conferees."

"Too dangerous," said her father.

Mark regaled them with stories of the travels from his home to Texas, then the long journey through the South into New York City and up to Boston. They were attentive and quiet. There was a break for coffee and cake; most of the cake was eaten by the large woman known as Betsy Ross. Between bites, she managed to put together the connection between their stop in New York City and Austin, Texas.

"We saw Marjorie White and our own Francis Flores on television last week." She took another bite of cake while looking over her half glasses at Mark. "She looked dreadful. Still a smart lady, photogenic, would have made a great president. Too late now."

Mark was trying to keep a neutral face.

"So, what were you talking to her about, Mr. Moneyman?"

Now he was in a dilemma. Denial would be pointless in this group. The truth was not his to impart. How could he tell them that he'd recruited the contender from the last election to be the running mate with the defeated Republican candidate? He opted for the truth.

"Too dangerous to disclose at this point."

"For us? Let us decide."

"No, not for you. Too dangerous for Marjorie White and her family. They've been through enough."

"What if we guess that you want her to run against Anders or whatever his name is this week?"

"I have no way of stopping you from speculating."

"You want her to mediate a return to the Union for Texas!" Paula suggested.

Mark laughed. "You'll be the first to know," he promised. "Thank you all for a good meal and for good conversation. I ought to go check on my traveling companion. Please excuse me."

He rose, shook everyone's hand, and went to be with Ginny.

\*\*\*

The next morning they woke to learn there were riots overnight in Boston. A nighttime curfew was imposed. As usual, there were conflicting reports. The television version was that a gang of drunken students had rampaged through the downtown area setting fires and looting. The police had arrested fifty students and some others had been treated at area hospitals.

The students' version was that there was a celebrating bonfire on Boston University campus to mark the end of finals week. At the celebration there was alcohol and some singing. The militia, two hundred strong, had gone through the campus with clubs, guns, and knives. Over one hundred injured students had been taken to local hospitals, and those transporting them had been arrested by the police. The militia, meanwhile, had taken any alcohol and drugs and gone on a looting spree.

Peter Doath wrote the latter version and sent it around the country.

\*\*\*

The conference was a huge success. Although many of those who had shown interest in attending, failed to show, it was still about fifty percent of the record number in 2012. To be fair, Boston seemed a great deal more attractive back then before the riots which played out on national television.

There were spies in attendance at each of the lectures. For the lecture to be briefed by Mark and Ginny, there were two versions. The spies were sent to the one which really presented on the topic advertised. They had filled out a questionnaire presented by two Harvard professors; if they had read the Peter Doath story in April and the latest one, then they knew the answers. If not, a few more questions sent them to room two.

In the primary lecture room, forty-nine people representing thirty-two states were in attendance when Mark appeared. He was instantly recognized, and the room gave a small gasp and then fell silent in awe that this meeting had been arranged for them to listen to the most wanted man in America.

Mark was nervous and a little scared. There might be a spy in the room despite the precautions. If there was an informant, then the chance of being arrested was only a matter of time. A very short time.

"Thank you all for coming here at great personal risk. We hope that you will feel that it was worth it when you get back to your own group in your own states. Communication, safe communication, is the biggest challenge that we have in our opposition to the present administration. We believe that we have solved that problem, or at least for now. I am not going to give you much detail of the workings other than it will route through a computer located west of the Mississippi. Now, if you will give your attention my colleague, she will give you instructions, which you may not write down."

Mark sat on a high stool so that he could observe the participants while Ginny stepped up to the podium.

It took Ginny two false starts to be heard. "I'm sorry to be so nervous. I was unaware when I volunteered to attend a seminar in Boston how dangerous it would be. The most danger before this trip was a day I spent in Galveston."

The laughter relaxed her just a little. It had been a nervous sound, as though everyone had been thinking the same thing. After that it was like attending a lecture on bank robbery with Bonnie and Clyde.

"You've already been subject to our new communication system. When you came in, each of you was asked to read a sentence; that sentence was transmitted and became a voice print. If anyone other than yourself attempts to use the phone that you are about to receive, then the computer will not give any information to the sender."

Mark and Ginny looked out over the audience. They were pretty sure that these dedicated people understood the importance of the message and the need for secrecy.

Ginny spoke for another twenty minutes and Mark wrapped up in time for participants to leave with their new phones and a brief summary of what had been covered in the other room so that everyone could speak knowledgably if approached. They left at the same time as room number two and mingled with them as they went to lunch. Since they had all been given the same packages, it was impossible to distinguish one from another.

Mark and Ginny, together with the organizers of

the meeting, left by a rear exit and drove away. Mission accomplished. Now back to Texas.

Instead of euphoria, the passengers were feeling a distinctly different emotion. Ginny was feeling relieved that it was over. Mark felt that it was a step forward but was anticipating a great deal of work ahead. The members of the Sons of Liberty from Boston had taken part in history but were now collaborators. They had taken on more responsibility than they'd expected.

The car travelled from the convention center back into downtown Boston, through Government Center, up Park Street, onto Beacon Street by the State House toward the Back Bay. A police cruiser blocked the street and the reason was obvious as there were fire trucks further up the street.

Mark was the first to react. "Get us out of here!"

## Chapter Twelve

"What the hell was that about?" the man known as Ben Franklin asked.

"We need a safe place to stop and find out," said Mark.

To the driver he instructed, "Stop at the first hotel and leave, then you will not be able to, when asked, say where we are."

"Is all of this necessary?" asked Ginny.

"People's lives are in jeopardy, even yours; especially yours," said Mark glowering in her direction.

"The Four Seasons okay?" asked the driver.

"Yes, pull around onto Newbury Street and let us out. Then leave."

"Do you think…?" Ben Franklin was afraid to ask.

"Yes," said Mark. "I think we have to prepare for the worst and hope for the best. It was not coincidence that fire trucks were outside your house, but let's hope they were not actually putting out a fire."

Ben withered. "My grandfather's trust fund bought that house. There was a lot of history there. I… I.." he stumbled.

"I'm truly sorry," said Mark.

Ginny and Hannah returned from the ladies' room where they had attempted to change their appearance.

"There's a television in the little room across from

the lobby," Hannah said. "I'll go see if there is any news of the fire or whatever."

"I'll go with her," said Ginny.

"No. We have to split up and make arrangements to communicate," said Mark.

Ben Franklin took out a cell phone.

"You can't use that," said Mark. "Switch it off. Who were you calling?

"A friend. He manages real estate rentals in this area."

"Let's use a pay phone…if they still exist."

Mark and Ginny were alone as Ben was using the phone and Hannah was watching television.

"You think that I brought them to the house." Ginny made a statement.

"It could have been anything," said Mark.

"But you think that it was because of me. I can see it in your face. You think that I'm a stupid, selfish idiot who was spotted out walking and led them to the house."

"It could have been anything," Mark repeated with less conviction.

Ginny stared past him, watching Hannah and Ben return.

Ben instructed, "We're going just around the corner. He's on his way to meet us. We can walk and talk."

They left by a side door and walked up Newbury Street to Berkeley and took a left turn onto Commonwealth Avenue.

While they walked, Hannah told them of what she had seen on the television. The announcer was saying that they had arrested two members of the Sons of Liberty and had a dragnet out for the rest of the terrorist cell. The broadcast indicated that this would break the back of the movement. Hannah had watched as Betsy Ross and the housekeeper were seen being taken from the house in handcuffs. Betsy Ross was shouting defiantly as she was led from the house. A large woman, it was with difficulty that she was manhandled into the police cruiser. The housekeeper, by contrast a very small woman, was quietly walking to the car when she was hit with a baton, then bundled into a different cruiser.

The camera shot then showed fire exploding from the downstairs windows and men in the informal uniform of the militia running from the back. A voice over informed the viewers that the Sons of Liberty had torched their own headquarters to prevent investigators from uncovering the web of terrorism which was spreading across the country. The gesture was futile, however, since a hoard of information had been recovered before arresting the occupants. The owner of the house, Professor Harrison Sanderson, was wanted for questioning.

Professor Sanderson listened with a placid, blank expression, but it was obvious that he was seething. The loss of his magnificent home and the fact that he had been placed on a 'wanted' list were both likely to affect his view of the world. This view, which until the last half hour, had been one of equanimity. True, he was affiliated with an organization at odds with the present government, but that he saw as his right to disagree, to oppose. Similarly he had seen the acquisition of firearms as guaranteed by the Constitution which he had sworn to uphold. He admired how his daughter had watched the television and recounted the story with strength. Now in the face of her father's stoicism, she dissolved into uncontrollable tears.

The story, of the original acquisition of the brownstone, had been told the previous night over a post-dinner glass of port. Back in 1964 the newly engaged, postgraduate student had been looking for somewhere to live in Cambridge, but he had visited close friends on Beacon Hill who said that their house was going to be on the market as the friend had accepted a position in California. The 'newly-weds,' or soon to be weds, were smitten. The house offered everything that they were looking for and was within walking distance of Boston Common, Boston Gardens, the Theater District, and waterfront. Harrison Sanderson called his father who agreed that he could invade his trust fund for the purpose of purchasing the house.

That was over forty years ago. Since then Hannah had been born in the Massachusetts General Hospital, where their obstetrics department was world renowned.

Hannah, Harrison remembered with a pang of remorse for his own self-pity, had never known any other home. It was where his wife, her mother, had died. He stopped and looked at her face; it was a kaleidoscope of emotions.

Now their home was gone.

The house that they reached on Commonwealth Avenue was four stories high with a basement living area. At one time the downstairs was where the servants worked, and the attic was where they slept. A conversion after the Second World War had created four large apartments. The second floor had three bedrooms, a large kitchen with a large table capable of seating eight, a dining room, and a living room with a grand piano and seating for twenty people. It was furnished in a manner of the nineteen fifties except for the kitchen appliances which were all new. The rental agent gave them the keys and, without comment, left them to wander around, establish that the refrigerator was empty, the linens were plentiful, and that the rooms had a view of Commonwealth Ave in the front, Clarendon to the side, and an alley out back.

"This must cost a fortune," said Mark.

"Less than you would think," said the Professor. "The owner moved to Florida, cannot sell it in this environment, and is happy to cover a few costs."

"What about the neighbors?"

"Private people, reclusive, wealthy; they're probably a target of the militia or other things and therefore subscribe to an excellent security system and low profile."

The four of them went into the kitchen. Mark and the professor sat at the table, evaluating their position. Hannah opened cupboards and cabinets, taking inventory of the apartment. Ginny sat, despondent, staring into nothingness.

"Ginny, you need to snap out of it," Mark said.

"But, I…This is my fault."

"Could be," agreed Mark. "Or they could have known about the house or someone else could have led them there, or there might be an informer among the members, or a dozen other reasons. We need to focus on now. We have to concentrate on staying alive. We have to have a plan. We have to work together."

"But…"

"Now, Ginny. Not tomorrow. Not when you get over your guilt. NOW!"

There was silence in the room, interrupted by the grandfather clock chiming four.

"Okay. What can I do?" she asked.

"That's better," said Mark. "I think we're going to ask you to do the most dangerous job. We need food; and we need it soon, before the authorities organize, so it must be today."

"But, what if…"

"They are definitely looking for militants. It's less likely that they'll stop a woman. The first instinct will be to seal off the city and check people leaving. If you shop in the city, walking across Boston Garden, you should be safe."

"I may be arrested," said Ginny.

"You have a better chance than anyone. The house was not a random attack; they know that the owner and his daughter were not home. If either of them was to be arrested, then hundreds, thousands, would be at risk."

"I need to think," Ginny said.

"Think quickly. The market where there are no cameras closes down about five o'clock, in less than an hour."

Ginny was back to thinking of her guilt in leading to the destruction of their safehouse and their present condition. The decision was therefore more to assuage her guilt when she agreed with the proposal.

It took five minutes to instruct her in finding the market and what to buy that could be carried while walking. Two large canvas bags were found, and she was dressed in a conservative manner using the professor's raincoat as a large, baggy figure-hiding outer garment.

Ginny left.

"What do you think?" asked the professor.

"Let's not think. Let's expect that she does her job and that we can do ours," said Mark.

"Hannah, can you make a list of people we need to

contact with telephone numbers and email addresses? Professor, we need transportation, an escape plan. Involve a minimum of people and expect that they are being watched. I'll contact Texas on our secure line and let them know the score."

Everyone set to work.

The grandfather clock chimed five o'clock and Mark looked up with increasing frequency as Ginny has not returned. At five thirty he sat looking at the clock face as though he might divine a scenario, from the inscrutable image looking down on him. The professor was watching television news stories and surreptitiously also watching the time. Hannah was sitting close to a garbage compacting disposal unit that would swallow her lists if necessary.

They collectively jumped when the doorbell rang. On the intercom Ginny asked for help carrying the packages up the stairs. Relief was palpable, but before going down they checked the streets on the three sides of the house.

In addition to the food, Ginny had bought a local newspaper. The fire was not reported. It was too soon, but the other articles were combed, looking for reasons for the raid and for any comment or conjecture regarding the conference.

One piece of information, a presidential visit to the area, led to a lively discussion. The most optimistic view was that the president had been alerted to the raid and chose to be in Boston. This was optimistic because it therefore led to the conclusion that the visit had indeed been planned days ahead of time. Clearly this was Ginny's favorite scenario as it exonerated her rash behavior. The others endorsed the premise since it was also clear that the way forward was going to require the cooperation of all, including Ginny.

Television coverage of the fire and the presence of the president topped the news and made for compelling viewing. Local coverage also showed the president attending services at the mosque off Tremont Street where he delivered a sermon denouncing those who would oppose his rule of law, the law introduced by his administration, to support the militia and the banning of inappropriate accumulation of wealth and status. He denounced Boston as epitomizing this inappropriate thinking with its emphasis on learning and, in particular, in providing an equal number of places in these institutes of learning for women.

Hannah, at some point in this harangue, stood and switched off the television.

Mark and Harrison had somehow fashioned a half decent meal from the bags of groceries brought in by Ginny. Since Ginny was a vegetarian, it was no surprise that the principal ingredients were green. The salad was fresh, the bread also. Chicken had been cooked and cut up into the salad.

Hannah found a compact disc player and Beethoven. The meal was eaten with little conversation and no dessert. They took coffee or tea and went their separate ways. Hannah went back to review the lists, Harrison said that he was tired and would try to read a little in his bedroom if he could find a good book. Mark sat at the dining table making notes, and Ginny had retreated to another bedroom and was working on her computer.

It had been a long, hard, eventful day. Everyone was tired and they were all in bed early, though it was very difficult to sleep. Mark had taken the smallest bedroom. Ginny and Hannah had twin beds in the middle room, while Professor Sanderson was coerced by the other three into the master bedroom.

Mark lay awake in the dark. The word from Texas was to get out of Boston as quickly as possible. Anyone compromised should also be strongly advised to leave. Intercepted internet traffic indicated that the president, backed by the governor of Massachusetts and his militia, intended to make an example of the Boston members of the Sons of Liberty.

The president had discovered that Joseph Lloyd, son of the executed, General Lloyd, former Joint Chiefs of Staff, was the military head of the uprising and had a cache of weapons that they were desperate to find. There was a price on the heads of several of the leaders, and they were also looking for the source of funding.

The news reports reminded everyone that Joseph Lloyd's father had refused an order from his commander in chief, the president, at his inauguration. It failed to explain why.

Mark guessed that General Lloyd had told the president that the withdrawal needed a great deal of planning in order to prevent loss of American military lives. Not liking that answer, the president had the general terminated.

The order, carried out by his replacement, to immediately bring home all troops from the Middle East had resulted in loss of troops as they were retreating to ships. Those troops had been attacked without the ability to fight back. The void in those Middle Eastern countries had also resulted in genocide. Anyone supporting or having benefitted from the American presence was slaughtered. The troops had been forced to abandon their camps along with large equipment, ammunition, and supplies. All of these were used against the retreating troops and the innocent population who might disagree.

Sometime before morning, Mark had fallen asleep because he awoke to a scream and could not think where he was. Dressed only in boxer shorts, he ran from the room into the living area and toward the sound of Hannah shouting for help from the master bedroom. Hannah and Ginny were both there.

It was obvious that, sometime in the night, Professor Harrison Sanderson had suffered a stroke.

"Call an ambulance," Hannah shouted.

"No," said Mark.

"Call an ambulance!" The shout now held menace.

"Not if you want him to live." Mark was trying to think and to calm down the hysterical woman.

"Call an ambulance. He's had a stroke." Now it was a plea.

"If he goes to the hospital, he will be tortured for what he knows until he dies. If you go with him, that will also be your fate."

"Then, what?" Ginny was emotionally supporting Hannah but was quickly grasping the precarious situation that they were in.

"Let me think. He's still alive, so unless he has another stroke, there may be some time."

"There is no time." Hannah was distraught. In the last twenty-four hours she had lost her home that she had lived in all her life and now her father. Her strong father was lying helpless in front of her eyes.

"Hannah, that list you were making last night, any doctors?" Ginny asked.

"Yes, a few."

"Medical doctors…heart specialists?"

"Yes…" She hesitated. "But…"

Mark jumped in sharply. "Hannah, you were going to call an ambulance. Let's at least give the doctor a chance to give us advice on the telephone."

She stood to get the information.

When she returned, Mark gave his cell phone to her. "Dial nine and then the number. It will appear to go through Nevada."

"Nevada?"

"Yes, or some other state."

They were all quiet as Hannah asked to speak to the doctor. It was clear that this was not going to happen without identification and that the identification would have to be recognized.

"Tell Dr. Cohn that Paula Revere is on the line and that it concerns Ben."

"Give me a number and I'll have him call you back."

In the room Mark was waving 'No' and miming 'hold on'.

"I'll hold. It's a matter of life and death."

"Yes; they all are," was said without irony.

They waited.

"Young lady?"

"Doctor Samuel Adams?" The use of the nom de plume created a silence. "Paula Revere. I believe Ben has had a stroke and there's no one to call."

"Right! Call back in five minutes to my private line. I'll have to make some arrangements."

There are five minutes and long five minutes but this one felt to all three in the room as if they would never end. Hannah went to hold her father's hand. He seemed no worse, no better.

"Doctor, what do we do?"

"No sirens outside, so I think that I have not been 'stitched.' I think that's the expression. Tell me where you are, and I'll be there directly."

Mark took the phone.

"Doctor, this is a friend, and I think that it would

be safer if you did not have that information."

"Fair enough. I do need to see Ben."

"Someone will meet you at the Copley Station. Come out and head toward the library."

"The underground? I haven't been on there since Harvard."

Things went relatively smoothly. It was an anxious half hour before Ginny brought Dr. Cohn from the station.

"Very interesting train ride but I think I will take a cab back to my car. Where's the patient?"

The doctor quickly confirmed the diagnosis and brought out a syringe and a bag of fluids. "I will give him a shot of tPA."

"What does that do?" Hannah was hovering close to her father.

"It's a clot-dissolving drug. It helps in many cases."

"What about the other cases?"

"I won't know without further tests. In any case, the tPA will do no harm. If it is more serious, a larger clot, then we can use another technology, deploy a stent, and remove the clot. Tricky but doable. For that, however, I'd need to get him to a hospital."

After completing a careful examination of the professor and setting the fluids to drip with the tPA administered, there was a meeting in the living room.

"He needs hospitalization," said the doctor.

"No," said Mark. "It's too dangerous."

"He needs hospitalization." The doctor held up a hand. "Trust me on this. We need to put him under an assumed name in a place where the militia, or whoever is looking, will never find him."

"And you can do this?" a now hopeful Hannah asked.

"I think so. Where would a Muslim militia never look and never get a straight answer?"

They recognized that the question was rhetorical and waited for the answer. "The Hebrew Rehabilitation Center."

"But, he's... he's not Jewish." said Hannah.

"He's a mensch," said Dr. Cohn emphatically. "A good man."

"Can you? Will you?" asked Mark. "We can pay."

"I can, I will. Who asked for payment?"

Fifteen minutes later it was arranged, and another fifteen minutes passed before a minibus with a reclined wheelchair as opposed to an ambulance with stretcher left with the professor, doctor, and a tearful Hannah.

Mark and Ginny were alone. It had been two days since there had not been people around and now there was tension.

"You blame me," Ginny stated.

"It doesn't matter. They knew about this group before we arrived."

"I can see in your eyes that you no longer trust me."

"I trust nobody."

"I thought..." Ginny didn't finish her sentence.

There was a long silence. Ginny was feeling guilty, was upset with Mark's perfidy, angry for having let her personal feelings intrude on what was clearly a mission or a quest and, she admitted to herself, she was homesick.

"We have to think of extricating our way out of here. I think it's time to go home, or back to Texas."

"Is that what the boss says?" Ginny retorted spitefully. She was ignoring the fact that she had been thinking the same thing.

"No. Actually, they want us to go and get Marjorie White out of New Jersey."

"Are they mad?"

"With some urgency," said Mark with a frown.

"There are only so many ways to leave Boston," said Ginny. "Air, train, bus, or car."

"Boat?"

"I think I've had enough of boats, and Texas is a long way to row," Ginny said, happier to be talking of going home.

"Air is out. Too many security measures and even more stringent in this paranoid administration."

"Rail and bus may have the same or similar limitations which means car, and we don't have one," Ginny stated.

"Let's think."

Mark did his thinking with a pad of paper, listing the pros and cons of each option.

Ginny wandered around the apartment checking the street though the window, examining the artwork, and eventually sat down with newspapers that she had bought the previous day. The financial news was virtually non-existent since the administration had made illegal all mutual funds, exchange traded funds, margin accounts, or anything that they interpreted as gambling or amassing great wealth. A complete joke to anyone who knew that the vast wealth had been accumulated through gambling, rigging elections, and always wagering on the successful candidate. Wall Street was just a shadow of its former glory. There was a small piece that said an investigation was still underway into the New York mayoral race. The national news was all positive and rosy – crime down, unemployment down, government ratings up. Even a casual reading could see the lies, the discrepancies.

Local news centered on fires and violent crime, usually involving militia, but never their instigation. There was an article on the Sons of Liberty and that manhunts had resulted in arrests with a few members still at large. The expectation was that all would be rounded up soon.

Ginny crumpled up the pages and threw them aside. She stood and went to the kitchen to prepare something to eat.

A knock at the door startled them and they were relieved to have Hannah enter the room.

Each sat with a cup of tea while she told them her father was safely ensconced in an intensive care unit under an assumed name. A patient had checked out and the professor had assumed his name so that the discharge was not recorded, nor was any new patient admitted. The attack had been severe, but he appeared to understand, without being able to communicate. Hannah had been invited and intended to move as a guest to a home closer to the Rehabilitation Center.

They chatted amiably about keeping in touch. Mark said they'd be leaving as soon as they could figure out how.

"You thinking of a cruise?" asked Hannah, picking up the travel section of the discarded newspaper.

"If it goes to Galveston," said Ginny.

"There is a Norwegian liner in Boston headed for New York, Miami, and the Panama Canal."

"Close enough," said Ginny, taking the paper from her hand.

"Let's not discuss this now," said Mark.

"That's right. You don't trust anyone do you?"

"Look, I trust everyone here, but the less people know, the less that can be tortured out of them."

Ginny headed for the bedroom, slamming the door.

## Chapter Thirteen

Tony Whittaker sat at a small table, in a small tavern, in a small town in north, North America. There was a small crowd of small-minded people drinking low calorie beer. A baseball game was showing on a small television above a small bar. All of this occurred to Tony as he was thinking why anyone might care about the fate of two small people.

The answer, surprisingly, was in front of him.

The bartender was obviously also the owner of the tavern. He was a man in his forties or fifties, medium height, wiry, lean, and he had never been good looking. He was dressed in old dark slacks and a dress shirt with sleeves rolled up to different lengths on hairy arms, which he now leaned on a cluttered bar top. At a remark, he attempted to smile and showed that he had probably never troubled a dentist; dark holes showed a ragged tooth-gapped grin; lines appeared, creating dark ridges down either side of his dark face. It was clear, however, that this bar, in this tavern, in this town, was the entire world of this dirty, inconsequential-looking, man.

There were two men in work clothes standing in front of the bar. They worked locally and from the conversation evidently had likewise never lived anywhere else but in this small town and had no desire to move onward, nor enough education to move upward. If the thought of moving had occurred to any one of them, it would have been laughed away.

To the men, in front of Tony, this then was their universe; to them it was big. The local politics were important, the schools, the sports teams were discussed with all the fervor of the big cities. Therefore the answer, why anyone would care about two little people, depended on where you were – physically, emotionally, or philosophically. Someone somewhere cared enough to want to find and kill Tony and Irene.

At the thought of Irene, Tony stood, and, with a nod to Al the owner, left the tavern. It was warm for May and still sunny and bright at six in the evening. He did not normally stop for a beer, but trying to fit into the landscape it also allowed a variation from his routine, a chance to see if anyone was following or paying too much attention to him. Standing outside, blinking, he looked up and down an empty street.

Tony and Irene had arrived in this backwater four months earlier after zigzagging through seven states for two months. Tony had tried stopping in other towns or cities, but something always spooked him and they moved on. Spooking could have been a police car slowing down, a rental agent not convinced of his history or suspicious of his willingness to pay in cash, or the feeling that he was being followed. A 'mechanic wanted' sign had provided the reason to stop and check out this dead-end town which was at the end of its useful life.

The rented house that he had found stood in a street of rental houses. The houses had been built in the 1930s by the company that had provided a large portion of the population with jobs, Marston Castings Inc. The company had grown out of the Depression, making large castings from various metals and was running three shifts during World War II. At that time to rent a property in Marstonville, the name given to the houses that the company built, was a privilege. Now Marstonville was spoken of as a slum, where half the houses were vacant or not paying full rent. It was a community which minded its own business and therefore was appealing to Tony.

Marston Castings was closed. The huge shed-like buildings stood brick red in the bright low sunlight. The walls of the plant came right up to the small pavement as though every inch was used, and expansion could go no further. The plant was a mausoleum, an artifact of a previous age, a victim of vertical integration. The factory was a monument to a time when large industrial complexes had sub-contracted work and were themselves just assemblers of machines. Now those industrial giants controlled vertically, from bare metal, through production and into the sales process. The sub-contractors closed. Towns that had grown with them died. Birds watched silently from the roof and from window ledges as Tony walked the empty street, confident that tonight no one was following.

"Hello, Sweetheart. How was your day?" Tony shouted as he entered the front door. He knew that Irene was still standing in front of the window, watching the street.

"I'll make your supper now," he said, then continued. "I stopped at the tavern; no one was following." He dropped his lunch bag on the kitchen table. "Not very busy today at the garage. I had to show Norman how to fix a thread on an oil filter that he had forced. I think he feels threatened so I gave him a hand and some praise."

Tony had been fixing his personal car and truck for a few years. Since everything that could go wrong had in fact gone wrong, he had enough practical experience to handle most automobile repair situations. "Hamburger alright?" He moved through the kitchen and Irene followed. "Cup of tea?" he asked, and Irene sat.

Tony went to the small noisy refrigerator and took out minced meat for hamburger and milk. "You didn't eat the sandwich I left for you. Never mind. I can take it for lunch tomorrow and make a fresh one for you." He tried to keep the concern out of his voice. Irene wasn't eating enough.

Tony made hamburgers and fried them while making a simple salad. He lightly toasted two rolls, set the table for two, made tea, and kept up a one-sided conversation. They ate while he talked about the weather.

Irene ate some salad and half of her hamburger; he ate the other half, after finishing his own meal.

Looking across the table at his wife, Tony still saw her as the beautiful woman he had always loved. When they first met, it was her feisty nature that had been the attraction – for him and a flock of suitors. She was a natural blond, although not at the moment, the result of a brown hair dye. Tony took note that the blond hair was working its way through the hair follicles. Her current identification, as Irene Whittaker, said light brown. He would have to do something about the color if they moved again…when they moved again. Where had the fire gone from her eyes? he wondered.

The fire, the explosion, the killing…that's when it started, or was that when it ended. They were supposed to be in the fire, killed by the explosion or by the hail of bullets that the thirty elite paratroopers had poured into the tiny cabin. The official story was that they had been killed while resisting arrest and had torched the cabin to avoid capture. One day they had been living a comfortable life in the country, the next day they were on the run. Irene believed that she had brought the pursuers to the door; that she had precipitated the carnage. At least that was his assumption. Irene had not spoken since that night six months ago. When they had silently stolen away, neither had spoken, letting the sounds and the fury etch into their brains. Tony still had occasional nightmares. For Irene they had never gone away.

He was still looking across the table and now he saw in addition to losing a great deal of weight, there was a grey pallor to her skin from the lack of sleep, lack of sunlight, lack of exercise, and the limited diet. "It was not your fault," Tony said for at least the thousandth time. "They were looking for me, may still be looking for me. It's too bad we can't call anyone."

Irene looked up, perhaps remembering that it was likely a telephone call she made that had led the government forces to their hiding place in the woods. It was a simple telephone call to her mother, to wish her a happy new year. It could hardly be a coincidence that they had been attacked the night following the call.

Tony saw Irene's reaction and was heartened. She had looked up. He had not imagined it. He decided to take advantage of this progress and say something to create a response.

"That political debate was interesting last week. I can't imagine Marjorie White going over to the dark side."

Marjorie White had been let out of her house arrest

to participate in a debate on foreign policy. She had been careful not to antagonize the current White House occupant. It was inconceivable that Marjorie White would support the present administration. The murder of her husband, made to look like a driving accident, and the kidnapping of her children had forced her from the presidential race.

Irene, in different personae, had been Marjorie White's media director and personal friend.

There was another spark of interest. Or maybe defiance. A comment about a friend would have sparked an hourlong debate in different times. Now it was sufficient to create a flash, some proof that there was a feeling returning. Marjorie White was a friend, and Irene had been her confidante.

The rest of the evening passed, as had the previous, almost two hundred, in a monolog which slowly petered out. Tomorrow would be another day, another opportunity to try to shake her from silence; tonight he showered and went to bed. Putting his arm around his wife, he wept, for her, for himself, for the United States of America.

Days passed. The routine was the same: work, cook, clean, shop, and sleep. Shopping was a challenge as it was necessary not to invite suspicion. It was getting easier since the stores had a limited inventory. Many items, especially in this lower end of the working poor, were not available. The explanations were always of temporary disruptions, of localized transportation issues.

Tony had a better grasp of the national and global economy and saw a pattern. Imported items were missing, indicative of a balance of payments problem. Also not readily available were items from the furthest parts of the country. Florida and California fruits were not making it to the northern states. The fruit could have been used as exports or they were remaining closer to their source. With a stated inflation rate of 7% and a real rate of probably more than 20%, it was hard for suppliers to wait three months and then be paid in devalued currency. Buyers were reluctant to pay for goods with no guarantee when, if, and in what condition they would be delivered.

The cracks were beginning to show.

The policymakers in Washington were being led by a Congress and White House that had been infiltrated and taken over by Islamist fundamentalists. The policy was now to dismantle the US armed forces, cancel all military contracts, all infrastructure projects were passed down to the states. The states' budgets were already trying to carry the load of unemployment and the subsequent loss of tax collections. Foreign support was being sent to the Middle East to continue the growth of an Islamic Empire. The US citizens opposing the government were branded terrorists in a bizarre twist of logic.

Tony and Irene were, or had been before their 'deaths' and disappearance, in the top ten of wanted people.

"Hello, Sweetheart. How was your day?"

Tonight he was tired. Tired of the same routine; tired of working for a pittance. Even the car repair business was off. Motorists were driving with broken parts, knowing that a badly undermanned police force was not going to stop them. Motorists were delaying repairs then having trouble paying a cut-price repair shop like Prime Motors. He was tired of shopping, cooking, and cleaning.

Irene walked into the kitchen.

Tony smiled at her blank, silent face. "I'll get your

supper," he said. "They had no bananas, no oranges, but I did get a few apples and a small pork roast."

The evening monolog continued about work, weather, and sports. Tony didn't talk politics or religion. And he didn't voice his fears for the economy.

"I think I'll watch baseball for about an hour." The television shows were mostly repeats of old variety shows since most of the current programs were either banned by the government watchdog, boycotted by the militia, or too expensive for sponsors' reduced budgets. The sports shows were exempt, but cutbacks meant just two cameras and limited slow-motion replays.

Tony fell asleep sometime in the sixth inning. The game had ended and the news was playing when he heard, "BASTARD! MURDERING BASTARD!"

Tony woke up with a start and came to his feet in one motion. He looked at the image on the screen. He looked at the source of the shout. Irene was standing behind his chair pointing at the television. Tony tore his eyes away from his wife to again face the television. He looked at the image of President Mohammed Al Adana and his chief of Homeland Security, Adam Fox. There was a burning building behind them that looked familiar. He turned up the sound.

"...here in Boston we have rooted out a cell of terrorists, made numerous arrests, and as you can see behind me, those opponents of this government have burned their own headquarters to the ground."

"Well, that sounds familiar. It's what they said we did in New Hampshire," Tony muttered.

The television cameras showed a brownstone in the Beacon Hill section of Boston, and the announcer revealed that it was owned by Professor Harrison Sanderson, the leader of the Sons of Liberty, a group opposed to the present administration. The Sons of Liberty, named for the original group of patriots, had been forced into hiding since the government-approved militias had come onto the scene.

Tony knew that the head of Homeland Security, Adam Fox, was also head of the militias. Ben Franklin was one of only two people in the world who knew that he, Mathew McDougal, was still alive. He had to think, to digest what he had just witnessed. The persons arrested or captured were likely turned over to the militia for torture. It was only a matter of time before they spread their net.

Did someone else know about him? Who had been interred? Where was Ben Franklin? Had the fight gone out of the movement? Was there no opposition?

More and more questions entered his mind. And he was hiding out like a coward. This was not the good news that he thought there might be. This was the worst news imaginable.

A bigger and decidedly more immediate piece of news was that Irene, no Helen, had spoken.

Mac was wide awake now; he needed to be. It was time to go. This time they wouldn't be running away. This time they'd be running forward.

They were headed back to Boston.

## Chapter Fourteen

Mark telephoned Texas and Las Vegas. He wanted to see if there were any better ideas, and he needed a new identity and papers if they were to be successful in leaving Boston in one piece. Texas gave him an added burden of getting Marjorie White and her family out of New Jersey and onto the ship. How did they imagine he was going to spirit five people, under house arrest, away?

Another twist was that the Bergen was scheduled to leave the next day on the early tide.

Mark wrestled with the problem for hours before calling Las Vegas and asking for more favors. Was it possible for Mark and Ginny to board as members of the crew, and was it possible for the line to invite Marjorie as a speaker and political debater in exchange for a free passage? The fact that the ship was leaving Boston tomorrow meant that Marjorie and family would have to join the Bergen when she docked in New York.

It was early hours of the morning when a message with instructions came through and he was able to go to bed, though not to sleep.

Over a terse breakfast of toast, fruit, and coffee, Mark announced that they were leaving.

"Did it occur to you to ask my opinion?" asked Ginny.

"No."

"Why not?"

"Because, number one, you are not in a fit state to make decisions, and, number two, you slammed the door as you left the room."

"That was because…Oh, never mind."

"No dispute then."

It was clear that the relationship that they had enjoyed in New York was ended for now, and maybe forever. Ginny was both heartbroken and felt guilty about possibly leading the militia to the headquarters of the Sons of Liberty and would resent that Mark knew this about her. There was also her jealousy over Hannah Sanderson which, irrational or with cause, had created the problem and led to the lack of trust, and possibly jeopardized their mission.

"What's the plan?" she asked.

Mark thought about not telling her, but there had to be some trust somewhere, and he still needed her co-operation. "We're going to board a ship, as crew."

"Dishwashers?" Ginny said sarcastically, forgetting for a moment her silent pledge of humility.

"Don't know yet," said Mark, either too tired to notice or too preoccupied and anxious to care.

"I'm sorry. I'll wash dishes if that is what it takes." Ginny was now contrite.

"We have to meet a man this morning. We should take what we need with us. There will be a laundry and toiletries on board. We'll need a set of casual clothes and non-slip shoes."

"And uniform?" asked Ginny.

"Provided," said Mark. "Probably taken out of your pay," he added in an attempt to lighten the mood.

Ginny gave him a small smile and bowed her head.

He couldn't help but feel love for this young

woman, but now wasn't the time for a relationship to blossom. They needed to focus. And they needed to stay alive.

Thirty minutes later they entered Syracuse, a restaurant on Hanover Street in the North End of Boston. The restaurant appeared small and insignificant. The interior was well lit, and an elderly waiter greeted them.

"Menus?"

"Not for me, thanks," said Mark.

"Yes, please," said Ginny who had eaten little breakfast and no dinner the previous night.

"No need," repeated Mark. "I'll have the rabbit and my friend a vegetarian antipasto."

"No rabbit. It's not on the menu," said the elderly waiter shaking his head. A younger waiter stood nearby shaking his head as well.

"Tell Mario that a friend ordered the rabbit."

"Who is Mario?" the old man appealed to the young waiter who shrugged and returned to the kitchen.

Mark and Ginny sat and waited. Five minutes passed, and no one else entered this early in the day. A man appeared at the kitchen door. He was probably in his fifties, dressed in shabby chinos, a long-sleeved shirt, and a tee shirt visible. He was heavy, overweight, and unshaven.

"Antipasto Italian, antipasto vegetarian, bottle of wine. How would you like your rabbit cooked?"

"Ten thousand cash, papers, and a means of catching the Bergen."

"Cash will be here with your lunch check; papers, you go across the street to the photography studio, they will take necessary pictures. Then you go to the Victoria for dessert and coffee. Half an hour a package with passports, driving licenses, and passes for the Bergen. You're both working on-board activities. The activities director and his girl, the headliner, are headed to Vegas for two weeks. A lucky break for them. I understand that a former politician has been invited to fill in." He paused. "Anything else?"

"How do we catch up and get aboard?"

"Here comes your rabbit, braised, with penne pasta. The Bergen is delayed until the afternoon tide. A union dispute that just cost you another grand."

The man, having eaten half of the small antipasto, tasted the rabbit and drunk half of the bottle of wine, all while talking, returned to the kitchen.

"Was that Mario?" Ginny asked, looking askance at Mark's plate.

"Who the hell knows?"

The photography and delivery of documents went as described, and no-one seemed to have paid any attention. It was not an area of town that the militia, or the police for that matter, had much jurisdiction.

"We should get to the ship," Mark said, pushing aside the now empty plate that had held an excellent tiramisu.

"What time is high tide?" asked Ginny.

"I want to get the lay of the land before we leave and in case we run into issues at the gate."

"Signore, a complication," the elderly waiter from the restaurant walked to their table in the Victoria.

Ginny gasped and grabbed Mark's arm. Her imagination streaked ahead with fears of their betrayal to the police, or worse. Was it for the money? Was there a problem with the new papers?

Mark was also stunned. "A complication?"

There seemed to be no way out. It was like being in a western movie, walking through the door would invite a hail of bullets.

"Another couple…" he gestured with both arms toward Mark and Ginny, encompassing them and showing that he was unarmed, "…came into the restaurant, ordered the rabbit, and asked to speak to Mario."

"A couple? A man and woman our age?"

"Maybe older, maybe forty."

Ginny was confused.

Mark was curious and cautious. What were the chances that they were being shadowed? "So, what does Mario want us to do?"

The elderly waiter spread his arms in a gesture that indicated that this was not his decision, that he was merely the messenger. "You must remain here until our 'friend' confirms."

"And if we don't?" Mark waved the papers at the man.

"Then the papers will not help you." It was said without malice, just a statement of fact. "This way," he gestured and led them through the kitchen into an alley then through the Syracuse kitchen and into the restaurant.

A man and woman sat in the same chairs that Mark and Ginny had occupied an hour before, but their faces were turned away from the door. Mark was unsure what reaction he might provoke by staring so he looked away. Ginny, with some naiveté, looked at the couple without recognition. She noted that the woman was pretty, but she also appeared tired and ill. This did not detract from the aura of beauty in her features. The man was dressed in work clothes and looked exhausted. The exhaustion, she recognized, was a tiredness together with a stress level that could be seen etched around his eyes. He looked slightly familiar, like someone she'd seen in an elevator or on the street. The thought made her grab Mark's hand. The sudden move made the man look up at them.

"Mark?"

"You're dead!"

"Mark!"

"Helen!"

The next half hour fled by and afterwards Ginny knew that her concentration had been such that she would remember every word. They had been shown into a room downstairs and assured they would not be disturbed.

Mark recounted how he had joined the battle after seeing the New Hampshire conflagration. Ginny immediately remembered where she had seen the man's face – on the television, in newspapers, on computer screens. She shrank into her chair. If it were known she was sitting in a room with the most wanted man and woman in America, what would be the consequence? It was reason to giggle silently because that could push her and Mark down two places in the most wanted if it were known.

Mark talked efficiently.

Mac asked few questions, mostly about people, including Professor Sanderson and his daughter.

Helen asked about Marjorie White.

Mark explained how the new political party was to be announced July fourth and endorsed by Marjorie, if they were successful in spiriting her away.

Mac talked about the last six months, leaving out Helen's silence.

"I have three questions," said Mark.

"Let me guess: Why are we not dead? Why come back to life? And why here and now?"

"Close enough!"

"First thing's first: I had suspected that the administration might be sending someone, so we moved into our neighbor's home. They were away visiting their daughter. The snow hid any tracks that we made. We watched the whole event from a hundred yards away. There were no guards on the road. Everyone was committed to the destruction. They were overconfident. I had earlier moved my old gas pick-up truck to the street; they blew up the diesel truck that I'd been driving.

"We came back from the dead after we saw what they did to the professor's house. It was reminiscent of what they had done to us, torching the evidence and then blaming the victim. Thirdly, we needed to help… help what might be left of the network."

"Next question. Telephone?"

"Yes, but we're afraid to use it." Helen spoke, fishing into a bag she was carrying.

"Give it to Ginny. She'll replace the SIM card. It's only good for outgoing calls; any incoming will be from us. At six-forty Eastern Time, dial zero to update headquarters in Texas; hit zero at any other time if you are compromised."

"Thank you, Ginny. And Ginny is…?" Mac asked.

"Ginny is our computer genius. You'll both remember her mother, Sheila Hutchins."

The telephone was turned over to Ginny with a few positive comments about her mother.

"We have to be going, Mark." Ginny tapped her wrist in emphasis.

"Yes, just a moment. Mac, do you have a place to stay, because we have the keys for a condominium in the Back Bay?"

"We checked into the Custom House."

"Are you crazy? The President was there last

week!" Mark couldn't believe that Mac would put a target on his back.

"So it is the safest place in Boston. The place is just about empty, and Karen Connors is a friend of ours and the Sons. Since they slowed, she is the general manager, concierge, and front desk. It was easy to register in our new names."

"Well, it may be the last place anyone looks, but take the keys and the address of an alternative 'bolt hole.' We have to go. We have a boat to catch."

There were hugs and 'good luck' all round as Mark and Ginny left. Mark and Helen held each other tight; Ginny gave a questioning look but was not enlightened by the others who were remembering that Helen and Mark had once been engaged. Mac held Mark's handshake as they silently renewed their shared knowledge of the financing in Las Vegas, engineered by Mac and being implemented by Mark.

\*\*\*

The ordeal of joining the ship was anticlimactic as both Ginny and Mark were distracted by their encounter with Mac and Helen. It was viewed as nonchalance by the guards at the dockyard and those on the deck of the Bergen. They had entered the yard separately and agreed to meet in the theatre to co-ordinate the greeting of guests already on board who might be exploring.

There were grumbles from the other staff and performers, none of whom associated the delay with the replacement members of the team.

Life on board the Norwegian cruise ship was different, and it was tempting to let down one's guard and relax. A summons to the purser's office brought Mark back to reality as his passport was taken from him and scrutinized together with his papers, with the ink barely dry. The purser explained that a copy went to Homeland Security as were all papers of new hires, and to anticipate an interview in New York. Luckily Mark had a chance to let Ginny know this was routine.

Mark surprised Ginny by being proficient in playing the piano and guitar. These were skills he had finetuned in college to augment his meagre savings.

"It was actually like earning triple pay," he explained. "They paid for the gig, threw in what you drank, and you were prevented from spending money that you didn't have drinking with people that you didn't like."

Ginny admitted that she could not play an instrument, and she couldn't sing or dance. She was, however, a superb organizer. The answer was to have her organize all the daytime activities – from bingo to table tennis tournaments, dancing contests, and teams of trivia. This was to keep her busy from early in the morning until the nightly cabaret started. Her roommate was a dancer in the cabaret and rarely returned before two am. This, to Ginny's relief, prevented any conversation between them.

Docking New York early in the morning gave Mark and Ginny a couple of hours to catch up with each other. Ginny had used the evening alone to communicate with Texas. The news had been mixed regarding the Boston Sons of Liberty. The group had been infiltrated and several important members were in custody, including Joseph Lloyd, who had been in charge of stockpiling weapons on behalf of the members. The militia announced that the woman known as Betsy Ross, actually a professor of anthropology at Boston University, had died in custody; the consensus was that she had been tortured to death and had not revealed anything. Sean Lynch had been arrested and then, two days later, he was released badly beaten.

"Where's the good news?" asked Mark.

"Well…," Ginny said, trying to remember everything. "Mac and Helen are again writing. Actually only Mac is writing, but it's given a boost to the whole national group. Turns out the Boston chapter is much bigger than we'd thought."

"And you know this how?"

"When Joseph Lloyd was arrested, there was a mobilization of over one thousand people after curfew. They moved the firearms from the hiding place in Arlington to four new locations around the state."

"Wow!"

"They're apparently growing so fast that they can be a force."

"I hope the rest of the country is seeing the same amount of growth. But…"

"But what?" asked Ginny.

"I hope it doesn't come to violence."

"Do you think that our Founding Fathers said the same?"

"But that was a foreign government that was being imposed," said Mark, now pensive.

"You now sound like I used to," Ginny replied with a little laugh. "The best news for last. Today is July fourth as you remember."

"That's the good news?"

"Yes, for three reasons. One is that Homeland Security is shorthanded and has no one to spare to check our papers; two, Marjorie White will come on board this afternoon; and three, during the nationally televised fireworks display, as we're sailing past the Statue of Liberty, the American Party will be announced."

"Tonight?"

"Tonight, as long as we can confirm that Marjorie White is on board ship and away from New Jersey."

"Will she have 'minders'?"

"I would think so. The bigger question will be whether she has her children and hopefully her parents with her," said Ginny, beaming with all of the news after the past few days.

"What about our stop in Baltimore?" asked Mark, looking for defects, looking for things that looked too good to be true, things not yet addressed.

"Probably good news on that front. The local Sons of Liberty have been asked to overtly threaten the docks. The hope is that we aren't allowed to dock or disembark the Bergen."

When the passengers disembarked in New York, Mark and Ginny stayed on board, making sure that they were seen working. Ginny went to the library and made charts of activities, the budget for prizes, etc. Mark sat in the theatre making flyers for Marjorie White's appearances. He discovered that putting excitement into political lectures was a challenge. It wouldn't hurt his career if he acted as protagonist, and it would help the cause to plant questions in the audience. There was enough in the news to provide entertainment for the masses and serious thought for the educated passengers interested in the direction their government was going.

Marjorie White and her family came aboard quietly. The routine was unchanged. The minders, there were four, objected to being housed away from the two-bedroom suite given to the family. Mark explained to the steward that they had been given rooms next to the communications center and next to the exit from the Bergen. The minders confiscated all of the White family cell phones, shut off the phones in the rooms, and retreated somewhat mollified.

Ginny bumped into Marjorie in the corridor and left her with a cell phone tuned into the secure satellite connection. She also gave her the cabin number and time she would be there alone. Finally, she told her to make herself known to the entertainment director through her minder."

The 'minder,' who did not introduce himself, found Mark at the piano in the theatre. He was rehearsing with a singer who had boarded in New York as replacement for a singer who had admitted that she was pregnant and had been put ashore per company policy.

Mark had seen the man several weeks ago in New York. The fact that the man failed to recognize Mark was due to the setting, the fact that he was doing something out of context, and to the small mustache. Mark made a mental note to stay out of sight as much as possible in case he triggered a recollection.

"Can I help you?" Mark had kept the impatient man waiting while he choreographed for the singer the moves for the next show.

"Marjorie White needs to see you."

"Have her come here then." Mark was concerned that the White suite might be bugged.

The man hesitated.

"It will be easier to show her how the room is set up." Mark was feeling confident now, "The acoustics."

"What's the schedule?" The man was attempting to re-exert control.

"I thought that we would have a show tonight, after the fireworks, to ask the audience what they would like to talk about in the future shows. Chat about the fourth, stuff like that."

"We will have to maintain veto over the content."

"I welcome Mrs. White's input," said Mark, deliberately ignoring the 'we' implication in the remark. "I should be free in about half an hour."

The minder left feeling a little confused since he thought he'd dominated the conversation, but the result was the opposite of his objective. The meeting would not be in the suite which he planned to 'bug' and the content of the talks was still open.

Marjorie White walked into the theatre twenty-five minutes later. She recognized Mark and started to speak until he rushed forward.

"Mrs. White, I'm Ted Webster, entertainment director. Welcome aboard."

"Mr. Webster, Ted, please call me Marjorie. We're pleased to join you for a few days. I'm looking forward to getting in front of people again. It's been a long time away."

Mark had taken the folder she had brought in order to take notes. He quickly found and showed to her the listening device planted there.

"Let me show you the stage and set up," he put down the folder on a chair and led her onto the stage.

They walked away, talking about the numbers that might be expected to be in the audience.

"It may be less than a full room tonight, but the nightly cabaret show follows, so there might be more people who come early to secure seats for that popular event," Mark went on. Once safely out of hearing and out of sight, Mark was all business.

"You have the new phone – same as the last one. Call on time and make sure you are away from your room and out of sight. It's critical that you call tonight. Ellie May Joseph will announce a new political party tonight. It should make an interesting evening and lead to a lively discussion."

"They'll block it; the present government won't allow her a free rein on something like that."

"Let's see! Just be as surprised as everyone else. We'll defer discussion on the subject until tomorrow; try to draw in a crowd."

"Okay. When am I supposed to endorse Ellie May?"

"Not yet, it's too dangerous."

\*\*\*

Ginny sent a coded message that the White family was all on the Bergen. She received a return message that all was now in place for the announcement.

The Bergen left the dock in New York on time with several groups, anxious, watchful, or relieved. Mark had all three emotions, the White family was relieved, the 'minders' were watchful, and the leader was anxious. A ship is so many things: a mini population, isolated, in a foreign environment, with layers of command, and a strict timetable with endless variables. The 'minders' were aware that watching five family members would be a challenge and were relieved to see them doing ordinary things – watching the ship leave, then going to a dining room together. The two boys were excited to watch the fireworks, so they ate efficiently.

Marjorie went with her sons to see the fireworks but was looking anxiously around since she knew what was being announced and that she was involved, but not in charge. Ginny, seeing her anxiety, came to the boys with pamphlets that she had prepared. One of the minders snatched the piece of paper.

"It's information on the Statue of Liberty, the history and some construction facts," said Ginny.

"Would you like a copy?"

Without a word the pamphlet was scrutinized and handed back.

"Some people," said Ginny "need to relax!" she was looking at Marjorie. "Just act normal," she whispered.

"Thank you. It's just…."

"I know, but everything is under control." Ginny moved toward another group of passengers with her pamphlets.

The fireworks were spectacular. A live show cannot be subverted, and the passengers saw the Statue of Liberty surrounded by sound and light. The colors reflected on the water, enhancing the experience for those on board the Bergen. No one noticed the 'minders' disappear, summoned below by an urgent message from their control. No one noticed that Mark was not on deck but was below taping the national breaking news.

The fireworks ended with a traditional crescendo. The cacophony of bangs was replaced by silence, then cheering, then the excited chatter of children of all ages exclaiming on the spectacle.

Passengers drifted from the upper decks to various pursuits. Some returned to their cabins where they failed to notice that their television programs were running ten minutes late. A few went to the casino, oblivious. Those who went into the dining rooms and bars were told by waitresses and bartenders that a strange interruption had taken place; that there was breaking political news. There were a few shrugs, but no one seemed especially interested in an event which likely did not affect them personally. Those who went into the theatre were hearing rumors and their numbers were augmented by others receiving messages via social media. Surely Marjorie White could enlighten and inform those interested in current events.

Marjorie White entered the room and, with nervous anticipation, walked toward Mark. The nervousness was due to her expectation that the press conference in Texas had taken place. She had no doubt that something had occurred when her guards disappeared. The anticipation was high, now she might contribute.

"It happened," said Mark,

"No glitches?"

"Not really, although the networks seem to be in a bit of confusion, not knowing whether to show commercials, go back to their regular programs, or give the news credence by reporting comments from 'experts.' It's great news all round."

In Texas the response was coming in from around the country. Congratulations, incredulity, and questions were plentiful, especially questions of how the announcement had been possible. Others who had missed the telecast were now receiving a reprise and copies of the speech through social media and through emails directing them to a secure web site.

From the White House there was fury. President Al Adana was calling all of the major network studios personally and demanding that each C.E.O. be fired.

He called the F.B.I. for an immediate explanation of what might have happened. He demanded an immediate cabinet meeting, even though most had returned to their constituencies for the Fourth of July celebrations.

Marjorie was simultaneously pleased, shocked, and scared. "What do I say? What do I do?" she asked Mark.

"Act as though the news is a complete shock;" said

Mark. "I'll show the announcement at the beginning of our program. By the way where are Larry, Curly, and Moe?",

"I don't know. They disappeared during the fireworks."

"Probably called away to get an update on the news and new instructions, I'd guess."

As if on cue, three of the guards appeared at the door and looked around the room. The leader detached himself from the doorway and headed toward them while the other two left.

"Where is everyone?"

"Define everyone?"

"Your parents, your children?"

"Ah, you excluded me as presumably you know." Marjorie was on edge and her tolerance for the constant surveillance was thin, very thin.

"Since it is late, Andrew and Ian have gone to their room with my mother. My father, once he has relieved his bladder, will be coming here to lend his support. Is that all right?"

"There's no one there."

"Then I can only assume that my mother was persuaded to detour by the ice cream parlor." She smiled and asked, "Will you be staying for the show?"

With a grunt, he wheeled away to take up a position at the back of the room.

Mark went to the stage microphone to comment positively about the fireworks and announce that the program would start in about five minutes when everyone had a chance to order drinks from the bar and find a seat. It was obvious that the news of the announcement had spread as there was a great deal of chatter between complete strangers, none of whom seemed to have seen the presentation, but all seemed to have an opinion. The theatre was filling.

There were two chairs on the stage. Mark and Marjorie entered to applause and sat.

"Good evening to you all. I expect that an almost full auditorium is a tribute to our guest and not in expectation of our cabaret special, which will begin at midnight. That is the end of our commercial announcements.

"It gives me genuine pleasure to introduce Marjorie White. Marjorie is a former Vice President of the United States, former senator, and a lawyer. She is the mother of two teenage boys. Marjorie has agreed to present programs on this cruise every evening at seven o'clock. She'll give us her unique point of view and answer your questions. Please welcome a truly great lady, Marjorie White."

There was generous applause while Marjorie waved.

"Marjorie, before we begin tonight, I think that you and many in our audience have not heard that less than an hour ago there was sensational political news. Perhaps we should join the audience and watch."

Mark walked Marjorie to two seats in the front row as a screen ascended and a fireworks display was showing. The guard rose from his seat at the back of the room in an impotent fury.

The fireworks played for a few minutes then the screen went blank. Stars and stripes filled the screen then panned back to show Ellie May Joseph seated in front of the flag.

"Fellow countrymen, please excuse the intrusion into your living rooms. I promise that it will be for just a few minutes and then your programming will return to where you were interrupted and started listening to my speech.

"It will come as no surprise to many that our great country is broken. There is no state in the Union with less than twenty-five percent unemployment. Inflation is rampant in spite of rent controls, which are not working. Armed militia roam the streets, which are unsafe in the daytime and deadly at night. Our foreign policy is to reward unelected dictators, juntas, and armed rebels fighting, not for freedom, but in order to enslave. This is wrong!"

There followed a listing of countries receiving aid and the amounts. All were Middle Eastern or African countries. After each amount there was the name and photo image of the present head of state or recipient rebel leader and a brief summary of atrocities, many against women and children.

"This cannot continue. We are, were, the strongest country in the world, the envy of the world. Now we are broken. We have been broken by our own hands. Our government, elected by us, has failed us. There are many, a great many, who are good people but some, Democrats and Republicans alike, have been subverted, bought, bribed, and threatened, so they no longer serve the people, the people who elected them.

"It is time for change, to do something. We, who care, all have to do something. I am going to do something! Today is the Fourth of July, and today, in honor of those brave men who stood up and signed a Constitution, I am announcing that I shall be running a campaign to become the next president of the United States. I shall seek every state's support up to the election in November of next year.

"Today I am announcing that I shall be running as a candidate of the American Party. We have already contacted candidates who will run for House and Senate seats in Massachusetts, New York, Nevada,

California, Florida, and, yes, in Washington D.C.

"Today, we celebrate those freedoms given to us by our forefathers.

"God bless you all, and God bless the United States of America."

The screen filled with the flag, went blank, then back to the fireworks as Mark stopped the recording.

There was wild applause from most of the audience while some sat in stunned silence.

Mark and Marjorie returned to their seats on the stage.

"Well, Marjorie, what do you think of that?"

"It's a surprise and will take a while to analyze. We've become so accustomed to basically a two-party system that we forget the fringe political groups."

"I would expect that many in our audience have questions, too. This evening is short because of the fireworks and because of this announcement, shorter still. So, I think that we should ask the audience what topics they would like to discuss in the next few days after we have given Marjorie a chance to speak about herself, her beliefs, and perhaps her future."

"Marjorie, you have the floor."

"Thank you, Ted." Marjorie recited her history, as she had so many times before, without notes. She went through the process even as her thoughts were elsewhere. Concern for her family was uppermost in her mind. What was she doing? How was this going to end?

After twenty minutes she was close to ending. "In conclusion, I think that you have a clear idea of who I am, my beliefs, values, and of my strong love for my country. My future, I don't know. I should like to serve my country again. Tonight it is unclear how and when that might be.

"Are there any questions?"

"We only have time for a few questions this evening with more time in the next few days." Mark interrupted in his role of coordinator Ted Webster.

An elderly man raised a hand. Mark and Marjorie both recognized him as Harry Taylor, the leader of the Sons of Liberty in New York.

"Yes, sir?"

"Mrs. White, will you join the American Party?"

Mark jumped in. "I think that question is a little premature as Marjorie, Mrs. White, has only just seen the announcement. Also, as I recall, Marjorie ran against Ellie May Joseph in the last presidential election."

"Next?"

"Does the American Party have a chance?" a small woman near the front of the room asked.

"It's largely a question of funding." Marjorie fielded the query. "In the last presidential election, each of the major parties spent over three billion dollars. Even spending that much money some states were ignored by the candidates. For example, there was not a lot of sense in my spending money or time in Texas."

"How can she contest every state?" someone called out.

Mark stepped in. "We have to leave in about fifteen minutes. Shall I presume from these questions that we should devote an evening to this topic? By a show of hands."

Virtually every hand was raised.

"What else?"

From the ensuing cacophony, Mark picked out the topics he wanted and got a majority of hands raised for 'foreign policy' and 'unemployment.'

"Let us see how that works for the next three nights. We're meeting here at seven pm. Please bring your questions. We will get honest answers and maybe raise more questions. I'm personally looking forward to the interaction and thanks again to our guest Marjorie White."

Marjorie turned and removed her microphone, silently mouthed a thank you very much, and squeezed Mark's hand, mostly in relief.

Mark watched her walking through the audience, greeting, shaking hands, nodding. She was a natural politician, and everyone seemed to be connecting. It was a practiced illusion. He looked around and saw Marjorie's 'minders' were watching. They were watching Marjorie, watching the room, they were watching him. He looked away. The 'minders' had obviously been informed and had received instruction. There was clearly concern in Washington and everyone knew there was a potential for people, voters, to side with an underdog. Mark needed a change of clothes in order to introduce and perform in the cabaret. He would have a break in the middle before he wrapped up the evening entertainment. He would have to try to talk to Ginny to see what she'd learned from their contacts in Texas.

The cabaret show ended late and the guests quickly left, as tired as the performers. Mark ordered a beer and strolled out into the moonlight. He chose the quieter portside, looking out toward Europe. It had been an eventful day and he was trying to digest the implications; to put them into place for himself, Mark Hughes. Or was it Ted Webster? Or was he someone else? He barely recognized the man he had been just a few years ago. He paused in his reverie, was quiet, and listened. Someone else was outside, nearby.

"Marjorie, what are you doing out at this time of night?"

"The last time I heard that was from my father, about thirty years ago," she smiled sadly.

"I'm sorry, I didn't mean that."

"I couldn't sleep; too much to think about."

They stood in silence, looking east at the vast ocean, the sky filled with stars, some small clouds occasionally blotting out the constellations, shading the moon.

"I was thinking of David. He was my strength. Now I'm afraid. What do people do who are afraid?"

"They carry on. It takes a different strength, an inner strength. I met your husband frequently, and he had inner strength but thought that you, Marjorie, were the strong one."

Once more they entered into a silence. Marjorie was quietly crying. Mark put his arm around her in sympathy and understanding. She rested her head on his shoulder in appreciation.

Another silent watcher made a note of the meeting, completely misunderstanding the act of friendship. It was a small event with major implications.

## Chapter Fifteen

In Texas the newly announced American Party was busy. There were calls from around the country and communications from around the world, mostly asking for interviews, some offering money, others with advice, and a few with vitriolic tirades. The tirades suggested that the proponents of the new political party were at best misguided and at worst completely out of their minds. All of the messages were logged. There were also telephone calls or text messages from supporters who had received access to the secure communications system in Austin. These were analyzed first and many were asking how they might help.

In the secure home of Ellie May Joseph a summit meeting was taking place. In addition to Ellie May and her husband Jim, Sheila Hutchins, media director, Allyn Cherwin, treasurer, and Alistair Kirk, chief of staff, there were several staff members and the head of security, Bobby Joe Williams. The mood was ebullient. There was much slapping of backs and congratulatory calls across the room.

Ellie May called for order. "To quote a great man 'This is not the end, it is not even the beginning of the end, but it is, perhaps, the end of the beginning.'"

She was interrupted by cheers for her quote of a war time speech of Winston Churchill.

"Seriously, we have thrown down a gauntlet. It will be picked up. We are in a very dangerous place which will be made more dangerous by complacency."

"We're insulated here, aren't we?" her husband asked.

"Jim, you are so naïve. I love you for it, but how many of the messages that we received were from people wishing us harm, not success? How many of the promises of money were attempts to gauge our capacity, or to locate our bank account, our source of funds? We're here to ensure that we are all on the same agenda and to determine our actions for the next year, and for the next week."

"Can we start with the immediate?" Alistair suggested. "What do we do with all of the phone calls? How do we screen them? And how do we get the money that we sorely need from people offering help?"

"Well, first of all, the response has been a little overwhelming. Even I was surprised; and you know that I am a cock-eyed optimist.

"We have a response sheet as the phone volunteers answer the phone. They are to be polite and ask for information, name, phone number, address, etc. The phone volunteers give no information except their name, which is a nom de plume assigned to them. We are recruiting more volunteers from the universities in Texas to deal with the large demand."

"What if they want to give money?" Allyn understood the need to get money early and often.

"They are told that they will be contacted and thank you very much."

"Why not take the money?" Alistair asked.

"One, it may be a scam. Two, we need to know if we can get more. More cash, host an event, hold a sign, etc." Allyn spoke up.

"A little cynical," Jim said.

"It's a cynical world. Everything costs a lot. It doesn't pay to not examine too closely sources of funds. We are no exception. Our campaign will be scrutinized, so we need to have a paper trail for every penny." He received a look from Ellie May. He blushed as he realized that even within this group of very close associates the fact that money was coming into the funds through Casinos in Las Vegas, at least one casino, was known to only a few of them.

Ellie May was back in charge. "Please understand: we give the information to the Sons of Liberty in the area in order that they might investigate our benefactors; they may also get a recruit. The findings are forwarded through our super secure server. Monies coming in will go through a bank that we have set up for the purpose. The bank account will be 'swept' daily. All collected funds will be swept into another account every day to avoid a cyber-attack on the account. Bills will be paid from a different account which will work on an impress system, money sufficient to cover those bills being deposited daily.

"What does that mean 'a bank set up to receive funds'?" someone asked.

"Just that. We've chartered a bank, a Texas bank; the campaign is to be the only customer."

"What if someone wants to open an account?"

"Minimum deposit $1 million."

"Leaves me out," one of the staff said with a chuckle.

"The next week will be a series of meetings with your staff, preparing reports, staffing needs, cash budgets by week, and other capital funding requisitions."

"How can we do this without knowing how many primaries, how much television advertising time, how much grassroots support we can count on? We are virtual prisoners here in Texas." Alistair's voice revealed his concern.

"Alistair, we need a positive attitude. We shall contest every state. We intend to match our opponents in television coverage, challenge debates. We need to assume a full presidential campaign." Ellie May had been ready with the speech since her own self-doubts had included all that was voiced.

"It can't be done. I can't do it," Alistair said.

"If that is a resignation then it's not accepted. Please stay after the meeting."

There was another hour of questions and information sharing on security – internal, external, physical, and cyber. Everyone promised to report anything at all unusual to Bobby Joe Williams. There were repeated questions related to the computer. The answer was that there was a director whose name was withheld, as was the location of the mainframe.

The meeting over, Ellie May Joseph moved from the center of the room to sit next to Alistair Kirk. The intimacy was to reassure and confirm the close friendship. In the trying years that they had worked together, the closeness had been tested in the heat of 'battle.' Never a bold thinker, Alistair had been an anchor, the anchor, and often the only voice of reason. When he had spoken, it was not lightly. His was a call which was never ignored. She needed him, but not if he had fears, not if he had doubts. If he left the team at this early stage, it could throw everything backwards.

"Alistair, what is it? What's wrong with what we're doing? You know that I rely on your reasoning. I depend on your solid thinking."

"It can't be done."

"You said that earlier; maybe it can't. But does that mean we shouldn't try?"

"You don't need me."

"I desperately need your sage advice."

"But you don't trust me with information, the source of funds, the location of the computer."

"I trust you with my life. I don't have the authority to trust you with other peoples' lives. If there is a breach, or if you or your family are compromised, kidnapped, there would be consequences, like a domino. Do you understand that?"

"Of course. It's my vanity, my self-importance…"

"Alistair, as chief of staff it may be necessary to travel to Washington. It is dangerous."

"Ellie May, I would go to the end of the world for you. The reality is that I am no longer young. You must find a replacement. I'm going to be seventy and am not as healthy as I was. Additionally, my wife has not been well lately. Both of us have lost a step."

"I am sorry, Alistair. I tend to forget that there are lives outside of these walls. Will you support me, find a successor for yourself, train and mentor?"

"Yes, in fact I was thinking of asking for an assistant, a deputy."

"You have assistants."

"Yes, that's why I changed it to deputy."

"Promote someone?"

"No; they are good assistants but not deputies."

"No 'Alistair Kirks' there?" She got the smile that she was seeking by the compliment.

"Are you using flattery so that I will change my mind?"

"Yes and no. It just so happens that to me you are irreplaceable. So who do you think?"

"I was remembering that meeting at the White House with Marjorie White and her team before the last election. You remember. It was an emergency and a highly unusual meeting after the funeral for Marjorie White's assassinated husband…to discuss our mutual fears and to combine in an effort to keep the White House out of foreign control."

Ellie May laughed. "Yes, Alistair. I do remember. I was there too." She smiled and sat back. "So, what are you thinking?"

"I was thinking…" Alistair paused, "since she is now supporting the new party that we might raid her staff."

"Her chief of staff is unavailable. The administration locked him up for speaking out against the domestic policy of arming the militia and disbanding whole battalions of armed forces."

"I know. But he was almost as old as me. No, I was thinking of that gal, I mean woman, who alerted everyone to the danger, then organized the meeting, agenda, press conference, everything."

"Helen Harvey?"

"Yes. We were talking about her recently. Her working with the Sons of Liberty."

"Right. She was supposed to be dead, showed up in Boston." Ellie May was pensive, remembering the beautiful woman of almost three years ago, trying to remember the efficiency that Alistair had seen. It must have been seamless, Sheila would know.

"Let me think," said Ellie May carefully. "We're pretty sure she was working with the Sons before she 'died,' but where has she been? Where have they been?"

"You're paranoid, Ellie May."

"Well, just because I'm paranoid does not mean

that someone is not out to get me! I'll check on Helen and also her husband Mathew McDougal. The good news is that they're already the two most wanted by the government, so helping my campaign can't put them in more danger."

They both laughed to ease the tension, but they also knew that she was right. Helen and Mac had nothing more to lose.

"Thank you, Ellie May. And thanks for the talk I will do everything I can for you as long as I can."

"Thank you, Alistair. We have a lot to do before the mid-term elections in a couple of months. There are a few seats up for grabs due to deaths and resignations."

As Alistair left, Ellie May breathed a sigh of relief. She exhaled, "Helen Harvey," and reached for the telephone. "Can you find Sheila Hutchins and ask her to come by?" Ellie May needed to research Helen Harvey quickly and she also needed to find out where she had disappeared to and how. "And when codename 'Sands' checks in, I need to talk to him," Ellie May said before hanging up the line. Mark Hughes might have just the information she needed.

The objects of this conversation, meanwhile, were on the move. Alerted by Karen Connors, formerly concierge, now manager of the Custom House, Helen and Mac were discussing where to go. They had strong clandestine ties to the local Sons of Liberty. They had a link to Mac's funds in Las Vegas and everyone believed they were dead. Mac saw no reason to change this state of affairs. It was true that Homeland Security was vigorously pursuing the Sons who they called terrorists. The local militia, acting as their agents, continued to harass the citizens of Boston. Local officials and police were often rendered powerless by the decisions of the courts and by corrupted officials. Added to this state of affairs was the needless violence against the populace and threatened toward any official opposing the gangs, their looting, and gratuitous violence.

It was amazing to Mac that there were still people standing up against the militia's rampaging indifference to the law. Daily acts of heroism or just acts of humanity took place. Where these acts were known, they were reported and distributed nationally. Mac was pleased to be a part of this communication. Often he said it was not enough. The local leaders always convinced him that, the pen being mightier than the sword, he was contributing more than anyone. Why didn't it feel like it? Writing these uplifting daily stories, to him, was diminishing as a man, and he often wondered if the same reaction was felt by the reader.

"Let's recap," said Mac. In truth it had been a monolog since Helen had contributed nothing more than frowns at most of the alternatives and scowls at the rest. "We can't stay in Boston."

Helen scowled.

"We can't stay at the Custom House."

She frowned.

"We can move into the apartment, the one that Mark used and gave us the key for."

He saw a flicker. Mac smiled and then wondered if Helen regretted choosing him over Mark.

"Then where?" he continued. "Washington?"

Her look became one of panic.

"Texas would be an option, opting out of the fight, or the front lines, assuming that we could get there."

"Texas is the epicenter," Helen said.

"Rubbish," he said. "It's here in the trenches."

"Ellie May is starting a new political party; the American Party."

"Maybe. And maybe it can only win seats in Texas." He was being argumentative.

"It's something; a start." Helen was adamant.

Mac was thinking of this comment and he joined the thought to his goal of restoring Helen to the committed political media relations director that she had been before. Before they had married, before they went on the run, before the current administration, before they had both 'died.'

"It looks like your former boss Marjorie White might endorse Ellie May."

"She'd better beware of helicopters, armed paratroopers, and militia." Helen was defensive again.

"What we really need is a daily blog regarding the progress of the American Party. It can show how to join, how to contribute, etc. I'm busy with the truth stuff, so I guess we would have to find someone. Unless…"

Helen was obviously not rising to the bait. He needed a direct approach, unambiguous. "I think that you could do a great job with a daily blog."

"Hmmm."

It sounded more doubtful than thoughtful.

"I know what you're trying to do. I know that I have been in a dark period. I don't like the expression 'dark place' since I am not psychotic, nor do I suffer from any other mental disorder. It's just difficult to think. My thoughts go back to the fire, back to the perpetrators. They were kids; they poured hundreds of rounds of ammunition into the lives of two people, you and me. Did they know? Did they care? These are the dark thoughts. These are the answers I seek, and they won't come. Why?" She paused with tears running down her cheeks.

"Why won't the answers come, or the other why?" Mac was exalted and wary. "My answers I have given to you over the last six months. I have a question; my question is when, when are you going to strike back? Maybe this is an opportunity to strike back, connect with good people. Maybe this is something that will help answer your questions."

"Maybe. Perhaps we should start with an article on the announcement; an interview with the founder Ellie May Joseph."

This was better than Mac might have hoped for. This was the first time that Helen had proposed anything in more than six months. He had to remain positive; small steps would have to suffice.

"We have the phone given to us by Mark. Why not make the call? Ask for Ellie May. She met you, she knows you."

"She knows that I'm dead." Helen was slipping back into remorse.

"If she has spoken to Mark, she knows that you are very much alive."

"Not very much use though."

"Depends what you are useful at, or useful for. I'm sure that's not very good syntax though."

Helen smiled – another rare occurrence that gave Mac hope.

When they called the number given, they were asked their names. Mac and Helen gave their nom de plumes Peter Doath and Leonard Vallice. The operator clearly had access to a very good computer system and a very good security system. After a wait of less than a minute, they were told they could continue to use these names or their real names. The request to speak and interview with Ellie May Joseph was received without comment, but with instructions. "Please call back in exactly thirty minutes and you will either be given another number or not."

Thirty-two minutes later, after receiving another number, the telephone call was answered.

"Ellie May Joseph."

Helen gasped. "Really?"

"Really, Helen. It's good to hear from you. I enjoy reading your news from Boston. I also enjoy hearing from that active part of the world. I hope to be able to go back there very soon."

"Peter, I mean Mac, he thought that I might put together an interview about the American Party."

"Good idea."

"You'll do it?"

"Yes, I will," said Ellie May. "In fact we were talking about you today. There had been rumors of your survival and speculation about the last six months."

"A long story."

"I'm sure. Apart from the interview which we can do tomorrow morning, is it possible that you and Mac could come to Texas?"

"Texas?" There was panic in the question, a slight hesitation, and then she responded, "Speak to Mac."

"Hi, Mathew McDougal here."

"Mac, good to hear from you. You have no idea how much I've enjoyed your writing and reporting over the years. I framed the money I won from you when my Dallas Cowboys beat your Washington team."

"With all this flattery, you must want something Ellie May."

Ellie May laughed, genuinely amused. It had been a long time since the days of banter, verbal maneuvering, as a sport. Mac was in a league of his own when sparring with words was involved.

"Mac, it is truly great to hear and know that I don't need our voice recognition software to confirm your identity. Yes, I have an ulterior motive. It can only be achieved in Texas and would not interfere with the excellent reporting that you're disseminating through the Sons of Liberty network."

"Can you tell me more? It will be extremely dangerous for us to cross the country."

"Not yet."

The hesitation, the concentration was picked up by Mac's interviewing and reporting acumen. "You want to know what happened. You want to know that we were not arrested, interrogated, and turned into spies for the administration."

"Not me, Mac, but there are other practical voices around here. They remind me daily that I am responsible for hundreds, thousands, soon maybe hundreds of thousands…citizens, activists."

"I understand, Ellie May. Intellectually I understand, but I cannot pretend that it doesn't hurt."

"Why would I invite you to my home?"

"Why not? How would we be able to get out?"

"Good point! The truth is I do trust you and actually need you both here. Is that enough pleading?"

"I get it. If you want to confirm that we were free and independent since January, there are two people who can corroborate our whereabouts. Unfortunately, one is a gangster and the other recently had a stroke."

"If you're saying…" Ellie May was thinking how this was going to sound "…that one is helping with our funding and the other is Ben Franklin?"

"I am."

"Then I will tell you that it is imperative that you

come to Texas and join my staff; both of you are invaluable."

"There you go again with that Southern flattery stuff. We'll be in touch."

Ellie May hung up the phone, laughing.

Mac put down the phone and looked across at Helen.

"Are you ready for this…stuff?"

"If not us, then who?"

"Are you mocking me?"

"Yes; let's make love and sleep on our decision."

"Sounds good to me!"

\*\*\*

It was good. All was well with the world Mac was thinking the next day as he looked out on a brilliant blue sky, cup of coffee in hand. He had enjoyed the best night's sleep in as long as he could recall. Remembering the previous night, he smiled. Remembering the telephone conversation, he turned serious. Thinking of what might be ahead, he was afraid. Not for himself but for the beautiful woman he had married.

"Good morning, Mac." Helen came over and kissed him, took the coffee cup from him, and drank it.

"Breakfast?"

"Yogurt?" asked Helen.

"Oatmeal," replied Mac.

Helen made a face of disgust.

"Fresh milk." said Mac. "Remember that there are a lot of people out there with much less to eat."

"I know. How did we go to a third-world economy in less than three years?"

"Some of it was inevitable," said Mac. "We never could sustain the growth and standard of living increases we enjoyed for so long. We were in a global economy but acting as isolationists."

"Next article?"

"No, not yet. We have to reach a bottom before people will accept that we are not going to bounce all the way back to business as usual."

"Heavy! Before my coffee and oatmeal." said Helen.

"You drank my coffee," he said with a laugh. "You have to prepare for your interview with Ellie May."

"When I get *my* coffee!"

## Chapter Sixteen

Mark was meeting with Ginny in his cabin on the Bergen. They had managed to avoid one another as their schedules were opposite. The regular meetings were related to the ship's schedule of events. It was easy to fall into the routine of games and entertainment. The Bergen had docked in Miami and in New Orleans, and now they were headed toward the Panama Canal.

Ginny had anticipated a scheme to have them leave the ship before they left the United States, since the next US port was San Francisco, the end of the cruise.

"So when do I get off and see my mother?"

"There were too many people in New Orleans watching the ship. Not to mention the transportation of seven people from Louisiana to Texas is nearly impossible, but splitting the group isn't an option."

"So it will be easier from San Francisco?"

"It would be absolutely impossible from San Francisco."

"Either you haven't figured this out yet or you don't trust me. Which?"

Mark could tell that Ginny was frustrated. "I do trust you. I only heard the plan last night. The problem is who to tell and when."

There was a silence. Ginny looked around the room which was different from her tiny interior cabin below decks which she shared with a dancer. In contrast Mark had a room with a tiny balcony. There was a view, an obstructed view. The sea was visible between the lifeboats.

Their thoughts were interrupted by a loud knock on the door. Mark put a finger to his lips.

"Who is it?" Mark shouted.

"Security!"

Mark, with a finger still on his lips, looked around, pushed a laptop computer under the bed, and ushered Ginny into his small bathroom. He opened the door to a large man who he recognized as one of the four men guarding the White family.

"Yes?" asked Mark standing in the doorway "How can I help you?"

"Well, perhaps you can explain how Mark Hughes is on a cruise under the name of Ted Webster?"

"You must be mistaken."

"No mistake. Inside," the man demanded as he pushed Mark backwards, propelling him into the room before him.

They passed the door to the bathroom. Had the door opened, they would have seen reflected in the mirror, a wide eyed, terror stricken, white face.

"What do you want?" Mark asked. "I'm busy." He pointed to the computer on the desk. The screen showed a calendar of events.

"Mark, I don't think you understand."

"It's Ted, Ted Webster."

"You see, Mark, face recognition never lies." He pulled out a photo, accompanied by a printout. "When I saw you lovey-dovey with Marjorie White on the deck the other night, I checked. I took the photo and sent it to Washington. They asked me to leave the ship in Miami, fly to Washington, and join the Bergen in

New Orleans. Here I am, and here you are."

"So you're here to arrest me?"

"Oh, no." The man showed his teeth for the first time – it was intended to be a smile. "No, you're wanted dead or alive."

"If I was as dangerous as you say, then you'd want to interrogate me."

"Actually the thinking is, my brief from Washington, to cut off the branch and twigs, to avoid someone warning others."

"Others like Marjorie White?"

"Well, she and her family won't be allowed to leave the ship, not alive that is."

"How would you explain all of these deaths? Even your twisted masters will have a hard time."

"Not really; you'll have killed them and committed suicide."

"How? By shooting myself in the back of the head?"

"I was thinking you'd throw yourself overboard."

"Voluntarily, or with a little lead in my head?"

"Either, though I'd prefer the former. Please open the door to the veranda and step out onto the balcony."

Mark, with no other plan, did as he was asked. He briefly thought of Ginny in the bathroom, but his thoughts quickly came back to his own dilemma. The balcony was small, and he stepped in and to his right in order for the gunman to follow. The gunman was well trained and made sure that he kept a distance from Mark and kept his eyes glued to his back There was more noise outside, from the wind, the bow wave, and the ship's engine.

Ginny had heard the whole exchange through the partially open door. She thought of all those deaths – Mark, Marjorie, Marjorie's parents, and particularly the boys, David and Ian. The boys had participated in all of her activities and had provided a great access to Marjorie. The threat to harm them created an irrational response. Ginny burst from the bathroom and hurled her one-hundred-pound frame at the back of a one-hundred-eighty-pound man.

A confluence of events followed. The gunman never heard the assault. He was in the act of stepping over the raised sill of the sliding door, and his attention was focused on Mark Hughes. The gunman staggered against the rail and made his second mistake since entering the room. The first mistake was not to have looked in the bathroom. The second was to hold onto his gun and try to stop his forward motion with his free hand. It wasn't enough. As his left foot left the ground, Ginny seized it and heaved upward. It proved surprisingly easy to propel his center of gravity forward, the one hundred and eighty pounds now counterproductive. He fell, bouncing off a lifeboat, into the sea, making no sound, holding onto his gun.

Ginny fell to the ground sobbing. Mark joined her, holding her trembling body for what seemed ages. As other sounds intruded, they could hear shouting, that a man had fallen overboard from down there. It was tempting to stand and refute or explain, but Mark pushed Ginny through the open door.

"Thank you. That was very brave." Mark was still holding Ginny.

"It was stupid!" Her eyes were glistening. "We could have both been killed."

"We were both going to be killed. We might still both be killed. They'll be here any minute since obviously the body was seen falling from the balcony."

"So, if you're here, it wasn't you," Ginny said.

"If I'm still alive, I'm still in danger. If I'm not dead, then who is, and, did I kill him?"

"So let's go!"

"Careful, think. I can leave my cruise phone and computer with the scheduling, but I need the stuff with the codes." He reached under the bed. "I don't need clothes. Did you bring anything in here?"

"Only my righteous indignation!"

"And an attitude!"

"And my attitude." Ginny agreed. "Can we go now?"

"Yes, I need a place to hide until tonight when we leave the ship. We have lots to do before then."

Mark turned to leave while Ginny stopped, looking through the open sliding door, to the sea beyond. With a visible shudder she followed him out of the door.

There was activity above them – voices, sounds, indistinguishable conversations. One voice was strident, insistent. Another voice, calm. It was easy to imagine a passenger insisting that a someone was overboard, a crew member trying to get information of how, when, and where.

"My cabin, below decks." Ginny led the way. "Suze will be rehearsing, then go with her boyfriend for something to eat. We'll be safe there for a while."

"We need a plan, a schedule. You'll have to do it Ginny. They are likely to eventually calculate the room from which someone left the ship. The conclusion will be that it was me. If the security guard is missed, if he told anyone where he was going, then they're looking for me to pin the 'accident' on."

\*\*\*

The plan was simple, the execution, extremely difficult. Everything depended upon confusion, coordination, misdirection, timing, secrecy, and cooperation.

Everything that anyone did was to act as if nothing was different. Marjorie White was to speak as usual. The topic was domestic policy and direction. The 'minders' were down to three – one was needed close to communications, one monitoring Marjorie, and one the other White family members. The ship was to suffer a problem with engines and radio for permission to be towed into Galveston, the nearest port. The Coast Guard would deny permission and suggest a repair crew come out of Louisiana. A repair crew just happened to be standing by and monitoring transmissions. They would offer to have the Bergen on its way by dawn.

The White family, led by the teenagers, proceeded to act normally, while disappearing. Grandma went to see Marjorie speak, but never arrived. Grandpa had gone to the library hours before and checking every fifteen minutes confirmed that he was asleep with a book in his hand until he was not there. The boys came and went from their room, keeping up a commentary about video games, movies, school, until the guard no longer listened.

In the theatre Marjorie was just about finished. The address system had announced hours before that the engine issues would be fixed soon and the rolling of the Bergen, dead in the water, alleviated. The generator kept lights and electricity working but there was a roll with the swell.

The guard at the monitors called his associates and asked for an update.

"Two boys in their suite; Grandpa and Grandma went to the theatre to watch their daughter. Marjorie White on stage; cannot see her parents, but they're probably here somewhere."

"Good. I need someone down here to check the repair team on board."

"I can lock in the boys and do that."

David and Ian had long ago decided that locked in was not a good idea and had two ways to escape. The first involved going onto the veranda, scrambling around the partition into the adjacent suite and exiting, the second they now put into play since the rolling of the ship made Ian reluctant to go around the partition. David refused to admit the truth, that it didn't appeal to him either. Besides, a call to the steward for more ice was just as effective and they could then be certain that no one was standing outside in the corridor.

Marjorie heard the announcement that the repair ship was alongside. It was the signal for her to drop her bombshell.

"I want to thank you for participating in my talks, not just tonight but for the last week. The first night, July Fourth, a new political party was born. It was born out of necessity. It was born out of patriotism. It was born to provide healthy discussions such as we have enjoyed.

"Tonight I want to announce, to you and through you, that I am joining the American Party and will be active in preparing a manifesto and actively supporting the party's candidates. I have been asked to consider the role of vice president."

There was a buzz and quite a few glanced to the rear of the room where the 'minder' sat. The audience seemed immediately to sense the danger to Marjorie. It was no secret that she was a prisoner.

The 'minder' ignored the glances and was animatedly conveying the news through his microphone to his relay. Deciding, he abruptly stood and, with a look toward Marjorie that said 'sit, stay,' he left.

Marjorie had no intention of waiting for a decision on her fate.

"Ladies and gentlemen, goodnight, God bless you and God bless America."

The assembly point for the White family, Mark, and Ginny now included the steward who had delivered the ice. They all rendezvoused at a life jacket locker. The locker was about thirty feet forward of the door at which the repair crew was now noisily coming aboard. At a bang from outside, David White and the steward turned the handle and opened the door into darkness. Ahead was the bow of the boat sent out with marine parts and nautical engineers.

David looked into the darkness at a man not much older than he was and, remembering his etiquette asked, "Permission to come aboard?"

"Get your asses over here!" was the brusque reply.

The steward helped them out into the darkness, locked the door and scampered off to provide himself with an alibi.

"Down the hatch!"

"Hump, what are you doing here?" Ginny was incredulous.

"I could ask you the same question pretty lady with no name." The smile was genuine. "By the way, my name is Henry or Hank. And somebody thought that you might like to see a familiar face."

"Were we seen leaving?" asked Mark.

"Doubtful. We had our lights all directed at the Coast Guard cutter out there." He waved an arm vaguely out to sea. "All of the ship's lights were on the stern and the cutter's lights were all directed at the upper decks. Make yourself comfortable here in the forward hold until we're underway and past the cutter.

They may just sink us anyway, like they did your previous ride." He looked at Ginny. Tears welled as he spoke, and Ginny remembered the young man who had flirted with her just hours before he was to drown.

"Ginny, my name is Ginny. Thanks for coming at some risk, at great risk."

"My pleasure!" A big toothy grin filled his face, visible even in the darkness.

"Are we going to Louisiana?"

"No, Galveston. It's too long a story. I have work to do. See you in a bit!" He was gone, climbing through a hatch which led to the engine room.

They were left in darkness.

A whispered voice instructed, "Stop that, Mom. It doesn't help."

"I want to be back on the ship."

"Looking at the wrong end of a gun? You heard what the plan was; we were all to die." Marjorie was taking charge.

"We're all going to die. At least I could have died sipping a martini, not in some dark place stinking of fish!"

There was no answer to this, so there was silence.

Sometime later the noise from the throbbing of engines was shattered by a tremendous roar. The boat shook, fixtures moved, a total wave of sound!

"What the hell was that?" Even Marjorie couldn't keep fear from her voice.

Ginny, Mrs. White, and the two teenage boys all moved closer to one another in the darkness. Ginny couldn't determine which was harder to bear – not knowing, not seeing, or not being in charge.

The noise was repeated but not as loud. Perhaps the surprise of the first time had now created a tolerance for the second event. The group was now straining for understanding, using only their ears. They could hear the sound returning, something coming back, was this to be their fate? No, it was nearer. The hatch opened and they saw Henry.

"Boy, that was summin!" The Louisiana drawl was emphasized by his excitement.

"For you, maybe, we all…" Mark glanced at the anxious faces, the inappropriate word died on his lips, "…wondered what was going on?"

"Texas Air National Guard, providing an escort. Didn't want us to suffer a boarding party and an accidental sinking by the cutter out there."

"I'm not sure that's comforting." Marjorie's father said laconically.

"Oh, and the captain says that you can come on deck now."

"Now that IS comforting," Ginny replied.

The final half hour of their trip in was in the soft, magical light of pre-dawn. Everything was calm – the sea, the sky, their minds. The rhythmic sound of the engines had even lulled some into an exhausted sleep. Others were moving slowly, whispering.

Mark stood, looking forward as the lights on land slowly multiplied, the shoreline taking definition. He was comforted by the occasional sound of a helicopter gunship flying behind them. The gunship had replaced the fighter planes about an hour ago. Apart from initial chatter, they had stayed off the air.

Mark was thinking, calculating, how long it had been since they'd left Galveston; it seemed years. It was only weeks.

"A penny for your thoughts," Ginny spoke softly, standing close to him.

"Just thinking about how long we've been away. Thirteen weeks, I reckon."

"Eighty-nine days actually," said Ginny. "Eighty-nine days of being chased, shot at, hunted. Eighty-nine days of hiding, eating on the run. Eighty-nine days...."

"What about the two-week cruise I took you on?" asked Mark, putting his arm around her shoulders.

"A cruise where there were people carrying guns and four homicidal maniacs. Four killers, who, if they knew my real identity, would ensure that I spent the rest of my days sleeping with the fishes."

"You're being a little melodramatic."

She turned toward him. "Me? You would have been forced to walk the plank if it weren't for me."

"Yes, thanks. By the way, why were you in my room? I guess you couldn't live with them killing us." His eyes twinkled in the rising sun.

Ginny kissed him on the cheek then playfully punched his arm and walked away.

Mark laughed and returned to his reverie.

## Chapter Seventeen

Dawn broke with a cacophony of sound. The helicopter flew directly overhead, low before rising and disappearing. Seagulls appeared from everywhere, complaining. The harbor at Galveston was alive with people shouting. There were boat horns and car horns competing to be heard. It was frenzy, a normal early morning at a seaport.

They were directed to a dock and tied up. Betty Jo was waiting, supervising.

"Are you down to give us a lift?" Mark asked after introductions had been made.

"No. You, Marjorie, and her parents are going with Bobby Joe. He's just filling up. I'll bring the boys, Ginny, Gump, and family as soon as they sign some papers and stuff."

"We need to sign?" asked Marjorie.

"No, ma'am. I signed for you all."

"Bobby Joe, good to see you again." Marjorie was in candidate mode, remembering names and shaking hands.

"You too, Mrs. White."

Other introductions and fond goodbyes took place. The boys were enjoying a freedom denied for two years. Following Henry around, they were given jobs tying up, washing down the boat, tidying the decks, taking away rubbish – everything was new.

In the first car to leave all was quiet. The seven-seater SUV was eating up the miles. Mark had sat in front with Bobby Joe and talked, but he quickly succumbed to the relaxation. In the rear seats there was also quiet.

Betty Jo, in the second car, was treated to a non-stop questioning from her passengers, who then learned everything about each other. Gump sat in front chuckling at the youthful exchanges.

The three-hour journey passed quickly. A telephone call ahead meant that breakfast was to be served outside. Bobby Joe had said that even driving with the window partially open it would still be a week before he could no longer smell fish.

"Pancakes, steak, eggs, coffee!" Ellie May greeted them on the veranda.

Breakfast was a convivial affair. Politics, though never far from their thoughts, were not discussed.

"Mr. Forrest, what do you intend to do in Texas?" asked Ellie May.

"Please call me Gump, ma-am. I only know fishing. Got me my boat. I'll find a slip then go fishing."

"We're friends now, and ma-am makes me feel old, so please call me Ellie May. What about your children. Will they remain working with you?"

"Well, Leon, he stayed with the boat. He wants to fish, I guess. The others, they are all growed and can answer for themselves."

Henry was the first to speak. "If I could, I would go back to school, to college. But with no scholarship, I guess I'll look for a job where I can go to school at night; learn about computing, become an astrophysicist," he blushed as he looked toward Ginny.

It was clear that in their two meetings some bond

had been forged. Ginny had impressed him with her knowledge, confidence, and maturity. It was not a physical attraction, more like a hero worship normally associated with athletes and sportsmen. Someone to emulate.

"I think I could look into a scholarship in Dallas." Ginny spoke since all eyes were on her. "We can always use people looking to learn, and there are jobs on campus that will pay a little."

"What about you Margaret, Richard?" asked Ellie May.

Richard spoke. "I think I would be a pilot if I had my choice, but I suppose I will fish." It was spoken without rancor and did not solicit sympathy, just a statement.

"Why fly?" Bobby Joe had been quiet, within a different set of thoughts until he heard the contradiction – a fisherman who would fly.

"When we were out there last night with the Coastguard cutter bearing down, I was thinking about that crew, that boat they shot out of the water. Then this plane, these two planes, came from nowhere…" He did not need to complete the sentence. All there knew what he was feeling.

"The Navy has a flight school. Get into Naval College, choose flying; see what happens." Bobby Joe said.

"Can you help steer me?" asked Richard hopefully.

"I think so, but first you have to have a shower!"

There was general laughter, and everyone realized the fish smell was still on the clothes of those coming from the Gulf.

"Bobby Joe, please take the boys down to the bunkhouse. Give their clothes to Marie to wash and dry. There should be some swim trunks by the pool."

Ellie May was in charge. "Ginny, your mother will show you to one of the guest rooms; Marjorie, you and your folks are going to be staying here. I'll show you to your quarters and have someone find clothes for you. Mark, can you go with the boys? I'll send the clothes you left here. Then we need to talk."

An hour later, in the lower bunker, Mark was filling in the assembled group on his and Ginny's odyssey. There were a few questions, but the group was attentive and quiet. Marjorie White was making notes, since most of the details were new to her. Mark had given her a brief overview of the events and the agenda for the group, but there were still a lot of missing details.

When Mark had finished speaking, Marjorie asked the first question. "Where is the money coming from?"

"Need to know basis. You do not need to know." Alistair Kirk's response was a reflex. He caught Ellie May's reproachful look. "Fact is, Marjorie, it is good. There seems to be enough, and we will all know, when we need to know."

"That is all well and good, Alistair, but…"

Marjorie was interrupted by Ellie May's hand in the air. "Not a subject on our agenda today. We have to keep the Sons of Liberty informed; we have to prepare for some House and Senate elections in November. Where do we have candidates, Alistair?"

"We can have candidates in about half of the states, next year. A few of them are incumbents. Some incumbents have decided not to run, the main reason being pressure and difficulty in dealing with the present administration."

"Can we ask them to reconsider – the ones who would be helpful?" Sheila asked.

Alistair looked at Sheila and voiced his thought. "Someone will need to talk to them, persuade them that change is coming. Anyone hearing of Mark and Ginny's adventure would be either brave or foolhardy."

"We need bold, brave people," Ellie May said. "How are the flow chart, recruitment, and responsibility chart coming along?"

"It was a quick start but is now bogging down on names. Recruitment is taking a lot of time. We have an office downtown; however, the fear of infiltration means we should have several places. Who goes where and how they are monitored is a full-time job. We need more security. Every security person we have is doing background checks on recruits." Alistair looked at security chief, Bobby Joe.

"True; we thought most of the work, checking references, etc. would be clerical, and we need to recruit liberal arts students and graduates who can ask questions and analyze answers. We need the officers, who are currently doing these jobs, free to be bodyguards and perhaps to fill the role of those bold, brave people, we need."

"Who will run that effort?"

"Perhaps me," said Alistair. "I cannot be chief of staff. I've resigned and I am filling the role until replaced. But I think I can still be helpful."

There was an immediate burst of sound as everyone asked questions at once. Everyone turned to Ellie May after hearing the shocking announcement.

"It's true that I've accepted the resignation of my dear friend Alistair, who has demonstrated his loyalty by volunteering for a post not yet on our organization chart."

"Who will…?" several people were asking at once.

"A replacement has been contacted, accepted, and is on their way here. I will not identify the person yet as it may compromise them and those helping us."

"When?" someone asked.

Ellie May gave a stern glance. "Soon! I think that is enough for today. Marjorie, Mark, let us adjourn for iced tea. Bobby Joe, can you make that happen on the veranda?"

"Yes, ma'am!"

The rest of the day was filled with meetings, people arriving and leaving. Gump and his boys left in the pick-up truck Margaret had driven from Louisiana. Margaret had been invited to stay in Dallas. She had readily agreed as she had been looking at the clothes worn by the other guests and decided that for her new life she would need new clothes. "New life, whatever that might be," she spoke aloud to herself. She spoke with an unusual amount of rancor. "They asked the boys what they were going to do. Not me. Might as well have stayed in Hicksville, USA!"

Mark was passing and heard some of what Margaret said to herself. He had already seen enough and heard enough of Margaret's resourcefulness, self-reliance and hard work to think she might be the staffer he was looking for.

"Margaret, Betty Jo is going to take you to a hotel in Dallas. I'd like to meet you there for breakfast in the morning, say seven. I have a proposal and want you to meet someone."

"Sure." Margaret was a little embarrassed, not sure how much Mark had heard of her mumblings.

"See Betty Jo. She'll figure it out. I'm going to be in meetings here until I collapse today."

Betty Jo was ferrying two of the participants back to the University and asked Margaret to ride up front with her. Within a few miles they were chatting about Texas, Dallas, working for Ellie May, the search for staff – all without breaking any confidentiality. The backseat occupants were whispering and looking at the spreadsheets on the laptop computer they were sharing.

"Do you know why Mark wants to see me tomorrow?"

"Two things, honey. No, I don't, and if I did, I wouldn't say. Secondly, this is an unusual organization. We're all safer when we stay on a need-to-know basis. Whatever you discuss with Mark Hughes is above my pay grade and none of my business."

"Sorry. I didn't mean…."

"It's okay, honey. We've all learned. I sleep with the head of security, and he never says who comes or goes, and we never talk business unless it is necessary."

Margaret wiped a silent tear from her cheek.

"Tonight you have a hotel bed. Tomorrow a meeting. I'll be around if you need a friend."

"Thanks."

"It's been a long, tiring day. How about I pick you up for dinner and, in the meantime you rest. Go to the hotel pool. Relax."

"Thank you. Dinner sounds good. What time?"

"Six."

"Okay, but I have nothing to wear."

"We'll take care of that tomorrow."

\*\*\*

At six there was a knock on the door of Margaret's hotel room.

"Who is it?"

"Betty Jo. I brought some things in case you were

desperate." She had brought a couple of blouses and skirts and two pair of boots. The blouses were flowery with long sleeves. The skirts were denim. The boots were high heeled with metal studs. They were clearly Betty Jo's as she was wearing something similar.

"Where are we going? A rodeo?"

Betty Jo laughed. "A little more color than you're wearing, honey." A pause, then they both laughed simultaneously.

A short while later they exited the hotel arm in arm. The boots were a little big but were snug with paper tissues in the toe. Both women were over six feet tall with the heels and were dressed as sisters.

"Oh, we invited a friend," said Betty Jo. "Well, more of an associate. You'll like him."

Bobby Joe was at the wheel of a large SUV and his companion filled the passenger seat. "Margaret, this is Eisenhower Patton Clark; his daddy was a student of the Second World War. His granddaddy drove a tank for General Patton, and his hero was General Eisenhower, and since his surname was Clark, it just made sense."

"For him it made sense," the newly introduced man stated. "*He* didn't have to carry it through school."

"Your daddy did carry George Patton Clark as a name through school, as I recall."

"So what do I call you?" asked Margaret.

"Call me Mr. Clark." There was a twinkle in his eye as this large black man paraphrased a line from the movie *Call Me Mr. Tibbs*.

The humor was not lost on Bobby Joe and Betty Jo, but Margaret was a little slow to appreciate the laughter. "Then Mr. Clark it is. I'm Margaret Forrest, and you can call me anytime you want to buy dinner."

The laughter lasted all the way to the steak restaurant where Bobby Joe and Betty Jo were well known. It was by then established that Eisenhower was called Ike by everyone.

The steaks, baked beans, mashed potatoes, and salad with beer were excellent. The conversation was lively until they had all declined dessert.

"So, what brings you to Texas, Margaret?" asked Ike.

Margaret glanced at Bobby Joe, unsure.

"Margaret is something of a refugee. We were out at the ranch today where she is something of a heroine," Bobby Joe said.

"I think that I object to both of those characterizations." Margaret was flustered. "My father, my brothers and I, we left Louisiana for more hospitable climes, and I just gave some help to people who were kind to us." She paused then deflected the conversation away from herself. "So, what do you do Mr. Bigshot?"

"Law enforcement."

"Ike is a captain in the Texas Rangers," said Betty Jo.

"Captain." She raised an appraising eyebrow. "Are you carrying a gun?"

"Everyone in Texas carries a gun," Ike replied.

"I don't," said Margaret looking around. "Can I see your weapon?"

"I never show my weapon to a lady on a first date." The mischief was back in his eyes.

"This is a date?"

"Let's dance," said Ike to cover the laughter.

When they returned, Bobby Joe and Betty Jo were still chuckling. Bobby Joe became instantly serious. "Ike, I need you to take a leave of absence from the

Rangers and come work on the campaign."

"Are you nuts? Do you know how long and hard I worked to make captain?"

"Yes, I was your captain when you started. We would guarantee your return, as captain, unless we go to Washington."

"Bobby Joe, this is me, Ike. Seriously? What are the chances of making the White House?"

"Well, if there are only two candidates, I would say mathematically fifty, fifty."

"Really?" Ike snorted. "What would I do that was remotely worthwhile?"

"Well, first I need help setting up a security command for the candidate, her staff, and her communication systems. Then you would make a perfect bodyguard outside Texas."

"You mean Ellie May would leave Texas and the protection of the Rangers and mosey down to Washington where there is a price on her head? Oh, and I am to guard her?"

"I could only speculate on that likelihood if you were a member of my staff."

"I'll speak to the chief tomorrow – give a month's notice."

"Done! Ellie May called today; you start Monday out at the ranch. Congratulations!"

"You … you knew I would accept?"

"Remember, I've known you for a very long time, since you were a cadet. You're ambitious, always looking for a new challenge, absorbing new trends and technologies."

"Guys, you can talk all night, but Margaret is dead on her feet and has a meeting early in the morning."

"I'm fine." Margaret yawned.

"Sure," Betty Jo said skeptically. "Let's go, boys."

"Okay. Margaret, can I see you again? Buy dinner or cook for you?" Ike asked quietly, seriously.

"I don't know…I don't know where I'll be. My folks, they're down in Galveston."

Seeing the disappointment on his face she continued. "I would love to if I am around. Tonight was fun."

"Well, guess I should take advantage while you're still here. How 'bout tomorrow night?"

\*\*\*

The next morning at a little after seven, Margaret entered the hotel dining room in the casual clothes that Betty Jo had given to her the night before. She looked around and saw Mark and a rather serious older man wearing eyeglasses. Both were wearing suits. The older man was wearing a dark blue tie with a single motif – the recognizable lone star of Texas.

Margaret, in a bright blouse and studded boots, regretted not having worn her own clothes. In truth she had been much more tired than she had thought and slept later than she'd intended. Her own clothes had also had an odor of fish and were being laundered.

"Good morning. Sorry I'm late; and also…" she waved an apology at the contrast to how she was dressed compared with their sartorial splendor so early in the morning.

"Margaret, this is Mr. Breakstone. We were using the time to catch up. Let's order, then we can talk about you, ask some questions."

Margaret was hungry, but the fact that this sounded formal and something of a test killed her appetite. She ordered toast, marmalade, and coffee. It took a while for George Breakstone and Mark Hughes to order, and they sat waiting for the kitchen to deliver.

Mr. Breakstone appeared to be a banker.

Makes sense, thought Margaret.

"Margaret, I understand you majored in accounting. Tell me, did you ever practice or pursue a career in an accounting office or use your degree in any way?" George went to his list of questions.

"No. I mean, yes. Yes, I studied accounting and no, I didn't pursue a career. When I came out of school, the political climate had changed; none of the women in my class were offered positions, not one."

"Did that upset you?"

"Yes, it did. But I was fortunate that I could help my family clean up their record keeping, collect money they were owed, make deals." She glanced at Mark. This time he spoke up.

"Margaret set up the deal that spirited Ginny and me out of Texas. She also provided transport at considerable risk to herself and her family."

"Not nearly as brave as you and Ginny." Margaret blushed.

George showed no emotion as he went back to his checklist. He was a gray man, nondescript, easy to forget. He had no distinguishing features, no emotion, no smile, no sense of humor. There was about him a suspicion that the questions he asked, he already knew the answers to. He appeared bored. Dangerous to not tell the truth to George, Margaret decided.

"So you did use your education, just within the family business. What are you going to do now?" asked George.

"Mr. Breakstone, it feels as though I am being interviewed. Do you have a job for me?"

"No. How do you feel about keeping secrets?"

"I can keep a secret." Margaret was confused, concerned. There was no job but secrets.

"How about danger? How about doing something

illegal?"

"Illegal? No way! You want me to run drugs because I'm a woman, because I'm black?" Margaret stood, threw down her napkin.

"Sit down, Margaret." Mark spoke softly.

"Not fair, George." Mark continued speaking across the table. "Are you satisfied?"

"One more question." George did not apologize or appear to have noticed that Margaret had stood. "How do you feel about President Al Adana and his administration?"

"How do you think? His administration made sure there were no professional jobs for women and my family's support of the policies of the new American Party meant that we had to abandon our home and move into exile, like refugees."

"Then you would not mind working for the American Party against them?"

"That's a different question. No, I wouldn't mind. I would break his new federal laws if it meant helping chase him out of office."

"It could be dangerous and illegal," Mark said.

"I get it. When do I start? What should I do?"

"You'd better hear what we have in mind first."

Mark and George nodded at one another.

"I run a unique bank," George began. "It has one customer, the American Party. Everything you hear from now on is known to only a few, and you must never, ever repeat any of it to anyone not at this table."

"A little strong for a banker," Margaret said.

"I need to be. You'll need to be too, even if you are tortured or if the information is extorted. There is no mercy in our competition. They would love to know where we are and who we are in order to destroy us.

"I'll leave you now. Mark wants to discuss things

beyond my pay scale." He gave them a small smile. "Here's my contact information. Memorize and then burn it. Sign this piece of paper; if you agree to join our campaign a credit card, debit card, and a check book will be delivered here to your hotel."

He stood and disappeared – a middle-aged man, good suit, walking without curiosity into the street.

"Where's his office?" Margaret asked.

"You don't need to know."

"Well, how will I get to work?"

"I want you to work for me!"

"For you? Getting shot at? Jumping out of boats? Are you joking? What happened to Ginny?"

"Ginny has gone back to…let's call is academia. She got seasick. We have logistical problems. Our money comes into the bank and George takes care of that, but we have to raise funds for campaigns all over the country and need feet on the ground."

"What about you?"

"I will of necessity be doing some of that, but my face is top of the most-wanted list. I cannot fly because of airport security, and public transportation would also be a problem."

"You want me to do this? Alone?" Margaret's eyes widened. She was suddenly aware of wearing borrowed high-heeled boots and a flowery shirt. Her effort to look small and blend in was futile.

"No. You'll have back-up and a contact in each place you go."

"By 'back-up' do you mean like a secretary, an associate…?"

"No, actually, I mean like a bodyguard, someone making sure you don't run into a burning building."

"I…" Margaret closed her mouth before making a further fool of herself. "Yes, I guess I can try it.

Nothing else has popped up."

"This is serious. This is not a try. This is not a wait and see if a better offer presents itself. This is dangerous, and you could put a lot of people in danger." There was a long pause. "Yes or no? If it's no, then we never met. I'll give you some time to think about things."

"No need to think. I'll do it."

Mark paid the check, shook her hand, told her he'd be in touch, and left.

Margaret went back to her hotel room and changed into the clothes that had been laundered. She stood looking at her image in the long mirror. She did not like what she could see. The clothes were not new. They'd been bought for working for fishermen and going to fishermen dances and dancing with fishermen. Her hair, clean, look old fashioned. Having been cut by the wife of a fisherman, it was cut in the style of…

Why had she said yes to Mark? Adventure? A new life? He had directed her to buy business clothes, whatever that meant. Also to put together a light suitcase to be ready at a moment's notice. How, why, and when were questions she had forgotten to ask.

Her thoughts were interrupted by the phone. "Miss Forrest, a package has been delivered for you. Shall we sign for it?"

"No, I'll come down." Was this a sign of curiosity or was she learning not to trust anyone? she wondered.

The courier had her sign for a package from Mr. Breakstone. There was no address. In the package, a credit card, a debit card, and a package of checks drawn on a local bank. The address was her old address, though she would have bet a lot of money that the statement would find her at her new address.

There was also a cell phone and a page of instructions. She went back to her room, spread everything out on the bed, and summarized. Credit card for business, debit card for personal and cash, checks in an emergency. No deposit slips. Breakstone would make sure there was money in the account. The phone was encrypted and monitored at all times, could not be traced, any calls to her old phone would be transferred.

Well, good so far, she thought. Now I need to get a haircut and style, buy clothes for my new job, for my new life. I just need a friend to shop with. I wonder if Betty Jo has time?'

Margaret looked through her wallet and found a cell phone number which she now realized that she would have to find a code for. She dialed, no answer, no voice mail. She sat looking at the phone and the card. Ike had given his number last night. She decided she would call him. Ike picked up on the first ring, a different Ike from last night.

"What do you want?"

"It's Margaret. I was trying to call Betty Jo and there's no answer."

"And there won't be. Her car was hit by a bomb or a missile, down on the ranch." There was the sound of a racing engine and muttered curses. "I'm trying to get there before Bobby Joe starts tearing people apart. Take care of yourself. Be careful. Trust no-one. Unfortunately, I'm going to need a raincheck on tonight." He hung up.

Margaret sat stunned, mouth open, realizing even more the severity of what she'd agreed to.

## Chapter Eighteen

In Boston a disheveled man moved uncertainly into the Syracuse Restaurant and ordered the rabbit pie.

"What do you want?" Mario came from the kitchen and asked.

"The rabbit pie."

"Oh, sorry. I didn't recognize you. How can we help?"

"I need a new identity as a truck driver and a union card."

"Let me get you lunch and a dish for your girlfriend."

Mathew McDougal and Helen were deliberately unkempt. Mac had not shaved since the decision to go to Texas, nor had he shampooed his hair which was uncombed. He looked tougher and harder than he felt.

"When you finish, go across the street to the photographer. He'll need money. Shall I arrange it?"

"Yes, please," said Mac. "The less anyone remembers me the better. I'd rather the photographer be beholden to you."

"The load you arranged for the trip west will be ready tonight. You'll leave early?"

"I am not saying when, how, or by which route. It's safer." Mac was alert, alive, ready for the challenge, ready to fight back. "Thanks for your help."

"For which I was rewarded and built some bridges,

I hope. Good luck!"

They looked each other in the eyes and shook hands. It was safe. They were on the same side. The same side, but different motivations. One was money, the other ideology.

When Mac reviewed the manifest paperwork, luxury automobile and truck parts from Europe. He discussed the route and stops to the West Coast with his employer. He had no intention of stopping at any of the truck stops recommended or taking the obvious route. It was partly what was expected by his cover but also part of his philosophy not to trust anyone. That had kept him alive, so far. Mac had decided on a longer, less populated route with unconventional stops. Although he was wanted for questioning and his face was well known, he trusted the law enforcement agencies much more than he trusted the local militias. They would rest close to police barracks, fire stations, active weigh stations. He'd be hiding in plain sight.

Helen had put together a shopping list of items which would sustain them for most of the trip. The list could be augmented along the way. The large coffee flask could be refilled, powdered milk, sugar, bread, butter, jam, salami, and tomatoes would get them past the fast food places.

Mac had his rifle hidden in the cab.

On the road Mac thought that the load they were carrying was not as attractive as if they were taking food, but a desperate population would take the parts regardless and sell them for ten cents on the dollar. The buyer would be willing to pass them to the legitimate owners for a handsome profit, even more profit if they had the patience to sell them piecemeal. These were dangerous times.

\*\*\*

The only incident occurred when Mac had driven further than he'd intended in one session and was near South Bend, Indiana. It was mid-afternoon and a checkpoint had been erected by a local militia group. Mac slowed and was waved over. He accelerated through the rag-tag gang of young men and boys. Aroused, two pick-up trucks, filled with youths, set off in pursuit of Mac's rig. It took them a while to catch up to the speeding tractor trailer. The occupant of one truck, which had pulled in front of Mac, indicated that he should pull over. The large eighteen-wheeler tractor trailer, with massive diesels, rear ended the pick-up. Meanwhile the other pick-up pulled alongside and waved a pistol at Mac and Helen.

"Give me the rifle and steer the truck," said Mac.

Having spent two years hunting rabbits, squirrels, deer, and duck, it was a simple shot from twenty feet to put a hole in the tire. "One down!"

The pick-up slowed to a stop on the median grass. Having seen the fate of their comrades, the remaining pick-up started firing at the large diesel with little effect. Mac was driving fast. The driver of the pick-up ahead was driving faster and was obviously nervous and receiving contradictory instructions from his passengers. He made a mistake, easing to the right lane to give his occupants a better shooting angle. Mac found some extra speed, touched the corner bumper, and spun the smaller vehicle.

It seemed they'd had enough. Self-preservation trumped their desire to confiscate the contents of a truck which was apparently not carrying food. There would be easier pickings back at the checkpoint.

\*\*\*

The nights were endless stretching highways. Trees appeared as ghosts in the headlights, getting larger then rushing past to be replaced by more ghosts. Mac drove, Helen slept. In the bunk behind the front seats, Helen dreamed her nightmares, reliving the horrors of being hunted, the insecurity of running, running. She cried out, woke herself, apologized, then slept some more. When Mac could drive no further, he found a secure spot and slept while Helen kept watch.

Mac slept little. He wanted to be finished. He pushed himself. Was it for himself, for Helen, for a cause, or, he wondered convincingly, against a cause? He had plenty of time for thinking. Thinking again and again whether there were more attractive scenarios than the one they had chosen. They could have stayed in Washington, in which case they would have been arrested, tortured, and killed. Instead they had hidden out in New Hampshire. They had been found there and targeted for assassination. Not really a surprise. A little drastic, but not a surprise. They had flown again, hiding out in Northern Ohio, or was it upper New York State?

Why had Ellie May Joseph invited them to join her campaign? Why had they accepted? Why? There were too many whys. Here they were, still running. Maybe this time they were heading toward the answers instead of away.

He turned his thoughts to Ellie May Joseph. She didn't have a snowball's chance in hell of being elected. She must have been really desperate to invite Helen and himself to Texas.

"What were you thinking?" Helen asked, now awake and watching Mac.

"How beautiful you are. How did I get so lucky?"

"Flattery will get you anywhere."

"That's what I'm counting on," he replied with a smile.

"Does Ellie May have a chance?" Helen always did have the ability to read Mac's thoughts.

"With you on her side, she's a shoo-in!"

"Seriously?"

"Seriously, no."

"Then why?"

"To have a voice, to have a choice. It's our democratic right."

"But democracy went out the window. Voter fraud is rampant. Candidate manipulation is a given."

"All the more reason to stand up and shout, 'We are *not* going to take this anymore,' right?"

"Not very original, Mac. But it is exciting in a self-destructive way."

Mac didn't care to comment as he'd thought the reason he wanted to do this was because Helen had become again the woman he'd fallen in love with. The Helen who had gone into shock and not spoken for six months was gone. The vitality was back. Life, whether short or long, was good again.

The patterns grew routine. Mostly contented silences, their disparate thoughts were on the future. The past was behind them in the East, although in truth, if they were successful, they were going to return East.

Mac's thoughts frequently focused on seeking a safe place to stop or on unusual traffic patterns suggesting roadblocks or observations from authorities. As they headed west, he observed there was less to fear, as if the administration was focused eastwards. This was an observation he could use to promote a grassroots revolt. No, not a revolt, an awakening; from the West Coast toward the East.

Finally they reached Los Angeles and delivered the trailer. Mac checked with the shipper and collected a draft form from the receiver. It was a nonexistent name, so he asked for cash. He argued the discounted amount and finally agreed on seven and a half percent. His next step was clean up and shave in a public toilet. He changed and dropped his old clothes in a dumpster. Helen joined him and they boarded a bus to Las Vegas.

They had made it. Almost.

# Chapter Nineteen

A week later Mac and Helen had resumed their real names and were meeting with Ellie May Joseph, Marjorie White, Alistair Kirk, Mark Hughes, and his new assistant, Margaret Forrest. Alistair had reiterated his reasons for his resignation and his delay on the official announcement until Helen Harvey McDougal could join the team. The small team was necessary because the subject matter was finances.

"First, I want to say that Betty Jo is doing better," Ellie May paused. "She's lost both feet, but the airbag saved the vital organs. Also the car was bulletproof, so the blast stopped the car but didn't explode upward. The damage was all underneath. We've ascertained that the device was carried by a drone and one of the passengers had a homing signal. The passenger appears to have been unaware of the plant. Bobby Joe, as you can imagine, is not doing as well as his wife. Ike Clark has moved into the compound temporarily as Bobby Joe spends time at the hospital. From this incident, we can assume that at least one anti-American Party cell is operating in Texas. Be vigilant.

"Next, introductions. Margaret Forrest is a new face and has agreed to work with Mark. Mark, as you know, is working with our financing source."

"Does she understand the risks, the consequence of being..." Mac paused, thinking of the rape and torture taking place in Washington. Of the women 'arrested' by the militia "…interrogated."

"Yes, I won't be caught," Margaret said vehemently. "I grew up black in Louisiana. We had friends and their boat was blown out of the water for transporting Mr. Hughes and now my new friend has lost both her feet. I think I know the risks."

"We've talked extensively since the missile attack," Mark interjected. "She knows that I'm on the ten-most-wanted list and the importance of someone to audit the money trail. She's willing to be that person. We're providing her with guards."

"That covers that," said Ellie May. "Next, Helen has agreed to be my new chief of staff. Mac will do press releases for us – media distribution and, most importantly, communicate with the Sons of Liberty and our candidates." Ellie May looked up as Alistair indicated that he wanted to speak.

"I want everyone to know that I am perfectly comfortable with Helen taking over my role. She's agreed to keep all of my staff. My staff have all agreed to stay, which is a great relief. It has taken the pressure off recruiting and investigating new people." Alistair looked tired and relieved. The role had developed far in excess of when he had first agreed to serve.

"Not to mention re-examination of any staff who wanted to leave." Ellie May was thoughtful.

"Perhaps," Ike interjected, having joined the room during Alistair's speech, "it's not a bad idea to look at everyone again."

"I was thinking that, and it occurred to me that Alistair, after a few days off, is the perfect person to run that review. Alistair?"

"We're off to my daughter's home for a week while Helen gets her feet wet, then I'll come back with a plan."

"I might be of some help." Mac was committed to this cause and anything that kept Helen safe. "I picked up a lot of information and tactics from the various Sons of Liberty groups."

"Now that that's settled, we need to talk money." Ellie May was back on agenda. "There are mid-term elections in November. Candidates are looking for direction and funding."

"We have candidates?" Mark asked.

"Some. We're not sure how many. And that is where Margaret will come in."

"Tell me how I can be of help. I appreciate that I've been treated quite well, royally in fact, and I know I'm to work with Mark. I also suddenly find myself in very elite company."

Everyone laughed.

Mark had talked to Margaret extensively, but she was still surprised to find there had been a conversation at a higher level of her role.

"Fair enough. Let's be specific with our first assignment. We have a candidate in Iowa who has requested funds. The Sons of Liberty aren't confident that he can win, with or without money. The leader of the Sons, and our contact, John Ford, was arrested and the group is fragmented or disbanded. We don't know which. We haven't heard any updates from them of late. There has to be contact with members and the candidate. We need to know three things. Is the candidate realistic and his budget real? Who is leading the opposition? And where do the Sons of Liberty stand?

"There must be face-to-face meetings with these people, secretly. It's a test of all of us. Remember, Iowa is the first caucus and therefore a barometer in the presidential race." Ellie May had everyone's attention.

The meeting ended after two hours.

Margaret was exhausted. How could she be so tired from just sitting? It was the tension and the concentration. She realized, with alarm, she was committed to another two hours, maybe more, with Mark and Mac on the details of her first assignment.

At the end of two hours, since no notes were allowed, she was asked to recap the plan, recite the names and addresses, and was then tested on her memory. Finally they were finished.

"When do I go?" she asked.

"Up to you. Tomorrow?" Mac suggested.

"So soon. I thought…"

"It cuts down on the thinking if you just jump in. Pack lightly. No Texas labels. Stuff that can be laundered or washed. Your identity will get you into hotels, etc."

"Transportation?"

"Work with your guard. If he decides that it's safer to drive, drive or take a taxi, bus, or train. Allow yourself to be guided – one thing less for you to think about." Mark had used all of these modes of transport and boats to get to Boston and back. "Guard will catch up with you in Iowa. He's leaving today. Use the secure phone tomorrow for the name of the hotel in Des Moines he'll have chosen."

"Okay. Can I go pack now?"

"Yes. Don't check out. Leave everything in your room. Someone will clean up for you."

Margaret packed, did not sleep much, and tried to spend the morning doing the things that she would normally do. At eleven she walked out with a canvas bag with clothes for a few days. She was surprised to see her old truck standing outside the hotel, even though she knew that the plan was to drive to Louisiana then fly from Shreveport over two hundred miles away. It didn't take long to realize that the truck had been serviced and filled with gas. The route, she had memorized, and she enjoyed being alone to think, to remember her instructions, and to marvel at the detail that went into a simple trip.

When she arrived at the airport in Shreveport, someone was waiting at the designated spot. She gave Margaret a plane ticket and took the keys for the truck.

Margaret was early with no bags to check, so she ate. She hadn't eaten all day and looked around anxiously to see if she was attracting attention. There was nothing out of the ordinary, and she forced herself to stop looking, in case her 'looking' attracted notice.

The security guard looked carefully at her and checked her ticket. "Chicago."

It came out as a challenge. Margaret was silent. It was the same every time she, a black woman, was confronted by authority. The authority could be black, white, Hispanic, Asian, man, or woman. A response always elicited questions. She nodded as she held out her hand for a return of her boarding pass. It was returned without further comment. Many families had left Louisiana and the South looking for work, a better life. Sometimes they could achieve both.

Margaret slept on the plane, glad that she had eaten since no food was served on the flight. The travel business was in crisis. Crews had been cut and airplanes were not upgraded.

The transfer to a different airline to Des Moines was designed to give her a sense of whether she was being followed. She had no idea. Trying to remember a face was a fruitless task.

When the plane landed in Des Moines, she called to find the name of the hotel and went to a taxi rank. Margaret didn't see the man following her, or notice that he watched until the cab in which she was riding pulled away. He got into a car that had been parked at the side of the road and followed.

While she was paying the cabdriver, he entered the small hotel and watched as she checked in. He continued to sit and watch.

The next morning at breakfast, the man approached Margaret.

"Mary Wilson? I'm your driver."

"Ike," said Margaret, jumping up.

"Have you forgotten everything already?" he chided.

"What?" she asked, then the smile slowly disappeared from her face. Ike had addressed her by her pseudonym and she might, no she had, blown his cover. "I'm so sorry. I've lost my job on the first day…."

"Shhh. Stop." Ike wasn't angry. "I signed the register Clark I. George and tend to use my name in variations with Clark, Isaac, or George, first, middle or last name."

"Then, no harm?"

"A lesson, maybe," he said with mock severity. "By the way, you weren't followed at the airport or here."

"How do you know?"

"I was following you."

Margaret laughed. "Then I guess I was followed."

Ike smiled. "So where are we going to this morning?"

"First I have an appointment with Mrs. Ford, then Joseph Polivar."

"Lesson two. I do not know, or need to know, who you're seeing or why."

"But I thought…"

"No. I'm your bodyguard. I work for you. That's all."

"All?" she smiled coquettishly.

"Yes, my job is to get you back alive. Hopefully myself too." He looked seriously at her. It was necessary to stay focused despite her beautiful eyes and smile.

"First, you need a sweater. It's colder here than where you came from. It'll give us a chance to see if anyone is interested in following us."

Ike was dressed in a black turtleneck, grey chinos, and a dark sweater. He was carrying a lightweight quilted jacket.

After a now quieter breakfast, they left and drove to a nearby mall. A gang of youths had gathered by the entrance but paid little attention to the tall black couple. They aroused no interest from those manning the surveillance cameras. Ike put his arm around her and tried to walk in such a way that Margaret was not seen or not clearly. He remembered that there may be infiltration of the American Party. It was always better to be safe than sorry.

Margaret exited wearing a cashmere sweater in which she instantly felt more comfortable. Ike was carrying, for her, another sweater and a down vest.

Mr. and Mrs. Ford lived on a quiet street near the college. Mrs. Ford was in her early fifties, plain looking, thin. The smile with a dimple disappeared as she opened the door to Margaret.

Was it personal? Was she expecting someone else? Or was there some other reason?

"Hello, Mrs. Ford. I'm Mary Wilson, and I've

come at the request of a political ally and friend of your husband." Margaret was unsure if other people might be in the house.

Mrs. Ford looked confused and leaned forward to enable her to see up and down the street. "How did you get here?" she asked suspiciously.

"I was dropped off." Margaret was vague, anticipating that the nervous woman would assume she'd arrived by cab.

"You, are you from…?"

"South," Margaret interrupted. "Can we go inside or meet somewhere?"

"Come in. I'll brew some warm tea."

Margaret followed her through the kitchen and watched as tea was brewed. She was learning to listen to the house. There was no one else home. And she kept in close proximity to ensure Mrs. Ford did not use the telephone or communicate with anyone.

Seated in the breakfast nook, Margaret sat facing the garden. "Your husband was arrested. Have you heard from him?"

"No. Someone said he was involved in…" she was unsure and did not want to incriminate her husband or say anything self-incriminating.

"Opposition?" Margaret volunteered, trying to be helpful.

The woman opposite nodded briefly without raising her head.

"Joe Polivar?"

Now the head came up, tears and a shaking of the head indicating there was nothing to be said.

"Could he have been involved in your husband's arrest?"

A look of fear, a half-question on the distraught face. "No." She took a long pause. "John, my John, was going to fund his election bid. He said that he couldn't fail with all that money. He was talking rubbish. We don't have that much money, and definitely not for a windbag like Polivar."

"Where was the money coming from?"

"I don't know."

Margaret's phone alerted her to a text message. She took it from her handbag and saw that it was from Ike. He'd written, "Now, north two!"

"Thanks for the tea. Wash the cup. I wasn't here. You may have other company coming."

Margaret left through the back door and garden gate. She was hurrying through backyards. Two houses, then she turned into the driveway and slowed down. She'd simply appear to have been a caregiver or cleaner leaving the house in whose driveway she was now walking, tired with aching feet. Ike was waiting at the curb, and she managed not to look up the street.

"What happened?"

"A police car."

"So?"

"So, I don't believe in coincidences."

"How would they know anything?"

"Don't know. Maybe a bug. Maybe a neighbor seeing blacks on the street. Maybe routine. Or maybe 'A wise guy's always right. Even when he's wrong, he's right' as they say in the movies."

"Maybe we just get on with the job, Lefty. Drive downtown. Park, then I can walk."

"Yes, ma'am." Ike said with a smile, then seriously. "I'll be close behind."

Entering the American Party headquarters, it was surprisingly quiet. Two people were working, packing flyers into envelopes and other shipping chores. A bank of telephones was unmanned. An unattractive, short man with a receding hairline came out of a rear room at the sound of their entry.

Margaret recognized Joseph Polivar, the candidate.

"How can I help you?" the question was addressed to Ike.

"Lady got some questions." Ike had deliberately adopted a servile tone. It generally suited his purpose to appear to know nothing. Today he had automatically sensed that Joseph Polivar was probably bigoted, misogynic or both.

"Mary Wilson, from national headquarters." Margaret extended her hand toward the pudgy five fingers that had been extended toward Ike.

There was a hesitation, and it was possible to see the gears grinding. No one had ever visited from the Ellie May camp. Why now? And why these huge black people? Maybe they weren't from Texas. But what if they were? Maybe they were here to refill his coffers.

"Welcome. How can we help each other?" he said, shaking her hand.

"First, tell me about your campaign. Secondly, share a copy of your budget. Then let me have a look at your books."

"Let's go to my office." He gestured to the back of the room from where he had appeared.

Ike went to talk with the two employees.

Three hours later Margaret walked through and out to the street. Ike followed.

"Coffee?" she asked.

"You say the sweetest things. There's a coffee shop at the corner. No one seems to have paid attention to us. No one is watching this candidate."

"If we start to see unusual things, we'll know

where and who."

"A view of the street then," he suggested.

They sat in the window with Ike facing the building they'd just left.

"What'd he have to say?" asked Ike.

"Nothing doing! I am *not* falling for that again."

Ike laughed. "Touché. Well done," he said. "Doesn't seem to be as much work happening as one would expect with only weeks until the election. I spoke with the young man packing flyers off to volunteers. They're running out of flyers even though the shipments are next to nothing. The woman was answering the telephone, making calls to potential volunteers and asking for contributions. Her comments were that the contacts were pretty positive but she can do little by herself with no follow-up. They seem to have the tools, but they need boots on the ground."

"When I asked for the budget and books," Margaret said, "I thought Polivar was going to have a heart attack. He recovered a bit and, after searching, gave me a copy of the request sent to Texas. 'Back up,' I asked, and he said that his chief of staff has that information."

"His chief of staff, in more ways than one, is Mrs. Polivar," said Ike.

"Can you do background on the staff this afternoon while I go back and rattle his cage?" asked Margaret.

"Including his chief of staff?"

"Yes. Pick me up at six, in case you are still out and about. I'm going to list the documents that I want to see tomorrow, including back-up to his request, financials to date, speaking engagements, fund-raisers…"

"Don't forget telephone solicitations and television

interviews," said Ike. "This is Iowa. Together with New Hampshire, they're early indicators for the presidential elections next year. We need to know if they're lining up the TV stations to give them access next year."

"Polivar is just standing to fill a vacancy," Margaret said. "Doesn't seem to be into this election."

"No matter. Groundwork is very important."

"Maybe we go to New Hampshire next."

"Let's get out of here first."

At six Ike waited anxiously in a no-parking zone, watching the front door to party headquarters. Just when he thought that he would have to go in, the door opened. Margaret had a fixed smile which disappeared immediately when she was on the street.

"That bad?" Ike asked.

"What?"

"Your face said it all, Sugar." He chuckled without humor.

"I need a shower."

One hour later Margaret and Ike sat in the bar prior to having supper. Both had reported separately to their superiors in Texas.

"Oh, I'm cleared to talk to you," said Margaret.

"And I am cleared to listen." Ike smiled, then added, "And to help with your investigation."

"There is nothing to investigate. Yet. I have a promise that I can see all of the books tomorrow; then I can begin my work. The schedule looks like a sorry piece of work with no direction. I know that I'm a neophyte, but I know more in a week of what is not right. Does that make sense?"

"Yes, you had an idea of what you might see and didn't see it."

"His chief of staff, Yvonne Fletcher, and his media

director, Joan Rodriguez, were both out today. I asked if they were setting up meetings, fundraising. He answered with a shrug."

Ike chuckled. "Yvonne Fletcher is his wife. Joan's their daughter. I found that out from David Hamilton. I checked, went to their home addresses. Joan Rodrigues was home with two children and is pregnant. Yvonne was at the hairdresser and then visited her sister."

"How do you know? Never mind. I probably don't want to know."

"Dinner?" he invited with a charming smile.

\*\*\*

The next morning Margaret, as arranged, was at the American Party headquarters. She was feeling much more confident, in herself and in being able to complete her mission.

She waited five minutes for the Polivars to arrive. She was smiling at memories of the previous night; first a positive conversation with Mark in Texas had quieted her concerns, then a pleasant dinner within walking distance of the hotel and then Ike had insisted on checking under the bed, on the bed, and in the bed. It would take a lot of lemons to wipe the smile from her face.

The books were presented, not up to date, together with the check register and bank statements. Margaret insisted that the bank statements up to the minute be produced, online, directly from the bank.

The office was again quiet with few telephone calls. At eleven Joe Polivar announced that he had a speech to present to the local Rotarians and left with his wife. Margaret stayed to continue working and asked Ike to cover the Rotarian lunch meeting.

At three o'clock they were seated around a

conference table. Ike sat as close to Margaret as the table would allow. Concern showed on Joe Polivar's face while his wife's body language was of defiance.

"How did it go?" asked Margaret.

Joe Polivar, who was unaware that Ike had been in his audience answered, "Quite well! They received the message of law and order and the questions showed a great deal of support."

"Turn out? Contributions? Pledges?" Margaret pressed.

"Good turnout, and we have a solid base for contributions."

"Not true!" Ike stood up, angry. "The turnout was poor for Rotarians, and some left before your speech due to threats from the militia to disrupt the meeting; the questions were watered down, as were the responses. Your chief of staff spoke to no one and solicited no contributions, nor did she ask anyone to host an event."

"What's the point?" Yvonne Fletcher Polivar retorted.

Margaret studied this plain-looking woman and wondered if she'd always lacked spunk.

"Taking the King's shilling!" said Ike.

"What? What are you talking about? I never took anything." She went quiet with the realization that the argument was going against her.

Joe Polivar stepped into the conversation in order to protect his wife from further embarrassment. "He means there is an implicit obligation to do your best for whoever's paying." He paused to see if there was an argument against, or an affirmation of, the definition. There wasn't even a nod.

"I take umbrage on behalf of myself and my wife. We've done our best for this campaign."

"That is disingenuous," said Margaret. "There are no meaningful appointments or interviews. The fundraising and solicitation of funds has been non-existent. Your chief of staff spends more time and money at the spa than on this campaign, and she talks longer to her hairdresser than the press – and not about you, I might add. The media activity, in spite of paying a media director, is non-existent. It is weeks away from voting day, too late to change the candidate, but not too late to change his staff."

"You mean… you mean…" Yvonne stammered.

Margaret and Ike turned their focus on the candidate.

"Where do I start?" Joe Polivar asked humbly, looking at that moment a broken man. The body language was of someone realizing, after a lifetime of failure, being forced to look hard and see his failings. It was like waking from a dream to realize it was a nightmare, to find it is light outside and that the day must be faced.

Margaret was now in charge of the room in spite of being the youngest and least experienced. "First, are you still a candidate?"

"Of course."

"Are you willing to put in the sixteen-hour days from now until the first week in November?"

"Alone?" he glanced at his wife, who wiped a tear from her eye and left the room.

"Are you in? You don't need to do this alone, but your wife doesn't have a clue what it takes to win an election. If she supports you, she'll be by your side at any and all campaign events. But she'll be there as your wife, not your chief of staff."

"I have to think."

"Think fast! We have a lot to get in order if you're

going to stand a chance at winning. By the way, fire your media director effective immediately." Margaret looked across the room to where Ike was standing. "Did David Hamilton check out? Is he capable of running a campaign?"

"Yup!"

"Then if Mr. Polivar is still in this race, he needs a chief of staff who already knows something, and he will know someone to work the media. It seems, with unemployment at twenty-five percent, it should be easy to fill these jobs with people anxious to work."

Margaret spent two days on the books and records and in preparing a budget. Ike spent those two days with Joe Polivar, who submitted to interviews on the radio and television. He met the new media director as they worked on making videos for TV and social media.

Polivar's first speeches were to law enforcement and firefighter groups. The message to return law and order and disband the militia was well received by both audiences. The experience in New York was cited. A commitment of safe conduct from the police for the candidate and his family helped smooth out the agenda. The police negotiated the release of John Ford from the militia, and the Sons of Liberty were again functioning.

At the end of six days in Des Moines, everything that could be set in motion was smooth. David Hamilton was in direct contact with headquarters and was receiving and sharing daily bulletins. The telephones were manned by volunteers who were receiving a great response to the solicitations after seeing the candidate preach on the daily news. The Democrat's candidate, by contrast, was asking for more time for the administration to turn around the economy without giving the voters any idea of how this was to be accomplished. He had been assured of no opposition and was slow in reacting to this sudden onslaught.

Margaret and Ike were back at the hotel after a successful day. She pressed the button marked six and the doors closed.

"You gonna check under my bed again?"

"Yup!" answered Ike.

As they were leaving the elevator, three young men with beards carrying knives and baseball bats appeared from out of Margaret's room.

Margaret instinctively stepped behind Ike, who in a reflex action pushed her back into the elevator as the door was closing.

"Call 911," Ike shouted as he turned toward the men.

"Militia!" said the man in front. "You're under arrest."

"Let me see your warrant."

"This is my warrant," the man said slapping the baseball bat into his hand.

Margaret staggered backwards and fell, banging her head on the back of the elevator. The doors closed and the elevator started to move downwards. She heard a gunshot, jumped to her feet, and hammered on the door with her fists in a futile gesture. Realizing the futility, she pressed the buttons on the panel, all of them. The elevator stopped at the second floor, then, as she stepped out, it continued down. Now what? She wanted to be in the lobby where there were people. She felt so lost. She looked down, saw the cell phone in her hand, and remembered Ike shouting 'call 911.' She had to call the police and an ambulance. There had been a shot.

Emergency vehicles were on their way. Margaret pressed the elevator button. She had to know what was happening on the sixth floor.

When the elevator stopped, she peered around the side and saw a man on the floor bleeding profusely from a wound in the leg. Ike was standing over him, assessing with his eyes the damage and the state of the injured man.

"I thought I sent you away! Did you call the police?"

"Three minutes."

"Then you have two minutes to pack and get out of here."

"What about him? And you?"

"Move; you now have a minute and a half."

Margaret moved fast without taking her eyes from the man who was leaning against the wall with a baseball bat at his side.

One minute later Margaret and Ike were again standing over the wounded man as sirens swept into the hotel foreyard. The man was still unconscious. Ike took a gun from the small of his back, wiped it carefully and put it into the man's pocket. Margaret had called an elevator and was standing to prevent the door closing.

"Parking garage," said Ike stepping in.

"Are we checking out?"

Ike chuckled. It was such a naïve question and was precisely the reason he was in love with this innocent for whom everything was possible.

"We'll check out online when we get to the airport."

"Where are we going?" Margaret asked, stepping into the rental car.

"Anyplace a plane is leaving for tonight."

"Are the police looking for us?"

"Not yet."

"Why not? What happened? Where'd the gun come from?"

"While I flew without a gun, I felt vulnerable and bought one before you arrived – a small one, a thirty-eight. The thug said, 'Here's my warrant' with a baseball bat, so I said, 'Here's my get out of jail card.' He swung the bat and I shot him in the leg. He fainted and the other two took off. The police are probably trying to figure out what he was doing with a baseball bat and how he shot himself twice in the leg."

"Twice?"

"I missed his knee the first time."

Margaret was horrified.

The rented car was checked in. They scanned the board for short flights leaving soon. They had two choices – Omaha or Las Vegas. A quick check revealed that there were seats to Omaha in thirty minutes and two seats on the Las Vegas plane leaving in one hour. After quickly conferring, Margaret overrode Ike's objection and he bought two tickets for Las Vegas. His concern was that waiting an hour to leave gave the authorities time to check and for the police to drive to the airport if they wanted to interview two missing, potential witnesses to a shooting. Or worse, if the militia were targeting them for interrogation, they might be looking and, even if not geniuses, it would take no time to check the airport.

Ike asked for two tickets, one way. The clerk looked up, peered over the desk at the small luggage, then looked at Margaret.

"Her brother's funeral," said Ike. "We don't know when we're coming back."

"I'm sorry for your loss," the clerk spoke to Margaret, who instantly burst into genuine tears.

"Is there a chapel, here at the airport?" asked Ike, thinking that it might be a perfect refuge.

"No, not allowed, religious places in a public domain, if you know what I mean." It was said with sympathy. "There is a quiet room, no cell phones, no computers, no televisions, and such. It's on the right down concourse A. Your plane is at C12, boarding half an hour before take-off, doors close ten minutes before departure. Have a nice flight."

The quiet room was also dimly lit, but there was enough light to show that they were alone. Ike and Margaret sat close to the emergency exit which led out toward the runway and was fitted with an alarm. They planned to wait until the very last minute and go quickly to the plane. After half an hour Ike stood, the door opened and two young men with guns were silhouetted. With the advantage of the subdued lighting and his eyes adjusted, Ike pulled Margaret through the emergency door which now emitted a shrill siren. He pulled her behind the door as the two men came barreling through. Ike pushed the second man into the first, then he pulled Margaret back through the screeching, body vibrating sound into the 'quiet' room and into the corridor as an armed response team arrived.

"How did they get those guns through airport security?" asked Margaret when she could breathe again.

"I don't know, but I think Homeland Security and TSA will have some explaining to do."

They were the last passengers onto the plane. Ike scoured the other passengers for someone who looked out of place. Margaret called Mark in Texas before they taxied out. "This is Mary. Change of plan. We're heading to Las Vegas. We had some uninvited guests show up to the wedding, so we decided to move the venue. Estimated arrival just before midnight."

"What last name are you using?" Mark asked.

"Wilson."

"You'll be met."

Mark was tired, he'd been working for the last sixteen hours and was ready to leave, but this was important. It also gave him chance to kill two birds with the one stone.

Margaret hung up the phone and after takeoff slept for the entire three-hour flight. Ike, seated three rows behind, was deep in thought. He would have liked to write down his thoughts but knew that this was frowned upon. His thoughts kept him watchful, watching from afar his sleeping companion.

In Las Vegas, in spite of the late hour, it was noisy. Exiting with their two carry-on bags, Ike mentioned that they should check the availability of hotels and possibly take a shuttle. A man in uniform with a sign 'Mary Wilson' caught their eye.

"You Mary Wilson and dude a Mr. Mark ordered a car for?"

"I guess." Ike was still wary.

"You guess? You better guess quick boy. This little lady got a meeting with my boss in one hour."

"An hour? It'll be one o'clock," Margaret said.

"Yes, ma'am, one o'clock."

This was Margaret and Ike's first time in Las Vegas. They looked up at the lights. The recession and the current administration's view on gambling, except for their own, had reduced the traffic and the number of hotels. Some of the other vices seemed to have lost nothing.

Ike voiced one of his thoughts. "Why did you say Las Vegas?"

"Two reasons. First, there were only two tickets so no one could be following, and, second, I knew that Mark and Mac had both been through Las Vegas before arriving in Texas, so there had to be a connection or a safe route. And when I called Mark to let him know about our new destination, he did say that he would send someone to meet us. So I think we're good."

"Honey, I'll follow you wherever you lead. You're the boss." Ike handed their bags to the driver. "Lead the way."

About twenty minutes later they arrived at the Vegas Plaza Hotel. Margaret and Ike were taken by the manager, who met them at the car, past the front desk to their room – a suite on the upper floor. As he was leaving, he spoke to Margaret. "At exactly one o'clock, go to the security desk. Do not speak."

"What about me?' asked Ike.

"That's all for my instructions." He shrugged.

At exactly one, Margaret presented herself as instructed. She had enjoyed a long shower in a bathroom as big as the family living room in Louisiana. She dressed carefully and applied modest make-up. Ike had snuck down and watched from across the room. The man at the desk looked up as Margaret approached. It was difficult not to speak. He turned away, and she followed through an electronic door invisible to the untrained eye to an elevator. The man reached in and pressed a number, then returned to his desk.

The door opened into an office suite where a man sat behind a huge desk. He was alone.

"Hal," he introduced himself. "Pleased to meet

you, Margaret. Please have a seat."

"You know my name?"

"Of course. You come with references from Mark and from Mac."

"You're the big boss?" she asked, maneuvering into the red leather club chair.

Hal laughed, spluttering at the thought. "Hell no! I am a small cog in the wheel, like you," he finished explaining while taking a drag to light his cigarette.

"You arranged the suite, the ride?"

"Those things I am guilty of," he said with a throaty chuckle.

"Thanks. What can I do for you?"

"Actually it's what I do for you."

"For me?"

"Um…." he was thinking. "Everything you hear or see in this room is secret. There are less than ten people in the world who know, but thousands would be affected if these things became known."

"Are you trying to scare me?"

"Just stating the situation. You've already seen, even today, how serious this is. You cannot mention this even to the lunkhead, who is waiting for you, stalking the lobby." He pointed to a monitor showing Ike pacing anxiously.

"That, sir, is a Texas Ranger. He isn't a 'lunkhead.' But I understand. He won't learn any information about you or this discussion from me. Neither will anyone else."

Hal nodded his approval. "Some funding for the American Party comes through this office."

"How does that impact me?"

"The reason given by Mark for this meeting is in the event anything happens to him. I will have met you and you'll know where to find me."

"All right. That must mean that you're a larger cog than you let on. Just how much of our funding comes through you?"

"The original concept was for five billion dollars."

Margaret sank back into her chair. "Five billion? Dollars?"

"Well, the way things are it should be less."

"From where?"

"Mark will have to answer that; I am just a bookmaker."

"A bookmaker?"

"Yes, I make book!"

"You make money on election results? Gambling!"

"No, we make a book, and we *never* gamble."

"How do we get back to Texas from here?" Margaret was on overload.

"The man who picked you up at the airport – Bruce – ask for him at the front desk in the morning. He'll get you where you need to go."

"Will I see you again?"

"Only if Mark Hughes is dead."

## Chapter Twenty

Three days later, Margaret was a little apprehensive in her debrief with Mark. She and Ike had already had a general debriefing with Ellie May, Marjorie, Mac, Helen, Alistair, and Bobby Joe. The general debrief was regarding the status of the election in Iowa and Margaret and Ike's on-the-ground impressions and thoughts. Since they had left Des Moines, the campaign had seen a positive swing. Meetings with police and firefighters had led to television coverage. Television coverage led to other meetings, mostly small but all potential sources of contributions and volunteers. Townhall-style meetings had been scheduled in different cities and towns. Joe Polivar's calendar was now filled with three appointments a day – anything from standing at the entrance of malls shaking hands and being seen to meeting with various movers and shakers in the community. A television crew was virtually following him around. Interest was growing. The message of change, not only to the present Congress but promising not to return to the old Congress, was resonating with audiences. The promise to take the unemployment issues and those related to law and order to Washington were met with considerable approval.

The proof that the American Party campaign was taking off in Iowa was when the Democrats' candidate took to the streets. Previously, with no competition, they had confined themselves to sending mail to previous contributors.

"Margaret, how do you feel?" Mark asked now that they were alone.

"Good."

"Just good?"

"Well, after being attacked in my hotel, meeting with gangsters, and playing heavy to some scumbag politicians, I think that's all I can muster. Yes, I think good is good."

Mark laughed at the serious woman who had come back from a strange initiation.

"Which part of that is funny?"

"The gross exaggeration. The scumbag politician is our candidate for the Senate, who you put back onto the straight and narrow."

"His wife too."

"The hotel attack is confusing as we're not sure whether you were the target or Ike, or it could have been a random attack. Ike, in his debriefing with Bobby Joe, thought that the matching bandanas meant they were militia or gang members, and that the motive was robbery."

"So we are just disregarding the fact that they were leaving my room?"

In answer, Mark ignored the question and moved on. "Hal isn't a gangster. Well, not that I know of. Not that I know what a gangster is."

"Hal! Well, finally someone you admit knowing. Is he a friend of yours?"

"Actually Mac introduced us."

"Mac? I thought…."

"Yes, never judge a book by its cover. There are hidden depths, there are secrets, there is much that I don't know. But what I do know that you did a tremendous job in Iowa."

"Not me." Margaret felt herself blushing, "It was mostly Ike."

"No, Ike did his job, getting you in and out safely. The rest was you. Assessing the situation, balancing the books, and giving us a viable budget and a viable candidate. That was Margaret Forrest."

Now Margaret was blushing a bright red.

"Now we need to know what you learned and apply those lessons to other campaigns."

"I have that. I should like to say that I anticipated your request but actually I needed to memorialize our experiences. I knew that I couldn't write anything like that down, so I listed what we need from all of our campaign managers and treasurers – sort of a seminar outline. It's on my computer. Shall I print it?"

"Yes, please. You can review and refine the list tomorrow with the campaign folks who can then distribute the memo to all of our financial members. I believe that the chiefs appreciated your assessment of the candidate and his staff. You and I can meet tomorrow to discuss future assignments. Anything I didn't cover?"

"Where is the money really coming from? Hal wouldn't tell me."

"I can't tell you where the money is coming from either."

"Can't or won't?"

"Both. I can't and I won't. Everything is need to know, and some things are even above my paygrade, which means that there are more above yours."

"And I knew that when I signed on. Just figured it couldn't hurt to ask…worst that could happen was you'd tell me what you did. And that's not so bad. I trust all of the people we're working with enough to believe that everything's as legit as can exist given the current administration. Thanks for being candid with me."

They both stood and finalized their plans to meet in the morning.

\*\*\*

In a basement office the conversation about the Iowa race continued. The congregation was in various relaxed poses. Only Ellie May sat behind her desk was in business mode.

"We have to show support for Joe Polivar and promote the American Party." Ellie May was stating the obvious and voicing everyone's thoughts.

"We haven't done much since the announcements; well not to the country as a whole. The Sons of Liberty are up to date, but that's like 'preaching to the choir' as it were," Alistair Kirk said.

"We need a national campaign on television." Sheila Hutchins could be relied on to state the publicist's view.

"Marjorie, how is your group coming along with a manifesto?" Helen Harvey asked.

"Pretty well; a couple of weeks. We sent a draft to Professor Harry Taylor at Columbia in New York. I'd like his input. Why?"

"It would make a major news item and we could take pieces and make them soundbites," Sheila suggested.

"We could take some pieces now, perhaps," said Marjorie.

"Let's hold that thought," Mac interjected. "I think that we have enough for soundbites now. It's a question of producing and distributing. Sheila perhaps could start with the young woman in Iowa that David

Hamilton hired for the campaign, the marketing major. She'll have a grassroots idea of what is on the state's mind."

"Good idea," Sheila agreed. "Then what?"

"Then we make soundbites of Ellie May and Marjorie since they are the recognizable faces."

"What about a video that can be shown by Joe Polivar at his meet and greet events? Ellie May welcoming new members, encouraging contributions, asking for support?" asked Joyce.

Ellie May paused in thought. "Can we make those videos here?"

"Sure, we need a scriptwriter and a filmmaker," Joyce said.

"I can do the script for that," Mac volunteered.

"Budget?" Allyn was concerned still about the money.

"Mark isn't here," said Mac. "But I can vouch for this outlay."

"Can we go back to the manifesto?" asked Helen, moving into her chief-of-staff role. "Where are the problems?"

"The Constitution," Marjorie declared.

"Explain," pressed Mac.

She continued, "The Constitution was written in 1776. It was the most modern, forward-looking document. How could the writers foresee computers, telephones, globalization, assault rifles, nuclear missiles, jet aircraft, satellites? It was gender specific: 'All men…etc.' It saw not a standing army but a militia to be summoned, now being misinterpreted and used against the people."

"You want to rewrite the Constitution?" Alistair Kirk was aghast.

"Maybe. Remember, there have already been a

number of amendments."

"Sure, correcting some of the oversights," Ellie May agreed.

"My point," Marjorie began, "our point, is to try to write a manifesto that preserves rights but can change with a changing world. Just because we have them, we should not have the right to bear assault rifles. I know that in Texas I am in the minority regarding gun ownership, but know that every citizen has an opinion on the subject and to sidestep it is only going to raise the issue."

"Marjorie, thank you. The job is yours. Bring back the document." Ellie May wanted to move from the specifics. "We've all got a lot to do, and I promised my husband and Marjorie's boys we could go horseback riding after school."

"Be careful." Mac, as usual, was the cautious voice.

\*\*\*

The next day seemed surreal to Margaret because it was so normal. Normal, surreal – they seemed contradictions. Here she was in a hotel coffeeshop eating breakfast, reporting to a stranger, who was looking through the checklists that she had printed out the previous night. The pages were now littered with changes and comments from their conversation.

It had been relatively easy to prepare the list as it started with the preparation notes she had made in order to meet with and confront Joe Polivar and his wife. To this she added all of the additional questions raised by the answers she'd received. Next were questions of relationships of employees – whether they received compensation, or other benefits of any kind, was prominent. Fundraising efforts with an emphasis on law and order and the various groups represented by law-abiding citizens.

Mark was pleased and outlined an itinerary for her to distribute the final product and then to monitor, physically, their implementation. It was going to be a lot of travelling.

Margaret was disappointed that her future bodyguards were not likely Ike. She was happier with two days off to go see her parents and brothers. The reminder to keep to her boring cover story was followed by the warning to 'be careful.'

## Chapter Twenty-One

The night was clear and crisp. The moon, a crescent, lit the landscape with pools of reflected silver light. Shadows cast by cacti looked like so many soldiers guarding the desert. It was quiet. It would be easy to consider the night silent, but a quiet watcher, listening, could discern the creatures of the night quietly trying to make it through to daylight.

The man stood still. He was some way off from the buildings and the lights of civilization. Looking at the stars, he silently checked them off by name from his memory. He turned and gazed at the constellations to the north. Thoughts crowded in, shutting out the sounds that the desert was whispering. Thoughts of standing in the same manner but thousands of miles to the north and east; there he had stood in snow, just ten months ago. Now he gave a shiver of remembering.

Mac didn't turn as he heard footsteps approaching the guest house behind him. He recognized the steps. Conscious of the intrusion, he was unsure whether he welcomed it or not. Like life, he thought, "things happen while we are waiting."

"A penny for your thoughts," Helen queried.

"You'd be overpaying."

"Why do you say that?"

"Because, Helen, you know every thought I have. Sometimes before I have them."

"You never verbalize." She was trying to draw him out. She had guessed what he was thinking and was afraid. Watching him leave the house, she knew his mood. She'd stood in the doorway as he walked to the desert and stopped.

"When?" she asked.

"Soon," he replied.

"Tomorrow soon? Next week soon? Next month?"

"Just soon," he replied.

"Why?"

"Because I'm an investigative reporter. I'm stuck here with secondhand stories – some true, some false. Most true ones are begging for a follow-up story, follow the trend."

"I know you're right." Tears rolled down her cheek. "I love you too much to beg you to stay. I've seen your frustration building. They will miss you. You've helped so much – the speech writing, the promotional videos. But I know it would be selfish to say that I will miss you and therefore stay." She fell against him, not holding back the tears.

"I love you, Helen."

"Come inside by the fire. It's getting cold out."

"Five minutes." Mac released her and watched as she walked back in the haze of artificial light. The hard part was done. Helen knew and understood. There was a fight, and he needed to be in it. He needed to be at the center, reporting.

That night Mac and Helen made love with a passion, fully aware that it might be the last time. Then a second time, with a certainty that it was not.

The next morning's meeting was barely begun when Helen took the floor.

"As you know, some of what we hear from the outside has no semblance to the truth. Some is good, but most of the news needs to be verified or expanded." There were nods.

"You all…" she stopped, realizing she sounded like a Texan. She returned the smiles of her audience, then continued, "All of you know that Mac was, and is, on top of the 'most wanted' by the present administration." She paused for a breath then said, "Mac, despite knowing this, has made a decision."

"I'm going to do what I do best – investigative reporting. I'm going to cover the primaries, just as I did three years ago. I'll take a cameraman, or hire freelance, and my reports can be broadcast through our station here. Written articles will be sold through my agent in Washington."

"It's suicide," said Mark with a sideways glance toward Helen, who stood stoically near Mac with a slight glistening in her eyes.

"We need you here," Ellie May countered.

"The world needs the truth." Mac's voice was without passion. He was certain that this was what he needed to do, but he also understood the potential consequences.

"It's suicide," Mark repeated.

"From someone who was in a shoot-out in New York, escaped a bombing in Florida, a firebombing in Boston, and who was almost pushed off a ship, I could question your right of dissuasion."

"You're right, Mac. I do have an opinion, and it is because of our experiences, and because I'm your friend, that I'm concerned. The reports of violence are increasing. The stories of unrest are escalating. There will be a confrontation, and I don't want you in the middle."

"Thanks, Mark. I appreciate your concern, but it's what reporters do – report. The attack, for example, on a Jewish temple on Yom Kippur. Three groups have taken credit and given three reasons, none of which sounds right. A Neo-Nazi group said it was for the killing of Jesus, another group said it was for Palestine, and the third group said it was retaliation for the death of a Muslim martyr."

"One of those might be the group and the reason," said Marjorie.

"It isn't a coincidence that the temple recently spoke in favor of the reforms in New York City and of supporting Ellie May Joseph for president. It isn't a coincidence that the local militia were manning a local roadblock which prevented firetrucks from responding. There are questions that need answers. There may be opportunities."

"Is that where you'll start?" Ellie May asked.

"Probably."

The premise had been accepted and, unenthusiastically, supported. Now it needed careful planning.

\*\*\*

A week later, Mac was ready. He'd sifted through reports from around the country and some reports of bombings in London, Paris, Brussels, and Berlin, of airports, train stations, schools, and museums. There was no consistency except in the intimidation of a shocked country. The only discernible pattern was that the retaliation for these attacks was against a legal opposition group. The object of each attack was clear: to crush and eliminate opposition.

Despite his desire to be in New York, Mac left for Iowa to cover the election of Joseph Polivar. He set out to report on the stance of each candidate.

The Democrat's candidate for Congress had been cleared and approved by the president's administration before Joe Polivar had changed campaign personnel and direction. It was thought that, as there was no, or exceedingly little, opposition, that anyone providing a singular, easily exploited dedication to President Mohammed Al Adana would be elected. And so the leader of the Iowa militia, Abid Rahman, was chosen.

This had been fine until the Polivar camp ramped up the fight with speeches and interviews. A reporter asked Abid to comment on Polivar's attacks on limitations and gun control. The question was whether Abid supported the Second Amendment. It should have been a homerun, but when he had to be reminded of the right to bear arms, he was adamant that only the militia should carry guns.

"So, Mr. Rahman, a citizen with a license cannot carry a gun?" Mac asked.

"No, only the militia."

"But the Second Amendment of the Constitution protects the right to carry arms."

"Then it is wrong. If we find people carrying guns, we take them from them, then arrest them, find them guilty, and punish them."

"And you get this right from where?"

"President Muhammed the Merciful, Al Adana."

Mac and the other reporters at the press conference jotted notes. Then Mac turned to a new topic. "Mr. Rahman, some co-ed students at the University have been attacked in the street by members of your militia. Would you care to comment?"

"I wasn't there."

"But you heard of it. And you are the head of the Iowa militia."

"I heard they were flaunting, not covered."

"Is this a crime?" Mac questioned.

"Why were they not home having children?"

"They were students at the University."

"Ha! Educating girls is a waste of money. There are no jobs for women."

"Did you go to college?" Mac knew he was pressing his luck, but he kept to the back of the room, behind all of the cameras who were focused on the candidate.

"I got a certificate," the now defiant candidate stated.

"For finishing high school?"

"This talk is finished," Abid Rahman said and walked out of the room.

Mac had done some preliminary digging and learned that Abid Rahman had not graduated from high school. He had received, by mail, a certificate that the school system was through with him and throwing him into the welfare system. He leaked the information to another news agency with airtime and tuned in to the six o'clock news where he watched the story unfold.

"This is Wade Roberts signing off and returning you to the studio."

"Extraordinary. Thanks, Wade," a newscaster stated from behind her anchor desk.

The clip was viral for three days until pulled. It was then kept alive by the Sons of Liberty.

The mangled body of Wade Roberts was found on waste land near the militia barracks less than a week after the interview.

Mac felt pained that he had likely contributed to the man's death. It was a message. He needed to lay low for a while, so he headed to Nevada.

"Mac, twice in as many months. You can't stay away, can you?" Hal said, looking up from his desk.

"Just passing through and thought that I might take

a look at my money."

"It's good. For the moment."

"Meaning?"

"We had a rush of money for Iowa."

"Not surprising that someone wanted to back Polivar," said Mac with some apprehension.

"The money was on Rahman."

"You took it?"

"Yes, we had some interest in the other side, from the East Coast."

"Where'd the Rahman money from?"

"Turkey."

"Is that legal?" asked Mac, knowing the answer.

The answer was a shrug.

"There must be a reason." Mac was speaking his thoughts. "They never bet other than a sure thing. Never! We've suckered them into a couple of losses, but we must not underestimate their resolve and cunning, their devious methods and illegal, felonious activities."

Hal laughed. "Like gambling?"

"Like killing that reporter." Mac was in no mood for playful banter.

Shifting back in his chair, Hal said, "So we guard Polivar. Put out that if anything happens, Rahman will encounter a similar fate."

Mac was surprised that this suggestion had been offered with such calm. "Why do you care that much?"

"Because the money backing Polivar is from friends of mine."

"They may just fix the election," Mac mused.

"That is definitely illegal," said Hal, causing Mac to laugh. "But your friends in the east don't have a monopoly on vote rigging."

"In England, local elections were stolen by write-in votes. A bunch of names were registered from a single address, by paper census, all requested write-in ballots, and all voted for the Islamic candidate. Despite being obvious that a crime was committed, it wasn't caught. None of the ballots were examined until the losing candidate looked at the mail-in ballots. He'd won with a count of the walk-in voters. One of the examples, there were nineteen voters, one apartment, all male, all voted with the same x for the Muslim candidate."

"So there was an investigation, criminal charges?"

"No again." Mac was smiling ironically. "The police wouldn't pursue the event because it was a 'victimless crime' and the pursuit would be viewed as Islamophobia, which is a crime."

"Now you're pulling my leg," Hal said.

"I wish. The militia will intimidate voters and meanwhile register as residents a whole telephone book of people and then fill out their voting slips for them."

"Then we need to stop them."

"We need to try."

They talked for the next hour until Mac received the second piece of bad news. Hal had laughed and then coughed clouds of smoke.

"Those things will kill you," said Mac.

"That's what the doctor says."

"Well, listen."

"Too late. He gives me two months max."

"And you haven't stopped?"

"Why stop now?"

"I'm sorry."

"Who for? Don't be sorry for me. I've lived my life on my own terms. I have loved and been loved."

Seeing the surprise on Mac's face, he continued. "Yes, my friend, I have loved. I've made mistakes. I have regrets. I have many friends. Actually, I have many acquaintances, several associates, and a few friends. It appears as though honesty has returned to me in my final days."

"I have always found you honest."

"And I you, which is why I count you among my few friends. I think that we have lived, or should I say I have lived, through the best of times. The best of times, from just after WWII when the standard of living started to improve and continued to improve until September 2001. We thought that it would never end. We were arrogant. We were wrong."

"Have you made your peace, made arrangements, transferred your business?"

"Yes, I'm Jewish, as you may or may not know."

"I thought you Italian."

"It helps sometimes. People fear Italian mafia more than Jewish." He laughed which caused a coughing fit.

Mac rose to get him a glass of water, but Hal just held up his hand and grabbed a bottle of Jack Daniels from his drawer.

"I saw a Rabbi recently. I think he was wondering how he could turn me into a profit." He laughed again and had another, longer, coughing spell. There was a silence. Hal looked at the cigarette; a moment of regret perhaps before he brought it up to his lips and continued.

"My sports book will be transitioned to some young buck, fresh out of school. He'll make his own mistakes. I won't be here to blame."

"Should I meet him?"

"No, no, no; my daughter will take care of your and Mark's transfers. They," he lifted his head towards the upstairs, "are better out of the loop; better for everyone. My daughter will take over some of my contacts, including the political 'book'."

"Your daughter?"

"A mathematical genius, an economist. She never wanted to be in my line of work. A good idea. I wouldn't put that on her. I don't need to tell you how dangerous it can be. But she believes in your cause. She's ready."

"Your daughter?"

"In Washington. Did I say she is a genius? She says that she will take care of things from D.C. Computers, I guess. I'll give you her name, address, and contact information before you leave. Please do nothing to jeopardize her."

It was a father's plea, a demonstration of a father's love. The gesture moved Mac. He had always thought of Hal as emotionless.

"You know that you are the only person in the world that I have not lied to." Hal blew reflective smoke into the air.

"Your daughter?"

"Ha! I lied to her last night, told her that I'd stopped smoking."

"Her mother?"

"Lied to her so many times that she left." There was a longer, reflective silence.

"Upstairs; they, they don't know about you."

"What do you mean?"

"I haven't told them about the money, the personal money, that I hold for you."

"I was here before. They know me."

"They think you died. They wiped you from their memory banks."

"A good thing?"

"A very good thing."

\*\*\*

Mac headed back to Iowa and was surprised when he finally arrived in Des Moines and checked into his room to find a message from Mark who was also checked into the hotel together with Ike.

"You must have gotten my message," said Mac.

"Yes, we had to see for ourselves what was happening and how."

"And?"

"Well," said Mark. "We arrived last night and there is no sign of the opposition party."

"Then it is not vote rigging." Mac was thinking back through the various scenarios. "It must be ballot rigging."

"Not possible," Mark said without conviction.

"Difficult, not impossible," said Ike. "Steal the boxes, damage some counts, intimidate some voters."

"Okay, I get it," said Mark. "Where do we start?"

"The media," said Mac who was now in his domain; his career had been reporting on politics. "A press conference."

"Who? The candidate?" asked Mark.

"No, law enforcement. How high can we go? Attorney general?"

"With what evidence? That someone is betting our guy loses?"

"No, we mustn't alert anyone. A general statement needs to be made to all law enforcement and to all those in charge of ballots and counting that they are going to jail forever if they mess around."

"They'll have been paid or threatened," said Mark.

"Then they must be persuaded to resign or accept the consequences." Mac was thinking, "Ike can you stay and help me with an outline. Mark, talk to Texas.

Get the Iowa Attorney General on board. Make some calls. Make some noise."

Two hours later they were seated in a quiet corner of the cocktail lounge. Mac and Mark were drinking beer, Ike was nursing a soda, and David Hamilton, the Iowa campaign manager, had a tall rum and Coke. David had arrived fifteen minutes earlier and Mark had brought him up to speed with what they were doing for his candidate.

"I don't get it," David said for about the fifth time. "How do you know this is going to happen?"

"The internet," Mac offered, feeling that everything good and bad, for the last twenty years, had come from the internet.

"The internet?" David was skeptical.

"Chatter," said Ike without emphasis which closed the conversation for now.

To move the conversation along, Mark added, "David, you and Joe have the best back room in the world. We are the messengers. As I told you, my friend here is familiar with the campaigns, has been for years, and we must use his experience."

"Yes, I know. I saw you on television at the last election. I thought you'd died."

"That's a common misconception."

"We're not sure how or what the opposition is likely to do. Your candidate, Joe Polivar, need not be included. It's up to you. I personally would leave him out of the loop. He has enough to worry about."

"You're right. He needs to stay focused," said David.

The three visitors exchanged glances.

"I think I can help you slip something into a speech somewhere. Something that will relate to the concern for the dirty politicking without specifics. Then we can leak the concern to the newspapers who, with a little help, can speculate." Mac was thinking and reached for a notebook to jot a reminder.

"Counting is supervised by town clerks here, right?" Mac looked at Ike. "Can you hook up with a reporter and interview a few. Background, how long in the job, family pressures? Maybe check for money problems or susceptible behavior?"

"You're a sick puppy, Mac," Ike said. "I'll do as you ask. Maybe there is nothing there."

"I hope so," said Mac, pensive. "I hope so, but I think that there is something somewhere."

Mark had been quiet. "I think that I'll spend a few days with Joe Polivar, help with some fundraising, pat a few volunteers on the back, recruit some more volunteers, if that's okay with you, David."

"Absolutely!"

"I have to leave day after tomorrow," said Mac. "I'm due in New Hampshire some time next week."

The questions were fewer and dinner was suggested, but David had to be back at campaign headquarters. Mark went with him to pick up food for the volunteers. Mac and Ike headed to the Holiday Inn dining room discussing Ike's role in checking the voter registers.

"You'll miss the president," said Ike. "He's going to speak at the University in support of his candidate."

"He's confident then. He wouldn't leave Washington if he thought that Abid Rahman was going to lose. Very interesting."

"Perhaps someone will ask him about the Second Amendment, that his candidate was unsure of."

"Perhaps someone should," agreed Mac. "Particularly since the American Party, our party, is suggesting a rewrite of the Constitution and all amendments would be null and void."

"Too cerebral for me." Ike was shaking his head.

"If we're to spread the message, then you must be current or no one will be convinced."

## Chapter Twenty-Two

Mac travelled to Washington DC by train via Chicago. There was less scrutiny than at the airport. It also gave him the time to write reports to have transmitted by the team in Texas.

In Chicago the mood was similar to that in other cities. If anything, the unemployment was worse than the national average. Since the figures were a guess and the numbers of local unemployed not available, it was a "seat of the pants" conclusion. The unemployed were visible from the train station to his hotel, sitting silently along the roadside waiting. Waiting for what? A job to show up? A food truck to pass by? He knew. They were waiting for something to change the monotony, the debilitating sitting, waiting, day after day.

Mac met the leader of the local Sons of Liberty in a bar close by the hotel. The man was black and very large with a smile that lit up the bar and a frown that made Mac check if the sun had set. During their one-hour conversation, the man named Edsel, in reference to the most famous dud car ever produced by Ford Motors, smiled and frowned a good deal.

"Thanks for stopping in Chicago, Mac," Edsel smiled. "You're the most famous, most welcome visitor since," a long thought, "...ever." Edsel laughed in amusement at his compliment.

Mac ignored the use of his real name. He was, he supposed, as famous as Jesse James, and as recognizable.

"Edsel, how is the state of your organization? Recruitment, candidates, members?"

"Good. Membership is up. Finding candidates is a little more difficult. We've resorted to finding a lot of candidates for local elections by making that course more palatable than supporting a candidate for national posts. The militia is well armed but internal squabbling helps us." He'd been frowning as he spoke. Now, with a smile, "We help them with their squabbles where we can. Pointing their illicit activities out to the police, with names, dates, etc."

"That's great. I can use that in one of my reports. It won't harm if they know I was here."

"Primaries in the spring – can we get a visit from the American Party presidential, or vice presidential, candidate?"

"Yes, you're on the list for both. Hopefully we can get the senator or local representative to introduce them."

"Hopefully. Hopefully we can elect a new congressman or convert the Republican members."

"We can probably help you with a foot in the door. Talk to Ellie May Joseph."

"Me?"

"Yes, you. You're on the front line. Leave a message with the idea and give a time that she can call you."

Mac left the hotel without going through the front desk, knowing the bill would be paid automatically. He bought a regular ticket for the train. From the conductor he bought an upgrade to a sleeper. The cash he had taken from his personal account in Las Vegas was useful for obfuscation. The tip he gave would grant him anonymity, with luck. The Amtrak staff were all augmenting their wages with gratuities. The militia were using intimidation, but the conductors were likely loyal to the money.

\*\*\*

Washington was brighter. The homeless and poor were not on the street – likely kept out of sight by a strong federal presence, Mac cynically thought. For the same thinking he decided not to check into a hotel. Mac took a bus then walked to the house owned and occupied by Carol, the partner of his former literary agent.

Carol opened the door to his third ring. She was still tall and blonde, but that is where the similarity with the woman he once knew ended. Carol was thin, emaciated. The clothes she wore hung from her frame – dirty, rumpled, old. There was no smile, no welcome. Dark eyes looked through swollen lids. Ugly bruised hands held the door.

"Can I come in?"

No answer, but the door was held a little further open. Mac walked in. The once familiar rooms were strange to him.

"Sue's not here," Carol spoke.

"I know." Mac hesitated. There was something in her tone that suggested Carol did not know that Sue was dead. Mac knew that Sue had been tortured and raped for not knowing where Mac was hiding. Sue had died more than a year ago. Perhaps Carol didn't know. More likely, she had not accepted the fact.

"She's well though," Carol continued with a slight brightening.

"How do you know?"

"Ralph comes by and tells me. We send messages

to each other."

"How do you know the messages are from Sue?"

"Because she says that she loves me," she replied with a faint smile.

"I brought you some food Carol – lettuce, tomatoes, some fish."

"Thank you, Mac. I'll make us a quick salad."

Mac asked questions but it was clear that Carol knew nothing. None of the old contacts had been around, no friends of Sue. She was running out of money – Sue's money really – and expected good times were just around the corner.

The salad prepared, they sat. Carol ate ravenously and returned to her main topic of conversation, Sue and her imminent return.

"Carol," Mac interrupted, "have you seen any newspapers or anything recently?"

"On occasion. I recently heard that the president announced that there's full employment with a couple of pockets still not enjoying the fruits of the recovery. Washington is one of those pockets, I guess. Ralph says there's more food in the stores."

"Who's Ralph work for? Do you know?" asked Mac carefully.

"FBI. I made him show me identification."

"If Sue went with the militia, then how does Ralph know?"

"He's FBI and he asks. Ralph wants to meet you."

"Really?"

"Every time he comes by, he asks if I've heard from you. I told him, no, you were dead. He's going to be pleased that you're alive."

"Let's leave me dead for the time being."

\*\*\*

The following morning, Mac awoke a little later

than he'd planned. He'd forgotten about the time difference, he reminded himself. He heard Carol before he saw her. She was singing an old song that Mac recognized but couldn't name. Mac followed the sound into the kitchen.

"Well, you're cheerful this morning," Mac spoke from the door.

The Carol he saw was nothing like the Carol of the previous night. Today her hair was freshly washed and shone blond and sleek. She was dressed in a light-colored dress with heeled shoes.

"I'm going to see Sue today."

"Carol, tell me that you haven't been speaking to anyone."

"Just Ralph. He told me that Sue was asking how you were, and he asked if we would both like to see Sue, and then she could come home. He's sending a car."

Mac wondered if he had time to grab his bag. Then the doorbell rang, and Carol ran to allow Ralph inside.

Ralph, if that was his name, walked into the kitchen. He was tall, in his thirties, and overweight with very short hair. There was an arrogant swagger as he walked wearing a self-satisfied smile.

"The lady was right. Mathew McDougal in the flesh and in my hands. I can just see a future promotion for bringing you in."

Ralph had a gun in his gloved hand, held loosely by his side. He gave a slight wave of his head to indicate Mac should precede him out of the door.

"Are we going to see Sue?" asked Carol, confused.

"Not you, sugar. Not today," he sneered.

"But, Ralph, you promised. You promised today."

"You're not seeing Sue. I needed to find this man, and I knew he would be in touch."

"When can Sue come home?"

"Never, you dumb broad. She's dead."

There was finally an understanding. Carol's comprehension spread from her eyes to her mouth and with a scream of fury she ran at Ralph with the knife she had been using to cut vegetables. Ralph had just enough time to raise the gun and fire at point blank range. Carol's impetus was slowed and the knife, instead of hitting the abdomen, sliced into Ralph's upper thigh and severed the artery.

Mac stood in shock as blood spurted over the two victims. Knowing there was nothing he could do for either of them, he went upstairs to grab his bag then left by the back door. The lawn at the house behind Carol's was overgrown, so he decided to head through that yard to the main street on the other side.

His timing was lucky. A bus headed out of the city came to a stop at the corner. There were few passengers. This was good and bad, he surmised. While he might be remembered, he was able to find an empty seat and no one talked to him. The bus had a camera, so he kept his head down and wondered if anyone else knew of his whereabouts and was looking for him.

The scene he'd left behind looked like a domestic dispute gone violent. Ralph, for all of his "smarts," had gone into the dwelling alone. No one rushed in when the gunshot rang, so he had obviously not brought anyone with him. He had wanted all of the glory of his coup in arresting one of the top ten wanted people. Arrogance and lack of understanding had gotten him killed. Misunderstanding the depth of feeling between Carol and Sue, he had been insensitive. Mac kept thinking back to how fragile love could make someone. Even someone strong. The need to connect with family, friends, lovers had caused too many slipups. People who never would have been so trusting, smart people like Carol, had made mistakes. And those mistakes had cost them their lives, had endangered too many.

When two or three people stood to leave the bus, Mac followed them into a suburban walk area. He waited until a taxi came by and gave the driver a street junction.

Mac was in a familiar area close to where Helen had lived, and he quickly walked to Paula's Café. He needed a cup of coffee and a plan.

The café wasn't busy, and Paula brought him a coffee, a little breakfast, and a telephone upon seeing him enter. He smiled. She knew who he was and said nothing. She anticipated his needs and was a silent ally.

Mac spent two busy days meeting many of the local Sons of Liberty in a wide variety of locations. He met a member who held a position in Congress and learned there were now several people sharing information with the Sons, including members of both the Senate and House. He visited a few and encouraged them to run for reelection in spite of intimidation, with a promise of help and protection.

It was interesting to Mac that every man and woman expressed doubts about the morality of opposing an elected government. They were swayed, or their doubts assuaged, by the fact that this was not entirely a legally elected government and that they were, in fact, contributing to this deceit, but it could only be corrected with their help.

Mac filed stories and contributed enough material to keep the supporters informed. He filed other reports for the candidates to use and special ones for Helen.

He told Helen about Carol's murder, but not that he had been there, a witness and the target. She had enough to worry about.

His last meeting was with a Son of Liberty who secured a ride for Mac to New York City. The city continued to be a beacon of hope, shining like the Statue of Liberty over the country.

\*\*\*

The driver of the tractor trailer was taciturn by nature and had nothing to say to his passenger. He moved his chin to indicate that Mac needed to climb behind the seats.

Once they were on the highway, the quiet rumble of the road gave Mac time to reflect on his meeting with Esther, Hal's daughter, earlier that day. It had been a revelation.

He found her ambiguous, contradictory – in looks, mood, and manner. Where Hal could have been mistaken for any nationality, Esther's dark hair, curly at the ends, and prominent nose didn't give her the same flexibility to have people wonder. She had a mood and demeanor which reflected her confidence in what she did, and it was apparent that she had fought to stay in front of an ambitious, competitive field.

"We need to establish lines of communication." Esther was all business.

"I'll have an encrypted phone delivered with which you can communicate through Texas to myself or with Mark."

"Only two of you?"

"Yes. There's an alternative to Mark in the directions of transfers from the American Party account. She will bring you the encrypted phone. In the event I'm unable to act, liquidate my account and transfer it to a bank account in my wife's name. This card has the information."

"No audit?"

"No audit."

"Trusting!"

"I've known your father a long time. We have no need of an audit or even communication. He has invested in mostly tech companies and real estate. It's worked. You know better than I do about where my money is now."

"How'd you meet?"

"On a flight. Seven years ago I was flying from Vegas to Boston, promoting my book and reporting on political matters. He was going to Harvard Business School, a graduation."

"Mine. I didn't see him."

"Were you angry with him?"

"Probably. I usually was."

"See him. He's very proud of you and loves you very much."

Esther gave a sound demonstrating doubt in the statement.

"Typical father-daughter relationship? Both afraid to say, 'I love you' first?"

"Mac, he doesn't love me or mother. Just those 'cancer sticks' he smokes. He told me he stopped, but I can hear him through the telephone." She shook her head as if to rid herself of the image. "So you trust me with your money?"

"And with my life."

"Good enough. I have to go to work." She stood and started to take a credit card from her bag.

"No, no cards," said Mac. "I'll leave cash. Be careful."

She nodded and left.

Mac had left money on the table then headed for

the rendezvous point. Having replayed it all in his mind, he pulled a jacket over his head and slept until he felt the rig stop.

\*\*\*

New York was active. A place for commerce, political fundraising could be centered on a mostly dormant Wall Street. There was no capital, new ventures were very few. The entire country was waiting to see what further taxation and limitations would be piled on the populace. It was freely acknowledged that the present administration intended to set in place an Islamic state. An Islamic state ruled from the Middle East. The new federal laws were aimed at deterring women and girls from being educated. Agendas included, for the time being, suggestions of dress code for women, and in many parts of the country lingerie stores were boycotted or targeted for attacks. It was suggested that women follow their husband's or father's instructions in voting. These were still suggestions, but many believed that they would find their way into future legislation.

For Mac, New York was a mine of information. Information was power, and people of New York were power mongers. Financial information had always been attracted like a magnet to Wall Street. The same people now gathered rumors and used them as currency.

Mac met with several harbingers of change every day. It was clear that most of the information was good, though much was unverified and, therefore, not usable. All of the information was entertaining.

The most startling rumors, confirmed several times, was that the changes in the U.S. were mirrored, even echoed, in other countries. In England there had been rioting in Birmingham and in Leeds. The riots were blamed on groups protesting against the erosion of free speech and the Islamic laws and rules introduced into schools. Widely adopted teachings from the Koran, restricted to boys only, started in Birmingham where the school board was one hundred percent Muslim. The trend had spread. Parents objected, agitations started fights, the police were called, and the protesting parents were arrested.

France had more arrests and unrest was increasing. Marseille and Lyons were confirmed centers of protesters receiving harsh prison terms. The jails were crowded.

In Germany and Sweden there were unconfirmed reports of militia, based on the Nazi brown shirts, beating people in the street with impunity while resisters were taken away. The German militia wore black and white checkered scarves which they could pull up over their faces. They enjoyed their name Schwartzweiss.

Mac had soon written enough reports to fill the month ahead. Marjorie was reporting on air daily, and many of Mac's stories were used. Questions were coming in from viewers. People were paying attention. People were asking how they could help. It was growing, expanding. It might work.

A revelation of a different kind in New York was the mayor Joyce Milner. Mac found her refreshing – if she thought it, she said it.

"So, Mac, why did you leave a cozy place like Texas?"

"To spend time with you, Joyce."

This remark brought great guffaws of amazement and non-belief. Joyce had, since becoming mayor, added at least fifteen pounds to her already full fifty-eight-year-old body. Mac was spare and forty. They sat in a busy restaurant with a group of New Yorkers under the guise of celebrating a birthday.

Unfazed, Joyce continued, "You left a beautiful wife behind."

"But the story is here…the East Coast," said Mac.

"It's everywhere. Where to next? Europe?"

"Plenty here to report on. I think of Texas and Helen, not necessarily in that order, every day. I'll go back. Celebrate the holidays."

"Not for Christmas you won't." A voice down the table had been listening.

"Why not, Harry?" asked Mac.

"Religious holidays and celebrations will be banned," Harry told him.

"Ridiculous. I don't believe that."

"True. Comes to Congress next week. Rubber stamp."

"I'll get that to Texas tonight for broadcast tomorrow," Mac assured him.

"Done. Comments sent," Harry Taylor replied. "I was on the Bergen when Mark spirited Marjorie into Texas. Wish I'd had a chance to discuss some of this with her then."

Mac nodded.

Harry moved to sit closer to Mac and Joyce. "It was interesting having research to do on the original writers and signatories. They didn't all agree, as we know, and their different approaches were rooted in what they knew. They wanted little to change. Across the Eastern States there were selectmen voted in by their fellow citizens. Eligible voters excluded slaves and women. Interesting that they thought of them in the same way, women and slaves. Remember, you had to travel to vote. The Constitution recognized this, arguably. The right to bear arms was expedient as there were no police or standing army. In England a landlord, in time of war, was expected to bring his serfs and arm them. England sent German mercenaries to do their fighting in another curious twist of history. Were the writers of the Constitution going to provide arms? Were the selectmen? It was not expected that slaves and women had the right to bear arms. Arms were muzzle loaders; not automatic assault rifles or guided missiles or computer driven drones. Follow?"

"Yes, professor. Now tell the NRA," said Mac.

"Do you suppose they've been infiltrated too?" asked Joyce. "I find it stunning that the NRA still hasn't issued comment on the pronouncement from the candidate in Iowa. And, speaking of Iowa, how does it stand?"

"Close. The president visited and gave all sorts of promises. He gave support to his candidate, saying he was inexperienced but a great American," said Mac. "He said that he agreed with his candidate that gun legislation was needed for a country which had hundreds of gun related deaths and thousands of shootings every day."

"Clever," Joyce acknowledged.

Mac continued. "It was noted that he was careful not to be seen at rallies or speeches with Rahman. The photo op was at a TV studio as they were passing."

"I watched that," said Harry, "The president was sparse with his comments, mostly assuming that he had five more years to get used to it. Abid Rahman looked as though he was under the influence of something."

"Probably was. It's in his past," said Mac.

"The message that Al Adana gave was basically 'I am in for the next five years. Vote for my boy or there will be consequences.'" Harry frowned as he said this.

"So Mac...." Joyce was changing the subject a little, "if the story is in Iowa, why'd you leave there?"

Mac was non-plussed and thought for a while. Could he admit that it was fear? He quietly reflected. The Washington machine was moving into Iowa. He might have been recognized or he might give reasons to be arrested or he may have retaliated against the politics that changed his life.

"I don't know. Stories are everywhere," he finally mumbled. Then he stood and left the room.

## Chapter Twenty-Three

Joyce was right. The story was in Iowa.

Mac was in New York, writing other stories. Helen was in Texas, working hard on the stories from around the country – encouraging, cajoling, threatening – trying to keep a sense of humor and a sense of objectivity.

The day to day facts showed a disapproval of government policies, a break down in law and order, a country spiraling out of the wealthy nation of workers into an unemployed 'third-world' country. As Mac wrote these words, he stopped. It was time for a reality check. What gave him a right to criticize and categorize countries as 'third world'? What did that mean? Though everyone knew to whom and what the definition referred.

Mac looked out his hotel window and thought that the democratic countries were all successful, had all been successful. Was it past tense? There were signs in many countries of a strong leaning right or left. Were autocracies the new wave? Benjamin Franklin had doubted that Democracies could survive. A two-party system would seek votes in the middle ground, look like each other, with indistinguishable policies. Then the people would look to a strong leader on the left or on the right. In South Africa the autocratic, with the wealth, held down a poor nation. The oppressed knew nothing else but poverty and were happy. Or were they?

It was too much to consider. He decided he'd better stick to reporting. But, if people were better off when ignorant and happy, then why not find a place to be with Helen? His thoughts were interrupted by a loud knocking.

"Time to go, Mr. McDougal," a policeman called through the door.

Mac quietly rose and looked through the peephole. "Wrong room," he responded.

"There's a federal warrant for your arrest. We need to get you out of here."

"I'll check."

"No time, Mr. McDougal."

"Why trust you?"

"Time to go!"

"Let me get my wallet and passport. Be right with you."

Mac went into the bedroom. Closing the door, he opened the bathroom window then hid behind the bedroom door. The policeman walked in, saw the bathroom window open and went to look as Mac scampered out of the bedroom and the hotel. He was paranoid, and he knew it. But then he remembered the expression: 'Just because someone is paranoid did not mean that someone was not out to get him.'

Safety first, he decided and headed to the lobby where there were people. He took the stairs, slowly opened the door halfway, and slipped out. Nothing extraordinary. The front desk was quiet, one of the two employees was on the telephone. The bellhop was reading the sports section of the newspaper.

Mac watched as the police officer came out of the elevator, then Mac went back through the door and back to his room. It was hopefully the last place anyone would look. He was confused and needed answers. There were few people he trusted. He looked at his cell phone as if the answer was there. It was, but he needed something else – proximity.

"Hello."

"Can you meet me M at minus twenty-four?"

A hesitation as the message was being interpreted. "Sure. A problem?"

"Maybe."

The whole thing had taken ten seconds. Now he had to get to Mario's as soon as possible. It was a gathering place for the Sons of Liberty, and Papillon, the New York leader, had agreed to meet with him. Harry Taylor, a professor of Political Theory at Columbia, was arguably the most important member of the American Party team outside of Texas. Mac knew Harry was careful and would know how to handle the crisis.

After a careful reconnaissance by both Mac and Harry, they were seated at the rear of the restaurant with coffee.

Mac related his morning visit and his reaction.

"It's what keeps us alive," said Harry. "Did you get a badge number?"

"Who's looking for badge numbers?" asked Mac.

"We do, ever since the attempt on the mayor's life last year. We look at badge numbers."

"So who? Is there a federal warrant? Would we know?"

"I don't know who. There is a federal warrant. It hasn't ever stopped existing. But I'm not aware that it was to be served. The feds pretty much leave New Yorkers alone. I can check with Joyce though. She knows who can be trusted in the NYPD."

"Time I left New York anyway." It had been Mac's intention, even before the morning excitement. There was still the uncertainty as to whether the threat was real or not. When you lived in a world of facts, evidence, proof, how could you accept a maybe conclusion? It was probably like faith: you accepted or not. "Marjorie get back to you on the new Constitution?"

"Yes. We're still ironing some things out. It's interesting the new challenges from the $21^{st}$ century. It's not a question, for me, how the writers in 1776 may have made mistakes as much as my fascination with how they got so many things right. Freedom of speech, religion, the right to be left in peace. We don't require people to wear crosses if Christian, Star of David if Jewish, Crescent Moon if Muslim, or…." Harry paused not wanting to leave anyone out.

"Ostrich if Atheist," Mac interrupted.

Harry laughed. "We may have been the first country to adopt these rights of freedom."

"And now?" asked Mac.

"You know your history. All empires fall."

"I thought we were different."

"So did everyone else – from Caesar to Hitler, Genghis Khan to Stalin," said Harry with a smile. He was in his lecture role, on his podium. "Remember, Benjamin Franklin said that Democracy could not last."

"You said that earlier. He was referring to a two-party system and referenced the amalgamation of ideas as being necessary to be elected," said Mac.

"Yes, he knew that there would be appeasement, complacency, a popularity contest."

"But did he know about the corruption?"

"Probably. That's not new."

"Now I'm depressed." Mac was thinking and quiet.

"Remember, to paraphrase someone else who was ahead of his time, 'It was the best of times, it was the worst of times.' That is as true now as it was then."

"Thanks, Harry. The start of the French Revolution, lots of bloodshed, and the beginning of my next newsletter. No question: time for me to go." Mac stood.

"Do you need help?"

"Yes, back to Texas. Somebody very important is waiting there for me."

"Okay. Call your hotel and have a maid pack your bag and leave it with the bellman. I'll have a taxi driver I know pick it up and we'll get it to you."

"Without anyone knowing?"

"Without anyone knowing."

"How?"

"You want to know?" Harry shook his head, paused. "We'll change out the name on your bags, then they'll go to Kennedy the next time he goes there, be dropped at a freight forwarder, and shipped to Texas. You'll receive a text that they are there. TSA may have been all over them, shipped without a passenger, but the freight forwarder is a legitimate, trusted transporter."

"And me?"

"Out of Newark. While someone watches your bags, you can buy a ticket and ship out. Let's check the schedule and timing."

"Second thought, can you ship to Iowa?"

"Sure."

The decision was made, just like that. Mac hadn't thought what he wanted to do next. Part of him wanted to go to Boston, then to New Hampshire. Mostly he wanted to go back to Texas, to Helen. He knew that she was worried about him. And there were other reasons for him to go there. Texas was the hub, where it was all happening. No, he was wrong. It was the hub, but everything was happening in Iowa, New York, Massachusetts, and California, in the rest of the United States.

\*\*\*

Iowa was in a chaotic state on every level. Mac was briefed by Mark on the way from the airport. A meeting had been scheduled and postponed in order for him to attend.

The room was full when he arrived and was loud from separate arguments. Joe Polivar was shouting at his campaign manager, David Hamilton. A woman called June was gesticulating to another staffer over something which had either not been done or not done fast enough. Margaret Forrest was taking verbal abuse from an older, heavier man, who instantly turned on Mark when he entered. Other staff were in angry, combative mode. Mac saw Ike, who seemed to be floating, making sure that no one was seriously hurt.

"Ike, what is this?"

"They're scared boss."

"Of what?"

"Everything. You'll see. Someone needs to take control."

"Me?" Mac asked.

"Uh, uh."

Mac found a chair, stood on it, and shouted, "Excuse me!"

When the room quieted, he said loudly, "Excuse me! Can we have a productive meeting? All staffers out. David, can you see that we have a point of order? And do you have an agenda?"

There was a return to the earlier cacophony, but

now it was directed against Mac. The level subsided as David Hamilton pushed some people from the room.

Everyone sat. Mac looked at Joe Polivar who sat at one end, then at his chief of staff at the other. Mac still standing needed to correct something right away.

"Joe, David, sit here in the middle. Mark and I will sit opposite. Margaret at the end. And, June, is it?"

"Yes, sir. Public relations," she spoke quietly unlike two minutes previously.

"Good, the other end of the table. Would you please take notes?"

"I want to know right now." The big man, who had been harassing Margaret, was on his feet. Red faced and angry, he was shouting and gesticulating at Mac.

"And you are?" Mac asked in a quieter voice.

"Tom Tobin, and..."

"And why are you here?"

The man looked startled by the question.

David Hamilton leaned toward Mac. "Contributor. He's on the agenda."

"Good," said Mac. "Sit next to Margaret, apologize for your bad behavior, and we can get started."

"I need to…" Joe Polivar looked like a deer in the headlights. "I need security, some authority."

"What's first on the agenda?" Mac could sense a retreat, a lack of confidence. It was palpable, and he feared it could be contagious.

"Polls," said David Hamilton, glad the conversation was back on track. "June?"

"Down again; not good with one week to go. Joe has 34% to 42% with 24% on the sidelines."

"Margin of error?" Mark asked.

"Four percent, I think. This election feels different," June said.

"You mean people are lying?"

"Likely. We need a big final push." June, although still young, looked tired and sat back in her chair.

David Hamilton took up his agenda and put it down with a resigned thwack. "The Democrats received a huge fillip with the president's visit. Since then the poll numbers have been down, contributions are down, and more of us have been subjected to verbal and physical abuse." He looked from Tom Tobin to Joe Polivar, then brought his gaze back to Mac.

"I want to know?" Tom Tobin was again shouting.

"Please, Tom." David Hamilton had heard it before. "If Ellie Mae Joseph could come to Iowa, she would."

Mac reached over and took the agenda, pulling it across the table. He scanned the headings – security, finances, speeches, dirty tricks, election day, other. Under 'other' was Tom Tobin.

"Security. Ike will sit with Joe and David. Finances, David meet with Mark and Margaret. Speeches, Joe coordinate with June. Let's speak with one mind. Connect with Sheila Hutchins in Texas. These other things, David, we can take a little further. Mr. Tobin, thank you for your contributions and your support. Thank you for your patience. How can we help?"

"Thank you for bringing order to our world." He was solicitous – maybe fake, maybe not. "After hearing and seeing for myself the last hour, I'm not sure that I should even continue. But I'm a businessman, and my business is being destroyed by the current administration. I had hoped that we could make a difference."

"We can and we will, even if only by bringing

attention to the problems that you and thousands of businessmen like you are facing, dealing with every day." This was not a typically Mac statement, but he realized that they needed the Tom Tobin's of the country on the side of the American Party.

"I've offered to put together a group for a dinner party at my house. A fundraiser, fifty people, ten thousand a plate. I was told…no, I was promised, a very important guest speaker." He stopped and looked at the few in the room before coming back to Mac. "And now it is to be Joe Polivar. I'm not suggesting that Joe isn't important, but with the polls as they are, he may be 'yesterday's newspaper' by next week."

"Who would you figure an important guest?"

"Well, either Ellie May Joseph or Marjorie White would be interesting. Even the governor would be worthwhile."

"We tried to get the governor," Mark interceded. "He chickened out last week right after the president's visit."

"I have a thought," said Mac. "Tom, I need a table plan. Leave one seat empty next to yourself and Joe at the head of the table. Let your guests know that the American Party will deliver and, to make sure they can, I personally promise that you will have an exciting evening."

Fortunately, for Mac, no one saw his fingers crossed under the table.

The rest of the meeting focused on the dirty tricks. Some election officials had been threatened. Since only a few had come forward, it was assumed that there were more. The ones who had provided the information on threats had, mostly, resigned. The attorney general had stated at the press conference that such interference was illegal. No arrests resulted. The candidate's family had been threatened. The death of the daughter's dog was suspicious, but no one was prosecuted. There had been a rise in voter registrations and random verifications had shown that ninety percent were phony. Phony names, phony addresses, and phony proof of citizenship. The number of requests for mail ballots increased tenfold. There were so many loopholes, plugging them seemed to be like holding back the dam.

Mac listened for over an hour and then interrupted.

"Remember, you need one more vote than the opposition. We need to either get the votes or identify illegal votes. Set up two teams – one to do each, then go. There isn't enough time left to discuss it. I have to line up something for the Tobins."

\*\*\*

The tension grew. In forty-eight hours, Mac had promised contributors that the American Party would deliver. It was more important than the million dollars that might be raised from the dinner guests and their friends. It was the access that these guests would open for this race and the presidential election.

The crew from Austin, Texas, included Henry Forrest, who was pleased to see his sister, even if only for a couple of days. He and the other two technicians were busy placing cameras and projectors in places around the dining room. Caterers and florists worked around the wires, and testing was limited to the hour before the dinner was scheduled. Tom Tobin was a wreck and sweating profusely. His wife Gerry was worse. Her voice rose with her nerves, and she had a snappy negative remark to everyone.

Mac had been invited, along with Mark and Margaret, to the cocktail hour. Ike would also be there in tuxedo and black tie.

"Mr. McDougal, this is going to be the most embarrassing night of my life." Gerry Tobin was a little younger than her husband, with a confidence of her position as a wealthy scion of Iowa.

"Please call me Mac. And I think that everything, now under control, means that you can dress for dinner."

"Mr., sorry, Mac, everything is out of control. I have no idea who these people are in my house...wearing blue jeans, sweatshirts..."

"Give them two hours. They'll be ready by the time your guests arrive. I think I saw your hairdresser come in a few moments ago," said Mac conciliatorily.

"Hair." Her hands instantly went to her head. She turned to go, then, as she passed Henry, "Oh, my god!" as though he represented everything that was wrong this day.

Mac wondered if it was the blue jeans, sweatshirt, sneakers, and Dallas Cowboys hat on backwards. Or perhaps it was his radiant smile.

The test of the equipment was a 'power on' demonstration. Helen had agreed to 'stand in' for the transmission, and Mac volunteered to test the output.

"Ready? Quiet everyone." Mac sat where Tom Tobin would sit next to the empty chair. The projector came on and Helen appeared to be sitting in the empty chair.

"Lighting. Check the lighting. That door must be closed. The drapes will be closed, and it will be dark outside, so close the drapes and put on the lights. No, no lights at the back. And dim those at the front. Candles are okay." There was a bustle as everything was changed.

"Helen, how's your view?"

"Good, but maybe not so dim at the end of the

table. It's a long way from here."

"Okay, one thing. There was a 'scratch' earlier. Mr. and Mrs. Sobotka cancelled – scared off maybe. So everyone to your right will move up. Mark and the Tobin's daughter will make up the numbers. Ready for a preview?" Turn to your left as if talking to the host and speak."

"Hi, Mac. It's me, Helen. When are you coming home?"

"Where is home these days?"

"Where the heart is," said Helen.

"Then I'll be in Texas soon."

The director said, "Good. Mac move further down. Helen pick him up and converse."

"Mr. Perry, you had a question?"

"You can call me Joe, Sugar," said Mac.

"And you can call me Mrs. Sugar, Joe," said Helen.

As everyone laughed, Helen picked out Henry at the end of the table. "That you, Henry? How is everything?"

"Fine, thank you, ma-am."

"I told you, no mams. It makes me feel old."

"Okay, Mrs. Ma-am."

It was obvious they were successful, as everyone had forgotten that they were talking to an image in Texas. The director tested for another thirty minutes before announcing it could work.

"Tidy up those loose wires. Everyone, get into a tux. Cocktails will be ready for the guests in half an hour, and we need to be too."

Everyone left Mac looking at the chair, which was empty again. "Time to go home," he said aloud.

## Chapter Twenty-Four

The cocktails were served starting at six-thirty. It was a very restrained group of people who met, and even the excellent wine and champagne could not break the edge.

Gerry Tobin was the source of the edge, as she worried and flitted among the guest groups. It was a political fundraiser, and so the topic was chosen with the occasional reference to business.

The presence of Mac was well known from his television coverage and many thought him to be the guest of honor.

Mark, formerly a political activist, was quickly in his stride, orchestrating conversations, introducing Joe Polivar and his wife, Yvonne, then moving seamlessly to the next group where he introduced Margaret to talk about finances. She quickly followed his lead.

Ike stood by the door, amazed at the scene. He admired the way Margaret looked in the dress, simple black with white belt and pearls, bought for the occasion. She looked as though she belonged. His eyes were also on the staff delivering the hors d'oeuvres. He had a lot of responsibility tonight – from the people parking the cars to the kitchen and the wait staff. He knew there was a police patrol car in the street, but they would be too late if anyone targeted this prominent gathering.

Henry, though slightly uncomfortable in formal dress, couldn't help walking by the gathering in his rented tuxedo. It was agreed that the technicians would try to blend in. Pulling his bow tie, he looked at his sister. He wasn't sure what she did exactly, but she seemed to be at ease in this group.

At seven-thirty people were being ushered into the dining room. Mark was pleased to note that he had met and spoken to every guest. He called Texas and quickly summarized the hopes and fears of the assembled group.

Ellie May and Helen worked feverishly on the names, to include them in the opening remarks. Everyone had to believe that their personal concerns were the most important concerns of the American Party. Everyone was finally seated ten minutes later as Tom Tobin stood to welcome them. His wife was tearing her napkin beneath the table.

"Friends and neighbors, welcome. This fundraiser for the campaign of Joe Polivar and the American Party is a first because of our guest. I am as anxious as you to hear what's in store for us."

There was a little shuffling and a few whispers.

"So let me please introduce the founder of the American Party and our next president of the United States, Ellie May Joseph."

Like magic, to gasps from the guests, Ellie May appeared in the chair. There was a smattering of applause led by Tom Tobin, who then sat.

Ellie May stood and placed a few notes in front of her.

"I want first to thank Tom and Gerry for inviting me into their home." She turned and smiled at the couple who responded with a tilt of the head, unsure how to address a compliment in Des Moines from someone in Texas.

"I'm inviting them to be among the first to be welcomed in the big house in Washington when we get there next year."

Ellie May then covered all of the topics talked out in the cocktail hour, singling the concerned guest with a hand gesture or inclination of the head. It was obvious that everyone was impressed and empowered by their inclusion. After about ten minutes she announced that she would remain for the meal and that Joe Polivar would speak before the main course. She was available after the main course and before dessert to answer questions, but, right now, soup was about to be served and salad.

The guests were impressed and began to speak among themselves.

Gerry Tobin was flattered and pleased when the three-dimensional guest leaned over and quietly complimented her dress.

Tom Tobin had promised that he had a surprise guest and had been perplexed and appalled by the intrusion of technicians. Even he had expected that Mac, the most recognized person in the room, would speak. That an announced candidate for the presidency should appear, albeit by satellite, was certainly something to be remembered.

Joe Polivar gave the best speech of his campaign. He was no doubt in awe of his company and reacted to Ellie May's confidence in his election and her assertion that she would be relying on him once he was in Washington. She made everyone, including Yvonne Polivar, believe that he would win with the support of those in the room. All this, as she introduced him before the main course.

During the question period, most referred to

personal issues that were surfacing in their particular businesses. Ellie May answered questions on inflation, supply, infrastructure, and cost of labor. The hardest questions came from the CEO of a large non-profit medical facility. His first question was on gun control, and Ellie May agreed that it was in her manifesto. She successfully side-stepped a definitive 'take it or leave it' stance as it was too early in the campaign. The second question was on the source of her funding. Mark and Mac locked eyes across the room, mentally remembering the guest, Quentin Somerby, small with a goatee beard. Ellie May stated that his and everyone's contributions would be confidential, that she and the Democrat's nominee expected to be the current president, would file returns as appropriate, and that she expected them to be similar.

Quentin persisted. "The election could cost three billion dollars. Does the American Party have the staying power?"

"Elections can cost either party that much, and, yes, I am confident that we can reach the finish line. I will personally write and deliver pamphlets if I have to."

"Where is your fund now? Who are your backers?"

"I will have one of my accountants speak with you after dinner. The questions you have may be of a personal nature, and I'm sure that they can help. If not, they will give you a number to call me directly.

"Thank you for the gentle reminder that political contests cost money. Please support your candidate Joe Polivar with your time and money. Thank you again, Tom and Gerry. I look forward to seeing you all very soon. Goodnight."

The image of Ellie May stood, walked away, seemingly out of the room, to loud applause.

"I suppose I should talk with Quentin." Mark had sought out Mac as soon as the party left the dining room for the after-dinner drinks and coffee.

"Do you think he's a spy, a plant?" asked Mac.

"Could be, or just someone skeptical."

"Or someone who likes to back only winners," agreed Mac, rounding out the possibilities. "Send Margaret. That will cause him to show his colors."

"How?"

"If he's working for the opposition, he'll dismiss a woman. She's familiar with the finances, is very bright, has shown her loyalty."

"And knows just enough to be dangerous," finished Mark, not entirely convinced.

"I'll keep an eye on them while you make sure that Joe and Tom get pledges from this well-heeled crowd."

Moments later, after Margaret had been briefed by Mark, she approached Quentin Sowerby with some trepidation. This job was much more challenging than she'd expected. 'I look good,' she reminded herself, and briefly thought of the looks and comments if she had shown up to the Friday dance in Louisiana in a backless long black dress with pearls over a modest neckline. She was now smiling.

"Mr. Sowerby, my name is Mary Wilson. I'm an accountant with the American Party. Ellie May has asked that I talk with you and answer any questions you might have." Margaret had automatically used the name on her travel documents.

"Ms. Wilson," Quentin passed his first test and was not surprised that a woman was the source contact. "You're a little young…"

"We're a young party." Her hand swept the room of young volunteers, slowing as she included Ike and her brother Henry.

Quentin was genuinely interested in how a party could get started and bring in funds. It was obvious after a while that he was in the fundraising business for his non-profit. Margaret advised that he find a guarantor and then pay attention to his expenses. He was satisfied and enchanted.

Ike looked less pleased.

"Not him, Mac," Mark said confidently.

"Well, it is someone." Mac turned toward his friend. "I was going to be in New Hampshire this week. A lot of American Party supporters were detained in Concord and Laconia, New Hampshire, and questioned about my itinerary."

"How did they know? How do you know?"

"An older acquaintance from Laconia, former Senator JR, called the number I gave to him. So the question would be, who told them. Everyone in New Hampshire still believed me dead."

"We'll have Ike investigate."

"No, that's a waste of time and resources. There is more than one person. This should just remind us again to be vigilant."

"We'll have Ike sweep the office."

"Yes, at the very least it will let people know that we're looking, that we are vigilant."

"Tonight was a success. We have several people offering to host dinners, lunches, breakfasts, meetings, for the primary and presidential ticket. More exposure more money, more party members." Mark was happy. It was like throwing a pebble into a pool – the ripples would reach out to consume, growing, expanding.

Mac, the pragmatist, was thinking that there was a long, long way to go.

\*\*\*

Election Day was a mess. Chaotic, confusing, contradictory. There was good, there was bad, there was very good, and very, very bad – sometimes at the same time.

Joe Polivar worked hard, as if it was his last day on Earth, which was close, when he had to be rescued by the police from a gang at one of the poll stations. He, surrounded by police officers, shook everyone's hand until the gang left, looking for easier pickings.

Mark manned the telephones while David Hamilton and his dedicated group of volunteers organized rides to the polls and fielded stories of intimidation, both physical and mental abuse.

Margaret wanted to be everywhere, which suited Ike who, armed with a list of polling stations and a reliable GPS system, drove by as many as he could during the hours they were open.

Mac sat and recorded the abuses as they happened. He was surprised that six John Wayne's and only three George Washington's had been refused ballot papers. The voting officials said that the limited vocabulary, or gang-based jingoism, had been the 'tip off.'

Proponents had decried the refusal of 'right to vote without documentation' practiced by those voting officials. Intimidation appeared to be the basic tool of the militia supporting Abid Rahman. Police had reported repeated attempts to infringe on voting location property in contravention of the law limiting them to the public pavement, voting signs and promotion.

There were fights and clashes with officials instigated by the militia. Militia members, entering voting premises with weapons, were arrested or ejected. The turnout was at historic lows as voters stayed home or turned around after seeing a melee.

The mood at the American Party headquarters was tense. Those staffers not in the field were busy or kept themselves busy. Phones were ringing, mostly asking about voting, many about their harassment ordeal. Mac had some of these calls directed to him, looking for a pattern, looking for a theme. If there was a theme, it was 'I'm right, so do as I say.' There was a brash confidence about the opposition. Unfortunately, for them, the average American does not follow a mantra, hates to be told what to think or do, and will therefore, given the choice, vote the other way.

Something there to remember when I write, thought Mac.

The balloting was all electronic. The ballot boxes, with evidence of the count, were escorted to the attorney general's office. Transportation escort was by police after the boxes were piled into the back of a police SUV. In some cases the militia had been able to forcibly take over the role and, without exception, had tampered with the contents. A re-count was going to be contentious or impossible. The results were in. Joe Polivar was elected by a narrow margin. The Democratic Party filed in court next morning for a re-count. The attorney general of Iowa denied the filing on the grounds of insufficient evidence and on the grounds that there had been tampering with the boxes. He ordered the arrest of the militia transporting those boxes which had been identified.

In an amazing reversal, the militia arrested were released by the attorney general of the United States on the grounds that voter fraud was a federal, not a state, offence. Also no evidence had shown that the boxes had not been violated prior to transportation. This decision was in spite of the seals attached and signed at the voting precinct. The attorney general of

Iowa was asked to resign. His answer was apparently unprintable but assumed to be negative.

The success in Iowa was isolated. Sadly the violence and offences were not. But there were gains and signs for optimism.

In the aftermath of the Iowa vote, Abid Rahman was found dead a week later. The official cause stated was a heroin overdose. Suspicion and rumor said otherwise, but neither party had proof. The police didn't spend a lot of time on the case, and the coroner ruling was quiet and unequivocal.

Two American Party headquarters in Illinois and Kentucky were attacked by bombs delivered by drones. Ike went to investigate since Margaret Forrest was sent to assess and to secure the finances. Ike concluded that the bombs were identical to the one which injured Betty Jo in Texas and killed her passengers. The bombs appeared to be military grade lightweight. The drones could only carry two pounds over a short distance. The drones were available at any large store. Walmart or Target, probably due to the stock and there was no verifiable address, if bought for cash. The trigger acted like a grenade and was simple.

Ike found some remains from the explosives had been saved. Mark directed him to a defense manufacturer with a vested interest in the American Party. The defense corporation passed the metal through their laboratory and identified the manufacturer.

The Federal Bureau of Investigation reviewed the evidence, interviewed witnesses, studied the externally prepared, independent reports, and made a finding. They found that the American Party volunteers killed in the explosion had been manufacturing bombs and had an accident. Case closed.

"That was a waste of time." Mark was despondent.

"It is certainly frustrating," agreed Mac. "That is why we do what we do."

"What is that? Bang our heads against a wall?"

"No. Fighting back with the truth," said Mac looking up from a newsletter he was preparing. "I'm going to put the evidence directly in front of the supporters of the American Party."

"Isn't that preaching to the choir? Our supporters, I hope, would understand that we are not manufacturing bombs."

"It doesn't help that the missiles came from one of our supporters."

"Don't start on that," said Mark defensively.

"So I shouldn't ask the question that everyone wants answered? I shouldn't answer that question? I shouldn't waste my time?"

"I'm sorry, Mac. I'm so tired."

"Then go spend Christmas with your brother. He's in Michigan, isn't he?"

"Yes, I haven't seen him since…" Mark stood rocking, thinking. "But who would…" He was interrupted.

"The graveyard is full of indispensable people," said Mac.

"I'll think about it."

"No. Do it. Primary season starts in January. We do *not* need tired people making decisions."

"Okay, Mac. You're probably right. I can spend a few days briefing my staff, then leave and be back end of December."

"And remember to be careful out there."

They both smiled with remembering the old line.

## Chapter Twenty-Five

"Mac, is this true?" Ellie Mae was frowning at the draft newsletter. She liked to add a comment to the final document to show she agreed and supported the information.

"Yes, the bombs in Illinois and Kentucky, and the one here in Texas, were all manufactured by one of our sponsors. They are military grade, lightweight, streamlined grenades, and they can be launched, or thrown, or dropped."

"Do they know who they were sold to?"

"Apparently they're new and have only been sold to the military."

"Our military? Our military bombed us?"

"Well, not exactly. The shipment has been identified. It was destined for the Middle East. When troops were recalled, the shipment sat on the dock in New Jersey. Troops and others coming back had been impressed with the product. Six months ago the shipment went from New Jersey to the armory in Washington."

"The militia headquarters."

"Yup! Your old friend."

"What can we do?" Helen asked.

"We can go public with that info," said Sheila.

"Unfortunately, we can't." Mac was speaking calmly in this emotionally charged room. "One, they would move the inventory. Two, deny. Three, blame the Sons of Liberty and accuse the American Party of fabrication and sedition." He had lost count of the number of reasons.

"What then?" pressed Helen. "Let them keep dropping them on innocent people, wait until they lob them into the meeting."

"No. I have an idea that the stockpile could be destroyed."

"Won't they order more?" asked Ellie May.

"Probably, and they can hide the purchase by use of third parties. But we would know who, where, when, and how."

"How?" Ellie May wondered aloud. She held up her hand almost immediately. "Don't tell me. I do not want to know."

"Wise, very wise," Mac agreed. "I'll have to go to Washington."

Helen looked up sharply, her body language asking questions.

"I'll be back for Christmas. Save me a drumstick," Mac spoke flippantly.

Helen answered by walking out of the room.

Mac caught up with her as she stood on the patio.

"I'm sorry. But if we don't, who will?"

"You want to be a boy scout, go ahead. Mac, Washington is a dangerous place for any of us. For you, it's a death sentence. For the people you're meeting, it's asking more than they signed on for."

"I am not asking anyone to do what I would not do myself. The French followed Joan-of-Arc, and she was a woman."

"Be serious. And that was not even funny. She was burned to death."

"Helen, if we do nothing, how are you going to

recruit for election campaign headquarters? If the party has one more 'accident,' how many volunteers will you have? Primaries start in earnest in January. You have to start finding locations and staff soon. What will you say when they ask how safe it is?"

"Mac," she laid a hand on his arm, "I know those are all valid arguments, but why you? I need you – your support, your strength, your counsel."

"Save me a drumstick. In January we will go to New Hampshire together and help win the state and plant seeds for the rest of the Northeast. I think we will be good in the Iowa caucus."

"How did you turn the conversation around?" Helen smiled thinly. "You are impossible."

"I take that as a compliment. I have always strived for 'impossible.'"

"Back to work."

They returned inside the house.

Mac sat at his desk, pushed the laptop computer aside, and pulled out a paper scrap and a pencil. In thirty minutes he had notes in several columns – transport, people, weapons, intel, timetable.

Looking at the list of names, he pulled forward his computer and sent the same message to three people. 'Call me.'

The first call came almost immediately. A guarded voice answered, "Yes?"

"You responded quickly."

"Sitting, waiting for a program to run."

"Have you time to help me out?"

"As soon as this download is complete."

"I want you to come out to the ranch."

"When?"

"ASAP."

"Not sure I like ASAP, but hey, my curiosity and

since you helped smooth my way out of Washington, be there in an hour. The download can finish while I'm in the car."

Mac called Bobby Joe. "Can you give me some time in about an hour?"

"Not much. I have to take Betty Jo for her daily walk on her new feet."

"How's she doing?"

"Unbelievable, but don't tell anyone. She wants to surprise them at Christmas."

Mac was informed that Martin Konrad was coming through the gate just as the telephone rang. He recognized the number.

"Can you call again from a secure line in five minutes?"

"Sure." Ginny Hutchins knew enough now that she didn't say his name.

Martin and Bobby Joe were both seated when the phone rang again. Mac held up his finger to silence them then answered on speaker.

"Ginny, can we get some intel from the satellites?"

"Like what?"

"A view of a building in Washington."

"Snapshot or real time?"

"Both."

I can get snapshot Satellite at five miles a second. For real time you'll need someone else's satellite."

"Easy to get?"

"If you can 'hack' in."

Martin Konrad nodded in the background.

"I have someone to do that."

"Have them ask for me at the desk. Astrophysical lab downtown. What building do you want? The White House?"

"No, the Armory."

"My pleasure. See you at Christmas, God willing."

"Amen," said Mac as he hung up.

"What on earth is that about?" asked Bobby Joe. "You know that the Armory is National Militia headquarters?"

"That's the reason you're both here," said Mac. "First, Martin, can you get me the intel that I asked for, from Ginny Hutchings. Secondly, can you hack into the Armory phone and computer system?"

"Number one, yes. Number two, probably."

"Why am I here listening to something that might be illegal. I may not now be a Texas Ranger, but as security head for a presidential hopeful, I have some moral responsibility to follow the law." Bobby Joe was clearly uncomfortable.

"This is about saving lives and protecting the law. Last I checked, the government using weapons to kill law-abiding citizens was illegal. The reason the information is needed is to confirm, if we can, that the militia is storing bombs from the same shipment that killed volunteers and our colleagues in Kentucky, Illinois, and here in Texas. We need to know if they are stored in that building."

"Same as the one that injured and nearly killed Betty Jo?"

Mac nodded.

Bobby Joe continued, "Then let's nuke 'em, the bastards."

"What happened to the moral indignation and due process?"

"That was before you told me."

"I want to have some proof before we act," said Mac.

"Act? Like ask them not to do it or act like blow

them to hell?"

"Now you have come to why I asked you both here. Are you willing to help?"

"Mac, you can count on me for anything. Let me go take Betty Jo for a walk, think some, then come back. Okay?"

"Thanks, Bobby Joe. Not a word, not even to Betty Jo."

As Martin Konrad stood to say goodbye to Bobby Joe, Mac mused at the pair. Both were about six-foot-four, both about two hundred pounds. The similarity ended there. Bobby Joe was a tough cop, a former football player who ate hard and ran ten miles a day. Martin had been a swimmer at college, ate foods that were healthy, swam for exercise, and would spend all night working on computer problems for clients. Mac wondered who was more dangerous in this new age.

"What I need to know from the satellite is any patterns of movement, how many ways of getting in and out of the building. The layout would be helpful, particularly if there are shipments in and out. Guard schedules and anything else you can tell me about the traffic, people, goods, telephone, emails, pigeons, anything."

"When?"

"Yesterday."

"Some things never change," said Martin laughing.

"A week, but then you have to bring it to D.C. Any problem with that?" asked Mac.

"If you're going to be there and it's no problem to you, then I will be there."

"Thanks, Martin."

"Better get started. A week isn't long."

After seeing Martin out, Mac called Edsel in Chicago. After a quick catch up, the conversation turned to the bombs in the campaign headquarters.

"So, what can we do apart from be vigilant?" asked Edsel.

"We think that we know where they're being stored," said Mac.

"So expose them."

"They'd be gone before anyone credible could look."

"Good point." Edsel was quiet. "Then what, we just hope we're lucky? Russian roulette with bombs?"

"We can't ask our supporters to do that. As a matter of fact, we would have no supporters, no volunteers, no candidates."

"So they have us." It was a statement of resignation.

"Not on your life. Can you bring four or five good people to Washington in about ten days?"

"For how long?"

"Two, maybe three days. I think that's all we can get cover for."

"Any skills?"

"Not really. Reliable, loyal, brave. It may get hairy."

"What are we doing?"

"Haven't decided yet."

"Hah!" There was a large garumph over the phone line. "Bring five people to Washington for a dangerous mission related to the disposition of bombs; but we don't know how. Have I got that right?"

"Yeah, I think so," said Mac.

A long silence. "All right. Let me know when and where."

Mac sat looking at the silent phone, picturing the very large African American with faith; faith in him, Mathew McDougal. Who the hell was he to ask for this? He reached for the phone to withdraw the request but halted. It was, he decided, his responsibility to bring home everyone safely. He had better re-evaluate his options.

Bobby Joe Williams had quietly entered the room while he was lost in thought.

"Interrupting?"

"No, I was thinking negative thoughts. How's Betty Jo?"

"Good. She is one determined lady. She's talking about coming back; says they damaged her feet not her brain. Her sense of humor is returning too. She says lucky it wasn't me because ever since I started playing football my feet and brain are those two pieces of my anatomy which are interchangeable.

"Did I hear you talking to someone?"

"Yes, I called Edsel in Chicago."

"Have you met?"

"Last month. Substantial asset."

Bobby Joe nodded.

Mac continued. "We need intel. Martin will get us some. We can contact a source in Washington. Edsel will bring people, but we could use more from out of town. The people in DC should be sheltered, if we can, in case…"

"Think positive, Mac. Nothing will go wrong. We are smarter and stronger."

"Didn't football teach you anything? Or is Betty Jo right? Never, never underestimate an opponent."

"You're right. And she's always right. Sorry," he said with a laugh.

Mac realized that Bobby Joe did not look sorry.

"We need a plan. A good plan. As foolproof as we can make it."

"You mean that we can't take the building by

force, plant a timed charge to destroy the inventory, fight our way out, and disappear after a high-speed chase."

"No, this isn't Hollywood. Let's wait until tomorrow and meet with Martin, who should have some drawings, maps, and stuff. In the meantime I'll find someone in Washington to help with local knowledge and logistics. Can you see if you can find one or two small groups, in say, Pennsylvania, Kentucky, Maryland, and Virginia to meet in Washington ten days from now?"

"Sure thing."

\*\*\*

The next day, to everyone's surprise, Betty Jo joined with Bobby Joe, Mac, Martin, and Ginny in a meeting on the farm estate. Helen walked in and greeted everyone, then went to sit down.

"Whoa," said Mac. "You were not on the list of invites."

"When my husband is talking about doing something that may be stupid, may be illegal, I think that the chief of staff should know what is happening."

"Precisely why you were excluded. This is not a good meeting to be at. Deniability is a great thing for a chief of staff. We have no intention of being stupid or doing anything illegal, but in case we stray close, it's best you not know our plans."

"Hmm." Helen was reluctant but recognized some sense to Mac's argument. "I've been thrown out of better places."

Everyone laughed, which eased the tension in the room. Once Helen had closed the door behind her, the chairs were re-shuffled so that everyone was around the one end of a large conference table. Ginny produced a large drawing and some smaller pictures and maps.

"Do you know how big this place is?" asked Martin to Mac.

"No, how big?"

"Big!"

"Informative but of little use."

"It can be used as an arena – basketball, indoor soccer, concerts."

"Inaugural balls," Ginny interrupted.

"And National Guard Headquarters," continued Martin. Large and gentle, he seemed to have entered the spirit of adventure and challenge present at this meeting.

"Meaning it is impossible," offered Betty Jo.

"Meaning it is a challenge," said Bobby Joe, squeezing her hand. "Sorry, Mac. She invited herself when she heard me talking on the phone last night to a leader in Dover."

"Good to see you back on your feet." Mac stopped and blushed with embarrassment at his faux pas, "As it were," he finished lamely.

"I want to be involved in identifying the cowards who launched a bomb at me." Betty Jo was defiant.

"Note I didn't kick you out as I did my wife. The more the merrier, but the fewer that know the better."

"A frontal attack is out of the question then." Bobby Joe was the policeman in the group.

"Too many doors," Ginny said to nods.

"Then subterfuge. Is there an event in the next three weeks?"

"No, all events were cancelled when the militia took over and booted the National Guard," Ginny again spoke after a glance at Martin. It was clear that they had enjoyed working together.

"National Guard. Bobby Joe can you connect and

get us some inside knowledge. Not just the parts we see but the heating, sewage, power source, contractors, etc.?" Mac asked.

"I'll do that," volunteered Betty Jo. "Bobby Joe, he is busy enough."

"Thanks."

"Do they keep prisoners there?" asked Betty Jo.

"Good question. Ask your guardsman if he knows. And ask if we can get help, if necessary."

"Will do."

"Prisoners? There shouldn't be prisoners, should there?" asked Martin.

"There shouldn't be. Let's hope there aren't. Not only is it unconstitutional, it would present other problems."

"Even if they were detained illegally?"

"Especially if they were 'helping' the militia identify terrorists."

It took an hour but, by then, after eliminations there was a skeleton of a plan. Enter the building with some subterfuge, steal the weapons, free the prisoners, and leave Washington.

"Really?" asked Betty Jo incredulously.

"It needs some work," admitted Mac.

"We need a truck, probably two. We need to know the payload."

"My job," said Betty Jo.

"Let's co-ordinate everything through Betty Jo. Ginny, Martin, we'll need to infiltrate or jam the communications. Bobby Joe, you go back to work; Betty Jo will take good care of us, I'm sure."

\*\*\*

A week later there was very little more to add. The Sons of Liberty had promised people. It was difficult to limit them to three per group but easier to keep quiet and for three or four people to be away for a few days. It had been determined that there was a football game at RK Stadium, next door to the Armory, on Sunday, just ten days away. This was good and bad. There would be less regular traffic on the weekend but more traffic focused around the area.

Mac had memorized the maps. Augmented by his ten years of living in the capital, he came up with a plan which required three things. First, they needed to blend in. He asked if any of the volunteers who might have been Marines could arrange to bring and wear their uniforms. Second, they needed a way to move the weapons. Mac asked that the groups travel to Washington in U-Haul trucks. Third, they needed to obtain information on Marine personnel. Fourth, Mac thought to himself, they needed a lot of luck.

It was decided that Mac, Martin, and Ginny would head to Washington with Betty Jo acting as a liaison and focal conduit in Texas. Bobby Joe was affronted at being left out, but the argument that he was invaluable running security was finally accepted.

Mac's next step was just down the hallway where Marjorie White was putting together a speech for broadcast about some of the Constitutional issues. This was not yet the time to announce potential changes but a time to start conversations and review how the present and previous administrations had viewed the Constitution.

"Hi, Mac. What can I do for you?"

"Am I interrupting?"

"Yes, and I want to thank you for that. I needed a break." Marjorie White was dressed in blue jeans and a blue collared blouse. It was a change from all of the formal dresses and suits that had been her 'uniform' for so many years. In a way it also seemed to influence her demeanor. Her voice seemed to be more casual, her conversation less measured.

"How are the boys?"

"Great." she said smiling. "You see them almost as much as I do, and I'm sure they tell you more things than they tell me."

"They're good kids. I took them to the museum once in Washington and they think I'm cool." Mac smiled back at Marjorie. The relationship was deep-seated from before Helen went to work for Marjorie when Mac had been a political reporter. A rarity in Washington was a political reporter one could trust.

"I'm guessing you didn't stop to discuss the kids. You want something. Does it have to do with this secret project that everyone is whispering about? Is Mathew McDougal going to share that secret with me?"

"Yes, I need something, and no, I'm not going to tell you why. I need the name of the highest ranking Marine you know."

"I know General Weir; he was joint chief of staff until he resigned. I think he stayed on as director of something. I can call and see if you like."

"I need to meet with him at Marine headquarters in Washington next Wednesday or Thursday."

"Use your name?"

"No, his phone is likely compromised – say a representative of yours."

"Won't that raise a flag?"

"Probably, but I'll have Ginny and Martin with me. They'll have me hooked up."

"Done."

"Thanks, Marjorie."

## Chapter Twenty-Six

Plan Day arrived with the weather forecasting cloudy skies and a chance of rain or snow later.

It was impossible to persuade those members of the crew assembled, particularly those from southern states, that snow was not desirable. The assembly point, changed three times, was a small suite in one of the hotels used by the group. The meeting was scheduled for one-thirty. People were drifting in at one to find Ginny and Martin with computers checking CCTV footage and checking the room for surveillance, internal and external.

There'd been several meetings during the week where each group had been assigned to a particular task. No one except Mac knew the whole plan. Martin and Ginny probably guessed most of it.

The group was mostly fit, aged from eighteen to forty. There were three women, including Ginny, and eighteen men. By one-twenty, all were assembled with the exception of Edsel, Mac, and another man from Chicago.

"Where's Mac?" a nervous man from Baltimore asked Martin.

Martin shrugged.

"You don't know? What if we're 'blown' and stuck here."

"Grab some water and sit down. We're busy," said Ginny. In spite of being busy and assigned an important, dangerous role, she knew that getting anxious for no reason was unhelpful.

The man looked as though he would argue when Martin stood up. With six foot, four inches standing between him and Ginny, the man knew it was time for a tactical retreat.

"Sorry I'm late," Mac stated as he walked in the door. He was, in fact, just two minutes beyond the scheduled time. "I needed to run through the district one more time. Nothing appears to have changed. They're not expecting anything. There are more ways in and out than we safely have people to cover, so who was on the front door?"

A large African American raised a hand.

Mac nodded. "We'll have to use you elsewhere and leave the front to surveillance." Mac looked toward Martin who acknowledged the change.

"Okay. Everyone here?" Mac looked at Ginny who nodded. "Next, check communications. All of your cell phones should be vibrating, and you should all have a message. Let me know if that's not the case."

The eighteen-year-old raised a hand slowly.

"Bring it up," said Ginny. She gave him a new phone and plugged the dead one into her computer, then signaled Mac.

Mac turned angry. "What on earth possessed you to think that a pictorial essay of your week away to share with your friends was worth more than the lives of the people in this room?"

A man stood up.

"Mac, I'm sure…"

"Sure what? That he didn't think! That if caught, it was a scolding? That you, pictured here at the Lincoln

Memorial, could explain what you were doing in Washington when supposedly in Orlando?"

The young man's abject apology was drowned out when the door crashed open. "Did we miss anything?"

"Bobby Joe, Ike, Mark – what are you doing here?"

"Had the weekend, so we decided to do a little fishing," Bobby Joe said with a smirk.

"You're insane. This could be tough, and it's getting tougher by the minute."

"How can we help?"

"Ali, back on the front door. Ike stay with him, take out the guard, then join us here," Mac said, pointing to a blueprint. "Bobby Joe with me and then to watch this door. Mark, join the Delaware team on retrieval."

"Here, ladies and gentlemen, is the whole plan. We're going to steal the militia's arsenal of bombs and hide them away."

\*\*\*

At two-thirty-nine, twenty minutes before the kickoff of the football game, a Hummer and a nondescript van stopped in front of the Amory. From the Hummer came Edsel and Ike dressed like militiamen with scarves up around their mouths. The back of the van opened with Ali and Bobby Joe holding guns on two women and a man with wrists tied. The three prisoners were pushed and kicked up the steps to the door. Edsel waved the van driver to leave. He'd return the van from where it was stolen earlier and pick up a U-Haul he'd parked nearby. Both places had been checked for CCTV cameras. There was no rush, but he had to be in place thirty minutes from when he left the Armory. When he was at the wheel of the U-Haul, he checked his phone. Martin

Conrad at his computer noted the time.

Edsel freed his three 'prisoners' as soon as they were away from the door. Ali stayed at the front watching the guard for any signal that the invasion was known. Ike delayed in case an emergency exit to the Hummer was necessary.

Edsel, Ginny, and the other woman went down a narrow stair into the basement. This location had been a storage area assigned to different teams, and there was a long row of metal cages. The sports equipment was gone. In the place of hoops, bats, balls, nets, flags, and practice aids, each space held an individual. All of the individuals were unclean. There were no bathroom facilities, so the stench was thick enough to cut. Some of the inmates sat, but most laid on the bare concrete floor. Some moaned, most were silent. Edsel held back a gag; the two women were not as composed and spit out vomit.

Edsel shouted, "Welcome to your new home." He laughed while they genuinely shrank back in horror.

"Bill Sykes, my man, see what sport I have for you; let them into your harem."

A man almost as big as Edsel appeared. He was armed and had keys at his belt.

"I ain't Bill Sykes."

"Likely didn't read *Oliver Twist* either. Ah well, here's your Nancy and your Bullseye. What's down here anyway?" Edsel nonchalantly wandered down the corridor from which the guard had appeared.

"A bit of sport." The goaler turned with his keys toward an unoccupied cage and therefore never saw the blow that hit him.

"Good hit, Nancy!" said Ginny.

"Hey, they don't call me Bullseye for nothing," the woman whispered with a wink.

"I thought I was Bullseye and you were Nancy."

"Bullseye was Bill Sykes' dog in *Oliver Twist* and Nancy was his girl. You're too young and sweet to be Bullseye. Plus, you don't have my military training."

"Thank goodness he never read the book."

Ginny took the keys and started to unlock the other cages. There was a stirring of hope. The moaning stopped and all stared in silence to Ginny's international signal for quiet.

Edsel advanced to the door at the end and looked through a small window into a solid room that was obviously used for coercion, questioning, torture, and elimination.

A young girl, naked and tied, was being raped by one man while another watched. The girl had lost consciousness which had not diminished the ardor, apparently the sport.

The rapist was unaware of the appearance at the door or the slowly advancing shadows. The observer watched in a strange fascination and was slow to react.

Edsel, now behind the rapist, felled him with a massive angry blow to the side of the head. The man hit the floor, tripped by the pants around his ankles, and only barely remembered a sized twelve boot hitting his groin.

The watcher, too late, grabbed for his gun, now in the hand of a woman he had never seen before. As he looked at the weapon, she gave him a swift kick on his knee. As he bent, she brought the gun down on his head.

"Tie them up. I'll bring the other guard in," Edsel directed. "Gag them, lock the door, and bring her with you."

"Her clothes?"

"Take his shirt," he said pointing. "It looks cleaner

than anything else down here."

"There are only eighteen people here," said Ginny.

"Nineteen." said Edsel. "They're very efficient.

"Eighteen alive, one dead," said Ginny seriously.

"Bring him anyway. How many can walk?"

"Two, three."

"There's just us. We have to bring them to the elevator at the end. Lock the door down here. We should have time."

"How much?" asked the other girl.

"Twelve or thirteen minutes," said Ginny. "I have to check in with Martin, then I can stay with the elevator."

Upstairs Mac and Bobby Joe took stairs up to the office of the director of the day. In the anteroom, a guard armed with a machine pistol was watching a computer monitor screen. It showed a cartoon show and his initial reluctance to look up gave him no chance as Bobby Joe chopped with the side of his hand.

"That's for Betty Jo," he said.

"Feel better?" asked Mac.

"Not yet!" Bobby Joe was smiling.

The man behind the desk in the next room was watching the six screens showing the entrances to the building, the cells downstairs, the loading area, and strategic hallways. Bobby Joe was aiming the machine pistol at him as he reached for the telephone.

"Relax," said Mac. "This is not going to hurt like downstairs."

"You won't get away with this."

"He watches too many Western Movies," said Bobby Joe.

The man was tied gagged and put into a closet along with the guard from outside. A call to Martin

Konrad and a few keystrokes and the images were under the control of an internet genius in a hotel room two miles away. After today he would fade back into his old workshop in Georgetown, destroy everything incriminating, and using any links he found to his advantage.

"Door number two, Martin."

"I see it," said Martin looking at the screen showing a U-Haul reversing up to the dock by the overhead door designated with a yellow two.

"Confirm door number two," Martin said into another cell phone.

Ike was now nearing the loading dock and knew that. Bobby Joe and Mac were very close behind. A guard stood at the pulpit door unsure of what to do. Ike surmised that a U-Haul van had stopped outside door number two, but no one had moved. The guard didn't want to go out and expose himself and become isolated outside, but he didn't want to call for assistance as nothing was happening. It was in this state of indecision that he saw Ike approaching.

"What's happening bro?"

"There appears to be a truck outside," the guard stated.

"So?" Ike countered.

"I wasn't told of a shipment or a pickup."

"Really? Let's find out. Upstairs watching?" he said, pointing towards the camera.

The guard looked up and that was the last thing he likely remembered for several hours. Ike pushed the button for door two to open. The U-Haul was backed up to the loading dock. When the rear door was opened, twelve men and a woman came out. The men were assigned to different duties, securing the entrances and securing the guards. Six men went in twos to disarm the guards, one stayed on duty by the truck, and another three men went to the guardroom to secure and search. The woman and one man, went to link up with Ginny and Edsel, guard their rear. and prepare for evacuation.

Four of the men quickly came back to head with Ike, Mac, and Bobby Joe to the weapons storeroom. They had been prepared by their intelligence for the lock and were soon inside looking at a vast array of weapons.

"Where the hell do we start?" asked Mac rhetorically since the others were picking up pistols, assault rifles, and looking at boxes of ammunition.

"Let's just get what we came for," Mark replied somewhat out of breath. "This place is huge. I just ran two hundred yards for the first time since high school."

"Can you identify the mortars for the drones?" asked Mac.

"Yes, I think so. My client manufactured them, so the box should have the name printed on the side." Mark was already scanning the boxes with an occasional low whistle.

"Here. Here," he said with some excitement. "Fifty to a box, two pounds each. That means each box weighs one hundred pounds. It looks like forty-nine unopened boxes. The remaining box has to be somewhere with whatever's left. We need hand carts."

"Let's take this lot." Mac saw a low-wheeled cart by the entrance. "One trip, two, will save us some time."

The men assigned worked quietly and efficiently, loading the four wheeled cart until it was difficult to push.

"Mark, take a look at the prisoner situation. We

have to get them into the same truck."

"Then what?"

"Depends if they can walk."

"And if not?"

"Beats me. Think of something."

Mark trotted off, shaking his head, muttering. When he got to the elevator he asked, "Edsel, how's it going?"

"Ginny went to get some blankets or clothes. Something we overlooked."

"Not back yet?"

"No, I sent a couple of men to the basement in case anyone tried to use the elevator and to cover our retreat."

"It's lights out if we're caught," Mark said unnecessarily.

Both men stiffened at the sound of approaching feet until they saw that the feet were topped by a stack of blankets and towels.

"Ginny, thank goodness," Mark said, wanting to embrace her but knowing it wasn't the right time.

"The ladies locker room seems to have been ignored by the looters. I've got blankets, towels, sanitary pads, and a first aid kit."

"Sanitary towels?" Mark asked skeptically.

"They work as sterile pads, Mark."

"Sorry. You're right, and I'm wrong, as usual." Mark blushed.

Ginny took control. "We have to get this lot to the loading dock ASAP. How many can walk?"

"Well…" Edsel looked over the group, most of whom were now paying attention. "More than when we brought them up from the cells. Hope seems to add strength."

"Those walking we can have safe tonight. The

others we can't take out of Washington."

Several of those on the floor now rose or attempted to stand up. Ginny walked through, dispensing blankets. Those standing now shuffled to the front.

"Ginny, can you lead these people out? No, never mind," Mark said. "You're more important here. Edsel, can you help someone and also lead them to the dock."

"Yes, sir, with pleasure. And I can take two, one on each arm. Probably don't need the fellas downstairs anymore. Can you tell them to come back please?"

Mark nodded, then ran to bring up the two men from the basement and asked for them to carry one each of the most injured people. The other woman who had accompanied them into the cellar pushed them away from the girl who had been raped and picked her up, walking toward the exit without a word.

The eighteen-year-old boy came running up.

"Pick him up," said Ginny pointing.

"But he's dead!"

"That's what happens here to people who should not be here, and he is going home. His family deserves to have a proper burial."

With some hesitation the body was retrieved from the floor and carried.

"Something you want to share with your friends?" Mark asked.

"No, sir," the young man said with a whisper.

Mark and Ginny took the last two.

"You're doing great," said Mark with admiration.

"I don't know why Mac picked me for this mission. This wasn't easy."

"I told him that he could trust you, that you are the bravest, toughest person I know."

"Flattery will get you everywhere, Mr. Hughes." She smiled for the first time that day.

"We are not out of here yet, Ms. Hutchins."

\*\*\*

At the loading dock, the final load of weapons was being put onto the truck. There had been room to load cases of machine pistols and semi-automatic guns too. The prisoners were also on the truck, as were most of the men. There was a cacophony as the tension released.

"Shut up!" shouted Mac. "We're waiting for Ali from the front door, then we'll be off. Quietly. One change – we have four cars, two vans. The cars will each take an ambulatory former prisoner and be responsible for taking them home. *Not* to their home, your home. Sorry about that. The vans will each take two. The car going to the game is to have first option."

"Are we carrying more weight than the truck can take?"

"Are you from health and safety?"

"Ali. Here at last. Everything okay?"

"Everything's going to plan."

"Marines ready?"

"Yes, sir." Three men and the woman who had been with Ginny were now in military uniforms. Their discarded clothes were given to cover and dress the former prisoners. Two men up front and nineteen former prisoners and eighteen vigilantes together with the bombs and guns were crammed into the back.

"One more thing." Mac went through the loading door, closed it, pulled a nearby fire alarm in the building, and exited the pulpit door. He stepped onto the back of the truck and pulled the door closed.

It was brutal inside the van, but it was only for two blocks. When the doors shut and the inside of the truck was black, the former prisoners started wailing. The rescuers were silenced by this demonstration of how quickly a human spirit can be broken. Ginny, in the dark, wondered how long it would take to mend.

They only had to travel two blocks, but it seemed to take forever. The overloaded truck was proceeding slowly, in part because of the crowds headed to the game and in part because of the realization that a pothole could break a spring and strand the merchandise and raiding party.

Inside the truck, unable to see the progress, there was a silent anxiety. Mac asked for their attention.

"Thank you, everyone. Remember to stick to your part of the plan, and stick to your stories. Take care of your charges. Travel safely. No tickets. Only the tolls that you cannot avoid. We will have more than a few angry people out there. Don't let them direct their anger toward you."

The truck stopped and the rear door opened. The man from the van was putting vehicle plates that matched the U-Haul on front and back, switching the ones used at the Armory to an identical U-Haul which he would drive back to a drop center in the opposite direction.

The mileage wouldn't show enough for a detour; the check-in time would be too close to have stopped. Just a little extra obfuscation to slow down any inquiries.

Ambulatory patients were directed and supported to nearby cars and vans. There they could be appropriately clothed.

A man and a woman in Marine uniforms were now in the driving position. Two others wearing similar uniforms were in a conservative black car. They had Mac in the rear seat. The black car led the U-Haul back onto the street and the two vehicles headed east. It was about a mile. At the Marine Corps base, the guard saluted and approached the car; two other guards stood at the ready. Mac lowered the rear window.

"Delivery." He handed a letter to the guard.

"Identification?"

"In the letter, of course." Mac gave his driver's license.

"We need to inspect the truck."

"No, officer. I'm sorry, but you will have to check the outside only."

"Every vehicle must be inspected."

"Could you ask your commanding officer to come to the gate?"

"Against protocol, sir."

Mac pointed to the letter. He knew what it said since he had dictated it to the general. The guard turned and told the other two to watch carefully. They immediately levelled their guns at the car. He returned from the guard house very quickly. "Pull over to the side, please."

Mac waited, window down. He watched and listened. He could hear footsteps, fast-paced, approaching. Four men appeared, two older men in the lead.

"Sir, it seems that the general was visiting the commandant," the driver informed Mac.

"You have something for me?"

"Yes, General. More than you bargained for I'm afraid."

Mac, the general, and the commandant went to the rear of the U-Haul. Two guards started to follow until Mac stopped them. Mac opened the door and the general saw the figures lying in the bed of the truck with Ginny hushing and giving comfort to them.

"What the hell?" The commandant gasped at the wounded and then at the boxes of arms.

"Can we get this lot inside?" asked Mac.

"At once." The commandant was all action. "To the infirmary. Follow me." He jumped into the car which moved to the rear of the building as he instructed.

Mac was left with the general watching two guards who seemed unsure of what to do but finally deciding that protecting a five-star general took precedence over curiosity.

The general leaned in to Mac and, in a low voice, said, "So, patriot, what is your thinking?"

"Even if they suspect, why would they? Even if they suspect their stuff is here, they're not coming to get it. To request it be returned is to admit they had it, illegally, then be questioned on how they got it. The militia would also have to admit they were breached."

"Good point. Those poor creatures. Were there five?"

"Six," Mac replied. "One is a dead body. I'm no doctor, but I think we can take two with us after some treatment. I know it's unexpected, but we were as shocked as you are. There's a young lady in that truck who was being gang-raped when we arrived."

"Her rapists?"

"Alive, but probably unable to father."

"Let's go to the commandant's office; we can talk about the rest of your exit plan."

"General, those people…We must keep them under wraps, incognito, not even let their families know."

"Consider it done."

\*\*\*

The plan took two single malts and an hour. First

the medical wing was placed in lock down. The doctors, nurses, and others were locked in and told that as a matter of national security none of the events were to be discussed, ever.

The dead man's body was taken to the morgue and a burial was scheduled for the next day. Mac filled out the paperwork giving the deceased's name as 'D.S. Cooper' and wondered if the name of the still missing airplane hijacker who'd disappeared in Wyoming would be recognized, but there was no reaction from the clerk.

Two ambulatory prisoners were given temporary military IDs, then were bandaged and wheeled to the car that took Mac, Mark, and Ginny from the compound. Three remaining patients would be treated as needed and then, if the hue and cry had ended, released carefully to family outside of the DC area.

"Mark, we'll drop you and Ginny up here at the corner. Take a cab to the hotel as if you are from the airport. I'll see you tomorrow. It'll give us a chance to see if anyone is following or showing interest in us. My new friends and I will go to Martin's condo for the night. I have a couple of people to meet, and these people need to rest. We'll plan on leaving in the morning."

"Where are you taking us?" asked one of the newly freed men. Even though the car had darkened windows, Mac could see the two shrink back into the upholstery at every corner, out of sight of police or military vehicles.

"Depends. Where do you want to go? Home is not an option." Mac faced them. "If you have particular skills and feel up to it, we can use you. If not, we'll drop you someplace or slip you away. Contact, at this time, with your immediate family can get them, and you, killed. I think you've seen what I mean. We need to work on a change in culture and return to some form of democratic law and order."

"Amen," one of the men whispered.

\*\*\*

In the cab, Mark leaned over and whispered to Ginny. "Um, looks like we may be registering as Mr. and Mrs. again."

"Mark, this is the twenty-first century. Nobody cares. Nobody does the Mr. and Mrs. thing."

"Well, maybe you care."

"Mark, I want to apologize."

"No, I should apologize to you. I was emotional in Boston and accused you, without knowledge or proof. I'm sorry, Ginny."

She took his face in her hands and kissed him.

## Chapter Twenty-Seven

The holidays were strange. It was unlike any that had been experienced by anyone gathered at the ranch. The strangeness was the favorite topic of conversation. For the Josephs the sheer number of guests was unusual. Thanksgiving had always been family only, the meal, turkey. For Margaret and Henry Forrest, they were without their parents and brothers. Mac and Helen had never really celebrated Thanksgiving as a married couple. Mark and Ginny, together with Ginny's mother Sheila, were in a conspiratorial mood. Other guests were in disbelief that they were giving thanks amid apparent doom and gloom.

A Thanksgiving speech was given by Jim Joseph. Here in the isolation of Texas, surrounded by hostile states, it was somehow comforting to hear thanks for the blessings and to not dwell on the problems, at least for the day. Thanksgiving dinner was roast beef on a spit over a large fire pit.

Mark and Ginny were again lovers and were moving in together, now with Sheila's blessing. In Washington with a bolster between them, the trauma of that day had finally overcome Ginny and she had eventually found sleep with Mark's arm around her. Daylight had brought a mutual dread of facing the day. By unspoken consent, they had left Washington as soon as they had concluded their business and tied up the loose ends.

Mark had spoken to Hal's daughter, Esther, who preferred not to meet. Ginny had picked up some back-up recordings from Martin since she and Mac had been wearing miniature cameras during the raid on the Armory, all captured by Martin two miles away.

After the Thanksgiving meal, Margaret and Ike travelled back to Austin from the ranch together. Both had the weekend off; Bobby Joe and Betty Jo stayed at the ranch providing security coverage. Everyone, it seemed, had a little something to be thankful for.

\*\*\*

Christmas came and everyone went their separate ways to celebrate. Mark took Ginny to meet his brother and family. Margaret and Ike travelled to Galveston for a celebration with the Forrest clan. Mac and Helen found a quiet resort near Corpus Christi.

Every one of the principals had been at a meeting a few days before Christmas and had revealed their travel plans. Each was made aware that the New Year would bring all shoulders to the wheel. Marjorie had completed a draft of new Constitutional ideas and asked for input at a meeting scheduled for December 31st.

After holiday greetings and farewells had been exchanged, Ellie May asked for attention. "Merry Christmas to all of you, and thank you."

"And be very careful," added Mac.

\*\*\*

Helen and Mac were packing an overnight bag for their trip.

"What's this?" asked Mac.

"Marjorie's draft."

"I know what it is."

"Then why ask?" Helen was confused.

"I meant, why is it taking up room in my overnight bag?"

Helen laughed. "I thought we might read it and be ready for the 31$^{st}$."

"No, no, and no way! We'll read it, disagree, argue, and spoil the first private days since we were in hiding."

"As chief of staff, I should be ahead," she argued.

"Which part of my two-letter word was difficult for you? And," Mac continued, "I doubt there is anything in there that Ellie May or Jim Joseph has not already leaked to you."

"That's not the point," Helen countered. However she didn't fight hard when Mac took the copy and put it in the desk drawer and locked it.

"So, Mr. Bigshot, what do you have in mind for four days?"

"The same thing I have in mind for four nights," said Mac with an exaggerated, lewd grin.

She laughed, gave him a swat on the arm, and then they each finished packing.

Once settled on the plane, Helen slept and continued to doze in the cab to the resort. After a swim in the pool and a cocktail, they returned to their room and took a shower together and made love. They showered again and had a light meal at the bar. Back in their room before nine, they acknowledged their weariness. When Mac came in from brushing his teeth Helen was asleep.

"Goodnight, sweetheart," he whispered. He watched her smile for a long time and reflected on his good fortune.

They spent their days seeing the sights, wandering around shopping areas, and walking the seashore.

Nights were quiet with long dinners, a little wine, then early to bed, lovemaking, and sleep. While Mac was ever vigilant, they felt more relaxed than they had in a very long time.

"This is the honeymoon we never had," said Helen on the final evening. "We've had time to talk about us and where we came from. We know how we got here, but, where are we going?"

"I don't know. And I don't care as long as it's with you."

"Mac. be serious."

"That's as serious as I can be, lest the glow fades."

"Lest? What kind of word is that?" Helen too was reluctant to break the spell of relaxation.

"I don't know. I just read it."

"In a book?" Her face wore an incredulous and playful look.

"There were a lot of pictures." Mac was laughing with Helen.

"Back to Austin tomorrow, back to work, back to working on our future. Tonight is the present. Let's make it a present to ourselves," said Mac.

"You'll get no argument from me on that."

\*\*\*

On December 31st, the principal decision makers were gathered in the large office that served as a conference room. Mark and Ginny looked shattered and everyone was either glancing at or away from them.

"Not what you're thinking," said Mark. "We just arrived back this morning. Militia was all over the airport, so we rented a car and drove, and drove, and drove."

"A reminder to be careful," Mac agreed.

Ellie May Joseph and Marjorie White came into

the room together and sat behind the side-by-side desks. "Today, on New Year's Eve, we need to record a television address to the large audience gathered to see the fireworks."

"Are they still on? I thought they were cancelled," Alistair Kirk commented. He was seated, a dour figure, at the back wall.

"All but New York. The networks are showing the displays from around the world, starting at ten Eastern Standard Time. We can steal ten minutes and no-one will miss their show."

"Are the networks being paid?" asked Alistair.

"My husband is working on a contract for our campaign which includes fees for interruptions. It's hard because the network executives believe the administration will boycott their network, harass the executives, close down the network, or all of the above. The papers being passed around – thank you, Ginny – have my speech. Please take a few minutes to look over what I've written. I'm open to comment."

Mac pointed out a few places where her words could be tightened up. Sheila suggested adding in mention of something from the day's events so that people would know she was broadcasting that day. A few other minor adjustments were noted.

"Thank you, all. Your opinions help me to be a better leader."

Marjorie picked up where Ellie May left off. "Which segues into our second reason for being here. Constitution, Article One: freedom of speech, thought, religion, political affiliation, and general pursuit of happiness."

Marjorie stood in order to be seen and heard. "This is not much changed from our Founding Fathers' original article. When we drafted the document, we accepted that the Constitution writers' thoughts were no different from today, but times have changed and are changing. In 1776 women couldn't vote, minorities were never considered, and even the working man had no expectation of an education or of having his thoughts or rights of religious preference considered."

There were few comments and additional suggestions as everyone prepared for Article Two, which was not numbered but instead was referenced by a single page.

"This won't fly, Marjorie," Alistair said. "The right to bear arms is as American as apple pie. The right to bear arms is a Constitutional right which will never be repealed." His voice was on of strident reproach.

"When was the last time you had apple pie, Alistair?" Mark asked in an attempt to lighten the mood.

"It's not on my diet. Gives me heartburn!"

When the laughter died down Marjorie said, "Exactly!"

"The revolutionaries had to provide their own weapons. Since there was no standing army, navy, or air force, it was important for citizens to bring their own arms. It does not say 'firearms' by the way, and it did *not* envisage a military or an armed police force. And there's no way our Forefathers could have foreseen the development of automatic weapons."

"So, no second amendment?" Helen asked, pleased that a head-on approach was being taken.

"No. We have a strong judiciary, a strong legal system, and a police force. Laws should be drafted by our next attorney general to legislate gun control. I advocate for banning automatic weapons, except for active military use. Handguns I would limit to police officers, and hunting rifles, kept in a secure location, such as certain police stations or gun ranges, to be 'signed' out by the owners for hunting trips or target practice. The police can require background checks and continuing demonstration of good citizenship."

"That seems draconian, Marjorie." Sheila Hutchins continued. "I grew up around guns and was taught that they're a measure of protection. Will the 'bad' guys have guns, leaving the 'good' guys defenseless?"

"That's a flawed argument. Think of it this way – the police can immediately identify 'bad' guys. Remember the judiciary will make and adopt laws. Police will have more power and respect. Sheila, last week there were fifty, I repeat, fifty, reported fatal shootings in Chicago alone. Automatic weapons were used. There were numerous injuries reported and who knows how many not reported. And it is escalating."

"What about the militia? We've all seen the arms and the abuse. The video from Washington is evidence that it's open to misuse."

"A standing, or casual militia, has no authority in the twenty-first century." Marjorie had clearly thought through the questions she might face.

"Can we convince the American people?" asked Helen.

"We only have to convince the American voter." said Ellie May. "Research has shown security is the number one concern. We must allay fears and show that we can be the party to make everyone safe…in their homes, in the classrooms, at work, and on the street."

The next three hours saw the balance of the manifests debated. With a good deal of time spent on immigration, the conversation drifted to the subject of unemployment.

"Not in the manifests as prepared by Marjorie." Ellie May ended the discussion as the attendees were getting a bit off track. "A lot of work still to do everyone. Back here same time tomorrow."

The only response she received consisted of unenthusiastic groans.

"I know it's New Year's Day, but there will be few days off in the next three hundred days if we can do well in the coming days. Tomorrow, Helen, we need plans for New Hampshire. We must show well or we all go home."

Helen nodded and began to jot notes.

"Marjorie, some tightening from the comments today then pass them by Professor Taylor. Ask him to have them back next week to report to group."

\*\*\*

At the New Year's Day meeting everyone appeared in the mood of a new year, a new beginning, an optimistic, forward-looking frame of mind. The old year was done and dusted, behind them. Even the news of a crackdown by the militia on teenagers celebrating the New Year with bonfires, fireworks, and music brought resolutions to make sure these events were legal next year.

Helen had center stage.

"My plan is to have many small meetings instead of one large gathering that can be disrupted. The problem is going to be the debates. We should go out of our way to avoid the president."

"Will he debate?" asked Sheila.

"I don't know. He's arrogant. He'll likely ignore our efforts as insignificant."

"Of course he is," Marjorie agreed. "Look at what he did to get into office last time." Her eyes became moist with the thought of her David. Losing him had been the most difficult thing she and the boys had ever experienced. She turned away, grabbed a tissue from a box on the desk, and walked over to look out the window.

Sensing that Marjorie needed a little time away from the spotlight, Helen continued. "We'll prepare speeches, record them, and have small teams of one or two people setting up screens. We can have questions relayed to the speakers, either Ellie May or Marjorie, who will be standing by in Texas at the end of the speech. We believe, with careful choreography, we can 'attend' up to three speeches each per day. Remember, New Hampshire, in many ways is a test for us. If this works, then we only have forty-eight states to go."

Helen waited for the nervous chuckles to die away and nodded to Margaret who seemed to have a question. "What about the holograph? That was a huge success in Iowa."

"Yes, we discussed that. The first problem is that we could only do one at a time. Two, it takes all day to set up. Three, if it were intercepted, we would have a problem. Four, it takes away a heavy weapon that we can use strategically."

Ellie May asked, "Teams? How many? Who?"

"We believe we can recruit and train local volunteers to act so that, even if there are disruptions and arrests, we can carry on. Margaret, I believe you're to participate in many of the events, luncheons, afternoon teas, dinners, breakfasts, social clubs, anywhere we can get larger groups together. Are you up for all of that?"

Margaret looked at Ike then back to Helen. "Yes, I'm up to it. I'm a social butterfly whose come out of her cocoon."

Everyone laughed.

Helen was glad that spirits were high despite the enormous obstacles ahead. "Sheila and her team are going through the lists of donors from our campaign last time. Whatever it takes, Margaret. Talking, cajoling, begging, soliciting..."

"Not to mention eating all of the food," Sheila said. "Just don't ask for Swiss on your Philly cheesesteak."

Everyone laughed, remembering how politicians could often be the focus of ridicule by media for breaking tradition.

"Sounds as if I will be putting on weight," Margaret commented.

Marjorie rejoined the group. "Not if you practice 'push-aways'. I'll show you the tricks I learned on my last campaign."

They were off and running before the end of the day with teams having been set up, hotel rooms booked, and secure venues and local contacts identified. These contacts would be able to recruit and supervise other volunteers. There had been a debate about the advisability of the candidates appearing at the traditional forum of 'kicking off' their campaign in New Hampshire at St. Anselm College. It was finally agreed that it was a 'must do' event, but the risk of a personal appearance early in the run for the White House was impossible. The final factor was that even if there were no incidents, every state committee would expect a personal appearance and that would be too irresistible a target for some fringe lunatic or enthusiastic militiaman.

Isolation on the ranch had provided a great experience for the leaders of the campaign who could work on their agendas without distraction. It also provided access to decision makers twenty-four hours a day. There was added pressure since no matter how hard someone was working Ellie May, Marjorie, and Helen were working harder, longer. It was impossible not to see that Mac, Mark, and Bobby Joe never seemed to sleep.

Mac and Helen were having their usual differences on deciding where they were most useful.

"Then come with me to New Hampshire. We still have our old aliases." Mac had been adamant about covering the campaign. He was convinced that even as a freelance journalist he could sell stories to some newspapers in the U.S. and abroad. He would approach news services and magazines.

"Mac, you know that as chief of staff I have to be here."

"Not so. Normally your candidate would be on the road and so would you."

"True, but…"

"New Hampshire and the other early states deserve a presence. Not me, not Mark; you're next in line – a natural choice."

"But, Mac…" Her eyes spoke the rest of the sentence. Helen was afraid a return to the Northeast would trigger the horror. That the terror would return her body to the rejection of rational thought.

"I know, sweetheart, but if not us, who?" It was a familiar mantra, one on which they had made so many decisions.

"I'll think about it and speak to Ellie May."

The decision was made the next day, and Mark secured a plane to fly Helen, Mac, and the main party to the Laconia airfield. The car rental agency had secured several all-wheel drive cars and trucks, rooms were reserved at the Margate Inn.

## Chapter Twenty-Eight

New Hampshire was a shock after Texas.

It was exciting to those who had never seen snow. It was depressing to those who had seen more than they needed to see. The sky was leaden; there was more snow to come.

Margaret, Ginny, and Ike ran out of the hotel onto the ice covering the lake. Then they ran back inside faster than they had left. Blue jeans and shirts with coats were no match for the cold. Mac watched, amused, anticipating their immediate return.

"Below freezing means just that! You can freeze or suffer frostbite in just a few minutes. There is a sports store in town. As soon as you can, buy thermal socks, thermal underwear, and thermal gloves, and a wool hat for outdoors."

"Just for a few days?"

"Just for a few hours outdoors anywhere in the North during this season. New Hampshire isn't our only cold weather state."

The party split up after dinner to avoid attracting undue attention. Mac had invited John Richardson to join Helen and him so they could tap into the political mood.

"Why ask me? I'm a has-been senator, no longer any use."

"John, what you and your group don't know is not

worth knowing," said Mac, understanding that a New Hampshire politician – present or former – was not going to give the whole story in one sentence.

"Well one of our group, can't remember who, he says the governor is not overly fond of the president."

"Because of his position on gun control?" asked Helen.

"Could be."

"What about our candidate's position on gun control?"

"Different. As I recall you want to ban handguns, semiautomatic stuff, and tighten controls on hunting rifles. I think most people will go along, though I would not want to test that in hunting season." JR laughed at his own thoughts.

The meal progressed and topics ranged from the economy and unemployment to education, retirement, and JR's golf game.

"Other candidates running?" asked Helen.

"The usual nine or ten 'no-hopers' on the Republican ticket. There is just Al Adana and some kid from New Jersey on the Democrats' side."

"I saw that. Does it make sense?" asked Helen.

"Maybe he has a death wish."

"Maybe there's an agenda to provide a debate," said Mac. "Too late to think about it tonight though. It will keep until the morning. I'm pooped! Thanks, JR. And good luck with your golf whenever you next see the course."

Helen stood as Mac shook hands with JR and each murmured their goodnights.

Over the next few days, the crews kept the hectic pace with an enthusiasm only the very young, very dedicated can muster. Mac was often to be found in bed asleep while these young men and women were still comparing notes from their day.

Mac visited television studios and newspaper offices where he was generally recognized. In spite of the recognition, he was rebuffed. Privately the studios and newspapers would love to have the business, but they saw too much risk. Democrats were not pumping money into advertising either, so all in all it was a decidedly bleak election season for those media enterprises used to surviving winter months on prior elections' endless candidate profiles and self-promoting announcements.

Driving back from Manchester, Mac was aware of being followed. He had sensed the presence of other cars on other occasions, but this time was different. He was alone and had misjudged how early in the evening it became dark this far north.

One car, two occupants, so far. He drove a little over the speed limit. Not fast enough to attract attention, yet quick enough to test his intuition.

Using his cell phone, he called Helen. "I'm being followed."

"What can we do?"

"Nothing that would be helpful. I'll take the highway to Tilton then try to lose them in Belmont. I could lose myself there."

"What if you pick up chicken for dinner?" asked Helen.

*What on earth is she thinking about dinner at a time like this?* Mac was confused until he thought of where he would get chicken. Where? It came to him.

"Good idea. Can you call ahead?"

"Delighted!"

Mac and Helen, while on the most wanted list, had delivered chickens to the Boston market from a farm above the lake. They had used the trips to Boston to meet with the Sons of Liberty and had become friends with the farmer and his wife. It was a chance to lose his pursuers. He focused his attention now on his mental image of a map of the area. Mac looked at the satellite navigation system in the car and wondered if it could be hacked. He decided yes it could, but it was unlikely. Worth the risk not to be lost, double back, and run into trouble.

The entrance to the farm was unmarked. The driveway ran straight, so Mac was able to switch off the lights of the car and try to remember not to brake until he was behind the barn.

There was a gracious welcome and the offer of a bed overnight which Mac accepted. He was deluged with questions which were still being answered when he realized they had been talking for hours past normal bedtime and farmers all had early morning chores.

"Sorry to keep you awake, Randy. I can help you in the morning and we can continue our conversation then if you'd like."

"What about me?" Patricia Scott asked.

"Maybe we can get Helen to come over. We need to leave New Hampshire now with the militia alerted to our identity."

Mac was hoping the Scotts would extend an invitation to include Helen. It would be good to have a couple of days to plan, to stop in Boston and catch up with their contacts there.

The next day Mac called Helen at the hotel. "Can you leave and come here?"

"Not easily. There are men outside in a car watching the entrance," said Helen.

"I thought as much. I'm getting too old for this."

"Not yet forty – what will you do when you're

really old?"

"Teach my grandchildren how to play baseball, soccer."

"Shouldn't we have children first?" Helen, always practical, asked sincerely.

"We decided no children into this crazy world, this screwed up country."

"Then let's start making it better!"

"Okay," agreed Mac. "Stay there and I'll see you soon."

"Mac, before I let you hang up, I want to share some good news. We're getting more coverage than everyone else combined. Even on television we're being noticed in a careful way."

"Even more reason to be careful."

"You too, sweetheart. I love you, Mathew McDougal."

Mac sat looking out at the wintry landscape. It was forecast for snow slowly turning to rain, and it was dark. The night and days seemed equally dark. There was little warmth from the layers of clothing he wore.

It was quiet. If he sat very still and listened, he might hear the boiler in the basement, a hum from the refrigerator, a utensil dropped in the kitchen. He loved it; he loved the fact that any vehicle entering the yard would crunch the icy surface and alert everyone to the fact that visitors were arriving – friend or foe. If foe, he was aware that they would be looking for him.

Another one of the benefits of being alone in the quiet countryside was that Mac could write and submit articles. From a vantage point away from the day to day, he could analyze and put into prose the mismanagement of the present administration. He could see clearly and could articulate the comments that were playing through the campaign.

He needed to talk to the opposition. Why would they talk to him? Because they were getting less coverage than they thought they deserved. If they knew, or suspected, he was closely affiliated with the American Party, why would they talk to him? Because they were hungry to win and feared no one. Arrogance and self-confidence, that was why they would talk to him.

They did. On the telephone.

"Senator, what is the first thing you will do when you are elected to go to Washington?"

"Thank you. I remind you that there still has to be an election."

"Not a problem I don't think. Do you?" asked Mac.

"Well, I will present myself to the White House and see how I might serve."

"Senator, I mean Senator-Elect, are you not elected to serve the people? And is there not a separation of power, executive, judicial, and congressional?"

"Of course!"

"Then how would you serve the people by serving the executive office?"

"The people elected President Al Adana. He serves the people we serve. It is very obvious that his will is the will of the people and that we serve them that serve."

The conversation continued but Mac was lost somewhere in that piece of logic. It became clearer as he spoke to other candidates, even those attempting to return to Washington, that there was control over Congress that would not be broken by returning those supporting the current administration.

How could the American Party change this? How did the supporters, the candidates, think that they were going to change the country? What kind of hubris possessed these people? Ellie May, Marjorie, and Helen were convinced, dedicated, fearless. It occurred to him, from nowhere, these three women would have volunteered to be with George Washington facing the British. A hopeless cause. Mac laughed out loud at himself and his analogy.

The thoughts, articles, were they making a difference? Was the American Party real and how was it to reach its goals? Were they realistic goals? The one good thing was that Mac, again, had access to politicians. Even though there were people looking for him, for now there seemed no energy to the search, few resources applied. This meant that either they didn't think him dangerous or they knew where to find him. Then he reminded himself; 'them' since Helen was on the wanted list too.

Helen? Where would they be safe? Probably nowhere since they had felt safe in New Hampshire and had been found. They had been safe in Texas until a drone had sent a rocket into the car driven by Betty Jo Williams.

His phone rang. "Mac," he answered automatically.

"Hello, my sweetheart. What were you thinking?" asked Helen.

"How did you know that I was thinking?"

"Well, I know you. You were not on the phone, you were not in mid-sentence, or the phone would have rung more than once, therefore you were thinking. Profound thoughts, I hope."

"I was thinking of you."

"Great answer, boy wonder."

"It's true. I was wondering where in this great big world I could take you to be safe."

"And the answer? Assuming that I want to be safe."

"No answer yet. Worried about you though."

"With good reason. Your two friends are outside watching me. Time to leave."

"I'll pick you up. In case they're listening, remember the inopportune comment that your mother picked up?"

"Don't remind me!"

"We'll meet down there in twenty minutes."

"Make it thirty. A girl has to look her best when she is being picked up."

"Be careful. I love you."

Thirty minutes later Mac waited at the Lyons Den restaurant. Helen's mother had overheard a reference to someone skiing down from Gunstock to the Lyon's Den, and had passed, innocently, the information on to someone and almost got her daughter killed.

No Helen.

He started to worry when another five minutes passed. The next five minutes were agony with the only noise coming from the lake being a noisy engine. The snow mobile finally stopped in front of Mac and Helen pulled helmet goggles and snowsuit off. She quickly pulled her bag from the back of the snowmobile, chucked in the outerwear she had discarded, then blew a kiss to the driver who noisily left them.

"Well; talk about making an entrance," said Mac.

"Safe and sound as ordered." Helen smiled. "Now get out of here before those clowns figure out that I'm here."

"Did they follow?"

"Yes, they drove onto the ice after us in their car but must have been afraid of the soft ice under the bridge to Governors Island. We were able to drive around, just enough snow for us, just too much for them."

"Next stop, Boston. A quick survey then we decide where to go next."

"All that thinking and you didn't decide?"

"Thoughts of you kept getting in the way." Mac was smiling.

"Two good come-backs in the same day." Helen squeezed his leg. "Never know what that might get you."

After driving numerous backroads, they crossed into Massachusetts and made their way to Boston, a city of contrasts. The militia was active – extorting, harassing, stealing, intimidating. People walking alone or even with friends at night would cross the street or turn back when militia members came into sight.

The Sons of Liberty were meeting regularly in smaller groups but growing. The Sons were divided into pacifists and militants, each with a healthy mutual respect and debates that were engendered. The pacifists were of the opinion that 'this too would pass' while the activists were generally those who was personally, or had some family member, affected by the roving gangs or by some arbitrary government policy. They wanted to strike out at the government. Which government? Local, state, federal? With the anger built from frustration, it didn't matter. They just wanted to strike something or someone.

Mac went to meeting two, sometimes three, a day, usually with Helen. It was Helen they wanted to see, to hear directly from the spokesperson for the American Party presidential candidate. The one they needed to support. Mac also spoke to them of the need to channel their anger and resolve into the primary vote coming soon. He repeated warnings of voter manipulation and vote tampering. It was like speaking a foreign tongue to these generally honest people. They promised to set up committees to monitor, scrutinize, and provide checks on the process.

Helen started her conversations with the Constitutional amendments in the manifesto, because it was always the first questions asked. The need for arms was made obsolete by the standing army, by a trained police force; hunting was now a sport not a means of providing food for a family. There were always "buts." The perennial "but" was 'if citizens are disarmed, only criminals will have weapons'!

Helen's answer, "And, therefore, more, not less, reason to arm and support police departments."

In the privacy of a hotel room or occasionally supporters' homes where they might be staying, Helen would express her own doubts. "Gang wars? Insurrection?"

"Well, it will reduce domestic violence." Mac being argumentative.

"Be serious."

"I am. The predominance of violent crime is domestic, or at least it was before our current president resurrected the militia."

"His militia," Helen corrected him.

"Well, I think politicians lost their credibility. In a campaign promise they might be left or right, had a voice; when challenged they said whatever would get them elected. Once in Washington they headed to the middle, no voice, no debate, just please everyone, get re-elected."

"Cynical, Mac. Very cynical and unfair. I could name dozens of hardworking, free-thinking politicians."

"I bet, Helen, that you cannot name ten or five percent."

"What do you want to bet, bigshot?"

"Usual stakes – loser buys dinner."

They were now smiling. "As chief of staff I have a report to write on how this campaign has to go forward. Let's discuss over dinner and a bottle of nice wine."

Mac and Helen were staying at the Custom House in Boston, renting a room on the twenty-second floor, which technically didn't exist. The laundry was off the elevator and another door led to a one-bedroom suite that looked north and east.

Hand in hand they exited the building by the north door, waving to Karen at the desk as they left.

As they were walking to the North End of Boston, Helen noted, "This campaign is fragile, but I see from being here in New England how important it is to have a named principal with their feet on the ground."

"I hope that doesn't mean you plan on going to every state primary and caucus." Frowning, Mac was sizing up the importance of what was proposed versus the danger. "I'm not sure my heart is up to the constant pressure. Even now we're walking unprotected in a city in which we have arguably more enemies than friends."

"Yes and no."

"Then that is cleared up."

"You wouldn't need to tag along anyway," Helen responded.

"Good. I was thinking of going to Washington to continue my daily writings."

"Safe as houses there." The answering sarcasm was heavy in Helen's voice.

"It probably is. I can re-grow my beard and

become whoever my identity says I am. In Washington I can contact the members of Congress, get the inside word."

"You're serious?" Helen was surprised.

"And you?"

"No, I was thinking Ellie May, Marjorie, Alistair Kirk, Sheila Hutchins, Allyn Cherwin, anybody recognizable from the inner circle of advisors could be at meetings. I was thinking that with planning and a protective guard it could be an effective way of showing we are real, unafraid, committed."

"Then what am I afraid of?" asked Mac.

"You're afraid they've sold out of rabbit, my sweet!"

"You're paying," said Mac. "I haven't seen your list of names."

Helen shrugged.

"Speaking of paying," Mac continued, "how are the campaign funds?"

"Not great. The sponsors are currently seeing no bang for their buck."

"Fortunately there is no cost or minimal cost of television or radio advertising or 'spots.' The talk shows continue to help in a negative-positive way but still the travel budget is a strain. The American party committees in each of the states will have to step up, particularly if they want an Ellie May or Marjorie White to drop in."

"Said like a chief of staff taking charge." Mac was smiling. Helen was unrecognizable from the woman who did not speak for six months.

"Keep your eye on the goal. The presidential ballot in every state."

"Next Tuesday the New Hampshire primary and Iowa caucus, then they come fast." Helen was thinking ahead. "Not much rest next few months."

After an excellent dinner, two hours later Mac asked Mario to provide them with a ride back to the hotel.

Mac and Helen had no more discussions on their decisions. It was just assumed they would pursue the objectives each had set. They flew with the regional airline out of Providence, Rhode Island, just to be safe. Flying into Las Vegas they were met by a limousine arranged by Hal. The driver explained they were going to a hospice to visit Hal. He was worse than the last time Mac had visited, much worse.

"How's my daughter?" The words were spoken carefully, slowly, in order to suppress the imminent cough.

"She's well," said Mac. "Very well. I'll see her in a few days' time."

"Give her my…" A hesitation, a tear, "She calls every day, but I don't speak to her."

"Why?"

"Guilt I suppose. I was a rotten father. I wasn't…. am not, a father."

"Speak to her."

"I don't want her sympathy."

"Maybe it's not about you," said Mac. "Maybe she needs you to say you're proud of her, you love her."

"Too late."

"It will be too late next week," said Mac.

"I'll think about it. Thanks, Mac, for being a friend. Goodbye now. I'm tired."

"Goodbye, Hal. Thank you."

## Chapter Twenty-Nine

Washington, city of intrigue. Center of the government, the country, and to some, center of the world.

Mac thought Washington was looking a little seedy. There was nothing too obvious, perhaps it had always looked tired. No, it wasn't the city. It was the people. There were no strollers, no sightseers, no children with their sense of anticipation or excitement. Pedestrians moved swiftly, carefully, making sure they attracted no interest, clothes blended, colors muted, pedestrian signs obeyed.

Washington was the center of information. It didn't take long to access the pipeline. Former colleagues, friends of friends, congressmen. All knew of his affiliation with the American Party. It was clear the American Party was not perceived as a threat. On bad days Mac could agree there was no chance whatsoever of making a difference. On the few good says he kept asking, *If not me then who?*

\*\*\*

Today was a bad day. Mac was calling parents about their public schooling. It was depressing as most were afraid to talk and the others gave monosyllabic answers. Not encouraging to an investigative reporter. Finally Elaine, she asked he not use her surname, agreed to talk. She had a faint brogue and confirmed that, born in Ireland, she had spent most of her life in America.

"So what is the difference in your schooling and your children's?"

"Everything. What they can wear. What they can eat. Sports. Lessons. Everything."

"How many children?" asked Mac.

"Five. Two of each in school and Mary Elisabeth should be in kindergarten."

"Should be?"

"Well, kindergarten is only for boys now. Soon no girls in twelfth. It looks like a plan."

"School clothing; school uniform?"

"Not exactly. The boys are generally okay, but the girls must have skirts below the knee, long-sleeved blouses, no low neck, no jewelry, no hair ties. There are new rules every week."

"Sports?"

"No sports for girls."

"Lessons?"

"Which subject? The only language lessons are Arabic. Geography is taught with maps from before nineteen hundred. Many of the African nations are ignored. The Middle East is one caliphate. No Israel. I can't remember the rest that Sean showed me. History is of the Middle East not America. Literature is the teaching from the Koran. The sciences are generally good, except every day there is a pause to face Mecca and the children are encouraged to pray."

"What about prayers to other faiths? The right to freedom of religion – who took that away?"

"The same people. The argument now is that those were prayers to idols, to false gods. There is only one God, and it is Allah."

"Who's making the decisions?"

"The school board." Elaine spoke in a tone of resignation.

"The school board, in my day, were well meaning people listening to parent's complaints."

"Mine too, but not now. The boards are now predominantly Muslim, predominantly male, and decidedly homophobic."

When the conversation finally ended, Mac had written down the names of the school board members and would call for a comment. He was in no doubt of the veracity of this concerned mother, but his ethics required the opposing view.

He got back to his desk and made a call, introducing himself and explaining his purpose.

"Sir, you were recently elected to your local school board."

"Yes, I was. Six months ago."

"How long have you lived in the community and why did you want to serve?"

"I've lived in this town for one year and saw how poorly educated were the children."

"You'd lived in the town for only six months before you ran for office. Did you have children in the school system?"

"My boys are not yet old enough for school."

"I saw that you won the seat by a large margin, beating out a popular incumbent. A lot more votes were cast in this election apparently."

"It was the will of Allah."

"It's the will of Allah that you introduce draconian rules, forbidding girls' sports and dictating dress code?"

"I do not know this word 'Draconian.' I know that we must save these girl students and teach them to become better wives."

"And prepare them for college?" prompted Mac.

"No. Girls will marry and have families."

"How can you and your board decide that?" asked Mac.

"We cannot. It is the will of Allah!"

"Who asked you to represent Allah on the school board?"

"The mullah. He said, 'You will be on the ballot, you will win, it is the will of Allah'."

"Thank you very much."

"Will you print that it is the will of Allah?"

"I most certainly will," Mac said with all the irony that he could demonstrate. He put down the phone.

A call to the town clerk confirmed to Mac that the ballot box had been stuffed with people voting several times and also an extraordinary number of postal votes, all for a stranger in town. She also confirmed that two Muslims had previously been voted in and that now they were a majority in a five-member board.

"Did you report this irregularity to the police?"

"Of course, local and state."

"Don't tell me. They have no time for a victimless crime."

"How'd you know?"

"Well. all of your schoolchildren are now victims."

"I know."

"Then file suit on their behalf."

"Who? Me?"

"If not you, then who?"

"I do know a couple of mothers with daughters and they are very unhappy."

"Start with them, investigate the votes. Start with the 'write-ins.' Guaranteed they're all phony, one hundred per cent. We've seen it elsewhere. An illegally elected board cannot set policy. Be prepared for the Islamophobia charges, and good luck."

Mac hung up the phone. It was depressing, like Washington itself, but Mac felt as though his work was contributing to the cause. Walking the streets he was constantly aware of people. He was watching them a little fearfully. They were watching him fearfully. There was no trust.

There was nothing more he could do in DC. He was needed at campaign headquarters – writing, directing, and featuring in campaign material. In truth he was ready. He missed Helen and he had completed a dossier of senators and congressmen, to be supported in the elections. There was a list of hardcore supporters of the president, some of whom were acting and voting for self-preservation. These politicians could be challenged and their opponents supported.

Mac had loved Washington before the death of democracy. The spring season with flowering trees, immaculate stretches of grass with couples sightless but for each other, hand in hand. The summer with the excited groups of schoolchildren tripping with their new-found growth, bigger feet, bigger hands, bigger voices. Summertime with its bus touring invasion following different colored umbrellas pointing defiantly at a clear blue sky.

Now DC held nothing. No bright spring dresses and shirts, no laughing schoolchildren, no tour groups. The trees seemed bare; the grass uncut. Mac knew there was nothing left for him there. He packed his bag and went to a small private airport where he hitched a ride with someone who was flying west to deliver supplies.

\*\*\*

Mac was welcomed back to Texas with nods as the

quiet group waited for Marjorie White, the last member to arrive. She entered the solemn enclave with a large stack of papers, recognized the mood, and nodded a good morning to everyone as she headed to a seat at the front of the room, to the right side of Ellie May.

"Good morning, everyone;" Ellie May started the meeting. "Well, Helen has a smile on her face, so let's start with her update."

Helen blushed. "That's thanks to Mac being back, not the news I bring. The primaries have been a disaster. The turnout's been poor and there is no energy out there; even our own surveys are showing that we have no chance. Good news in Florida – we got about eighty per cent of the vote, four times what the president received."

"That was the elderly coming out in poor weather," said Sheila Hutchins. "The president is planning on cutting the social security allowance."

"Just a proposal, a bill before Congress to slash Medicare," Alistair said.

"Same thing to the retired and the elderly. And when was the last bill submitted by the president voted down? He definitely has found a way to ensure he wins on all fronts," Sheila stated.

"Maybe not all fronts. At least we can count on Florida to vote the American Party at the November elections," Helen replied, trying to get the weekly conference back on track.

"I think I prefer the good news," Ellie May said. "Any more?"

"Not much that's new," Helen confessed. "We're on every state ballot in November and, in most states where we have identified a Democrat running unopposed, or with weak opposition, we've recruited and helped candidates."

"So we've won the first battle?" asked Ellie May rhetorically. To emphasize the fact for the glum faces in the room, she continued. "We are in the running?"

"Yes, you and Marjorie are going to be on every ballot, probably at the bottom after the Communists, Greens, Tea Party, etc., etc., but you'll be there."

"It's not where you start but where you finish." Ellie May was trying to be positive. "Mark, money?"

"A problem we're working on. The poor primaries don't help. Grassroots is showing some promise. Those who thought we'd be 'New Hampshire and out' are slowly coming in. It's hard work, and we need more volunteers."

"We're working on that," Alistair, who was in a petulant mood, grumbled. His role of recruiting and investigating potential workers was taking its toll.

Mark continued. "The PACs are experiencing some backsliding. Our reservoir of funds is drying fast. We, Margaret and I, are covering that next week; could use some positive news."

"Marjorie?"

"The manifesto," she said dramatically indicating the stack of papers. "Everything we stand for is written down, here. A copy for all, each department, numbered. Share them, but be careful until they are officially in the public domain."

"Which will be when?" asked Sheila.

"The videos have been made and will be released every few days, starting today and ending September 30$^{th}$ with the gun control legislation we support and which will be the first order of business in January."

"Two questions," Alistair interrupted. "One, do we have the funds to promote? And, two, is there a significance to the September 30$^{th}$ date?"

"The answer to number one is yes, barely," Ellie May replied. "Two, the president has invited all candidates to live debates in October."

"You're kidding me," Ginny said in a louder voice than she'd intended. "How many? On what?"

"How can anyone go anywhere? It's suicide," Alistair warned.

"Three debates – domestic policy, foreign policy, and the economy," Helen answered.

"The president is going to debate policy, foreign policy, and the economy? The sitting president is going to debate policy?" an incredulous Mark asked.

"Well, I suppose he is expecting no one to show and then say whatever he wants to say on live television and have everyone believe it," said Ellie May.

"Very likely and very, very likely that no one will show who would prefer to not be arrested or worse," Alistair Clark voiced loudly, supported by the other pessimistic voices in the room.

"We shall of course accept. We're working on a plan as to how, preferring not to be arrested or worse." Ellie May spoke positively but her voice and body language showed apprehension and less sure telltales.

"How about on Labor Day, which is just next week, we have a Texas barbeque? Jim has a steer that can feed everyone."

"I'll bring beer." Mac wanted to leave on a positive note.

"There's a band at Uni who'll play for food," offered Ginny.

"We'll need pies." Betty Jo was already counting in her head how many people would be there. "And ice cream."

A few other people offered to contribute items, as

long as the stores were supplied with what they needed.

Ellie May thanked everyone for their updates and asked them to go about the next items on their checklists.

When the meeting ended and dispersed, everyone left to return phone calls and to handle other typical campaign work. An hour later, the central cabal met by mutual unspoken assent on the porch. Iced tea was available in large jugs next to a tray of glasses.

Jim Joseph broke a thoughtful silence. "Gonna rain."

The other occupants on the porch looked to the sky then resumed their silent contemplations.

"How bad is the money, Mark?" Helen had made notes during the meeting and focused on the one subject that, although she looked at the budget regularly, she was unsure of. She had the feeling that it was incomplete and wondered what outstanding liabilities there might be.

"Bad. We're over budget, no surprise there. A number of candidates are asking for additional funds that we do not have, and we've just added three debates."

"We eliminated a convention," Sheila offered.

"And added a barbecue," Ellie May chimed in. "Good thing Mac's bringing the beer."

Mac didn't smile at Ellie May's comment. "Sorry, all. I got some more bad news. One of the phone calls was to let me know that Hal Rabb passed away."

"Who is he? Important?" Sheila asked.

Mark, Ellie May, and Helen looked with shock, knowing that the PAC monies on which they depended were being held in Las Vegas.

Mac looked across and answered. "A friend.

Funeral is tomorrow. I need to go."

"Do you want company?" asked Mark, although his eyes were conveying a look of desperation. "Will Esther be there?"

Sheila was about to ask about Esther then changed her mind.

"I'm counting on it," said Mac. "Gotta go!"

"Be careful, sweetheart." Helen was visibly upset. "I liked him too."

Mark followed Mac across the rectangle in front of the house. There were several pairs of eyes following them. Bobby Joe watched as he was trained to do, but with only an idle curiosity. Alistair Kirk and Sheila Hutchins were wondering if each was the only person who did not know, who had never heard the name Hal Rabb. Ellie May, Marjorie, and Helen knew the significance to the funding and to the campaign.

"Mac!"

Mac continued walking and without turning said, "How bad?"

"How bad is what?" asked Mark, knowing very well the answer.

Mac turned. "How bad is the money situation?"

"I just answered Helen." Mark was annoyed at being asked again. "I was hoping that you could ask your friends in Vegas for a loan, since you are going there."

"Are you out of your frigging mind?" Mac had raised his voice so that the six pairs of eyes were now looking directly at the two men. Now quieter Mac continued. "The rate of interest would be exorbitant but, more importantly, would put one of the loan participants in the cabinet, a seat in the White House. Or worse."

"Worse?"

"Can you imagine a member of the mafia running the FBI? Find another solution."

"Like what?"

"I don't know. You're the PAC man. What would a political action committee do?"

"I need your help, Mac. I'm begging you," he shouted at Mac's retreating back.

"I have my own problems. I have to bury a friend."

The exchange had been watched and the sight of two associates arguing and shouting was out of character.

"You don't care," shouted Mark. "You're an investigative reporter, and you'll report whoever is in the White House, the FBI."

Mac stopped, turned, and saw that they were on display. He walked over to Mark and firmly stated, "I do care; I always cared. I may have reported both sides of the issues. I cared that both sides were represented. You, Mark, gave money to both sides, not because you cared, because you were paid, handsomely, to give away other people's money."

"That's an unfair characterization and you know it." Mark turned at right angle and walked toward the desert needing to clear his head.

Mac regretted the exchange, hesitated, then headed in the opposite direction.

Helen had started out of her seat but was pulled down with Marjorie touching her elbow. Helen knew the two men – one she had been engaged to and she was married to the other. They would get over their spat. Or they wouldn't. But Marjorie was right – neither would appreciate her interference. Still, she was chief of staff and a 'happy ship' functioned better than an unhappy one.

Everyone else could sense that Marjorie and Helen

needed to be alone. They quietly headed inside to resume their other responsibilities.

"Will it be okay, Marjorie?"

"The guys? They'll work it out. I've always admired that about men – they get mad, say what needs to be said, and move on. Women tend to hold grudges."

Helen smiled. "That can definitely be true. I meant the budget though. I mean, we knew it was always going to be difficult to start a new party on a shoestring budget."

"More than difficult. Impossible," said Marjorie.

"Then why?"

"I think it was to awaken the American public. I don't think we were realistically aiming for this election; maybe the next, or more likely the one eight years away against a weaker incumbent."

"But…"

"I know things in America have deteriorated over the last two years. The problem is Congress. For years they have voted party lines. We elect individuals then one party votes the presidential line and the other votes with the leader of the opposition, making it not a two-party system but a two-person system."

"Not true. They debate and amend."

"They debate on behalf of amendments which will serve their geographical or demographic constituents' purpose. Until we have representatives who forget party once they're in, then we won't be able to succeed as a nation. This is why term limits are so important."

\*\*\*

The funeral was a very small event. In addition to Mac there were two women – one recognized as Hal's daughter Esther and the other Mac presumed had been

Hal's wife. Standing back some was a young man dressed in black, including a black shirt and tie, together with four representatives of the funeral home.

With a quick look at the clock, the funeral director stepped forward. "Are we expecting more people?" After a pause he asked, "A priest perhaps?"

"No," Esther responded.

"Would someone like to say a few words?"

No one offered.

He looked expectantly to the rear to no avail.

"Shall I say the Lord's Prayer or the Twenty-third Psalm?"

"He was Jewish," Mac whispered.

"Twenty-third psalm is fine," said Esther's mother.

The service was quickly concluded, the necessary papers completed, and Mac walked slowly out followed by the two women who were both silently crying.

Outside was warm and sunny in contrast to the cool dark place they had left behind. The stocky man in black was now wearing reflective dark sunglasses.

"Who are you?" the man asked Mac.

"A friend. And you?"

The man responded with a small smile. He turned to the women and asked, "Relatives?"

There was a long pause. Finally Esther's mother replied, "Friends," while putting on sunglasses.

"A quiet man with so many friends." He gave a chuckle.

Mac disliked the man on sight and the reflective sunglasses were another reason to mistrust him.

The man stood waiting for a reaction. Getting none, he turned and walked away with the swagger that said that it was 'job done.'

"Can I buy you lunch?" Mac asked.

"No."

"Mother, Mr. McDougal is not affiliated with the casino or with any of Daddy's associates. Yes, we would love to have lunch. We need to talk. And we may have company." Esther nodded in the direction of the retreating black suit.

"Then a noisy fast food place," Mac suggested.

"Perfect. I know just the one. Follow our car."

\*\*\*

Seated in the middle of a busy local burger restaurant, they were the best dressed patrons and a black suit would have brought inquisitive stares.

"Susan, Susan Schaff, my maiden name. Hal mentioned you, Mr. McDougal, when we spoke. Apparently he thought enough of you to talk about his health."

Susan Schaff, was, Mac calculated, about sixty years old but attractive and slim. This was in contrast to her daughter who was short and overweight but with bright intelligent eyes.

"Mr. McDougal…"

"Please, Esther, call me Mac."

"Mac, Dad transferred your portfolio to me last week and there are a few things I'd like to change. I don't have his insider information and it would be illegal for me to use it anyway, so I think that a more 'blue chip' approach would be appropriate, or you can use someone else."

"That's fine. I never knew what investments were bought or sold. I just know I was doing well. I understand your reluctance to continue and will understand if you ask me to find someone else. But, please, can we delay that until after the election? Depending on how that goes, I have no idea what I'll do."

"The other money has about dried up and no one is looking to 'book'." She glanced at her mother. Susan pretended not to be listening. Mac could see that she had done a lot of pretending to not listen while married to Hal.

"The action will increase with the debates. We hope to have increased the coffers by then. It's a genuine worry."

Mac was extremely worried about every aspect of the campaign. The obstacles were mounting – it was becoming more dangerous, and the financial situation was dire. Looking back the idea had come from anger; was it anger at the administration, on behalf of the people, or was it a personal anger? He could and did find merit in all of those thoughts, so chances were it was all three.

The scores on the wagering, New York then Iowa, were fortuitous and might not be repeated. The people who had wagered on behalf of Mohammed Al Adana becoming president and won had been burned in New York and Iowa. They'd lost a few minor contests too and would be more cautious. Besides, anyone putting their money on Ellie May Joseph was putting her life in further danger.

The gun policy was a gamble. Something had to be done about street violence and the killings were mostly by gunfire. Time and again, in surveys and conversations, it was agreed that with over a billion personal guns on the streets, a billion could be scrapped, 'as long as I keep mine, just for my family's protection.'

"I understand," said Mac, taking a bite of his burger. "Guess we'll have to hope for some good luck to come our way then."

Esther nodded, then said, "Mother and I will be

returning East late this afternoon. You know how to get in touch with me should you need to."

Mac stood as the two women rose. They all shook hands, and then they left.

With a great amount of despair – at the loss of his friend and the bleak financial status of the campaign, Mac sat back down and decided to focus on his food. There was little better than a greasy burger, too-crisp fries, and a thick shake to drown one's sorrows in.

These thoughts were still occupying Mac an hour later. His usual, careful observation was missing as he entered the hotel room. Sitting in a chair facing the door was the black-suited man.

"One of us must be in the wrong room." Mac was buying time, organizing his thoughts.

"I had a couple of questions," the man said quietly, without menace.

"Then ask." Mac was equally quiet.

"Who are you?"

"You know who I am or you wouldn't have found my room. Who are you?"

"How do you know the deceased?"

"A friend," Mac said.

This response was met by a snort. "Gambler?"

"I never gamble." Hal told Mac that knowing the result before making a wager was not gambling.

The man moved in a practiced manner, exposing a gun holstered under his arm so that Mac would see it and be afraid.

Mac did and was.

"Who are the women?"

"Ask them."

"I did."

"And?"

"You heard their answer. Friends." The man

smiled, amused by something he knew but would keep to himself. He stood to leave then looked hard at Mac.

"Man had a lot of friends," Mac replied.

At the door the man turned. "Be seeing you!"

While it was said pleasantly, Mac was aware that it didn't mean that the next meeting would be pleasant.

The door closed.

Mac sat thinking. He needed a drink and called Esther to meet him in fifteen minutes in the small bar of the hotel next door. He showered and changed into casual slacks and shirt. Looking more like a tourist, Mac was seated at the far end of almost deserted bar with a beer for himself and a sparkling water for Esther. They would have looked out of place anywhere in the world except Las Vegas. Esther was wearing dark glasses covering eyes puffy from crying.

"Did you have a visit from the dark suit?" asked Mac.

"Yes, what does he want?"

"Everything. I think he believes there's a second black book with information they'd like to have. Information is the bitcoin in this community. This black book has politicians' dark deeds in it as well as a good deal of background on the political book."

"Does it exist?" The dark glasses masked any unwanted hints of obfuscation.

"Oh, yes, it exists, on a memory card." Mac was guessing about the computer memory card, but he knew that Esther had the only copy.

"I've made a decision." Mac continued, "We probably will not participate in another political book. It's too dangerous, hasn't enough return for the risk, and has provided a crutch for too long. The disk is therefore worthless and should be destroyed for the safety of all who know about it."

"I see. You're scared?"

"Damn right I am. I'm out of here first flight in the morning."

"I am on a redeye leaving tonight. Be back at my desk by eight-thirty."

"Good. The other money and mine can be transferred by wire to the Bank of Texas as needed. I have a card with the bank numbers in my hand, encrypt and destroy this card. Is this a problem?"

"No. I put your investments with my other clients in a coded account. The monies in the Political Action Fund is in a segregated client's cash account. Don't worry – there's a lot of money in there, just coming and going. A lot of clients are hiding money in trusts, offshore accounts, etcetera. But some have indicated that they may want to invest in the new party."

"That's more than you should be telling me…more than I should know. Mark will need to be in Washington; he should meet with some of these people if they have political ambitions or a stake in America's future."

"Mac, you never stop."

"To rephrase Gorbachev, 'If you stop, you're going backwards!'"

## Chapter Thirty

George Breakstone was not in a good mood. Seated opposite Mac and Mark in a breakfast shop in a hotel in Austin was not how he had planned to start his day.

"You're telling me that new funds aren't committed, and the payroll is growing?"

"In a nutshell." Mac was straightforward, honest.

"There are some outstanding pledges. The party has volunteers on the telephone around the clock." Mark was more optimistic, a typical salesman.

"I see the numbers, Mark." George was not relenting.

"Okay, the poll results published, even our own assessments, aren't encouraging. We hope for a boost in interest when the debates begin."

"No boost for about a month then? The PAC is just about dry too." George persisted.

"Working on that," Mark said. "A quick visit to see where the unpaid pledges of support are, then to Washington to do what I do."

Mark and Mac had patched their differences, for now, and simultaneously agreed that Washington was still the power base and was the home of many ambitious men and women.

"And in your absence?"

"Margaret Forrest, the woman you interviewed, is a fast learner." The inference that Mark might be arrested, or worse, was not spoken.

"By the way, George, are you coming out to the barbeque on Monday?" Mark asked while Mac looked quizzical. It had been assumed that George would be known to only a few people.

"Wasn't planning to."

"Bring a friend. I've invited a couple of heavy donors. They've expressed some interest in contributions, money raising efforts, and one asked about our bank's strength."

"Wise?" asked George.

"Legit?" asked Mac.

Mark feigned a shocked look on his face. "One hundred per cent and one million dollars sure."

\*\*\*

Monday the three potential donors arrived in two separate helicopters. A reassuring sight was the occasional Air National Guard flights, instructed to practice in that air space. The three principals had joint meetings and half an hour each with Ellie May Joseph and Marjorie White. They were informal and no notes were kept.

Mark stayed away and ensured that the travelling companions were entertained. One had an interest in horseback riding, so a stable hand and a Texas Ranger accompanied her into the desert, investigating a couple of canyons. One headed for the pool in a very small bikini, while the third parked close to the bar.

Mark headed to the bar to provide conversation and monitor excess drinking in the hot weather. He had a note in his file that she had been in the Betty Ford Clinic.

"Mrs. Chambers, I'm Mark Hughes."

"Sent by my husband to keep an eye on me?"

"Not at all. Although, to be honest, it does benefit

me that everyone has a good time. I sent an invitation to you both."

"He wants to be an ambassador."

"Not mine to give or to decide."

"But you still will take his, our, money."

"Well, you have two choices. You can hope that the money given to the American Party will help provide a stable and economically viable country for your grandchildren, or you can leave it to your son-in-law."

She laughed at the thought. "Done your homework eh, Mr. Hughes. How does one get a drink here?"

"It's Mark. This is an informal barbeque for the employees, volunteers, and families, so one goes to the bar."

"I like you, Mark. Call me Judith. No, call me Judy. That takes me back to college and the last time I was this relaxed."

"I'll have spritzer, tall, lots of ice," she told the bartender.

"Same for me," said Mark. "Ever seen a steer roast, Judy?"

"Haven't been in a kitchen since before college. What is that?" A large wood-fired grill had skewers of fish and shrimp tended by Gump, his son, and two women.

"Gump, what are you doing?"

"Grilling shrimp with Cajun sauce and shark with a sprinkling of this and that. Good to see you, Mr. Mark."

"Good to see you, too. This is Judy. What do you think, Gump? What should we have?"

The normally taciturn middle son was known to Mark as Pump. He was particularly tongue-tied and nodded to the attractive young woman next to him.

"Hi. I'm Sandra. Leon's not usually so quiet."

Gump suppressed a laugh. "Not with Sandra anyway. This, by the way, is Tanya, my wife. Margaret was supposed to come down for the weekend with that Ike fella. Anyway, said we should come up see them here, do a little dancing, do a little eating, do a little drinking."

"Is the fish fresh?" asked Judy.

"If it was fresher, it would still be in the gulf."

"Can I try some?"

"Help yourself, honey."

Judy laughed, it sounded as though it had been a long time since she'd been treated as Judy instead of Mrs. Chambers.

"Gump, can you direct Judy to the steer roast? I have to mingle." Mark left.

"Why do they call you Gump?" Judy was engaging with the Forrest family as Mark left to check on the swimming pool.

\*\*\*

Throughout the afternoon there was the sound of occasional gunfire from the desert. Ellie May was curious and went looking for Bobby Joe who had a communication bud in his ear. "Rattlers!"

"Rangers?"

"I got some off-duty Rangers to volunteer, keep an eye out. Getting some practice shooting at rattle snakes. This party is a pretty tempting target."

"Good thinking; and…"

"All quiet."

"Get some food out to them."

"Yes, ma'am. I think I know the men for the job. Mrs. White's boys are getting a little antsy, not into two stepping yet."

Ian and Andrew were more than happy to load a

quad bike with steaks, fish, and shrimp, corn on the cob, bread sticks, and a container of beans, along with plates, napkins, and utensils, and head out to the various pick-ups parked about half a mile out from the ranch. This was fun, as they had also loaded cases of beer and water.

They'd been gone half an hour when Marjorie asked Bobby Joe if they were okay. In answer to his radio request, a laughing trooper with teenagers said they were heading back and would be fine as long as they didn't fall out of the quad.

"Fine, Marjorie."

"Have they been sampling the beer?"

"They're fine, Marjorie," he assured her.

As she tried to find words that would describe their punishment, there was a large explosion in the desert.

"What the hell? Report in."

Silence. Marjorie screamed and started running toward the smoke that was now visible.

Helen reacted first, grabbed Marjorie, and forcibly dragged her in the house.

"My boys!"

"Marjorie!"

"My boys!" She was struggling in the grip of Helen and another staff member.

"Marjorie. No one knows what's happened." Helen was facing her, holding Marjorie's hands.

"They've killed my boys!" Marjorie was hysterical.

Outside there was an element of confusion, although by and large people were calm and headed indoors. The potential donors called for their helicopters but were persuaded to wait until more was known, particularly since the Air National Guard was due for a fly by.

Mark went into damage control mode, suggesting that they wait downstairs in the conference room. Ginny and her mother set about getting drinks and food. The guests were shown the electronic gadgets that were being used and on a map screen where the American Party support was currently. The male donors had seen some of this. Judy showed interest in the map of Texas and asked where the noise had come from, and was it normal?

"Appears to be about here." Mark pointed at the map about twice the distance from the ranch then where it might have been.

Judy's husband harrumphed his disbelief. "Sounded closer than that."

"Sounds travel a long way in the desert," Sheila explained then picked up a ringing phone and listened.

"It was a drone shot down by a ranger."

"And the bang?"

"They didn't say." She knew and Mark and Ginny knew that it was a device similar to the one that had taken two visitors lives and Betty Jo's feet in the attack on their car. It was clearly one that had not been in the Washington Armory.

"Marjorie White, is she okay? Seemed shaken by the bang," one of the donors asked.

"On edge. We have a very busy schedule, crossing the country in the next three weeks. She's protective of her sons." Mark was playing the diplomat. "If you have friends who would like to meet her, have a speech, we could put together a party, any size, get ten thousand a plate. The schedule has some flexibility."

"Ten thousand?" one asked.

"Why not? Who wouldn't want one of America's most famous women to speak? One who is proposing one of the most radical agendas any party has ever published."

"Good point. I know at least six who would pay in order to say they were there."

"Sweetheart," it was the woman who had been in the desert and was now clinking an empty glass of ice cubes. "You would embarrass them into being there. How would they feel at the club if every wife had been at a party showing their diamonds, except their latest wife?"

Mark was smiling. They had forgotten the explosion and were focusing on their money. "Contact Sheila or Ginny and propose some dates."

Ginny brought another glass of bourbon to the ice rattler and Sheila was handing out cards and contact information.

Upstairs the door crashed open as two excited teens dashed in. They were oblivious to the looks, oblivious to the silence that fell over the people. Some gathered around Marjorie.

"Mom, you won't believe it. There was an explosion, knocked us off the quad."

"Knocked *you* off, I hung on," Ian clarified.

"Don't you ever go off again."

"Mom, we just went to take stuff to the Rangers."

"And drinking!" Marjorie was crying again, this time with relief. She was trembling as she stood and enveloped them.

Slowly the party got back to normal, or almost. The band started playing, the guests started dancing, the grill was again doing business. The difference was that a group around the beer keg was talking in less strident tones, dismissing the explosive event and the implications. Taking the microphone between tunes, Bobby Joe addressed the crowd to update them all on the event. "A drone was spotted that was not one of ours and shot down. Turns out a grenade was attached and exploded harmlessly in the desert. It was a meant to create panic and confusion to damage and deter our support for this campaign. It did not do that. Eat up, drink up. And it's time that my wife, Betty Jo, and I show you how to two-step."

Betty Joe stepped up on her artificial feet to applause as the band played their version of "Yellow Rose of Texas."

\*\*\*

It was late and quieter. The band was on a minibus heading back to their school. Rubbish had been collected and compacted, leftovers taken away or stored. A few of the guests, having made new friends, were reluctant for the magic to end. Marjorie caught up with Ellie May as she said goodbye to the latest leaving guests.

"Ellie May, I need to apologize for my breakdown and to resign as your vice-presidential nominee. My behavior was unacceptable."

"It was understandable behavior."

"Not as a vice president. Can you imagine if this happened when we were in office? Unacceptable!"

"Let's talk in the morning. We need a forum anyway, a re-cap of all we learned today. We'll get a report from Bobby Joe on the drone, Mark on the funds, and Helen on the fall out."

"I won't change my mind."

"Sleep on it."

\*\*\*

The next morning's meeting was held as usual in the secure room beneath the house. The mood was unusually quiet. Some were quiet as a result of excess celebration, some with the knowledge that there were important decisions to be made which would affect their future.

"Bobby Joe?" The directive came from Ellie May as an indication that the meeting had started. Today no preamble.

"The drone was the same type as took Betty Jo's feet. Same explosive, same as we…" He caught himself just in time, "…same as we understand was in Washington Armory. Directed from a vehicle, camouflaged, in the desert with a camera, probably linked to some federal agency."

"Conjecture, unsupported, guesswork." Ellie May rarely spoke so firmly. She was clearly angry. "Enough shillyshallying. This is all important. We had guests could have been injured and the entire staff in one place. The party is over as we said last week. There are exactly nine weeks to an election. We will all be putting in a minimum of twelve hours a day for all sixty-three days. Anyone who cannot, or is unwilling to do that, either in this room or on your staff, let them go now." There was a silence as she examined every face in the room. A few shifted slightly, and some could not hold their gazes.

"Ellie May." Marjorie spoke.

"Not now, Marjorie." It was again the lawyer's courthouse voice. She continued, "Fundraising. I want every phone manned from eight in the morning on the East Coast until nine at night on the West Coast."

"We don't have enough people," Alistair protested.

"Get them and remind them to ask for their vote. Mac, work on a telephone speech."

"Yes, Ma'am." The tone of voice was noticed by everyone in the room. Officially Mac was not part of the team. He was Helen's husband, and as such was generally asked to do things, not ordered. The newsletters he would have done whether he was involved or not.

Ellie May affected not to hear his response or his tone. Mac understood; she was committed to the campaign. It was clear now that it was a two-dog fight, and that one of the dogs was willing to fight unfairly.

"Mark, you're moving to Washington. That's good, we need to have some distance. If you proceed as a political action committee, then you need space and to expand your base. We need support. In an ideal world, you'd have no function, but this world is far from ideal."

"Marjorie and I are planning to visit some important sponsors this week," said Mark.

"Important?" asked Ellie May.

"Critical," Mark replied.

"Then your staff can work on having an office in D.C."

"But, Ellie May…"

"Not now, Marjorie."

"You have my resignation."

"It's too late Marjorie. We have committed to your being with Mark. You heard him say that. When we are in the White House, we can talk. Until then, we need you. We need you committed. We need you to go with Mark this week then back here to prepare me for the debates."

"What's next, Helen?"

"We must not forget the Senate and House races. The candidates have all received notices that there can be no funds at this time for their campaigns. They'll have to raise the money, pull in favors, and work like we are, to stay solvent."

"What about the opposition? The Democrats and, to a lesser extent, the Republicans?"

"Republicans have almost shut up shop or are American Party candidates or supporters of our party, afraid to put the name on their literature. Their fundraising is okay. The Democrats believe they will win every seat one way or the other and are not bothering."

"Go hard, Helen! No letting up. Give them support, read them the riot act if you must. Do we have anyone out in the states?"

"Margaret Forrest was doing the audits. She was recruited and paid for by the PAC money Mark brought in. Is she going to Washington, Mark?" Helen asked.

"Doesn't have to. I can pick up my old staff or recruit in Washington."

"Good, then we'll keep her with her permission, to take on a role for the party."

"I underpay her," said Mark, looking over at an embarrassed Margaret.

"Good, then we'll have no problem matching her salary."

"You'd better pay Ike, too," said Mark, while Margaret flushed an even deeper red. "He's overpaid!" Mark was chuckling. In truth he would have preferred to keep them both, as talented, hardworking, dedicated staff was hard to hire in even the best of circumstances.

"Helen?" Ellie May prompted.

"Yes, I'll take care of it. George will do the paperwork, etc."

George Breakstone was overseeing the banking for the campaign now, in addition to having the PAC contributions channeled through his bank. The conflict and issues were confusing and interrupted his night's sleep. Lawyers and consultants were reassuring but it was still a gut decision when it came down to it.

Helen was aware of this conflict as she talked with Allyn Cherwin, the campaign treasurer, every day. She added, "…or George will reassign the responsibility," a nod to Allyn Cherwin made the administrative function his responsibility.

"That's it for today. It's ten o'clock and there is much to do. If you have something for the agenda, talk to Helen. We have two months. Nine weeks, three debates, and fifty states to fight a corrupt, mentally deficient opponent, and there's no money." Ellie May was somber. "I want to take this opportunity to let you all know how special you all are, and I could not have a better team to work with."

There was a brief round of applause, then the staff filtered out of the room, motivated.

Alone now with only her husband Jim and Helen, Ellie May stayed focused. "Helen, follow up. Did you take notes? Debates, we need to practice."

"Yes, yes, I spoke with Professor Harry Taylor in New York, and he thought the students might be educated by simulating debates on the topics and then he has them writing a critique of the actual debates for credits."

"Great idea, Helen, and we can see the student debates by video."

"Actually, it was the brilliant idea of Hannah Sanderson. She's going to orchestrate a similar debate at Harvard."

"Maybe we can float the idea to the other colleges and universities. They're all old enough to vote."

"Even high schools. Speaking of which, there have been a few debates recently on the Second Amendment. Former Supreme Court Justice Stevens has been speaking of the gun control legislation,"

Helen spoke while furiously making notes to herself.

"I must tell Mac for his writings and also for his speech writing for Marjorie and yourself."

"Will Marjorie be okay?" asked Ellie May.

"You mean after her non-resignation speech?
"Yes, I think so. She's a professional. One of the best!"

## Chapter Thirty-One

Marjorie and Mark had meetings with the sponsors of the active political action group that Mark was representing. Marjorie spoke at rallies organized by the unions and other locally active groups in Oregon, Wisconsin, and California. In every case the meetings were hastily organized and the participants were amazed that they were facing a candidate for the vice president who was not intimidated.

The intimidation was also in evidence at each meeting. The local police were not interested in breaking up a meeting of their neighbors. State police generally found something else to do in spite of orders to arrest Marjorie, an alleged fugitive from justice. There was no legal case for entering a meeting without probable cause, so it wasn't high on the agenda. The police were also quick to answer any inquiry with a question of why their funding was being changed, lowered, while crime increased. The militia, while interested in disrupting and intimidating, were disorganized and reluctant to take on large crowds while there was more profit for them in individual harassment, extortion, and kidnapping. The militia did vandalize parking areas where the meetings were held and proved a menacing presence to participants. This worked in favor of the American Party. Donations and contact information was gathered by Marjorie, Margaret, and their team. Volunteers were easier to find at every stop. The geography planned by the headquarters included skipping and doubling back which, while exhausting, was proving effective. There would be three meetings scheduled and local or state representatives would speak at two of them, Marjorie at the third, chosen randomly.

Mark, with vague promises of additional funding and data, moved to Washington.

Everything was set in motion that could move the campaign forward. Political debates became the campus fad at colleges and universities across the country. Ellie May watched them all. Mac analyzed each, noting geographical concerns, gender issues, rising inflation, and how the economies were affected. But the overwhelming issue was job related. Where were the jobs? Mothers and fathers were unable to pay fees due to redundancy and short work weeks. Mac wrote the concerns down. He was back doing the job he loved, investigative reporting. He wrote daily blogs which went out, wrote summaries for Ellie May, answered local candidates seeking new ways to reach their constituents, and worked on ideas for the upcoming debates.

He saw very little of Helen as she was putting out fires with both hands. They passed in the hallway.

"Dinner tonight?" he asked.

"Alistair wants more money. Marketing is looking at a new poster…"

"Wine."

"Marjorie needs to conference from Tupelo, or is it Tucson. Mark, I forget what he wants…probably to gloat."

"Candlelight."

"Ellie May has a meeting with Senator…" a pause as Helen stood, a pencil in her mouth. "Okay, what time?"

"Six, so we have plenty of time afterwards." Mac gave his imitation of a Groucho Marx leer. "What got you? Me and the candlelight?"

Helen walked away, "No, you had me at wine." She laughed in a genuine trilling way that Mac hadn't heard for a long time.

***

Entering the office, Helen announced, "Ellie May, I'm out of here at five-thirty."

"Meeting with the senator?" asked Alistair.

"No, dinner with Mac. The senator can meet with Allyn. One is our treasurer and the other, unless I am mistaken, wants money. They will either solve each other's problems or give us all a solution."

"Helen, you could be good at this."

"Only if I get some time with my husband. You too."

"You're probably right. I'll have Jim fix something for the two of us on the verandah and hire that stable hand Jose to play his guitar. Jim loves the Mexican guitar music.

"Great idea. I haven't looked forward to anything like this since I was in college." Ellie May was smiling. "Let's get Marjorie on Skype or whatever we call it. She's doing a fabulous job and we must tell her. Funds are coming in, candidates are volunteering, people are offering to canvas, drop off leaflets, hold signs. It may just come together."

***

In Washington Mark was bombed out of the first two store fronts he rented. Fortunately the firebombs were at night and no one was hurt. The damage was also limited to campaign material. A message.

"So, where to now?" Mark asked the assembled staff.

"What if they bomb when we're here?" asked an anxious young staffer. "We could be hurt."

"I was thinking last night of *Guys and Dolls*," said Mark waiting.

The blank questioning looks from the three people facing him confirmed his suspicion they had likely never seen the show.

"Longest floating crap game in New York."

"Ah! In a mission. You want us to move into, or join a mission, join the Salvation Army, or something?"

"Or something!" Mark smiled, trying to give confidence to this team. "How about we rent a couple of buses, fit them out with copiers and load our materials in the baggage area. We're all using cell phones anyway. We would have transportation, park in garages with surveillance, pick up and drop off volunteers. What do you think?"

"Like one of the buses that rock groups have with kitchens and bathrooms?" a young staffer asked.

"Big screen TV's?" another pushed.

With a frown at the last speaker Mark agreed. "Something like that. Let's see what we can find."

\*\*\*

The plan turned out better than could have initially been expected. A former Marine drove the first bus. When the campaign moved to Washington, a campaign bus was rented and, with its success, the format was replicated throughout the country with instant recognition. All of the advertising, newsletters, and pamphlets included shots of the buses in the background.

The campaign was in full gear and gaining momentum. There were still attacks and harassment from the local militia groups, but the law and order groups and the local law and order departments had had enough. They pushed back and arrested and harassed whenever they could. It was a stalemate for now.

In Austin refinements were being made to the technology needed for the debates. Practice was in full swing. Mac helped Helen and a team to anticipate questions, then Helen worked as moderator and Mac stood in for the president. Mac had interviewed President Mohammed Al Adana when he was Senator Arthur Anders hoping to be vice president to Marjorie White. He hadn't liked him then and his opinion had dropped steadily since that day. There had always been the underlying feeling that he was lying, about everything or anything, but Mac acknowledged that in reality it was just a different agenda.

The questions would be slanted toward the incumbent. Domestic policy was the first debate, scheduled for Washington. Alistair Kirk was still negative but, persuaded that his negativity was an asset, offered questions, points of view, and general criticism.

The college debates had yielded a plethora of material. Overriding every other domestic subject was the unemployment or, as some colleges debated, the lack of employment opportunities. In some of the more liberal colleges, the debater representing the government quoted the low government unemployment rate to jeers, estimates of high rates by the challengers to cheers. Other colleges had a mixed reaction to both.

"We must anticipate this question and act

decisively to secure the unemployed or under employed voter." Ellie May was stating the obvious.

"The president will lie," said Mac.

"Our message must be slick, practiced, and given every time, whatever the original question." Alistair Kirk had been through many such television events. "Like the Clintons or Trump – pick any recent debate and the question is twisted to the answer that has been practiced."

"But the public doesn't like that," said Mac.

"Depends," said Alistair with a shrug. "Subtle and strong, it is heard, and once out of the bottle, we can build on it with messages for several weeks."

"Statistics?" asked Ellie May.

"They have limited usefulness. They can be boring, confusing, and not suited to television," Sheila contributed while making notes for press releases.

"Okay. Two days from now, a full-dress rehearsal. Alistair in the role of questioner. Mac, will you be president?"

"Delighted!"

"Helen, Marjorie, Sheila, Jim, help me prepare and practice my answers."

"Any audience?"

"No, top secret. I debated sending a video to Harry Taylor, but the fewer the better."

"You're the boss." Helen closed the conversation.

\*\*\*

The mock debate was a debacle. Alistair set out the rules to the non-existent audience and then introduced the speakers.

"The President of the United States, Mohammed Al Adana." Mac appeared and approached the podium. He was dressed in a long robe and gave an Islamic greeting as he stopped.

"The challenger, representing the American Party, Ellie May Joseph." It had been decided to use the holographic image technology, and a lifelike image approached the other lectern.

"Good evening."

"What is this crap?" shouted Mac. "I'm supposed to talk to a cartoon. I might as well be on the Simpsons."

Alistair Kirk looked around for guidance, and Ellie May jumped.

Alistair recovered somewhat but was left shaken as he read his opening remarks and guidelines for the one hour allotted to the candidates with opening speeches, questions provided by the live audience, then concluding remarks by the candidates.

"Mr. President, you elected to speak first."

"My first remark is to protest this character, the total lack of respect for the American people."

The remainder of his remarks were related to achievements of the last four years, the peace around the globe, the demilitarization of the armed forces, and gave evidence of the billions of dollars saved by reducing armed services, scrapping bases, and by reducing armament purchases. These billions ploughed back into the economy into infrastructure, job training, etc.

The figures were accurate, but the use of funds was fictional.

Ellie May was still shaken and was scribbling notes as Mac spoke but was far from confident in her opening remarks.

"I apologize to those Americans offended by my unorthodox appearance and the circumstances which made it necessary."

The rest of the opening remarks were rehearsed

and grew in strength but were delivered in a wooden, self-conscious manner. Questions and answers went as rehearsed for Ellie May. Mac continued to throw off the routine with references belittling the candidate, women in general, her choice of women staff and a female vice president. He took no notice of questions in order to attack the gender issues, quoted statistics to support his point of view, and loudly harrumphed when Ellie May made a point. Eventually the hour was over.

"What on earth was that?" Helen was red faced.

"An absolute disaster!" Alistair loosened his tie.

"Where did you get those facts?" asked Ellie May.

Jim slowly applauded. "That was brilliant, a tour de force. Unbelievable, but believable! Now, let's go sit down and review the recording."

Mac sat at the conference table and stated, "Two immediate comments before the playback. One, we've been stressing to expect the unexpected; in this case not far from possibility. Two, I fabricated all of the statistics which, again, we have stated is probable. We have to be ready with counter arguments. And never, never apologize!"

"That's three things," said Helen.

"When you see the playback, you'll see a dozen or more issues." Mac took a long drink of water. "Alistair, great recovery."

"Seeing you in the bed sheet almost gave me a heart attack."

"Do we still go holographic?"

"Do you want to be in jail or wind up dead?"

"We go holographic for now."

Ellie May was horrified at how the initial tirade had made her static, wooden looking. She had never turned a question to her advantage. She was too nice.

The next few days were geared to the voters she needed, women, out of work people, law enforcement officers, those victims of crime, ex-military personnel, and those in manufacturing worried about keeping their jobs.

\*\*\*

The first debate was at Georgetown University. The militia were there in force, surrounding the campus with orders to take into custody Ellie May and her entourage. There was an attempt to stack the hall with militant Islamic supporters of the president. Virtually all were turned away by campus police who were backed by local police after setting off alarms in the metal detectors. The audience was made up of students, alumni, curious government employees, and media personnel.

The president arrived in a dark pinstriped suit and refused to make eye contact with Ellie May's image. It was in such stark contrast with the rehearsal that Ellie May relaxed and gave an outstanding performance. The president had not expected any opposition and had prepared a speech, not a defense of his administration.

Margaret Forrest and volunteers handed out brochures and pins at the exit, slowing the flood of students long enough for Henry and his helper to remove the holographic projectors.

\*\*\*

The pro-presidential newspapers decried the use of holographs and reiterated the party line. Word of mouth, however, praised the honesty of unemployment, of the underemployed, of chronically unemployed figures presented by the American Party candidate. Crime and associated gun violence, the role of the militia, all of the answers from Ellie May felt better than the president stating that crime was going down thanks to the efforts of the militia. There was an overwhelming blitz of telephone calls pledging money, promising support, and giving encouragement. There were many less-pleasant calls stating what might happen if anyone tried to disarm them. Overall it was encouraging, and many said that after the original surprise they had not noticed the holographic image. The message was more important.

The telephone operators had a checklist and were mostly successful in soliciting a name, address, email, pledge of vote, and willingness to canvass friends, neighbors, and associates. It was heartening, but short lived. The next debate was only two weeks away and was to be held in San Francisco on foreign policy.

"It won't work. I'm weak and vulnerable on foreign policy."

Ellie May was struggling to write an opening remark and closing summary.

"But we, the American Party, isn't weak on foreign relations," countered her husband, Jim.

"Everyone says we are."

"We have the strength all around us. Marjorie, as former VP, travelled the world on behalf of the U.S.A.: Have her write your opening remarks."

"I suppose…" Ellie May paused. "I suppose I could replace her on the campaign tour for a few days, find out what the country is thinking."

"Dangerous!"

"It's been for Marjorie, too, and I can't ask someone to do what I should. She hasn't seen her boys for weeks."

"You're right, sweetheart, as usual. I'll go with you."

"No, you'll be distracting. Best I take Bobby Joe."

"Oh, now I'm distracting?" Jim teased.

Ellie May gave her husband a wink and a smile. "The timing's perfect, actually. Marjorie's in Nevada and had planned to go to New England next. She can come back here. I can leave early for Boston. Where's Helen? She knows all about that area."

***

Faneuil Hall in Boston was full for a televised debate between students from the University of Massachusetts and students from Harvard. It had been publicized as a debate between the generally poorer state-subsidized students and those from wealthier parents or alumni-sponsored scholarships.

In the presentation it was difficult to distinguish who was who. The subject was 'foreign intervention, financially, politically, and militarily.' UMass had won the toss and took 'in favor of the motion' in order to speak first; Harvard was delighted to speak 'against.'

After two hours, everyone in the building was enlightened and sure that the intervention, if at all, should be financial and political but not military. It meshed perfectly with the American Party manifesto.

Hannah Sanderson had introduced the teams and moderated.

"Thank you, both teams, and congratulations. You have split the vote and the voters. Therefore, I have a surprise judge who has watched with us all tonight. I've asked her to comment in person. Please give a warm Massachusetts welcome to Ellie May Joseph, presidential candidate, representing the American Party."

There was a stunned silence until some realized this was a live, confident woman – a woman that some media outlets had labelled too timid and weak to leave

Texas, let alone lead a country. When the realization rippled through the historic building, there was immediate applause and everyone stood.

"Thank you, all. I want to thank these two teams for an exciting evening. An event such as this proves that Democracy is alive and well in America. That these young men and women can engage in conversation on opposing sides of a complicated foreign policy issue is commendable. This country should be using the wealth to help lesser nations in some of their needs as we should be helping our neighbors who may have temporary difficulties. We should also use our strength as arbiters, not our military strength as aggressors. This is what the American Party will do."

The audience and debaters stood and applauded.

Regaining the attention of those in the room, Ellie May continued. "I'd love to spend the whole evening with you and answer all of your questions. Some of my people will be here even after I have to go, but now I think that the two teams should each ask a question which I will attempt to answer as clearly as they have expressed themselves."

Forty minutes later Ellie May had the audience in the palm of her hand.

"Well, I'm getting the signal from my staff. They're anxious for me to go raise some money."

The audience laughed. They loved how personable, how human she was.

"To you panelists I say, come to Washington, join my administration after you graduate. Write me directly.

"God bless, y'all. God bless America."

A standing ovation, a shaking of hands with the panelists, a wave, and the Ellie May was taken out of a side door. Her next stop was a dinner party in the suburbs, then a midnight meeting with the Sons of Liberty, and finally sleep in a suite that Mac had secured at the Custom House. A suite, she was reminded, that did not exist. Since the hotel was President Al Adana's stopping place, it was hopefully the last place anyone would look to find her.

\*\*\*

"I'm so tired. How do you do this day after day?" Ellie May was sharing a ride with the same staff she'd seen only a few hours before. They were headed north in a large popular brand of SUV, armed with a Thermos of coffee and a box of breakfast sandwiches.

"Practice," said the young man driving.

"Where to today?" she asked.

"Long day. First Portland, Maine, and then Concord, New Hampshire."

"Why Portland, not Augusta?"

"Because as Willie Sutton said about why he robbed banks, 'That's where the money is'."

"I'm so tired."

"You have time for a one-hour nap before we hit Portland, then a one-hour nap after lunch before we hit Concord."

\*\*\*

Upon her return to Texas, everyone wanted to see Ellie May. There was a quick meeting before she finally surrendered to her exhaustion.

"I slept on the plane from Providence and I'm still tired. We stayed outside Concord then to Newport, Rhode Island, not Providence 'because of the hostilities.' How do you people do this? The logistics are mind boggling."

"That's what we're underpaid to do," said Ike.

"Goodnight!"

## Chapter Thirty-Two

"Disaster!"

"Bad!"

"Tragedy!"

"Embarrassing!"

"Time to fold the tents!"

A group was discussing the debate on foreign affairs which had been aired on television the previous night.

Ellie May entered the room to silence.

"It may have been all of those things, but we are not folding our tents, Alistair."

"Sorry, Ellie May, it's just…"

"I know — anything that could have gone wrong, did. We must accept that was a disaster. Mac had warned us of overconfidence after the first debate, and we believed we knew better. So!" Ellie May stopped speaking and looked at the lowered faces in front of her. "What's next?" she challenged.

"The vice-presidential debate," Sheila informed them.

"First we have to look for anything favorable, any positives from last night." Mac wanted to try to lift the meeting.

"It was like something out of a TV show," Sheila confessed. "We know what happened – someone kicked an electrical connection and Ellie May faded away. The president picked up on it and made fun of the non-existent candidate. The papers and social media are ridiculing our campaign, our candidate, her advisors, our engineers, everybody."

"It was a tragedy, a disaster."

"Did anything positive come out of last night?" Mac persisted.

"Whatever we do from here on out can't be any worse."

"The president will be overconfident now."

A quiet descended as the group reflected on the pathetic nature of the 'positives.'

"It was a shame," Sheila Hutchins spoke into the silence, "that no one heard the brilliant foreign policy closing statement composed by Marjorie and her team."

"Finally," said Mac. "Something useful. Marjorie can use the speech in her debate with Vice-President Flores."

"But it was tailored for me," said Ellie May, "and the president."

"Two things," said Mac. "First, there will be a bigger audience watching to see a new 'screw-up', the speech works because Flores was also visiting those camps in the Middle East where presumably he was brain-washed while 'diddling' little boys and leaving himself open to blackmail."

"How do you know this?" asked Alistair Kirk.

"I am an investigative journalist."

"Then print it."

"I am an investigative journalist with principles. Even though people have told me things that I believe are true, I still need corroboration or for someone to be willing to be quoted."

"I think this has great possibilities." Helen had

been quiet. She had watched the previous night's debate and had the same misgivings as Alistair. "It's worth a shot. Let's get to work on it. The debate is in Kansas less than a week from now and this is in addition to our present overload."

Ellie May nodded approval and typically had the final word. "Voting in a month. Anybody with finances, or financial concerns, stay behind. Everyone else, stay on track! Thank you."

Mark had called Mac several times before they were able to speak on a safe phone.

"Problem?" asked Mac.

"Problems!" replied Mark. "One, the debate last night was a freaking disaster. The senators and congressmen and women we had on board are calling in alarms. Two, the PAC monies are trickling in and I haven't heard from the West Coast yet. Three, I hear someone is betting even money that Marjorie White will not even show, that the American Party is done. So, how's that for a start?"

"Remind those politicians that they took the King's shilling."

"What?"

"When men accepted a shilling from the King or his representative, they were conscripted into the Navy. They've been taking PAC money from American Party funds and help from party headquarters. Tell them Marjorie White will debate Flores next week, a not-to-be missed event."

"So, we should take some of the even money?"

"No. I guarantee it's a set-up."

"What do you mean a set-up?"

"It's a book, right? At the moment, it's some nitwit in Vegas who's trying to get lucky with mafia funds. On the other side is a bunch of very nasty terrorists gambling with US aid payments. I suspect they may both be looking for our conduit, for different reasons. It's not worth jeopardizing Esther. Let them have their fun. We won't play their game by their rules."

"Were you always a cynic, Mac?"

"I was always careful. You be careful too. Invite your senators around to watch Marjorie next week. Should be fun. Maybe serve popcorn...a theatre experience."

"You can be one strange dude sometimes." Mark hung up the phone trying to remember and analyze the conversation.

The call reminded Mac to telephone Esther.

She was at her desk and answered guardedly, since the secure phone rang so rarely.

"Your investments are doing well. Do you need any funds?"

"No, just checking in."

"I saw the last debate. It didn't go very well, did it? By the way, I understand there is some money being invested in Vegas. Are you planning to participate?"

"No, to both questions. Thank you."

"Very wise."

"Be careful."

"You too."

\*\*\*

The vice president was surprised to see Marjorie White present herself to the audience and to the television cameras on cue. He hid his surprise with a little smile and lifted one eyebrow. Flores was smartly dressed in a dark suit, blue shirt, red tie. He was an average looking man and had been well prepared. Marjorie was aiming for a similar reaction in a long-sleeved dress up to the neck, off white with blue accents.

The venue was the Kansas University auditorium. It was packed. Anticipation had been heightened by Mac's leaking of the betting that Marjorie would not show. Both candidates had earpieces for instructions or prompting. In front of each podium was a bulletproof screen.

Marjorie spoke first and in a confident manner, quickly turning a central, generic political speech into an attack on the presidential policy of abandoning long-term staunch allies in London, Paris, Madrid, Rome, and Tel Aviv and replacing them with dubious ones in Istanbul, Rabat, and Kabul. "These bedmates..." she said for emphasis, "...were nurtured in a special relationship on the annual vacation Francis Flores and Arthur Anders..." she deliberately used the president's given name, "...spent in those remote regions of the desert. These relationships were conceived and nurtured in dirty tents. Are America's citizens now paying the price in foreign aid to countries and regimes whose sole aim is an Islamic world?"

It was brilliant, stunning. The audience heard the nuances and watched as the color of the vice president's face turned from red to blue. His futile attempts to stop the attack added credence to the speech which fell just short of slander.

"Vice President Flores." The moderator introduced the ashen man, no longer resembling the confident politician who had entered the auditorium just twenty minutes earlier. Seeming bewildered, he appeared to still be processing the thinly veiled attack on his illegal and immoral adventures. His head was spinning, his mind processing, wondering what the other side knew.

Was there any photographic or video evidence?

Yes, yes, he knew there was evidence. He remembered the turbaned intelligence officer showing him a photograph. He and the little boy clearly seen, a large smile on his own face, no smile from the boy.

"Mr. Vice President?"

"Yes." He looked down at his notes. Unable to focus, he started from memory.

"Thank you, Tom, for moderating, Kansas University for hosting. This is a new era, a new beginning, a new…" He froze, unable to recall what came next. He looked at the papers in front of him and then looked heavenwards, a look appealing for deliverance.

It was clear that he was receiving instruction through the earpiece. Now a little more composed, he finished his opening remarks with a recitation of the accomplishments of the present administration. He noted reduction in military spending, jobs for all, and more spaces in higher-level education for men of ambition. These were all topics agreed to be included in the debates.

The moderator now asked each candidate the questions. On employment, while Flores gave his party line that there were pockets of unemployment, Marjorie White countered that the real number countrywide was at least twenty-five percent and that she would be happy if all those out of work or who feared for their job would get out and vote for the American Party. The audience loved it.

It was clear who was growing in confidence and whose answers were getting more defensive. Marjorie pointed out that more seats in colleges and universities were places for men at the expense of places for women. The audience erupted in support. Frank Flores, with nowhere to go, argued without conviction that it was merit based.

As Marjorie stood smiling, the screen in front of her shattered. The sound of the shot, though recognized by just a few, created a panic. A second shot was heard, and Ike could tell that it had hit Marjorie.

She swayed a little but continued to stand, unshaken.

The aisles were full of people pushing and shoving for the stairs. Everyone was on their feet. The moderator had ducked behind his unshielded podium. The Secret Service had quickly surrounded Frank Flores and whisked him backwards off the stage and out of the building.

Ike, standing behind Marjorie, stepped forward. He stopped suddenly just two feet away, expecting to catch her as she fell; instead, she was standing straight, her left hand extended, palm backwards. He stopped, she turned left and smiled, then she turned to look forward to the chaotic scene and spoke with a calm confidence. "Ye though I walk through the valley of death, I shall fear no evil."

The cameras were still on. The microphone was open. As she spoke the first words, people stopped where they were. The shouting slowly subsided. The words were familiar to all Catholics, Protestants, Baptists, Jews, Agnostics, and Atheists. Kansas was Bible Belt country. Everyone knew the words and turned to see the speaker, unmoved from being shot at.

"For thou," she paused and turned left, smiled again, and continued, "thou art with me." She stopped to an ovation. Everyone had been standing. They applauded, cheered, some even whistled enthusiastically. It gave the shooters time to disappear.

In the communication center outside, Mac watched

in amazement. The scenes were like none he had ever seen. After the initial shock, there had been panic, then a miracle. The audience returned to their seats but did not sit.

Mac asked for to be connected to Marjorie's earpiece.

"Marjorie, if you can hear me, nod."

He saw her give a small nod.

"Marjorie, give them your gun speech."

On the television monitor she gave a quizzical look.

"Flores has gone, you have prime time television," Mac encouraged. "You could read a train schedule and they will listen. Go!"

Marjorie told Ike she was fine and wasn't leaving.

"Guns," she said, forcefully but with meaning, "have no place in our schools." A minute of ovation followed. "Guns do not belong in our places of worship, in our workplaces, where we are entertained, or in the streets of this country." Another minute of ovation. "Guns will not win this election."

It seemed that the noise would never die down. The cameras showed the audience enraptured. They showed Marjorie confident and comfortable. She spoke for another fifteen minutes to enthusiastic applause and covered the bases of her campaign. She spoke on gun control, foreign policy, of supporting the police and firefighters, promising to support the military and abolish the militia, provide jobs, and return the foundation freedoms to the United States – religion, freedom of the press, and equality for fringe groups and minorities. It was the manifesto in fifteen minutes.

After closing remarks, Marjorie thanked the moderator, university, and auditorium. Finally, she moved the microphone and turned to Ike.

"Are you all right?" he asked.

"Did you see him?" asked Marjorie, just as urgently.

"The shooter? Not until it was too late."

"No, David," said Marjorie, with a desperate tone.

"David who?" ventured Ike.

"My David, he held my hand."

"But…"

"I know he was murdered four years ago, but he held my hand."

"Yes, he did Marjorie," said Ike, forced to turn away.

The aftermath of the event was that the studio political commentators had to abandon their "canned" comments to talk of the extraordinary debate. They were careful not to talk about foreign policy comments and struggled to find something positive to say about the vice president or the administration. Social media was less concerned with the political correctness and openly speculated on the ties to the Middle East and any complicity by the president.

Mac was feverishly at work. He sent articles to every newspaper. The articles had been partly prewritten, knowing the essence of the opening remarks. But now he was writing as fast as he could. The headline which had found its way to the top of all papers looking to sell, read, "Thou art with me!" It was to be the rallying cry for the rest of the campaign.

\*\*\*

In Texas, the reaction was similar to the rest of the country. "Jeez Louise!" Ellie May was unapologetic in her praise. "I thank God I'm not running against her! That was an election-winning performance from start to finish."

Sheila had been watching with Ellie May; the media director was saying as the phone rang, "I'm speechless for the first time in my life."

An aide who had picked up the phone said, "Well, time to get over that. Alistair Kirk says the switchboards are overwhelmed. He would appreciate help and suggestions."

"Can you all go to the media center and volunteer? Sheila, have Alistair and crew direct any newspapers or politicians up there, and, of course, any heavy, heavy contributors. Jim and I will try to cope."

It was a phenomenon which was unabated for three days. The local offices of the American Party were inundated with volunteers. Major organizations, unions, national groups of engineers, lawyers, accountants, bankers – all were asking for Marjorie to speak with them. These groups were offering support, money, and advice. It was energizing, liberating. Volunteers were able to quickly pick out the crank callers and had no time for the lunacy of their wild assertions.

\*\*\*

On the flight back from Kansas, Marjorie asked Margaret if they could switch seats for a few minutes so Marjorie could speak with Ike.

"Ike, what I said at the debate…"

"It's all right, Mrs. White; I'm here to protect you."

"But if people thought I was seeing things, people…"

"When I protect, it is protection. It is personal. No one, not even Margaret, will hear what you said to me until you say it."

"Thank you," she touched his arm in gratitude. "He was there you know."

"I know," Ike whispered.

"You saw him?"

A long pause allowed Ike to relive those minutes of history. "He was there." It was clear to Ike there was some force, some reason Marjorie wasn't dead. She'd had a bulletproof vest on under her dress, a new design, super light titanium, but someone, he decided, with more power was watching over her. He unconsciously felt in his pocket for the spent bullet he'd found on the floor under the podium. It spoke of assassination. One day it would lead him to the gun.

\*\*\*

Closer to November 5th, the tempo was furious. All around the country money was still being donated. Television was covering the American Party campaign, in part because the Democrats were confident enough not to need the coverage and the Republicans had already conceded to the Democrats. More corporations were offering support, not in the hope of a win and access, but as a way of being in the game, gaining access to speakers of Marjorie White and Ellie May Joseph's caliber.

Tempers fueled by fatigue flared. Helen with little sleep proved her worth again and again, persuading people to not only stay but to work even harder for the common good. Everyone had to be convinced they were the cog making the wheel spin. It was true in an organization with no spares.

"The final debate on the state of the economy is sold out." Alistair Kirk was in a positive mood. "Scalpers are having a field day. New York police are promising protection for all participants and the audience. Hope there's no problem with the equipment."

"I'll be there." Ellie May was chair for the now

daily early meeting.

"But, Ellie May…"

"Two things, Alistair. First, we don't want a repeat of the last fiasco I was involved in. It may be that it was sabotage. If so, they will do it again. If not, they may have been given the idea that all technology is vulnerable. Second, how can I not appear when Marjorie stands to take one for the team?"

"It's not the same," Alistair said weakly.

"It is the same." Ellie May closed the subject.

"We need an East Coast blitz. Media, speakers, dinners, cocktail parties – whatever it takes." Helen took over the meeting. "We've arranged a big event in Boston incorporating Boston College, University of Massachusetts, and Boston University, and have asked Hannah Sanderson and some of her team to arrange the Harvard Club for the event. This should raise the interest of graduates, alumni, faculty, and the local non-profit television station at the very least."

"What's the topic?" Alistair asked.

"That's a great question," Helen responded. "And here's the answer: 'Is the American Party, or any new party, viable?' Only a few of us know Marjorie will be in Boston, so it will be a surprise when she appears and speaks after the short intermission. And, to show that she is still connected, we're going to let her subject herself to questions from the panelists."

"Marjorie is attending as many events as we can find for her in three days."

"I'm tired just thinking about it," Sheila said.

"Well, rest up. You're going with her to do publicity."

"What about Ellie May and the debate?" asked Sheila.

"Covered. Well, that's it for today."

## Chapter Thirty-Three

The last two weeks went by too quickly, or at times too slowly. Mac and Ellie May were to practice answers to the expected questions for an hour each of the last three days prior to the New York debate. It felt impossible. Interruptions were constant, even when they were to be stopped only for the most dire emergency. Everything that close to voting was an emergency.

On the plane east, it was impossible to escape the questions. Mac had finally given up trying to anticipate the president's responses and concentrated on drafting answers to anticipated questions and challenging weak spots in the administration's last four years. All of his facts were checked by assistants and confirmed.

"Mark, Mac here."

"Keeping busy, old son?" Mark was in better mood now that money was again flowing in.

"Import figures. You have anything on that?"

"As a matter of fact, one of my people just got the numbers for the East Coast."

"Verifiable?"

"Teamsters, Newark docks. Reckons they are down fifty percent in and thirty percent out — something like that. I'll have the exact tonnage later today and send the report down to you."

"Does your man want tickets to the debate?" Mac wanted to show it was a two-way street.

"Send me half a dozen if you have them. I owe plenty of favors this year. Thank you, Mac."

"One more thing. West Coast?"

"I will find out and let you know."

"Thanks. Be careful. Not long to go now." Mac's routine reminder to be aware and observant was appreciated.

\*\*\*

The final presidential debate was much tighter than any of the others. Introduced by the moderator, the two candidates met and shook hands.

"Good to see you, Mrs. Joseph. I wasn't sure you really existed."

Ellie May smiled at an obvious reference to the holographic debates.

"Good evening, Mr. President. The American people weren't sure *you* really existed after the last four years." The remark earned nothing more than a wry smile.

The president's opening remarks were predictable. The economy was doing very well considering the major reduction in Armed Forces, the spending curb, and the reduction in social services. These cuts had created small pockets of unemployment and the administration, with broad bipartisan cooperation of Democrats and Republicans, was addressing those areas.

It was impressive. He was well coached and looked presidential in a trim blue suit, white shirt and small patterned blue and red tie. President Al Adana was appealing to both major congressional parties. The Republican candidate had withdrawn from the debate, claiming a slight cold. The fact that he was trailing in the polls to both of the other speakers meant that he would not further damage his standing. Since he was likely going to parrot the president, his absence ensured no loss for the audience.

"Ladies and gentlemen, I trust thou art with me in recognizing an overwhelming amount of hogwash." Ellie May waited for a small applause. There had been polite applause for the president.

"These *small pockets* of unemployment are in every state, in every city, every county, and every village in America. The economy which we are debating here is stagnant. Exports are down, except for arms to the Middle East, by over fifty percent on the East Coast and a staggering sixty percent on the West Coast – a third of what we were shipping four years ago. Imports are down over fifty percent since there is no money to buy anything. Americans are starving to death in cities like Detroit, Chicago, and Minneapolis. And winter is about to bring more misery to those cold areas that cannot, even if they could afford it, find fuel.

"We need change. We need it fast, and in ten days, you can make that change."

"Mr. President?" the moderator found his job much easier than he had anticipated.

"Facts and figures with no substance – a noisy can of marbles. In our northern cities with disruptions in the automobile and military equipment areas, I will be asking Congress to approve special treatment. Shipments of food, essentials, and subsidized fuel will soon be on its way. Figures I have received from my ministers indicate that imports and exports are running slightly ahead of four years ago and that our balance of payments with both Eastern and Western hemispheres have never been better since 1945."

"Liar!" a man in the third row blurted out and quickly sat down.

The president was clearly unnerved. The moderator quickly turned to Ellie May.

"Mrs. Joseph?"

"Yes, thank you. I believe that gentleman just said it all." She waited until the little laughter in the audience subsided. "My facts and figures come from the source, those men and women working on our docks on the East Coast and on the West Coast. I would be happy to share them with your ministers, but I suspect they have them and 'sugar coat' them for your consumption." She paused giving television cameras time to show the anger rise in her opponent. "Perhaps they are afraid of their fate if they present bad news." Ellie May was deliberately goading the president.

He pointed at her and said, "You're finished, you're dead!"

"On the contrary, you are finished. They are with me!"

The auditorium filled with resounding applause. The president only listened to half before he left. There were a few formalities before the broadcast ended.

Ellie May walked into the audience, thanking people, especially Alan Bedford who had called out the president. "You and your wife must come to the White House for dinner when we get there."

"What about me?"

"You too, Joyce."

Joyce Milner, mayor of New York City, had walked up behind Ellie May.

"Joyce Milner, meet Alan Bedford. You will make for a great dinner conversation. Gotta go. Y'all get to know each other."

Mac was still speaking in her ear from the sound truck. "Great job. Time to go. Problems out here. Bobby Joe close? Just nod and get him closer."

"What's the problem?" Helen asked as she and Mac made their way to the front of the building. A limo was parked with two police cruisers behind it. Mac directed staff members into the limo then walked over to the head of security.

"Bobby Joe, get Ellie May into the second police car. Wait until you're halfway to the White Plains airport, then redirect him to Penn station. Amtrak to Boston."

Bobby Joe, without questions, affected the change in plans efficiently. Mac and Helen left in Mayor Joyce Milner's limousine with an escort. Other staffers were directed to cabs.

At Penn station, tickets were bought for business class and arrangements to be boarded early were made by the chief of police.

Finally seated and moving, Ellie May with Bobby Joe very close cornered Mac and Helen.

"What the hell was that about? Where are we going and why?"

"Ellie May, I made the decision as your chief of staff. The monitors in the television truck followed the president out. He was furious, arms waving, frothing a little. His security was getting the brunt of it and his enforcer took over directing six men to go with him."

"Did you have sound?" asked Bobby Joe.

"Didn't need it. Anyway, the president heads out to JFK and two cars, seven men, head off to White Plains where we left the plane. So, since we were going to head north anyway, I decided we should take the train."

"Business class your idea too?" asked Ellie May.

"No. Mac's."

"First class is the wrong image, and steerage is too noisy. Here we can get a drink, mingle a little, pick up some votes, maybe lots of votes since these are generally businesspeople with money and influential friends."

"Thought of everything, Mac," said Ellie May. "Accommodations?"

"Custom House. Spoke to Karen, the manager. She'll be there when we check in to make sure we're incognito. She had already gone home, but she's coming back in."

"Then I had better freshen up and shake some hands."

\*\*\*

The next day was a flurry of interviews and meetings with supporters – some influential, others wealthy. It seemed to the participants to be more of a statement against the current situation rather than a confidence in proposed radical changes.

A town meeting-style forum had been arranged. The popularity of the debates on campus had heightened the interests in politics this year. Unable to reveal who might speak, Hannah Sanderson had invited students from the local universities and the request for tickets to the free event was so overwhelming that she'd had to relocate it to Faneuil Hall in Boston.

In order to provide a basis for the inclusive society and to avoid any charges of bias, the invitation had been to all of the parties with candidates entered in the current election. The local politicians who were secure in their victory and busy collecting monies, not votes, declined. The presidential candidate for the Democrats had declined. Francis Flores, the vice-presidential candidate had initially accepted, a chance to return to his home state, but after his disastrous appearance on television had not been seen and had withdrawn. It appeared to those streaming into the hall that Marjorie White was in town and it had leaked that she might appear. Most were fine with that premise as the debates and people in Massachusetts in general had all favored gun control legislation.

The local public television station had asked to show the meeting live. Other news outlets had asked for feed, and some were taping for future editing and showings. National television franchisees were stationed outside as news gatherers and in case there was a disturbance. The presence of cameras and reporters were almost a guarantee of disturbance.

Police activity was evident with dogs patrolling the Quincy Market area.

Faneuil Hall has been the site of debates and meetings for presidents, would-be presidents, governors, and mayors, as well as providing a platform for activists. A capacity of three hundred students and academics were in the seats. Hannah Sanderson had solicited interest in asking questions from the assembly and ensured that all the schools were represented in the questions.

"Ladies and gentlemen, students, faculty, and our television audience, welcome. Welcome to this location famous for progress. Sons of Liberty met here. Julius Caesar spoke here..." She waited for the laughter to subside. "No, the Romans did not discover America. Julius Caesar Chappelle was a black legislator who, in 1890, advocated voting rights for all black men. He spoke here and was responsible for the reputation of this building as the 'cradle of liberty.'

Mitt Romney introduced a Massachusetts Health Bill here, and President Barack Obama came back to introduce his Affordable Care Act for the country based on that Massachusetts model.

"Tonight another historical first. Following in the footsteps of Samuel Adams, Susan B. Anthony, Oliver Wendell Holmes, and others, please welcome the American Party candidate for vice president, Marjorie White."

Marjorie took the stage to a raucous welcome. She gave a short speech highlighting her career, accomplishments, and her reason for running again for office, in spite of the hard work and risks it entailed. It was brief and did not anticipate any of the questions the audience might have.

Hannah said, "Thank you, Mrs. White. The first question we have is regarding your gun control proposals. Here in Faneuil Hall above us is the armory of the Ancient and Honorable Artillery. Isn't that a little disconcerting, given your vociferous opposition to guns?"

"Not at all. I visited with them today. Wonderful people, doing wonderful work. All the guns are registered, and not one has been used to commit a crime. Let me outline the proposed legislation..." Her words came right off the campaign speeches she had been making for at least four weeks, four times a day.

Other questions followed and, with the knowledge of having watched the debates from these schools, the answers were smooth, professional. After an hour the audience was relaxed and entertained. Marjorie finished up an answer on climate change from a Tufts University student.

"Helen, I should like to introduce to you and your audience a friend of mine, a very close friend of mine and the next president of the United States, Ellie May Joseph."

The applause was loud and continued while Ellie May hugged first Marjorie then Helen and walked along, greeting the front row of the audience. Security was obvious but not intrusive.

Ellie May finally returned to the stage and a microphone and addressed the audience and television cameras. "Thank you for that warm New England welcome. I had heard y'all were reserved, cool. All I've seen in my visits to New England and these few hours is warmth and welcome, so thank y'all.

"I know you weren't expecting me. Truthfully, I wasn't expecting to be here. But here I am, no holograph. If you have questions, let's see if we can work a New England town meeting."

Hands flew up and Helen recognized and chose a face from M.I.T.

"What will your administration look like and, as an engineer, will I have a job after graduation?"

There was a contrast in style between Marjorie and Ellie May. Where Marjorie had been smooth, Ellie May gave illustrations, told stories. It was a tour-de-force. Another hour had passed when Helen said they would have to close. She had claimed the last two questions for herself. The first she directed to Marjorie.

"Mrs. White, you were shot last time you were on television, and we all have that image of your courage and strength. Can you remember what it felt like being the victim of an assassination attempt?"

"Well, yes, I think that being shot is something one remembers." She waited while the nervous laughter subsided. "And, yes, it was an assassination attempt. I heard both shots, both were accurate to within one inch. That type of accuracy is professional, practiced. David, my husband, once told me, 'If you hear the shot, it missed. You're not dead.' Knowing, knowing that you're not dead is incredibly calming and immediately, without thinking, the Twenty-third Psalm came into my head. 'Thou art with me.'" Marjorie held up her thumb, forefinger, and little finger in the international sign for 'I love you.'

The audience responded with the sign, some shouting out, "Thou art with me."

"Mrs. Joseph, how, given the odds against you, how confident are you in winning the election next week?"

"With this strong lady beside me, anything is possible. Let me illustrate. Just today in New England two very powerful individuals asked for positions in Washington. There was no doubt in their minds and there is no doubt in mine."

Helen closed the meeting over the noise of the audience with the exhortation to vote.

The major news channels showed the last two questions all night and all of the following day. Some even reshowed the footage of the shot intended to kill Marjorie White.

## Chapter Thirty-Four

The two politicians with different entourages separated with Ellie May taking a path through territory less familiar north and west. Portland, Maine, for breakfast, Manchester, New Hampshire, lunch, and Burlington, Vermont for dinner meetings. The days were merging, it was difficult to track where they were and the name of the group being cosseted, petitioned, persuaded. They rode overnight in a coach car to Indiana then doubled back to Pennsylvania. It was confusing.

Marjorie, meanwhile, took the southern route. She met with more urban, working class people in Rhode Island, Connecticut, and New Jersey.

The coverage of the campaign was better, the crowds better, the militia less obvious. The presence of television crews previously ignoring or censoring the brutality now showed the world the bullying tactics against unarmed citizens, women, and children. The message was filtering through. Shootings were still at unacceptable levels, but less than they had been just six months earlier when the media had been afraid to show the militia in the true light.

\*\*\*

On Election Day, Marjorie voted in New York and campaigned until the East Coast polls closed. She and her crew were exhausted.

Sheila wanted to complain, but how could she? She was spent and then looked to see Marjorie doing twice as much. The support team had travelled with Marjorie, had spent their days speaking with local officials about voter fraud – how to find it, catch it, and deal with it. They spoke to the police, who were less interested but agreed to address the issue. Never did it translate into 'prosecute it.' The easiest crime to prove yet it was one never taken to court. Other crimes were always seen as more important, more serious. In voting fraud it was assumed there was no victim. Then why provide police details at the polling stations? The answer was in order to prevent a crime. Not a very satisfactory answer.

When the polls closed in New York, the entire crew went to the airport in order to be in Texas for the results. Since the West Coast polls were three hours behind, it would be a while before meaningful data could be assembled by the watching candidates and television stations.

Walking through JFK airport in a loose group of twelve people, Marjorie, Margaret, her brother Henry, and his media crew, Sheila was talking to two assistants. All were watched over by a small security team led by Ike. The mood was happy. Tired but heading home for a few days' rest. The election results were now out of their hands. They had done their best, but was it enough?

Marjorie was talking to Sheila, Margaret to her brother, and Ike was close to both a few feet behind Marjorie, some six feet behind Margaret when something odd, something it took a moment to register into his security conscious brain. He was tired and relaxing a little too. A tall black man walked toward Margaret smiling with recognition. Not incongruous, but he was walking toward them, against the flow, away from the departure gates, with no luggage; Margaret knew few people outside Alabama. Ike in two strides was now just in front of Marjorie, his prime concern. He reached back for his gun. It wasn't there as it had been temporarily surrendered coming through security.

The man pulled out a nine-millimeter gun and, as his primary target was blocked, turned toward Margaret to create confusion as Ike shouted, "Margaret, down!"

Margaret was turning to hear the familiar voice shouting her name as the shot hit her.

Ike hurled himself at the assailant as a second shot hit a technician in the group. The impetus of a large object hitting an equally large object dislodged the gun. The men fell to the floor. Ike tried to establish a grip as the man was starting to stand and took a foot in the face which produced an angry bellow.

The man was up and running. Ike tackled him to ground and took another boot to the face. He turned to check on the team. He could see that with their training the security men and women had Marjorie and others at the wall while surrounding them. The man he had tackled had turned a corner and disappeared. He went back, retrieved the gun, and put it into the back of his pants.

He staggered to where the group was huddled, a few bent over Margaret, the rest at the wall. Airport security was arriving and talking on their communications links.

His Margaret shot on his watch!

Henry was at his sister's head. He had taken the second bullet in the arm. Henry pushed away people trying to tend to his wound, holding a handkerchief against a gaping hole in his sister's chest.

Ike fell to the floor, putting his hand on top of Henry's to help staunch the blood. Alternatively he was praying for help, promising everything, and cursing the shooter and whoever had orchestrated the attack.

An airport security guard appeared at his elbow. "EMT on the way, nearly here. Anything else?"

Ike shook his head, then told him, "Hold the plane. Get these people out of here."

"You expect more shooting?"

"I don't speculate!"

"I can't stop planes."

"Call the mayor."

"I can't call the mayor.'

"I'll call the mayor." Sheila had stepped forward and was now grateful to help.

"Thanks, Sheila. You," Ike said to the guard, "is moving the crowd something you *can* do?"

"Is she…?" Henry's voice was breaking.

"Still breathing, but not for long at this rate. Where the hell are those medics?" Ike was shouting.

Running footsteps answered his question.

"What have we got?" a breathless medic asked while pulling on latex gloves.

"Gunshot, chest, bleeding heavily, bleeding out!" Ike choked on the last word.

"Not if I can help it."

"Blood type if anyone knows." It was asked more to keep people thinking than in the expectation of an answer.

"B positive, I'm afraid."

"That's a good help. The hospital will have it available as soon as we step in. We can verify while on route. Meanwhile, start an IV with plasma." This last remark was directed at his assistant who had already attached a heartbeat monitor to the finger and to his computer.

"How much you got?"

"Two units here."

"Not enough. There's more in the ambulance." He was cutting around the entry wound and applying gauze pads. Talking seemed to relax him to the severity of the wound as he worked efficiently. "Anybody here B positive by chance?"

"I'm pretty sure I'm B something," Henry spoke quietly without looking up from his sister's face.

"That's something if we are desperate. And I mean desperate." He looked up at Henry. "You're bleeding like a pig yourself. You're no help."

Henry looked up at the medic. "She's my sister. You take every ounce of my blood if it saves her. Got it?"

The EMT hesitated. It was not the time or place for an argument. "Got it! Where's my stretcher?"

A stretcher and electric cart appeared. Another cart took Henry, the second medic, and the balance of equipment not attached.

Ike went to follow until Sheila grabbed his arm.

"I have to…." he tugged.

"You have to get Marjorie to Texas." She was looking into unfocussed eyes. "Besides," she patted the back of his pants where she had recognized he had put the gun after picking it up, "security is still looking for this. Airport security and New York's finest are wanting a statement."

Ike seemed to be coming back to the present but frequently looked back to the airport exit where the ambulance and police sirens could be heard.

"Right! I'll put him in the ground."

"Not today, big boy. Let's get these statements done. They have a room down here. Plane is being unloaded, all baggage rechecked, x-rayed per orders from the mayor's office to security. Should delay the plane by not much more than an hour."

"Security?"

"Yes, you were gone again."

Ike was walking in the direction indicated while dialing a number in Austin, Texas. He had finished by the time they reached a room with a security guard at the door. It was some time before the door opened, witnesses exited, Marjorie was inside after giving a detailed statement.

"How is she?" Marjorie asked.

"I don't know. Good hands, I think."

"You should be with her."

"I have to be with you." Ike felt guilt sweeping over him. "Sheila said so!" He gave a lopsided grin.

Marjorie nodded.

"Thank you, Mrs. White. We need a statement from Mr. Clark."

"She stays and does not leave my sight until we arrive in Texas where my Rangers take over."

The men introduced themselves. The head of airport security and his assistant with a recording device, a detective inspector from the New York Police Department, and a sergeant by the door.

The preliminaries were name, address, flight number, reason for being in New York, all handled impersonally while Ike assessed the two men in charge. Then Ike was asked to go through what he had witnessed and his role. He did in some detail, omitting the evidence in the small of his back. The next question, a description of the assailant, and would he recognize him again.

"Yes, I generally recognize people who point a gun at me. Tall, over six feet, black, trained, military."

"That's a lot in sixty seconds." The security chief was skeptical.

"Wearing some type of uniform under a sweatshirt which you will likely find discarded as he melted into the structure of the airport. But you know that as you have the surveillance tapes. Nine-millimeter." Ike stopped. That was enough information for them to pursue if they were inclined.

The detective inspector from NYPD was watching Ike carefully, quietly. "Some witness thought he had dropped the gun. We haven't found it." He waited and, getting no response, he asked, "I don't suppose you know the manufacturer?"

Ike shrugged. "Lots of nine mills."

"Okay for now," said the security chief. "We may have more questions. Don't leave the area. We will question all of the cleaning crews."

"Number one, you don't have jurisdiction over us. Number two, I'm taking this lady to Texas. And three…" Ike stopped himself. He needed something and saying anything else would guarantee his not getting it. "Could I have a copy of all the statements you've taken?" he nodded to the recording device.

"Well, I don't…"

"Me, too," interrupted the detective.

"And a copy of the CCTV footage."

"Me, too." The detective handed over a contact card. Ike took one too and read, 'Detective Inspector Vozzella, NYPD.'

Walking out of the interview room, the detective caught up with Ike and walked down the departure corridor. "What did you not say in there?" His question was met with silence. "Okay. Are you coming back to New York? I'd like to help."

"Because your chief ordered it?" asked Ike.

"Partly." He smiled. "Mostly because it's my job."

"Check the surveillance. Let me know." Ike gave him a contact card. "I'll be back on the next plane. Take care of that woman in the hospital. Make sure you have guards 'round the clock."

\*\*\*

Ike sat with Marjorie in the business class section of the plane. The rest of the crew was scattered around. Most were asleep before they left the gate. There was blanket over Ike's knee. Underneath the blanket was the gun he was holding. He would not sleep.

"Are you Captain Clark, Texas Ranger?" a stewardess asked.

"Yes, ma'am."

"Captain Mueller's compliments. A message came from an Inspector Vozzella." She pulled out a piece of paper and read, "Ms. Forrest still in surgery; CCTV footage missing."

"What a surprise," Ike said angrily.

Ike slept at the Texas airport after handing control of his detail to a waiting Bobby Joe. A ticket was purchased. The boarding pass on his phone, he never left the departure area. He was asleep again before they finished boarding the plane for JFK. When they landed, he placed a call to Detective Inspector Vozzella to find out if there was any news from the hospital and for him to meet at the arrivals gate.

\*\*\*

Vozzella was standing back watching the arrivals. A security officer in a distinctive yellow jacket stopped Ike at the door. Ike signaled with his eyes that Vozzella should stay back.

"Chief wants to see you. Follow me."

"Follow me." Ike spoke loud enough to be picked up and transmitted by the phone in his shirt pocket.

"News on the shooting, the CCTV maybe?"

"Didn't say."

They entered a now empty room, the same previously used for interviewing. Ike took out the gun as the security officer turned while unclipping his holstered gun.

"Looking for this?"

"Yes, yes. It's evidence."

"How do you know that?" asked Ike with a little smile. "Because you dropped it while trying to assassinate a vice presidential candidate?"

"Give it to me."

"I think not."

"I think so," said a voice behind Ike.

"Hello, Chief." Ike spoke without turning around. "I wondered when you would show."

"You suspected?"

"When I mentioned uniform, you said janitor. When I asked for CCTV, you made sure there was none, the camera damaged retrospectively. Not bad, just not good enough."

"Yes, but I have the gun in your back."

"True, but who will believe suicide, shot in the back?"

"He has a good point chief!" Vozzella stated as he and a uniformed NYPD officer had entered.

There was a moment of silence as each interpreted the scenario. Ike felt a move on his spine and spun as the chief fired. The chief died in a hail of bullets from the doorway. Two steps and Ike punched the hitman twice with as much force as he could muster, once with the gun that shot Margaret.

"Thank you," said Vozzella.

"Thank you!" Ike shook his hand. "You'll find this is the gun used in shooting Margaret Forrest and this man's prints will be on the bullets and on the clip."

"I think I heard enough on the phone. Not too pleased that you held onto evidence until now."

"Two reasons, maybe three. I thought it might disappear or be exchanged. I recognized the uniform of course. The security people knew it was missing and never mentioned it to your lot. I also wanted to be armed in case there was another attempt on Marjorie White."

"It will just be a bit more paperwork, maybe. Let's get you to the hospital."

## Chapter Thirty-Five

In Texas, as in most of the country, everyone was anxiously watching the results of the election.

There was early euphoria as the better policed voting states' results came in. New Hampshire and Vermont were predicted to be won by the American Party; Maine and Massachusetts were too close to call.

"Amazing!" Ellie May Joseph was constantly on the move – sometimes sitting comfortably next to her husband Jim, then near a bank of computers. Each computer and operator was in communication with local results and updates around the country.

"Isn't it amazing that we've won two states?"

"You didn't enter the race to lose, sweetheart." Jim squeezed her hand. He was nervously eating any snacks left on the table in front of him.

"No, but this is special."

"It turned when they tried to kill Marjorie."

"Where is Marjorie?" Ellie May's strident voice carried to the back of the room.

"En route from the airport." Several voices gave different versions of this small piece of information.

"How is Margaret doing?" Ellie May asked.

No reply.

"Then somebody better find out! Where's Helen?"

"I'm right here. Stop shouting!"

"Sit and tell me realistically where we are."

"Some seats in the senate, some in the house, not many. Our easy states are okay. There are some shenanigans here and there but generally not as bad as we'd feared."

"Why do you think that is?"

"Lack of seats is due to lack of candidates, though the Republicans are doing better and may support the American Party agenda."

"The enemy of my enemy is my friend!"

Helen shrugged as an aide came up to them. "Margaret is in an induced coma, not much hope, and virtually no hope of returning to a normal life."

Ellie May's tears came spontaneously but no sound, no other acknowledgement that he had been heard. Ellie May grabbed a tissue to dry her face.

Another aide at the door gave the updates and brought Ellie May back to her feet. "New Jersey is predicted to the Democrats. New York is going to need a miracle. Connecticut went to the president."

"Don't go far, Helen. I need you."

A big cheer announced the arrival of Marjorie White, Sheila Hutchins, and entourage.

"Marjorie, I want to hear everything."

"Not before I go to the bathroom and have a large strong drink in my hand. I've never consumed so much water in my life."

There was a core group gathered around a conference table. A television set sat silently transmitting on the wall. Everyone at the table was looking away from the conversation every few seconds for any news updates. Only through the advertising minutes was there one hundred percent concentration.

"Hey you," Ellie May gestured. "I'm sorry, what's your name?"

"Wayne."

"I'm sorry, Wayne, for calling 'hey you'. Wayne, could you possibly do two things for me in addition to whatever you're working on. One, have someone bring me two gin and tonics. It will be my only drink tonight, but Marjorie shouldn't drink alone. And secondly, can I put you in charge of calling the New York hospital every half hour for updates?"

"Yes, ma… Mrs. Joseph."

"Thank you, Wayne."

The rest of the group had gathered in a disorderly fashion in the conference room. Marjorie, now freshened up, sat with a thump next to Alistair Kirk. Helen sat opposite, Allyn Cherwin at the far end from Ellie May, Bobby Joe – as usual – stood at the end of the room.

"Where's Mac?"

"Writing two speeches."

"Ah, Wayne, thank you," Ellie May said as the drinks arrived.

"No change in New York, I'm afraid. She's still in an induced coma, very grave."

"Wayne, are you busy? Sorry, yes everyone is busy. You're one of our volunteers. What's your degree in?"

"Liberal Arts, minor in finance, graduated in June. No jobs really, thought I may be able to help."

"You can. Sit next to Allyn learn from him. Margaret Forrest should be in that seat. You will have to do."

"Do what?" Wayne was stunned.

"Explain to us, or get the answer to, any financial matters that Allyn needs. Sorry, Allyn."

"Needs must," Allyn said. "Been here before."

The silent television at the end of the room showed

New Jersey definitely a victory for the Democrats. A groan accompanied the breaking news.

"Update, Helen."

"What you see. Early yet."

"Florida, lots of electoral college votes there?"

"Heading for a recount."

"No surprise there," Alistair snorted.

"Apparently they lost some ballot boxes – a whole county they're saying. Officials are reporting them as 'en route,' the press is saying 'missing,' and one official is saying 'stolen, lost.'"

"Broward?" Alistair harrumphed.

"How'd you guess?"

"All of those retirees were bound to vote for the American Party. They voted Democrat last time, all of their lives probably, until it hit their retirement savings. They see and feel the stock market down fifty percent in four years, know they can't survive another four years with social security cut drastically, cut completely if one has savings. Likely the boxes will appear tomorrow twice as full as when they left the voting precincts."

"Solutions, any?" Ellie May was trying to hold back anger at the matter-of-fact manner she was receiving this information.

"First will be to warn the other state's committees," Sheila decided. "I'll take care of that." She rose and left.

"I'll call for the recount." Helen could already feel the amount of work entailed in requesting a recount. "And ask for voter audit on Broward. I can call their attorney general tonight. Will you talk to him, Ellie May?"

Ellie May nodded. "Allyn?"

"We're broke!"

"Call Mark to cover your overdraft."

Allyn scribbled a number on a piece of paper and gave it to Wayne. "Call!" was all the curmudgeon needed to say for Wayne to leave the room to make his first foray into the murky world of American politicking.

"Marjorie, up to your story?"

"Not much of a story. I think I was targeted from the beginning because of what happened to David." She was now comfortable talking about her murdered husband. "Everybody knows I dropped out of the race last time, letting what's-his-name become president."

"Inside information on your whereabouts?"

"No, I think it was opportunistic. I trust everyone on the team."

"Me too!" Bobby Joe was paying attention.

"But Margaret was shot," Alistair interrupted.

"Opportunity! I think I was the target to kill or scare. Ike stepped up, so the shooter had no shot at me and took the easy target. Someone shouted a warning, I remember it sounding like Ike, then Ike launched himself at the man. There was utter chaos, and the man got away."

"Marjorie, can we win New York?"

"I would say yes. The Sons of Liberty are well organized in every downtown precinct and the police are with us. There will be very little hanky-panky."

It was going to be slow. There was no pattern, no direction. Coffee was still in demand but more and more water as dehydration took over. The air inside was being used and started tasting stale, air conditioning was barely keeping up. Positives were still being cheered and groans greeted every set back.

Analysts were poring over charts with past races compared with the current voting, vindicating every nuance, every vote. Strong local candidates, or weak, large turnout or small, strong policing of the polls or none, historically left wing or right.

Helen stepped outside picking up a light coat on her way. The desert was cold. She needed air, needed to think without interruption. The cacophony of overlapping conversations and voting announcements was mind numbing. She stepped to the outer edge of noise.

The American Party was a protest, designed to question. It had not seemed possible that in less than two years it could be a viable option. Was it possible? Was it possible the same questioning, the discontent with the present political situation feeding the party, could *that* questioning result in the replacement of the source of that discontent? It had been impossible until the assassination attempt. Everyone in the country had seen at least once the five minutes of drama. The moment Marjorie had stepped forward to speak, the seemingly single shot, the panic, the abdication of his podium by Vice President Flores. Then calming the situation 'thou art with me' before launching into a speech on the need for gun control.

Extraordinary!

What was next? If the election was lost, she and Mac would be hunted again and would need to go away. Where? How? She would leave that to Mac.

If the miracle held and the American Party went on to win, then her life, their life, would become infinitely more difficult. Ellie May would likely ask her to lead the transition team. Meeting with cabinet members, advisors, any number of presidential appointments would almost certainly end up divisive and needing a firm hand. Agreements for trade and international relations would be transitioned. There were implications far beyond her knowledge and expertise. She must make a list of names to help. Would Ellie May consider Mac a source? Probably, after all he was writing her next speech.

Helen had been vaguely aware that she wasn't alone. There was another figure silently taking in the desert air. He was in his usual position for contemplation, forty yards or so in front of where she was standing. Walking quietly, she put her arms around him.

"Penny for your thoughts, big boy!"

Mac remained silent.

Helen recognized the mood since normally he would answer that he had been thinking of her and how lucky he was. This was serious so she stood beside him and they gazed together at the stars. Mac slipped his hand into hers.

"Carl Sagan says we are a speck of dust, referring to Earth. If Earth is a speck of dust, what are we? A group of countries, divided by language, different beliefs, different climates. We have a limited lifespan. We share our speck of dust with different species. We fight, wage war, with and within countries, within neighborhoods." Mac paused. "Why?"

"If Mathew McDougal, the smartest man I know, doesn't know the answer, then no one knows."

"Why are you sweet talking me?"

"Will we win?"

"Yes!"

"No doubts, no reservations?"

"None. California will be a landslide and Nevada, Oregon, Wisconsin, all late states."

"Still…"

"Unemployment. The film industry cannot get anything past the censors. Silicon Valley cannot sell computers or software to people with no money. The other states have no militia, food costs are soaring, they're at the end of the chain and can't get their food to market or supplies in. Ellie May and Marjorie both asked those unemployed or in danger of being unemployed to vote for the American Party."

"And you know all this because?"

"Because I am a political analyst and the smartest man you know," he replied with a grin.

"So, what happens next?"

"Ellie May will try, with your considerable help, to form a working government and move to DC."

"Interesting choice of words. You said 'try' and then you put the move to Washington, later."

"Indeed," he agreed.

"Ellie May will want you in her government. What would you be? Secretary of State, Secretary of Defense, what?" Helen asked.

"Nothing. Not going to happen."

"Because?"

"Conflict of interest, too many enemies, primarily because I have a job."

"What conflict? What new job?"

"You didn't offer Ambassador to St. James Court?" Mac was smiling.

"You're not leaving me and going to England."

"See, conflict of interest. A decision maker in a powerful position."

"So what will you do?"

"My new book will be out; I'll be doing the rounds, television shows, book launch and signings, working on the movie."

"What new book? When will you start?"

"The Birth of the American Party. It's almost finished."

"When have you had time to compile that?"

"All the time, the meetings, I kept notes, the stories I heard, then at night I would transcribe. The hours on planes, waiting for planes – lots of time. It just needs the last chapter and then I send it to my publisher. He loves it so far, talking six figures, perhaps seven figures if we can get it launched in Europe."

"All the time I thought you were watching sports and drinking beer," she teased. "Can we go back to your 'try' comment?"

"I just can't see it being easy. Democrats will still control the House, together with Republicans they outnumber your party in the Senate."

"So?"

"So, many of your appointments require approval from Congress, and many of your appointments will replace friends of someone. It will not be easy to tip-toe through the tulips!"

"Hmmm. Can I read your book?"

"Hmmm," Mac imitated Helen. "When you take a week to go with me to the shore."

"Mac…" She was about to say, 'I can't,' stopped at the implication, then asked, "A few days, and can we go to Florida; see my mum?"

Mac recognized a negotiation, the sacrifice. "Five days!"

A very slow, "Okay, next week, four days," she offered.

They spontaneously embraced and kissed to seal the deal. A promise of a hiatus from the mad whirl. As if on cue, a large cheer erupted as another state was projected to be won by the American Party.

"Indiana, maybe," said Helen turning to the noise.

"Illinois probably. By the way, put Edsel from Chicago on your list of candidates. He would be excellent in urban affairs and stick in my friend Sean on the list for Attorney General."

"I think that Ellie May as attorney general here in Texas may have a better handle on that," said Helen defensively. "She'll look at the states' attorney generals for a candidate."

"And what have they done in the last four years?"

"I'll see that his name is on the list. He was active in Sons of Liberty. Now, I have to go I may be needed."

"Clear next week," he reminded her.

"Yes, sir!" She gave a mock salute and was gone.

Mac watched as she walked into the pool of light marveling, not for the first time, at his good fortune in finding Helen and her saying 'I do.'

## Chapter Thirty-Six

The next morning, Wednesday, Mac was at his desk analyzing a very detailed chart of election results. It was very early, so he was alone with his coffee. Helen had quietly entered their bedroom in the early hours, and he had awoken only long enough to hear the news. Good news or bad, he would analyze for himself.

In summary, the American Party had won the presidency. In the detail, President Mohammed Al Adana had lost the election. The evidence showed a generally low turnout. Probably, Mac thought, due to voter intimidation. In the areas where there was high unemployment, there was generally a better turnout and there they generally voted for change. Democrat senators and congressional candidates suffered even if they were incumbent. Where candidates were actively identifying with change, they were more likely to have won a seat. This was prominent in areas with large unemployment. People wanted change, they wanted jobs.

The telephone rang.

"Yes, Brad? How come you're in the office so early?"

"It's after seven here and, as your agent, I'm already hard at work on your behalf."

"Rubbish! You've never been at your desk before

nine. What gives?"

"Okay, so I'm not strictly in the office. But I am getting calls from the network shows in New York. They're asking for comment from the American Party camp. They want you to appear on a live feed or on a telephone feed."

"And what is in it for me? Or for you?"

"Exposure."

"Can't spend exposure. What has the White House said?"

"Nothing!"

"Nothing? No concession, no congratulations, no well fought? Nothing?" Mac was thinking hard. "I'll talk to them after the president speaks. Gotta find the news program. Keep in touch and enjoy your breakfast."

Mac turned to one of the New York television stations and listened as the 'talking heads' spoke of the extraordinary result without ever saying anything. A note was finally passed to one of the anchors. "A spokesman for the American Party, who we had invited to speak with us, has replied saying he would be delighted to speak with us after we have heard from the White House. Where are we on that, Grant?"

A split screen showed Grant stationed outside the White House. "We've tried all morning to reach someone in the administration, a member of the staff or spokesperson. So far we've been unsuccessful."

"Surprising given the circumstances and the apparent overwhelming, if unexpected, victory by the American Party."

"Very. Protocol is generally there that we hear a concession speech unless there is to be a recount. There's a time limit for a decision to recount. It has to be made within two days."

"No doubt here though, is there? We'll take a break and, when we come back, we'll have a professor of political science from Columbia University as our guest. Professor Anthony Barber will be in the studio when we return."

"Who the hell?"

Mac could hear Ellie May as she disappeared into the downstairs conference room.

"Who the hell spoke to the media before we have a statement?"

Mac followed her as he was anticipating the exact words she was going to say before they were said.

"Not enough sleep, Ellie May?" he asked.

"No sleep, no telephone call, nothing."

"I'm probably at some fault for the incorrect reporting on television this morning. I told my agent I wouldn't appear on air until after the president had spoken."

"Has he?"

"Not yet."

"What if he doesn't?"

"Well, television has a political genius on the set now, so why not listen while I go and rewrite the opening of your speech."

"Like what?"

"Well, instead of praising a fair fight, start with 'President Al Adana can take a flying leap into the Potomac and take his bully boys with him.'"

Ellie May listened, frowning with concentration, then burst into laughter. "Okay, Mac, write something and we'll get it out."

"Let's shoot for top of the hour."

"That gives me how long to get rid of these bags under my eyes and look presidential?"

"Fifteen minutes, then we can run through the

announcement."

"No time to think about it, that the plan?"

"Something like that."

Mac went back to his computer and passed Wayne who was diligently carrying bulletins to the conference room.

"Wayne, what are you doing?"

"Posting bulletins on Ms. Forrest." In answer to a quizzical look he continued. "No change, resting comfortably, still in the induced coma, a Mr. Clark is with her."

"Okay, thanks. I need you to wake Mrs. McDougal, Mrs. White, and Mrs. Hutchins. Down here tout suite."

"But they're sleeping."

"Precisely why they need to wake up. Take coffee."

"Yes, sir," Wayne replied, not entirely convinced but anxious to be a part of whatever was to be next. His mother had not believed his story the previous night that he had met and talked to all of these famous people and that he might well have a job paying him for what he would do for nothing.

Ten minutes later he was back.

"All done?" Mac asked.

"Yes, sir, but I don't think I'm very popular."

"While you're on a roll, go and roust the camera crew and computer techies."

"No, sir. Don't make me do it! They were the last to leave…they were waiting for champagne."

"Tell them champagne for breakfast. They have fifteen minutes to set up."

Mac called his agent and gave him a green light to gain points with the major networks. They could interrupt their morning news show for a live announcement from the leader of the American Party and next president of the United States, Ellie May Joseph.

The room was full. Ellie May Joseph looked conservative with a white blouse tucked into blue, velour pants. Her high heeled boots were just barely visible.

"Is this…" she gestured to the cameras, "… necessary at this ungodly hour?"

"Yes, and it is eight in the East, in Washington and New York," said Mac. "Al Adana is playing games. Screw him!"

"Perhaps we should have called first?"

"We did. Helen called their chief of staff. 'Not available.' Press office, 'not available'."

"Okay, let's do it!"

"My fellow Americans, good morning. Yesterday was a historical day. It was a special day for me and my family and support team…"

The speech was more than ten minutes, praising those candidates who had won seats in Congress under the American Party banner, congratulating all the winners, Democrats, Republicans, the lone Green Party winner, and hoping they would work with her and each other to bring her party's vision of America to all the citizens of the United States. Finally she came to the part of the speech which had been modified and was contentious.

"Although you the people have elected me and my vice president Marjorie White by a considerable margin, it is not my intention to claim a victory until I have communicated with my president, President Al Adana. We have reached out to the White House but as yet have not received a reply. We can only hope the president has not suffered an accident or is ill in any way.

"God bless you all. God bless America."

\*\*\*

In New York the news anchor stated, "Well, lots of questions and we'll be right back with Professor Barber after this message."

\*\*\*

In Texas the surprise and euphoria had not diminished, the celebrations were becoming more muted but high fives were still the preferred method of greeting.

The conference room was a hive of activity as the realization sunk in. Each person had processed the news in a different way. Some had logistical obstacles to overcome, some geographical, and for some it was over.

The whole campaign had become a life to those volunteers and those directly involved in campaign funding, for example. Campaign funding included campaign requests for donations, receiving donations, sending out campaign literature, party brochures, answering requests for information, supporting materials for cocktail parties, luncheons, breakfasts. These volunteers all over the country were now to return to their previous lives. These volunteers were looking now for letters of recommendation if they were going off to school, letters of thanks for resumes that might help in applications to law school or some doctoral program.

Others were content to return to a previous life, believing they had been part of something good, that their part had been pivotal, at least a small cog in the wheel of progress.

Wayne approached Alistair Kirk who was compiling a list of cabinet positions and candidates for

Helen. Alistair looked up with his usual look of annoyance at being interrupted and turned towards the irritation. As he saw the irritant, the young person who had been placed into his life, he smiled, a smile of recognition.

"How can I help you, Wayne?" he asked pleasantly.

Wayne was initially tempted to look behind to see who was behind him. "Just stopped by to say goodbye and thank you, sir."

"Thank me? Thank you for stepping in to help an old man keep things straight. It's a different world for us old folk. We're trying not to screw it up for you kids. You stepped into a crisis and helped, worked without sleep I bet. That's something."

"It was a privilege, sir."

"What now? Do you have a job to go to, graduate school?"

"No, sir, nothing really. I was thinking of finding a job with a brokerage house, or in finance of some sort. Perhaps you might give me a reference and some guidance."

"Better than that, maybe. Willing to move to Washington?"

"You mean with the new president?"

"I mean if Margaret Forrest recovers, she is going to be invited to Washington in a senior position and will need an assistant who is smart, hardworking, and loyal. That you?"

"Yes, sir. That's me."

"Good. Meanwhile she's in a New York hospital and you will have to handle her backlog."

"Will I be on a payroll, sir?"

"Yes, well paid too."

"My landlord will be pleased to hear that, and my

mother."

"Go to Margaret's office to keep things under control. I'll put the paperwork through. You may get a call from George Breakstone, our banker; good guy. Be guided by him. Any questions?"

"None right now. Thank you, sir.'" Wayne was confused but enthusiastic. "Are you going to be our boss in Washington?"

"Me and Washington are like oil and water. I'm staying here where the oil is. Too old for that nonsense."

"Thank you again. I was on my way to the conference room with the update. No change in Margaret Forrest's condition, still in a coma but they will bring her out tonight, evaluate, and operate tomorrow. And Mr. Clark is there and will take care of all future updates and bulletins."

"Ike is there, in charge. Good."

In the conference room an aide was adding appointments to one board and candidates to another while a different aide was filling a third board with the names of people calling into the American Party headquarters. The people were requesting, cajoling, begging, and sometimes threatening in order to be considered for a position in the new administration. A shorthand synopsis listing the accomplishments or some other reason to be considered accompanied the names. Most of the resumes and reasons for appointment were embellished to the point of bringing howls of derision, scorn or disbelief at the chutzpah.

"If she delivered so many votes, how could we lose that state?" Or, "Just Googled the guy – he didn't graduate Florida State, he took a remedial summer course."

It was a light mood but deadly serious too. Ellie

May, Marjorie, and Helen were talking on telephones. A group of aides was contacting the list of potential candidates on the board and then passing the call to one of the principals available. All the call recipients wanted to congratulate the team, and most were surprised to learn they were being considered for a post. As a new party, there were no standouts. Since they were a new party, Congress was going to be brutal on any new face, no longer partisan politics, where votes were traded. Everyone would have knives out for anyone foolish enough to put their head above the parapet.

Ellie May told each person she spoke to that she would like to put their name forward and, if there was anything in their past that might not face a close scrutiny, now was the time to say 'thanks but no thanks'. The objective was to pre-screen as many as possible.

There were requests for interviews from media groups around the world. Sheila fended off requests with a statement indicating interviews would be granted after the president had accepted the results of the election. Some said they had contacted the White House and been unable to find anyone speaking on behalf of the administration either on or off the record.

"How can we break this deadlock?" Fox News asked.

"Go with the story you have. The president silent in the White House, American Party anxious to be heard."

\*\*\*

"Professor Barber is a leading academic specializing in Political Science at Columbia University." The television host sat opposite a distinguished gentleman who looked no different from two days previous except for wearing a different color bowtie. The bow, without doubt, added gravitas to a rather unexceptional face.

"Professor, we had a general election, a nationwide election on Tuesday. It is now Friday and still no word from the White House. We listened on Wednesday to a speech from Mrs. Joseph which filled no holes in what is rapidly becoming a political vacuum."

"Yes, you are right. Unprecedented I would venture."

The announcer, anxious to have the camera focused on himself jumped in. "Do you think there was anything in the comments to the press that the president might be ill?"

"No, I don't think speculation of that kind is necessary or helpful. Remember, they are still counting in Florida and recounting in Wisconsin."

"But, with both of those states, even if they were both resounding victories for the president, wouldn't they still be insufficient for him to win the election?

"Now a break; we will be back with Professor Barber and ask why we have not heard from the White House and play again Ellie May Joseph's non-acceptance speech. Be right back."

\*\*\*

Mac submitted his manuscript to his publisher, promising a final chapter on the acceptance speech and the expected political appointments within the week. He was trying to have it finished before he and Helen left for Florida. He watched with only mild interest as the political analysts continued.

"So, Professor, why have we not heard from the White House?"

"The president has seventy-two hours to respond, particularly since there are two states not finished. He can also request recounts in other states."

"But all week we have heard other experts discuss the futility of other recounts, not to mention the cost."

"Quite."

"And why not send a spokesperson – Vice President Flores, for example, to make a statement?"

"Well, we can only speculate on Flores. He is damaged goods in this campaign; he was savaged by Marjorie White. Someone else could have made a statement."

"What, Professor, is going to happen next?"

"Well, I think it is up to Congress. They will give the seventy-two hours, then come back Monday to verify and validate the election results."

"Very interesting. Let's watch Ellie May Joseph's speech again."

Mac muted the television. He'd already heard the speech he'd written several times.

\*\*\*

It was the question on everyone's lips. Where was the president, the leader of the country, commander in chief? Was anyone minding the store? The vice president was reported out of the country. Speculation was rampant, mostly unkind. He had not surfaced in any of the spots covered by a very hungry media.

Congress adjourned for the weekend with the same questions. Many senators and congressmen were also 'lame ducks,' having lost their seats in the recent election. Others owed their seats to dirty tricks, extortion, bribery, blackmail, or worse, and wondered what was going to happen to them.

Some of the lawmakers were making whispered plans to meet. Aides were being dispatched to find like-minded congressmen.

Media trucks were parked as close to the White

House as was permissible. Interviewers, their aides and newspaper equivalents from around the world, questioned anyone they could see. Shouting to security personnel, questions, studiously ignored. Questions ran the gambit from whether the president was home, to whether he was ill, to was there a statement, or did he have meetings and what was his view on the election. All questions were met with the same stony silence.

## Chapter Thirty-Seven

The answers came Saturday night, or early Sunday morning, depending on what part of the country one lived in.

During the day the weather had turned cold, adding to the bleakness of a steady rain. Many of the media had left and most of those electing to stay repaired to the closest bar. One first year reporter remained together with an otherwise empty transmitting truck. She had taken refuge with a flask of coffee and a package of chocolate chip cookies. The screens were lit. Facing the White House was a roof mounted camera. Intriguing was the number of lights burning in the White House and the occasional car entering and exiting.

It could be changing staff as none of the cars were special, none were escorted, she surmised. There was nothing to report, not yet. She would include the facts in her first report, live at about five o'clock.

In Texas the switchboard, manned twenty-four hours a day received a call from General Weir. The general had been invited to take a post in the American Party government after his help and understanding in the Washington raid by Mac and friends.

"I need to speak with Ellie May Joseph, important."

"Sir, it's a little after two. Can it wait?"

"It's early here too, son. General Weir needs to speak to her now."

"Yes, sir."

"General?" Her voice was sleepy, but Ellie May was immediately alert.

"I've been ordered by my commander in chief to assist the militia in arresting the members of the House and Senate. There is apparently a long list of people to be arrested. I refused to comply and presumably joined the list. The barrack gates are locked and my next calls, unless I am blocked, will be to my fellow officers and other service personnel."

"Thank you, General, for the warning. God be with you!"

The night switchboard, generally quiet, wasn't. The operator was instructed to wake everyone on the premises for a meeting in five minutes.

"Where's Helen?"

"She and Mac left last night for Florida."

"Well, wake them. I need them both now."

"But…"

"Now! On this speaker."

A whisper. "This is Helen."

"Wake him!"

"Ellie May?"

"Who else would wake you in the middle of the night when you have a few well-deserved days of freedom?"

There was a sound of thumping and a decidedly annoyed bellow as Helen tried to cover the phone.

"Okay, we're awake. What's the national emergency?"

"The president just ordered the Army to help round up all the members of Congress."

There was a gasp from all the listeners, including Mac who was now fully awake.

"Can he?" someone asked.

"Commander in chief," Alistair replied.

"But the Constitution, separation of power."

"It looks ominous. General Weir thinks we might be on a list. He joined the list by ignoring the orders to back the militia. His rationale is that the militia is not a military unit and the regiment is not taking orders from anyone not subscribing to the codes imposed on the men and women of our Army, Navy, Air Force, Marine Corps, and Coast Guard."

"Do we know if other branches of the Armed Forces are complying?" Marjorie was worried.

"Let's plan for the worst and hope for the best," Ellie May suggested.

"We're sitting ducks for a missile strike from Army, Navy, or Air Force," Bobby Joe warned.

"Then we split up, set up separate headquarters." Ellie May was directing. "Jim and I will stay here. Mac and Helen, are you good in Florida?"

"Not too many people…" Mac started.

"My mum, inadvertently, last time…" Everyone knew the story and was reminded that it was imperative to be careful.

"Mac and Helen, I need a statement for broadcast, then move, stay in touch."

"Marjorie, you should be safe in New York City. Joyce Milner was re-elected there."

"Margaret?" someone asked, fearfully.

"I'll let Ike know," said Bobby Joe. "Betty Jo and I will be staying here."

"Alistair, take Wayne and pick up George Breakstone in Austin. Video conferencing will have to stay in Austin."

"Can I, should I set up in Washington?" Sheila asked.

"Why on earth would you do that?"

"Ginny is there with Mark."

"Oh, shoot. I forgot about Mark."

"We'll get the message to him," offered Helen with a look at Mac.

"Let's do it," Ellie May said. "I'll be here if anyone has additional questions or suggestions."

Ellie May sat silently with her head in her hands, trying to think of everything at once and going nowhere. Her husband Jim sat waiting for the next stream of consciousness, the next brilliant thought. It was a long time coming.

"Jim, why did I think I could do this?"

"But you did do what you set out to do."

"The lives of all those wonderful people I put in danger. Put at risk all of the people in this great country who believed in us, believed in me. A fraud!"

"You did not put them in danger. Their love of freedom put them in harm's way perhaps. Everything worthwhile is worth fighting for. I am sure someone smarter than me said that."

"Jim, what are we to do?"

"The only thing we can do at the moment. Wait and see."

Bobby Joe walked in with a draft for Ellie May. "From Helen and Mac with a message. They're moving north and will be in touch and said to tell you to be careful."

Ellie May looked quickly at the concise language used and the assumption, with which she agreed. This was not a long-winded diatribe but a quick repudiation of the acts against elected officials. Illegal acts in violation of the Constitution.

"Let me read this to you, Jim. Bobby Joe, you will have to critique."

Ellie May had almost finished when there was the now familiar sound of Betty Jo running down the hall. She burst into the room.

"Television and radio stations are being taken over and they're putting a message on the screens or on the air. 'This station is closed due to a National Emergency. The president will address the world at six o'clock this evening, Eastern Standard Time.' What does it mean?"

"It means he is giving his militia time to round up the list – politicians, Supreme Court, and anyone else he has identified as a threat," Jim answered.

"A little fantasy, a little fantastic?" Betty Jo asked.

"No, it is a proven ploy in communist and certain African countries. Separate the people from information then give them what you want them to have after removing all dissention."

Ellie May broke in. "We need to record this statement and be ready to interpose into an opportune moment. Betty Jo, can you find out, from our techies in Austin, what our options might be?"

\*\*\*

Mac contacted Ike in New York. "How is Margaret? Can she be moved?"

"Not good, probably not."

"Change the name, her records, move as soon as you can. Go somewhere safe, like Harlem for now or Park Avenue, then head south where your accent is less likely to be identified. Don't tell me where and don't ask me. Only use your cell phone in an emergency. Buy a disposable with cash."

\*\*\*

A helicopter landed and discharged a platoon of

ten men then took off. The platoon double timed to the front of the ranch where they spread out covering the area. Ellie May and Jim were seated on the verandah waiting for the president to speak.

"Are you James and Ellie May Joseph?" a young man, clearly nervous and sweating in excess of that necessary in the heat, asked. "You are under arrest and we are authorized to use force if you resist."

"Under what authority?"

"The president of the United States."

"Allow me to see the warrant." Jim Joseph held out a hand.

"I can see you are armed and resisting arrest."

"You have no orders to arrest. You are ordered to assassinate a duly elected president of the United States." Ellie May could see it clearly. "Y'all can rot in hell."

"Squad ready…" a clearly nervous commanded.

"Think it through, kid." Bobby Joe was behind a pillar at the corner of the verandah. "First, you won't survive. Neither will we, but do you seriously think you will be allowed to live after this? You and your squad are expendable and will all disappear one way or another."

"We shall have performed our duty as commanded."

"Wait, we surrender to you," Ellie May shouted.

"Fire!"

As some of the platoon fired, Bobby Joe cut down the squad leader. The men turned to Bobby Joe as Betty Jo fired a shotgun from the other corner of the porch. It was over in less than a minute. Ellie May and Jim Joseph bled out on the floor. Bobby Joe and Betty Jo were dead. Half of the young men were also dead, five injured, one was miraculously untouched. None of them – the dead, injured, or healthy – saw the missile, guided by a beam from the fallen leader, which buried all the evidence. The watchers in Washington smiled with the conclusion. Who would know? They would spin a story later.

They might not have celebrated if they had known a lone security drone high above the ranch was transmitting live feed to Austin.

## Chapter Thirty-Eight

The president took the closure off the television networks at six in the evening, Eastern Standard Time, in order to speak to America. It had been anticipated with quick online announcements all day to ensure a maximum coverage. Many of the people listening merely wanted to know when their favorite television show would be back on the air. There was an expectancy which had been fueled by speculation since there were troops in the streets. Citizens venturing out had been warned to stay indoors. There had been a number of arrests – politicians, chiefs of police, and women in federal government positions.

There was no introduction. At six o'clock the image of the president appeared from the Oval Office.

"I am here this evening to explain some extraordinary behavior of the past week since a general election was held.

"I was shocked to hear that the election, November fifth, was fraught with fraud. There was rigging of ballots, missing votes, and intimidation of voters and candidates. I was skeptical until my aides assured me of the facts and brought evidence. It was clear to me that we could not allow candidates elected by fraudulent means to govern.

"Therefore, under powers granted to me as your president, I have declared a state of national emergency. I have ordered the disbandment of Congress and the arrest of all senators and members of the house. I ordered the arrest of members of the American Party, including Mrs. Joseph and Mrs. White and their staff.

"We went to great lengths to address the issues with Mrs. Joseph and my ambassador, sent with my invitation to a meeting, was brutally murdered by an employee of the American Party who also killed his employer. I am now authorizing the showing of a video of this murder, with a warning that it shows graphic violence."

There followed an edited version of events from a body cam of the squad leader. He addressed the couple on the porch and asked if they would accompany him, he had transportation. Jim Joseph was seen to ask who he represented, by what authority, to which the man answered President Al Adana. The camera switched to show Bobby Joe with a gun. He shot and then Ellie May and Jim Joseph are seen falling. The 'ambassador' is heard calling for Bobby Joe to surrender before falling, apparently shot. It was a brilliant editing of the events with words dubbed in and out, the sequence of events showing a distortion of the facts.

The president was now showing sympathy for the fallen. "As you can see the peaceful transition of government was not anticipated by the American Party who wished to repeal gun laws while espousing violence. I shall therefore remain your president until we have rooted out all of these rebels and dismantled the discredited terrorist cell calling themselves the Sons of Liberty. I shall be steadfast for as long as it takes. Congress has been terminated and I shall take council from my advisors and from imam around the country.

"Allah be praised."

\*\*\*

In Boston there was a silence as the news was absorbed by Mac, Helen, Hannah, Sean Lynch, and other Sons of Liberty gathered to hear the speech.

"Did he really dissolve Congress?" asked Sean. "He can't, can he?"

"He did and declared himself president for life." Mac saw the facts as they were.

"But we know what actually happened at the ranch." Helen was looking positive.

"We can try showing the real time, real life version, but how many will believe it?" Mac asked the stunned group.

"We also have Ellie May's speech stating that the ballot fixing was militia orchestrated. And that she had waited the requisite time for a concession speech, and that she was asking Congress to recognize her as the next White House occupant."

"All very interesting, but, not helpful from where we are," Mac said. "We should have the Ellie May speech and footage aired anyway in order to refute the claims. But it's not going to alter the facts. The fact is we are being hunted and there is a price on everyone's head. We are a line of dominoes ready to fall."

One of the members of the Sons of Liberty stood to speak. "Two things. There is a price on Al Adana's head too, and I am not waiting for them to gun me down like they did Ellie May Joseph."

"We amassed arms, but I never thought we meant to use them." Sean was pensive. "Killing Al Adana is not going to kill the snake. It will grow another head. There is one goal, one only, Islamic domination of the world."

"Then what? Do you think there will be peace?"

"No, they will overrun Israel, accept a nuking as part of the collateral damage, then take the Western world apart. Christianity, then the East, Hindu, Sikh, etc., and finally the indigenous tribes. They will then find themselves back to the beginning and fight each other." Sean had thought a great deal of the future. It was not a future he had wished for himself or for his children.

"The military," Helen spoke. "They are the only ones to stop this madness."

"I think the generals are all arrested," said Sean.

"Then the next down, they cannot arrest every man and woman in uniform," Hannah firmly replied. "I'll go see my father. He'll likely have thoughts about the day's events."

"Mobilize the women," a female graduate student offered. "We have the most to lose – our education, all the inroads we have fought for in the corporate and political fields."

"Mobilize how?"

"What we do best – motivate our menfolk to repudiate the ideas. Do they want to see us in burqa? Maybe. If so, maybe they don't want us educated. Do they want to go back to having sex by rape? I think not. I think the vast majority of modern man understands the strength and contribution of women."

"Not bad. Can you explore, think, and give us a plan?"

"I can speak to a commandant in Washington and gauge the military option," Mac offered.

"I'll get the Ellie May speech and video on the air," Helen told them.

A quick survey showed everyone offering to do something positive.

"Be careful out there. It's Sunday. I'm guessing there will be a curfew imposed soon. Let's plan on meeting in the basement of the Custom House Tuesday evening at five. Hopefully we can beat a curfew." Mac saw the gathering safely out the door.

\*\*\*

The basement of the Custom House had once been a tunnel to transport cash for customs duty up to the banks. It says much of those turbulent times that there was insufficient trust to transport the money through the streets, Mac thought to himself. The posting of guards with guns in the balcony above those collecting and counting the monies likewise illustrated the security precautions of the day.

Mac called the gathering to order. He was not sure how he got the role. He had the respect hence the duty. A quick look around and he had settled on an agenda. Most people had shown up. There was no sign outside of militia. In November it was already getting dark at five o'clock, and they were likely looting he thought cynically.

A report on recruiting and encouraging women through social media, social groups, and flyers received warm applause and the proponents were encouraged to pursue. The inventory of arms hidden by the Sons of Liberty received less of a reception. It was clear this was a last option. Mac had contacted the commandant of the barracks in Washington.

"Commandant, you never did ask or receive my name. We delivered armaments and badly damaged goods to you a few weeks ago."

"Yes, I remember. We had a drink with General Weir."

"Are your lines compromised? And where is the general if you know?"

"We're in lock-down. Our lines are limited but this one should be secure. The general was arrested, vague charges of collusion. He's being held in the Amory by a strange coincidence, and tortured I dare say. Unfortunate, nice man."

"Did you see the president and the president-elect presentations?"

"Yes. I was impressed by the one from Texas, declared by the president as phony. We had our communications expert verify the doctored presentation was the president's. The missile obliterated any evidence."

"We need to bring back Congress. Free them and your general. Restore order."

"Amen, but how? We are a Marine unit. Our commander in chief, the president. Also we would need support for any military operation. Air support!"

"I'll try to find air marshals and admirals to support any efforts to free illegally imprisoned members of Congress."

"What about my oath?"

"What about the presidential oath? An illegally declared national emergency?"

"My cousin is an admiral. I'll give him a call."

There was progress. Professor Sanderson had largely recovered from his stroke and was still the most wanted man in Massachusetts. He brought a wealth of common sense and common-sense planning to the proceedings. The Hebrew Rehabilitation Center where he had recovered had been a revelation. He attended as many Jewish services as there were and found many friends.

"If he stays much longer in the White House, Israel will be no more, then they will eliminate the Jews in America. It will make the Holocaust look small! We must have the Sons of Liberty protect the state house when the governor and local officials return. In other capitals too."

"Why not the police?" one of the pacifists asked.

"Why not indeed? Can we put you in charge of contacting law enforcement? They should be happy to help given the current wave of violence."

The team members were all anxious to do something. Some were contacting women's groups, police, Jewish communities, Christian church groups, college students, sports teams, men and women. The strength was in the diversity, the safety in the concentration. The people visiting police, for example, had no contact with the other groups. Other states were encouraged to follow the model. All were encouraged to have restraint when it came to force. The arms remained hidden. There were setbacks and arrests. When the arrests were by the police, lawyers were quickly provided to release the unfortunate on bail before the militia could extract and torture them.

The president issued orders from the White House arbitrarily. Mandatory head covering for women in public incensed the women's groups and increased membership to the American Party. Orders for police to arrest and punish women disobeying the ban were usually ignored by law enforcement agencies, which meant there were numerous vacancies in the ranks.

The issuing of arrest warrants for the leading figures of the American Party was done personally by the president. He had named the guilty parties by the use of playing cards, mimicking the Al Qaeda listing. The queen of spades was shown as Ellie May Joseph with a black diagonal line across. The queen of hearts was Marjorie White. The other queens were Helen McDougal and Sheila Hutchins. The 'jacks' were predictable. Bobby Joe Williams with a diagonal cross, Eisenhower Clark, Mark Hughes, and Allyn Cherwin. The latter two presumably because they would lead to the money. There were other names – Alistair Kirk, Margaret Forrest, and Ginny Hutchins among them. The president had, however, kept the kings in his hand. He revealed the kings with a flourish and said that he would personally pay the reward for the apprehension, dead or alive, of the following – Papillon, last seen in New York City, Professor Sanderson, using the pseudonym Ben Franklin, and Mathew McDougal, believed to be writing and contributing scurrilous lies under the by-line of Peter Doath, the Deep Throat of the discredited organizations American Party and Sons of Liberty. The final king was an outline and referenced an unknown money launderer in the Las Vegas area. The money on the kings' heads was one million dollars. The queens' heads were only half, representing their status in the eyes of the president. The president had a self-satisfied smile as the screen faded. The activists in Texas quickly put on the tape of Ellie May Joseph's speech.

There were immediate repercussions to the president's request for the population's help. Social media was divided – some saying take the money in these times as it was so hard to earn; others offered sanctuary to any of the named names. The 'cards' were now on notice and doubly vigilant.

Helen was concerned, less for herself than for Mac. But he had lived so long under the threat that he was examining a copy of the speech for flaws.

Mac was examining the tape again and making notes when a news bulletin broke that the University of Texas Astrophysical Laboratory had received a direct hit, a missile attack. There was no information regarding the launch site or reason or even speculation on the rationale. He made two notes and returned to his task. The first note was to exhort the person speaking to colleges to use as a rallying cry that the president had now targeted innocent citizen students. The second note to include in his daily newsletter. Knowing that Helen would correspond with the Texas staff, he returned to his task. There was something here. They knew about the Astrophysical Laboratory. Did they know the transmissions were in the basement or were they targeting the antennae on the roof? Perhaps the space dish?

The pen is mightier than the sword, he surmised. At least in his hands. Mac wrote and then wrote again as if the duplicate message could point his pen, his keyboard, in the direction of truth, action! There was no mole or spy. He reached this conclusion as the cards which he had copied were in front of him. They did not know Papillon's identity, though he had been active. They did not have a name in Las Vegas. The president was obsessed with the money. Three major playing cards were money, not political threats.

The president was willing to put up his own money. Wait a minute, Mac stopped writing. What money? Mac knew or could find who lost and who won. This reminded him to talk to Helen, talk to Esther, a quick note to himself then back to his newsletter. He needed to goad the president into further mistakes.

Finally, the newsletter was ready. Published, it read,

> Friends, it is no secret that the president and the American Party are not compatible. It is an indisputable fact the American Party won

the presidential election in a landslide. A landslide victory; a vote for change from the present state of affairs.

The completion of counting in Florida merely emphasized the margin in favor of the American Party. The president and his advisors are looking for a King of Diamonds, a bogeyman in Las Vegas. Perhaps they should look closer to home. Oh, sorry, devout Muslims cannot gamble.

The president had four million dollars to put on the head of four kings, two with no name or face. The other two kings, a Harvard Professor and an investigative journalist. So what do they have in common? A love of country, defenders of democracy, and both are pacifists.

So what can these two do to harm the current, illegal, occupant of the White House? Call to the attention of similar USA loving pacifists the hijacking of your democracy!

When people say it is not about the money, it is ALWAYS about the money. How then did the current occupant of the White House amass this amount of money in a short amount of time?

Being an investigative reporter, I investigated. A great deal of money from offshore accounts was wagered on the elections this time. There, were winners and losers. When the stakes are high there is a temptation to 'sway' the vote.

Illustration, in New Jersey nearly one million dollars was wagered on the American

Party candidate. This was matched by an even larger amount because there were odds of three to one. The American Party candidate canvassed unopposed with strong support of local monies. The Democrat's candidate, someone handpicked by the president, won on the basis of stacked ballot boxes. The same day as the election results, a large check sent to Washington was deposited offshore.

I wonder? Who double crossed whom?

Yours in hiding for now, Peter Doath.

\*\*\*

"Mac, I just read your letter today. Any of it true?" Mark had called from Washington.

"All true, although for most I could not give you written proof."

"So why?"

"For a reaction."

"He may double the reward."

"So what? If they want me for one or two or ten million, it doesn't matter. I will go down writing.

"There were boys in New York putting up money for the American Party candidate. They had the unions. Paradoxically they had law enforcement, they had the unemployed, they had the election officials. How could they lose? What they did not have was the desire to be seen. They've been doing this for years. There were ballot boxes stolen, emptied, enough votes taken out or put in to ensure a Democrat victory, so they lost. Now I point out to those 'boys' that they were hijacked. They will not be best pleased. Also, there was only about five hundred thousand at even money in the real 'book.' I inflated the amount and odds. People interested will want to know where the other money was from and who put it in."

"You're suggesting it was Al Adana."

"Did I say that?"

"No, but…if someone else thinks that…Devious, Mac, very devious. I bet if I read the article again there are no assertions of fact "

"Thought it might give some people thought and Al Adana some loss of sleep."

"He will slither through."

"Maybe today, but I bet he checks his off-shore account. Martin is looking for it as we speak. Tomorrow I should know the island it's on, then I can report to my friends in New York and Al Adana's friends in Turkey where it is."

"Good luck. Stay safe. I'm not sure I like the idea of you being worth more than I am."

Mac chuckled. "You be safe too. We are only worth the same amount to the undertaker!"

Helen entered as Mac hung up. "Who was that?"

"Mark. We were talking about my letter today. Which reminds me, I have to talk to you."

"About the letter?"

"Sort of. You know how I told you about the West Coast wins?"

"Dead on!"

"Well, I did go nine out of ten at even money."

"What do you mean?"

"Another reason I'd never get approved by Congress. I took ten states and backed the American Party."

"Not the ticket?"

"No, too much scrutiny. Then I sent the winnings offshore and brought them back to Washington."

"Why didn't you tell me?"

"Conflict of interest."

"I have to report it now."

"To who? The illegal president, non-existent Congress, imprisoned Supreme Court, or to the American Party in hiding?"

"Not funny, Mac." She left, slamming the door behind her.

"Another satisfied customer," Mac spoke aloud. "Didn't even ask how much?"

Mac spoke to Admiral Cook brother of the commandant. He had read the letter and they chatted about it a little. "Admiral, are you and your fellow admirals deployed?"

"Three are in agreement, others I left out of the conversation. We agree, however, as long as the president is commander in chief there will be no mutiny. Three aircraft carriers are stationed as you suggested in the Chesapeake Bay, off Galveston, Texas, and in the Pacific off San Francisco and the Presidio. We have various reasons for inactivity, from orders to lack of fuel, all legitimate if stretched."

"Thank you. Something has to give soon."

The next day President Mohammed Al Adana appeared before the nation to introduce his advisors. They were three imams in flowing robes and an older expensively dressed Turk with a large diamond ring. All were introduced with extravagant praise.

Mac recognized the name of the older man as Arthur Anders, Al Adana's father-in-law. The president then went into a rambling diatribe against gambling and offshore bank accounts. He reiterated his assertions about his cards, with reference to his kings, vehemently stating his net was closing and he knew the identity of the persons making illegal book on the political race and that agents were in Las Vegas about to make an arrest.

Mac phoned Martin.

"Already on it, boss." Martin had anticipated his asking for up-to-date information on the three imams and the father-in-law. "The father-in-law is quickly wealthy. I remember he was a local official in Turkey from the city of Adana."

"Well, I already know he was smuggling people into Turkey for years and selling them. Little boys by chance?"

"Let you know in the hour."

Mac's new newsletter was similar to the previous day but included veiled references to the missing monies from Las Vegas. He now reminded his readers of the annual visits Frances Flores and his friend, then Arthur Anders, now President Al Adana, had made to the Middle East and his meetings and friendship with the man at his side, his father-in-law. Was this all coincidence? Was this man going to continue his people trafficking business into the USA? Would his business continue to specialize in little boys sold into prostitution? Would his money continue to be held in a numbered account in Switzerland? Stay tuned!

The president could not resist. He had taken Mac's bait was red with fury when he appeared on television the next day. The letter from Mac had been sent out as a viral message on the internet. The harder the president tried to argue, the worse it sounded until he exploded in a threat instead of an explanation. "I know you are in Boston. Boston will look like Aleppo when I am finished unless you turn over your Deep Throat! You have forty-eight hours."

The threat had an immediate effect as the Peabody Building on the Harvard campus was hit by a missile. Simultaneously the Science Building at the University in Dallas, Texas was hit and destroyed.

"He is out of control. He is doing an Assad. Has he

no sense of responsibility?" Helen was white with fury and fear. "He really wants you and Professor Sanderson."

"Then what? Then who? It's like the Nazis without the style. He intends to destroy everything, everyone in his path. Or is it the path of the radical Islamists?"

"We have a meeting tomorrow. Let's wait until then," Mac continued as he viewed the images now showing the burning building in Cambridge and the militia keeping the firemen at bay."

The newsletter the next day was short and somber, written by a man who had been unable to sleep.

> The present state of affairs is to be deplored. Deplored for the innocent lives lost. Deplored for the American service people raining the carnage down on their neighbors. Deplored for using the illegal seizing of the presidency to deploy the might of the country on its own citizenry. Deplored for the arbitrary personal vendetta of a man, ignoring the teachings of his own faith. A faith of love, not murder. Hiding behind false imams and a foreign father-in-law whose aim is profit. The profits of these thugs earned by controlling elections in this country and throughout Europe. In the last year elections were rigged affecting Britain, France, Germany, Italy, and Greece. How? I will explain tomorrow. Today my heart goes to those killed and injured in two cowardly attacks and also to those military people involved. We have military personnel caught between carrying out orders of their commander in chief and their conscience. I should like to appeal to your conscience, since your orders are not in

accordance with the Bill of Rights and would be countermanded by Congress if they were not illegally incarcerated. God bless America.

*\*\*\**

There were protest marches in the streets of Boston and in Washington. There were protest marches on the campuses of every college in the country. They were nervous, not rowdy marches, as if a loud noise would bring a missile on their heads.

There were meetings in support of the president, asking for the surrender of the traitor and agitators. These were attended by militia and their families, televised with added soundtrack to emphasize enthusiasm.

Outrage over the bombings came from New York City. New York had come to a standstill, knowing after September 11, 2001, how vulnerable the city was.

The telephone rang and Mac jumped. It was a reaction to his thoughts and his sleep deprivation.

"Mac." It was his automatic reaction.

"Some of my father's friends are heading out West to find out what happened to money they won on the election."

Esther hadn't identified herself nor did she need to.

"I get it but not sure I get it. Explain?"

"It seems as though they ran a primary 'book' through my father's employer and there was a reneging of the odds. They were paid but the odds were changed. They want the difference one way or the other."

"But that is against the code. There will be consequences even if they get the money. We participated from Washington, right?"

"Right! It's not us, of course, because we were

winners. It seems as though the foreign gentleman in your letter today has never been to New York." She chuckled a little at the thought of them doing business. "And I think our New York friends believe the money we invested, you invested, came from the White House and the president let the American Party win California for his own profit."

"That is so preposterous, but makes sense if you want it to. Thanks for the information. Keep your head down in case the New York folk come looking. At this point they are almost as dangerous as the president."

The missile hit the Boston campus of the University of Massachusetts and the Kennedy Library. The strike was symbolic with little loss of life due to an anonymous warning that they were targeted. A military person in the chain had a conscience.

The meeting was not as well attended as previous meetings. When someone asked where certain people were, if not there, the answer was 'Mac'.

"There are people, not here, who would have you give yourself up to the authorities," someone shouted.

"Good idea," Mac said sarcastically. "Then I can be tortured into giving them your names."

"You could negotiate an amnesty for us."

"Not worth the spittle from your mouth. It's not about just me, I am merely the one poking the tiger."

"I know and you can depend on us and the ones not here in our rationale moments. Peter, though, knew someone at Harvard who was injured."

"I have to keep poking. The military are conflicted and fear repercussions. Anything we do must be in a coordinated, legal manner. Still working on that. The president is putting his supporters in military roles as fast as he can."

\*\*\*

Time was passing. Mac was running out of ideas and planned to visit the island bank holding his money and stay there, Helen at his side.

"Mac, Mark here. You know I have someone in the White House."

"Not until you just told me."

"Well, anyway," Mark said without apology, "he has reported to me that the president is in a coma."

"Common knowledge? How does he know? Anything unusual?"

"More information, Mac. It appears he collapsed after a Mr. Bonanno had an audience. The meeting was to help neutralize certain people for the reward money. Speculation would make that a whole 'deck of cards.' Symptoms would suggest a nerve agent."

"A Russian product?"

"Yes, likely novichok. He had a runny nose before collapsing. The FBI are in and focusing on the telephone. More info." Mark paused. "Not as good news, I'm afraid. He had apparently named his father-in-law as his deputy. He now has hands on the nuclear trigger."

They hung up and Mac sat for ten minutes digesting and organizing his order of actions.

He called Admiral Cook and asked him if he could bring his aircraft carrier up the Potomac as close to the capital as safely possible in support of his cousin. The next call was to Commandant Cook.

"Commandant, the president is dead or dying. There is no commander in chief until Congress appoints one. The country needs you to free those elected officials held in the Amory and take them to their chambers. Do not let them slip away until they've done their duty. If they don't vote, Al Adana's father-in-law, who is Turkish, will no doubt will be pulling the strings. Congress needs to ratify the election results as soon as possible."

"Sounds like herding cats."

"Yes, but your cousin will be in the Basin. His missiles will be trained on the militia, his jets on deck in case someone tries to stop you."

"I will check on your news on the president first if I may be so bold?"

"I understand. I wouldn't trust me under these circumstances either."

"What should we do with the militia in the Amory? Any suggestions?"

"Any exiting and leaving their weapons, let them go home. If they have committed other crimes, the legal system will prosecute. Resistance? Up to your discretion. Hopefully there will be none if you call up your cousin."

Mac's next call was to his agent. "Brad, can you open up the television stations. The president is dying, and the fleet is in the Basin."

"On our side or the other?"

"Ours. Also, the members of Congress will be released and vote on ratification of the election."

"And you know all this because?"

"I am an investigative reporter. The best you know."

"Okay, don't tell me any more. I'm on it."

Mac immediately dialed the next name on his list. "Marjorie, you need to be in Washington overnight." He brought her up to date with the happenings.

"I'll find Ike, ask him to arrange things," she replied. "Joyce Milner has been very kind with providing off-duty police officers for me and my family. Glad there is a resolution."

\*\*\*

At the Amory, supported by armored vehicles on each side of the building, Marines stood in riot gear at the steps to the front door.

"Lieutenant, take six men and knock on that door. Ask the men inside to come out and surrender their weapons. Give them exactly two minutes before we come in and take them. Not negotiable. They are not being arrested. They may return home."

"Yes, sir."

After less than a minute the door opened, and twenty men came out carrying rifles which they placed on the floor. A quick body search resulted in knives and guns being added to the pile. There were clearly armed men still inside.

The voice of a spokesperson called, "We want to keep our weapons and we want compensation. We have hostages."

"Go," the commandant ordered. The doors were blown from the hinges and Marines entered from four sides. Bombmakers in the basement had not completed timers or detonators and, taken by surprise, quickly surrendered. The armed part-time militia was no contest for the heavily armed, trained Marines. It was over in two minutes.

\*\*\*

Emilio Gonsalves found that he was the ranking member of Congress. He was also one of very few American Party members as any new members in the election had not yet been sworn in. Understanding the urgency of the vote, he suggested a joint session. No one had a better plan. There was a roll call, made difficult by continual calls for order. Everyone excited to be freed wanted to talk. Banning cell phones was not successful either as family members and friends, seeing the news, checked on the status of loved ones.

"Members of the House and Senate, we are here with one agenda item which, when voted, will mean we can go home until tomorrow morning. The one item is the ratification of the election results of November 5th. Discussion?"

A hand raised and permission to speak was given to a senator from Virginia.

"Do we have a quorum? Can we transact this business and by what authority?"

Shouts and conversation filled the building. Hammering of the gavel quelled the noise.

Another hand was raised. "What if we obey our president and believe that he was acting in the country's best interest?"

More noise, more gaveling.

Emilio finally quieted the noise. "Look," he said staring directly at the timid congresswoman from Kentucky, "you have a vote on the motion. We have a quorum because we are all there is. Some of our members have disappeared, some voluntarily and some not. We are voting here for the country and for ourselves. We can vote and ratify the will of the people or…" He paused, "Or we can vote to put ourselves back in prison. I need a motion.

"The chair recognizes the senator from Massachusetts."

"I move that we ratify the vote of November 5th and declare the American Party candidate the rightful president-elect of the United States of America."

There was a chorus of 'seconds' and 'so moved'.

"So that there can be no doubt," Emilio was trying to follow as much procedure as possible, "I want to confirm that since Ellie May Joseph was murdered the president-elect will be her vice president, Marjorie White. Also, can the clerk please record the individual votes?"

This took a great deal of time due to recording votes from both the House and Senate and the noise. Finally nine people had voted against the ratification and Emilio called it passed. He admonished the members to be in their respective chambers in the morning to transact further important business and asked for a motion to adjourn. This was met with a clattering of feet toward the exit.

Meanwhile the Supreme Court justices had been released. Six were taken to their homes and three needed medical attention. They were transported to the Walter Reed Hospital.

Commandant Cook left a small contingent of men at the Amory. There were bodies in the Amory basement and a coroner had been called. The rest of his command and his armed vehicles he now, with the vote of Congress, moved to the White House where they asked the occupants to leave. The secret service units met with the commandant and agreed in principle that they were relieved of duty and would therefore stay in place and facilitate the evacuation of the building. The head of security also guaranteed he would confirm the status of Mohammed Al Adana. In thirty minutes he returned.

"The president is dead. Some foreign bloke told me he was now president and we should prepare a grand parade of the military to celebrate the life of his son Mohammed 'may his name always be praised' Al Adana. I asked what he had been smoking. He gave me a signed declaration of his succession. I told him that he should find on the wall a copy of the Constitution and a copy of the Bill of Rights, and I explained that he could never succeed if not born on these shores. I then suggested he might have overstayed his visa."

A parade of vehicles entered, after inspection, and one hour later departed the White House. The gates were opened and left open. A gunship from the aircraft carrier in the basin followed the line of cars to Reagan International and the occupants filed onto a private jet. A host of baggage and a coffin went into the hold.

It was a much more somber assembly of senators in the chamber the next morning. Scheduled for nine am, it was after nine-thirty and there were still members missing when Emilio Gonsalves declared that, with a busy agenda, they must start. He suggested a timetable for a general meeting until eleven-thirty then a recess to allow the House to join them together with the members of the Supreme Court to meet the president-elect, if there were no objections, at twelve noon. He then asked a member from Maryland to bring up to date the chamber on the happenings of the previous twenty-four hours. There would be no questions allowed. This was everything known. The new members were all sworn in and then Emilio asked that all members repeat their oath of office.

At twelve noon Marjorie White entered the room alone. There was a standing ovation.

She walked confidently to the front and shook hands with Emilio Gonsalves with a whisper and a nod. She moved to the microphone.

"Before my oath of office, I'd like to address you and the American people watching, as well as the citizens of countries around the world looking for examples. We must set a *good* example. I should not be the person standing here. Ellie May Joseph founded the American Party as an alternative to the politics of two parties sometimes lost, alienated from its citizens.

She should be here. She will be here as long as we remember her. In her memory, I ask that you work together in a spirit of bipartisanship to correct all that has gone astray. It starts here. It starts today. Many people, great patriots, brought us here today and we know them. I was spared and will have a copy of the Twenty-third Psalm on my desk to remind me that 'though I walk through the valley of death, thou art with me.'"

There was a standing ovation then Emilio asked that they stay standing as the oath of office was administered in front of the Supreme Court justices, the Senate, and House, bringing the legislative, judiciary, and executive branches of government together with the people standing in the public gallery.

Andrew and Ian proudly held a family Bible for their mother.

"I, Marjorie Harrison White…"